WATCH US SHINE

Also by MARISA DE LOS SANTOS

I'd Give Anything

I'll Be Your Blue Sky

The Precious One

Falling Together

Belong to Me

Love Walked In

WATCH
US
SHINE

A Novel

MARISA DE LOS SANTOS

𝒲ℳ
WILLIAM MORROW
An Imprint of HarperCollins*Publishers*

WATCH US SHINE. Copyright © 2023 by Marisa de los Santos. All rights reserved. Printed in the United States of America. No part of this book may be used or reproduced in any manner whatsoever without written permission except in the case of brief quotations embodied in critical articles and reviews. For information, address HarperCollins Publishers, 195 Broadway, New York, NY 10007.

HarperCollins books may be purchased for educational, business, or sales promotional use. For information, please email the Special Markets Department at SPsales@harpercollins.com.

FIRST EDITION

Designed by Bonni Leon-Berman

Library of Congress Cataloging-in-Publication Data has been applied for.

ISBN 978-0-06-309560-1   8254991

23 24 25 26 27 LBC 5 4 3 2 1

For
Helen and Tim Boulos,
with love and gratitude

Chapter 1

CORNELIA

MY MOTHER IS A GARDEN.

My father is a street overlaid with gold on that day in fall when all the ginkgoes drop their leaves at once. My husband, Teo, is a salt marsh soaked in dawn and the Blue Ridge from a distance and our backyard and the star-riddled night sky in the desert. My stepson, Dev, is a shining creek running through woods. My friend Viviana is a rooftop museum café. Her daughter, my almost daughter, Clare, is a meadow: bee balm–starred, fringed with goldenrod, milkweed floss skirting the grass tips like ghosts. My sister, Ollie, is a laboratory, gleaming. My brothers are both beaches in July. My friend Piper is a kitchen, immaculate, with white cabinets, white marble countertops, and oversize appliances that beam like the moon. My children. Oh, my children. Rose and Simon. My children are everywhere I am or have ever been or have ever dreamed of going.

When I was a kid, I assumed everyone's brain did this nifty trick: conflating people with places. And then in fourth grade, in the middle of class, in a preamble to answering God-only-knows-what question, I piped up, "You know how people are places and when you're with them, it's like you're in the place or, you know, you go to the place and the place is *them*?" and then paused before continuing to look expectantly at my fellow nine-year-olds only to find that they did not, in fact, know and could not even imagine, and thus learned that the people/place thing is my own little weirdness. Like most of my weirdnesses, I can't help it. It's reflexive, immediate, more synesthesia than simile. When I hear my brother's name "Cam," I picture his face, yes, hear his big, sunburst laugh laughing, usually at me, but also, a little window in my brain opens out on yellow sand blooming with umbrellas; white lifeguard stands; dipping, looping kites; the ocean green as a bottle.

My mother is a garden.

A mild, Upper South garden where butterflies clap their wings in the lavender. You can picture it; I know you can. Clouds of asters. Riots of roses. Shaggy peonies staked into perfect posture. Espaliered magnolia against the garage wall. Delphinium spires, the blue of which . . . well, you know that blue, don't you?—the one that makes you want to climb inside it and live out all your days. In the garden that is my mother, there is always a trellis strung with morning glories. There is always a mockingbird in a tree.

What my mother, Ellie Brown, is not, not in the slightest bit, is a place where you could plant your boots on snow crust or a frozen lake, tip your head—in its tasseled and probably also ear-flapped hat—back, and watch the northern lights. I am not entirely sure where those places are, except for very far away. Iceland? Finland? Lapland? I'm not even sure if the northern lights are something you watch or merely look at: Do they waver and ripple or just stand still and shine? But I do know that she has nothing to do with any of it, with snowfields or ice floes, with fjords or reindeer or auroras, with any place where people believe in elves. In the garden that is my mother, there are four equal, equally undramatic seasons. And I can see how you might think this all sounds a tad crazy, but I swear if you met her, within five minutes of meeting her, two minutes, you'd know exactly what I mean.

But there she was, in her hospital bed in the rehab center, just out of a physical therapy session, with her spindly hands—never had I thought of them as spindly before, but now they were—kneading the edge of the quilt we'd brought from home, light from the westward-facing window illuminating the tears spilling, spilling, spilling down her tired face—tired in that taut, wasted, frightened way it always looked after a long physical therapy session—her eyes sunstruck with grief and staring straight into mine, pleading, "Bring me the northern lights. Would you please, Cornelia? Bring them to me? I can't believe I left them."

And because none of this, not the request or the halting, blurred-edged voice she gave it in, not the exhaustion or the crying or the regret or the worrying hands or the northern lights, had a single thing to do with the mother I had known for my entire life up until the past eight weeks, I, too, behaved in a way I never had before, at least never toward her: I got down on my knees beside the bed, gently unlatched my mother's fingers from the quilt, kissed her hands, pressed them between my own, and said, "Tell me how."

She was my mother and she wanted the northern lights; I was her daughter and would have given her anything, anything.

We almost lost her.

I WAS STANDING IN MY kitchen unpacking a load of groceries that had just been delivered, while my friend and neighbor Piper commandeered a counter stool like Cleopatra—if Cleopatra had shopped at Talbots and scorned eyeliner—on her throne, watching me, although "watching" was far too benign a word for what Piper was doing. So are "scrutinizing," "surveying," "peering," and "eyeballing." "Glaring" comes closer. Piper's eyes were lovely, round, and the blue of June skies and forget-me-nots and truth, but they could tear, raptor-like, into a guileless bunch of bananas with a single glance and rend them limb from limb.

"*This*," Piper pronounced, stabbing her finger at the bananas. "*This* is what happens when you let those feckless barbarians at the grocery store do the choosing for you."

I dangled the bananas from two fingers.

"What *this*?" I said. "This is not a this. It's just a bunch of bananas. Also, remember how we don't call people barbarians? Remember how that's not okay to do?"

"In what sick, twisted universe do three bananas make a bunch? (A). And (B) they're overripe. Look at those spotted peels. Inside, they'll be bruised mush covered with strings. You watch."

"They're fine."

"They're garbage. May as well take them out back and stick them in your ridiculous grinder right now."

"It's a composter, Pipe," I said. "It doesn't grind. Not everything with a handle that turns grinds. It tumbles."

"Maybe," said Piper, shrugging.

"Definitely," I said.

"All I know is it's garbage rotting in your yard. But let's put that aside for the moment."

"It's in a container," I said. "It's contained."

"Since when do you buy orange juice with no pulp in a plastic jug, may I ask?"

"Are you asking if you can ask? Because: no."

"Since never. And I guarantee you those salmon filets were in the prewrapped fish section. They did not come out of the seafood case. The fish woman wraps them in brown paper; those are not wrapped in brown paper."

I wanted to remind Piper that we did not call people "fish women," that it was not okay to do that, but I couldn't right at that moment think of what else in the world those women would be called, so instead I said, "How can that possibly matter?"

"I can almost promise that salmon was not properly iced. You'll probably get salmonella, all of you, the entire family."

I smiled.

"Is that funny?" said Piper. "Salmonella?"

"*Sam*-monella."

Piper threw up her manicured hands.

"Other people shouldn't choose your food," said Piper. "They make stupid choices and then they manhandle it and then they shove it into a bag and who knows how long it sits in their car after that. Their car or—what do you call it—their *van*, for God's sake, with, what, some kind of *logo* on the side. Do they put the air-conditioning on in the back of the van? Do those kinds of vans even have air-conditioning in the back? We have no way of knowing, do we?"

"Delivery vans," I said. "So distasteful, yet shrouded in mystery."

"You know what I'm saying. People should go to the store and do their own shopping."

I set the trio of bananas on the counter and looked at them. Piper was right. They were freckled. They were soft. I sighed and lifted my gaze to meet Piper's.

"I can't."

"You can't what?"

"I tried. I keep trying. I drive there and sit in my car and imagine being inside that giant store, waiting in the checkout line. And I can't do it. I can't go in."

We sat with this, with my inability to enter a grocery store, for a few seconds, and then Piper said, "Well, of course you can't."

She lifted her right hand, moved it in my direction so her arm was completely extended, and then set the hand down on the countertop. She didn't expect me to hold it or give it a squeeze. She expected me to not, under any circumstance, hold it or give it a squeeze, would've been mortified if I had, but I recognized the gesture for what it was: a Piper hug. Then, Piper lifted her hand and slapped the counter.

"Okay! I'll do your shopping for you. I'll make Carter go with me and push the second cart. I've been thinking I should teach him how to shop before he goes to college," she said.

"Carter's fourteen," I said. "He just started ninth grade."

"The child is not a quick study, takes after his father that way. Don't get me wrong: Carter is at least eight *million* times smarter than Kyle. Algae is smarter than Kyle, but Carter's legitimately bright and sweet as he can be. You just couldn't call him quick."

Piper's ex-husband, Kyle, had never struck me as particularly stupid or particularly smart or particularly anything apart from smooth and shiny and monotonous. If Kyle were a place, he'd be one of those moving sidewalks at the airport.

"Still," I said. "Four years."

"Enough time to at least scratch the surface."

"The surface of grocery shopping." I smiled at her as I lifted a head of lettuce out of a bag. "Thank you."

She swatted my thanks away in annoyance. "It won't be forever."

Because I couldn't in all honesty agree with this assessment, although I hoped with my whole soul she was right, I tossed the lettuce into the air like a basketball and caught it.

"If you actually ordered that, this friendship is over," said Piper.

"Why do you think they call it iceberg?" I said. "It's round."

My phone started to ring. Piper recoiled.

"Who would be *calling* you?" she said. "What kind of maniac calls people?"

"And green," I continued, eyeing the head of lettuce. "Actually, not that green."

I picked up my phone, saw the caller's name, and my breath skidded to a halt inside my chest. Like Piper, both my parents believed that calling someone's cell phone unannounced was the equivalent of banging on their door in the dead of night just to say hello. They weren't texters, either, not conversational texters; they called but always texted first to schedule a convenient time. Always. I answered.

"Dad," I said, "everything okay?"

"She's alive," he said. His voice was high and rushed. "I just want to say that to you first. No one here has died."

SHE HAD BEEN LEANING OVER to pull weeds from the edge of a stranger's yard, which for her would have been a long and careful process, no mere, superficial yank. When it comes to weeds, my mother is deliberate, eagle-eyed, and murderous, a sniper. She goes for the taproot, if weeds have such a thing as taproots, a fact I would know if I had followed, even for a few steps, in my mother's gardening-clog footsteps, which I had not done. I can imagine her in the foggy early morning, her fingers burrowing deep into the soil, pale pink manicure be damned. She had been out for her morning walk, had leaned over to pull the weeds, when a car jumped the curb, hit her, and kept going. We knew this because there'd been a witness, a young man named Landon Smith. He'd been delivering newspapers, tossing them from his car window. He had tossed a paper, then turned back to drive to the next house and saw it happen.

"It jumped the curb and hit her and kept going. It was so quiet. Just this thump in the fog."

It's what he'd told the police officer. When he said it, he was crying, wiping his face and then looking at his wet hand, like people do when they aren't used to crying. That's what the police officer told my dad, in those exact words, and it was all so odd and kind and human: Landon crying and staring at his hand, the police officer including this detail, my dad in turn including the detail in his recounting of the awful thing that had befallen his wife, I knew I would never forget if I lived to be a thousand.

"She was hit by a car?" I said to my father on the phone.

"No, no," he said, and I could hear the wince in his voice. "Not *hit*, I don't think. They were driving slowly. Bumped. A glancing bump. But you know, she's just very small."

I did know, but it was a thing you could forget about my mother, with her brisk certainty, her state of constant and efficient motion, her crisp voice and laser gaze. My mother is tiny, like I am, five feet tall, narrow with practically nonexistent bones, and still, she takes up a lot of space in this world; she stands tall. But Landon Smith hadn't seen her standing, so at first he'd thought she was a child, maybe ten or eleven, lying facedown in the dewy grass in her walking sneakers.

BY THE TIME I'D HUNG up the phone, Piper had finished putting away the groceries and there were four packed overnight bags for me, Teo, Rose, and Simon lined up next to the back door. I had been on the phone for roughly twenty minutes, yet I knew that each bag would contain clothing items for every weather contingency; Rose's would include whatever book had been sitting on her bedside table; Simon's the notebook where he kept his sports' stats (MLB, NBA, NFL, ACC, and whatever other three-letter, ball-involved acronyms might exist) and his eyeless, threadbare stuffed dalmatian named (by Simon at two years old) Pothead. If Piper had not folded sheets of tissue paper into Teo's ironed dress shirts, it was only because we didn't have a packet of tissue paper squirreled away in a closet of our house for just this purpose, an oversight I knew Piper would remedy on her very next visit.

I dropped, shaking, into a kitchen chair, struggling to catch my breath. Piper placed a cup of steaming tea—paper-thin disc of lemon drifting on its surface because her friend Cornelia liked lemon in her tea and Piper would be damned if she didn't have her tea exactly as she liked it—on the table, and then she stood before me, backed by light coming through the windows of the French doors, ablaze with love and fury, her hands in fists on her hips, her blond bob incandescent.

"Your mother will be fine, do you hear me? One hundred percent fine. Because this is too much," she said. "It is one thing too many, and I won't have it. I will not have it. Your mother will be *fine*."

TEO CAME HOME AND WE all drove down to Virginia, and in the hospital, I saw my father and then, later, my mother. That's it, all the description I can manage. Language is basically my religion, always has been, and my storytelling style has forever been marked (or marred, depending on who you ask) by leaps and ambles and asides and tangles and tangents. My stories take the long way home. And prior to composing the above sentence about the drive and the hospital, I would say that I had never distilled an entire experience— even an insignificant one, which this one was not; it signified and signified and signified—into a single sentence, but that wouldn't be accurate. I didn't distill anything; that flat, lusterless little sentence was built, word by painful word; I laid it like bricks, heavy ones, the kind that strain your back and bruise your hands. For the second time in six weeks, and for possibly the second time in more than forty years, I lived a thing—people I loved lived a thing—I could not instinctively put words to. Could not. Would not. Standing in that hospital room after the first of two surgeries my mother would have,

Teo just outside the door, talking to the doctor, my mother there, too—there and also not there—I felt that words were unreachable. That's what I said to myself. But the truth is I didn't try to reach for them; it would have been like touching fire.

There are some pains that evade shape and order. What had happened in the checkout line of that, not quite a grocery store, what they call a big-box store—the one I will never enter again—six weeks earlier was one; my mother in the hospital room was another.

THE DAY AFTER WE ARRIVED, I opened the door of my parents' house to find a man and a woman standing on the front steps. They looked to be about my parents' age or maybe older, and it wasn't Sunday, but they were dressed for church. The man wore a suit; the woman wore a cream-colored tweed skirt and low beige pumps with a T-strap; her blouse had a pattern of violets and a bow at the neck. A rectangular beige pocketbook dangled from her wrist. At first glance, they looked like the "nice elderly couple" from central casting. At second glance, though, I saw their faces, which were stricken.

"We didn't know," said the woman, beginning to weep. "Not until this morning when we read about it in the paper. We thought it was just the bump of going over the curb. We would never have left her. We are so sorry. Oh, when I think of her lying there—"

The man took a white folded handkerchief from his pocket and handed it to his wife. She pressed it to one cheek and then the other.

"I'm Thomas Hall and this is my wife, Katie Hall," said the man. "We live just a few miles from here. We were going to visit our kids up in Baltimore, so we wanted an early start. But we shouldn't have gone out in the damn fog. It was damn stupid of us. Terrible call. I'll not soon forgive myself for that. I will not."

"Oh," I said.

Thomas Hall smoothed his red tie with one hand and placed his other hand on Katie Hall's waist.

"We are heading to the police station to turn ourselves in," he said. "But we wanted to stop here first to say we are responsible for your family's hardship, and we're just sick about it."

"Yes, we are," said his wife, her eyes brimming again. "I hope it's all right that we came by. After we read the article, I called my neighbor Eloise, who I remembered knows your mother from garden club, and she took the liberty of telling us your address. We maybe should not have come barging in on you in your hour of distress, but we just had to. Please know we are holding your mother in the Light, just as hard as we can."

"Thank you," I said.

If there was something else I should have said in that situation, some more apt response to Thomas and Katie Hall, who had bumped my mother with their car and then materialized on my doorstep, I could not for the life of me imagine what it was.

I pictured the two of them getting dressed for this solemn occasion, dignifying their confession—this one and the one to come—with a tie and wing tips, with heels and a matching handbag and a blouse with violets. I pictured Thomas knotting his tie in front of a mirror, Katie taking care with the bow at her throat, her fingers shaking just as they were shaking now. Then, I pictured her ironing his handkerchief, and something already rickety inside me broke, shattered and fell to flinders, and I started crying, gulping, helpless, heaving, core-of-your-body crying like I hadn't cried in ages. I stepped out and pulled the door shut so my children wouldn't hear me, then leaned back against the door and quaked with sobs. Katie reached out and touched my shoulder, then ran a hand over my short hair.

"I'm sorry," I said, gasping, "I didn't mean to do this."

"Nonsense," said Katie. "You cry all you want. When it comes to our parents being hurt or sick, we're all kids, aren't we?"

"It's just that it's so like her," I said. "So exactly like her."

And the woman said, "Yes, of course it is," even though she couldn't have known what I meant, and if she had, would have certainly thought I was slightly deranged, although I knew she would sweetly chalk up my rantings to stress or exhaustion. Because that would be so like Katie Hall, so exactly like her.

But I knew what I meant, knew that deranged or not, I was right: leave it to my mother, Ellie Brown, to get injured by the nicest people to ever darken a doorstep, to sustain breaks and dislocations and a terrible concussion in a manner adding nothing to the world's stockpile of rage (because not even avenging angel Piper could get mad at these two), and to hand her stressed, exhausted, soul-jarred, woebegone younger daughter, a woman at the end of her rope, a little more rope and a chance at giving—and getting—grace.

"Can you do something?" I asked. "For my mother?"

"Anything under the sun," avowed Thomas.

"Do not, whatever else you do—and I mean I really need you to promise—do not go to the police station and turn yourselves in."

Thomas drew back; he looked stunned.

"But it's the right thing to do," said Thomas.

"It isn't, though," I said. "Maybe in some moral universe, a lot of moral universes even, it would be. I can see that; I really can. But not in this one. In Ellie Brown's universe, it would be the exact wrong thing to do."

"I just don't see how—" said Thomas, shaking his head.

"Is it what she would want?" said Katie. "For us not to? Truly?"

"I swear it is," I said.

"What about our checking in with you about her?" asked Katie. "From time to time. I might be wrong to ask such a thing, but would there be room for that in your mother's universe?"

"So much room," I told her. "Acres and acres. Or—what are pieces of universe called?"

"Solar systems," said Katie. "Galaxies."

"Galaxies and galaxies," I said.

THEY CALLED IT SUNDOWNING.

A pretty word for a not-pretty thing: those near-daily bouts of confusion my mother experienced in the rehab center, usually in the early evening. Asking, always politely, where she was and why someone had brought her there. Mistaking a nurse for my brother Toby: "Jasper is too young to be on a surfboard, Tobias. I know you don't want my advice, but there it is." Answering questions about gardening that her physical therapist had never asked: "The problem with your Virginia bluebells is they're woodland, they like shade. You should replant them around that big oak in your backyard." Pleading for her daughter to bring her, *please, please, oh please, Cornelia*, the entire swirled, pleated, satiny, draped, and iridescent majesty of the aurora borealis.

After the first time the sundowning happened while I was with her, I sent a text to my family's sibling chat, a chat that had included my sister Ollie only since my mother's accident. Prior to that, multiple times, Ollie had been added, had stayed for a few days without making a peep, and then had removed herself after a friendly little sign-off like: Gotta get off this, guys. You should, too. Total waste of time.

CORNELIA: Today, Mom asked if I wanted her to take in my homecoming dress.

CAM: Like to Goodwill? Nice thought but you were two feet tall in high school. Who would buy that?

TOBY: Someone dressing a squirrel maybe. A child squirrel.

CAM: And hold on, did you even ever get asked to homecoming?

CORNELIA: YES, I DID. Senior year, anyway. And no, idiots. She mentioned darts. Running in some darts.

TOBY: Harsh. Go run in some darts and then play in the traffic, honey.

CORNELIA: It's SEWING. And Mom doesn't even sew. Plus, I don't need a homecoming dress. I'm not sixteen.

CAM: 18 you mean. 16 was you sitting home on homecoming night, remember?

TOBY: And every night.

CORNELIA: I'm just going to give you two galoots a minute or an hour and wait for what I just told you to sink in.

CAM: Oh shit.

TOBY: But Mom's never had dementia. She has, I don't know, what's the opposite of dementia?

CAM: She's like hyper clearheaded. Nothing gets past her, not even when you want it to.

CORNELIA: It's something that can happen to older people sometimes when they stay in the hospital for a while. They have confusion, often in the evenings. It's called sundowning.

OLLIE: Or hospital delirium. Sundowning is a stupid and unscientific term. And often not accurate.

CORNELIA: Thanks, Ollie. I think the sundowning will go away when she comes home. I hope.

CAM: It better.

TOBY: It will. Definitely will. She'd never put up with it not.

CAM: It's kind of funny though. Typical Mom. Other sundowners are probably cussing out the doctors or howling at the moon.

TOBY: Haha. And Mom's version of a werewolf is to turn into someone who thinks Cornelia actually got invited to homecoming.

MY SOJOURN AT MY PARENTS' house had begun with my coming down on the weekends, but then one Friday, I told Teo I thought it would be better if I stayed.

"Not forever," I added quickly.

My husband smiled at me. I had known Teo Sandoval since I was four years old—so forty years (*forty years*)—and his smile still felt like a revelation every time I saw it. His mouth, period, was a gift, but his smile was a waterfall and a row of streetlamps coming on at once and a perfect grilled cheese sandwich all in a single flash.

"Well, that's a relief," he said.

"They need me," I said. "My dad might be a doctor, but hospitals make him sad, at least hospitals that have my mom in them. And the rehab hospital, too. The rehab hospital *more*. It's the sundowning. He can't bear to see her like that, but he also hates leaving her alone in those moments. Plus, he needs me to keep everyone else informed about what's happening; you know how he doesn't text. I'm—what do you call it—the eyes on the ground."

"They're my favorite eyes," said Teo.

"I know you all need me, too," I said, although as I listened to myself say it, I could tell I didn't sound convinced. I didn't add "Even though I let you all down so grievously, back there in the checkout line of that damned, damned, accursed big-box store," but I could tell Teo heard it anyway.

"We do. You're the love of our lives," he said. "And you take the best care of all of us. But we can let you go for a little while. They're your parents."

Argh, I couldn't do it. I thought it would be better for everyone if I did it (a little sidestep, a little whitewash), but I couldn't. I couldn't stand there and feed this good man a half-truth, even though the whole would hurt him to hear and me to say. I couldn't have him thinking I was just a kind and altruistic daughter. As terribly imperfect a wife and mother and woman as I'd turned out to be, I wasn't as lost as all that.

I thought about how it was to be my mother, to be a person so rooted, a person whose sense of home ran so deep, that being away from home—night after night, going to bed, morning after morning, waking up somewhere else—caused you to lose your place in the story of your life. Displaced you. I used to be a person like that—just weeks ago I was. But not now, not anymore.

The point wasn't only to be there; it was also to not be here.

But how could I tell Teo what I felt? "Even when I'm in the same room with my children, even when I'm holding them, I am far, far away." Or "The difference is that my mother is healing; her broken bones are knitting back together like a film in rewind, and I'm helping that happen. But here the film just plays the same moment over and over and over, and I can't fix a single thing." Or "I need an escape from all of this impossible love, this piercing, shattering, disorganized, powerless love."

Who could say such things? Just to think them made me a traitor to everyone and everything I loved. Maybe a braver woman would have just hauled off and said them, but, as everyone now knew, I was not a braver woman.

Instead, I said other true things. True but easier.

"It's not just that I want to help my parents. It's that I haven't been myself for so long, ever since, well— And I feel like a fraud being here when I'm not who you all think I am. I need to figure out how to get back to being the person who deserves all of you because there has to be a way, right?"

"Cor," said Teo. "Stop with deserve. What does deserving have to do with anything? We belong to each other, the four of us. But you need to feel at home here again. And of course there's a way to do that. Definitely."

My husband Teo put his arms around me, and, for an instant, the distance between us healed like a cut, knitted like bone. I put my ear to his chest and listened for his heartbeat and, in the space of that fleeting moment, did not pull back from him, not even inside my head.

"We'll be here," said Teo, "Simon, Rose, and I. When you bring yourself back, we'll be right here."

Chapter 2

ELEANOR

September 1964

Eleanor looked up from her book, and there she was.

Martha. Walking toward her, still so far away that Eleanor could not make out her features or which of her few dresses she was wearing. For most people, a figure at that distance could have been anyone, but for Eleanor, instantly and unquestionably, it was Martha: the span and set of her shoulders, her rangy, beeline gait, the particular way she displaced light and cut through space. And as she approached, what always happened happened: everything else fell back a little, diminished. Even here, marveled Eleanor, even here on her sunlit campus with its columns and patterned brick walkways, its lush old hardwoods and lacquer-leaved magnolias, and everywhere, walking or sprawled on the grass, the lithe and lucky, boys with their shirt collars open, girls dressed as if it were the 1950s and not the 1960s, pedal pushers and twin sets, the cardigans discarded in the late September sun, tied loosely around still-tanned shoulders or littering the ground along with book bags and schoolbooks.

It's like being in love, thought Eleanor, *like in movies and poetry.* The beloved appears and the rest of the world fades. Eleanor did not know if she'd ever find love like that, wasn't even sure she wanted to. All the high drama and upheaval and pounding hearts and staying up late, pining. The very thought of pining made her impatient. The boys she knew seemed trivial—sweet, loud, and puppylike—and although she knew she might see them differently one day, she also knew that, as she watched her sister walk toward her, so far and for as long as she could remember, this was her truest—her only—love story.

And so it was that all the elegant geometry of academia, the great billows of emerald grass, her schoolmates resting lightly and shimmering inside their youth and beauty, all of it dimmed as Martha marched up, plain features and heavy brows, awkward and staring straight ahead, all angles in the old green dress Eleanor had made for her. Even across the distance, Eleanor read nervousness in Martha's gait, a hitch of tentativeness, and she wondered if Martha's nervousness might mirror her own, that same uncomfortable pang of worlds colliding. But Eleanor knew that if that were the case, if Martha was feeling out of place, she would set her jaw and lift her chin and step with extra certainty. It's what she usually did when she visited Eleanor at school, a display of bravado that made Eleanor proud and also hurt her heart. So Martha's nervousness meant something else. But it didn't matter, not at that moment. What mattered was Martha was there. Martha was *here*. Eleanor's older sister, Martha, strode closer and closer, her long shadow preceding her, and as quickly as she came, as purposeful her strides, it was not quick enough for Eleanor, who shut her book and stood up to close the gap between them.

When they were sitting on the bench together and Eleanor could take her sister in, she saw how even Martha's angular face softened in the afternoon sunshine. The lakeshore college town in North Carolina's Piedmont was not even a day's drive from where they had grown up, but it had struck Eleanor from the very first time she saw it that the light here was different, mellowing as it sifted through leaves or turned the white columns honey colored or ran like a gentle palm over the smooth hair of coeds. In Eleanor's memory, the light of home was stark and bright, garish as a camera flash in the kitchen, turning her mother's face, her hands, her teeth, and the whites of her eyes to marble. Until Eleanor had left home, she hadn't realized she noticed things like light. She thought she must have picked up the habit from her sister, whose eyes drank in everything, always had, subtleties and shadings, textures and variations and tints.

Eleanor's hands were clasped in her lap, and Martha wrapped one of hers around them both. Martha was tall and lanky like their father had been; Eleanor was tiny like their mother, Susan (they called her Susan more often than Mother because they thought Mother was too personal). "Look at you two," their mother had said once, laughing. "A crow and a wren. Caw, caw. Twitter, twitter." Even though Eleanor knew she herself was supposed to be the pretty one—certainly their mother had pointed it out often enough—when Martha was excited about something—her cheeks pink-stained, her brows leaping, her black eyes brimming with emotion—Eleanor thought there had never been, in all the world, anyone so splendid.

"What it is?" she asked, laughing. "Your eyes are practically shooting sparks."

But Martha didn't smile. She placed her hands in her lap, right over left, and then shifted them, left over right.

"Listen, Elsbee," she said. "I'm leaving."

"But you just got here," said Eleanor. "I thought we'd get sandwiches for dinner and sit by the lake. I made lemonade. With mint, the way you like it."

Martha sighed.

"I got a new job."

"But that's wonderful! Something good I hope."

"Yes."

"Something that will really draw on your gifts?"

Martha and Eleanor's father had saved enough money for both

of his girls to go to college, funds in their names that their mother couldn't touch. He had died after a brief illness when Eleanor was barely out of babyhood, but it was as if he'd known even then about the chaos to come. He left his wife money, too, but a man named Cyrus Burke, his father's oldest friend and their family lawyer, kept control over it. Susan received an allowance, and, to her vicious and everlasting fury, if she wanted extra money, she had to ask for it.

Martha was six years older than Eleanor, and she recalled the years when her father was alive as tranquil and happy. She told Eleanor how she could remember going to bed at night and hearing, from somewhere in the house, her father's low, steady voice like a hummed lullaby. She remembered going to sleep quickly, not staying up late listening for the sound of things breaking. She didn't remember whiskey on anyone's breath. All of that came later, came after. Even so, even then, for their father, there must have been signs of the storm gathering—and gathering and gathering—black clouds and roaring wind and stabbing shards of lightning—inside their mother's head.

So he'd put their education money into safekeeping, but Martha had decided on the local secretarial school instead of college. Eleanor could remember coming home from school to find her practicing, the staccato music of it, Martha's long fingers playing the secondhand typewriter like a piano. Martha was good with her hands, could draw like an angel, but her talent as an artist went deeper than deftness. She'd make art with her entire body, curving herself over the paper, leaning back to look, going in close to build a forest with charcoal swipes or blend pastels into a layered radiance. From Martha's hands, fields, skyscapes, bowls of plums, even Eleanor's own face appeared entirely new and crackling or seething or quietly breathing with life. It wasn't imitation, Eleanor recognized, it was birth. Like God in the Bible. Let there be light.

All that brilliance inside her hands and head and for the past three years, Martha had worked as a secretary in an insurance office, a fact that galled Eleanor in her soul. Time and time again, she'd told her to quit, leave, go to art school.

"I don't need to go to school to learn how to make art, silly," Martha would say. "I just have to make it, again and again and again."

But Eleanor knew this was only part of the truth. Now, here at college, now that she'd gotten away, whenever Eleanor pictured the three of them in the same room, even when they were both children, Martha was always between Eleanor and Susan, her arms outstretched like a crossing guard's, throwing herself up like a wall. Stony-eyed and flaring, fiery and loud, even as Eleanor could see her skinny shoulders quaking inside the cotton of her dress. Eleanor understood this was why Martha had stayed: to come between, face off, intercept. To take the brunt. Absorb the blows. Blows did not often come, but sometimes they did.

"Will you get to make art at your new job, Marthy?"

"Yes! That is, I've been promised time and materials. It'll be part of my pay. He even put it into the contract."

"He?"

"You know how I went back last year and took that bookkeeping course? Well, my teacher, Mr. Gillibrand, he's so kind. He called me a few days ago to say he had an opportunity for me. A friend of his from college, a rich guy named David Olson, had just moved with his family to live full-time at what used to be just their summer home and was looking for a personal assistant. He'll work from home as much as he can and will need someone to write correspondence, do some accounting, make travel arrangements, things like that. Mr. Gillibrand, God bless him, thought of me."

"You'll be so good at that, Marthy. You've known how to run a household since you were ten years old."

Martha smiled. "More like eight. And, yes, I think all those years is why. So many years."

"Why what?"

"Why Mr. Gillibrand offered the job to me."

Eleanor met her sister's eyes. "He thought it was about time you got away," she said.

"It's perfect timing, really," said Martha, briskly. "You're in your second year of school. You've got lots of friends. That professor's family has taken you under its wing. I can leave, knowing you're settled, and there won't be a reason in the world for you to go home once I'm gone."

As Martha spoke, Eleanor wanted to jump in and say so many things, things like "You should've left a long time ago." And "You don't need to worry about me." But then Martha's voice said *gone*, and that single word, the tone Martha said it in, sent Eleanor spinning and drove every other thought out of her head. Martha reached out and brushed back a stray lock of hair from her sister's face—a thing she'd done many times over their life together, her most tender gesture.

"Don't worry about her," Martha said. "She's taken care of. She's got the Sunday school job and her church people and is still doing bookkeeping for the church. I gave the minister's wife your address here and the main phone number of the college, but I've told her not to get in touch, not unless disaster strikes. And it won't. So don't worry. Just soak this up: school, your friends, being here in this beautiful place. You hear me?"

Eleanor knew as well as Martha did that the books didn't always balance, that the Sunday school children sometimes sat fidgeting in their seats, waiting for a teacher who never arrived until someone else showed up, flustered, to tell them about Moses in the bulrushes, to make macaroni art or string god's-eyes. But it wasn't her mother Eleanor was worried about, not yet.

"Where is the summerhouse?" she asked, her voice coming out small.

"Way up north," said Martha. "The North Shore of Lake Superior. Minnesota, if you can imagine that."

Eleanor could not, but she said, "You've always wanted to live up north. You've always said so."

"I have," said Martha, laughing. "Even back when I had no idea of the points of a compass or a map of the United States. All I knew was that it was far away. I imagined it was the exact opposite of where I was."

Eleanor smiled. "Well, if you're going, you'd better stock up on the white paint. For the snow. And the icebergs. And the polar bears."

Martha's laugh rang out, happy. "All those polar bears on icebergs in Lake Superior. But, yes, I *know*. And I think the light will be different, too, don't you? I bet everything will be different."

Martha was Eleanor's best friend, her protector, her truest love, her only home. Without her, Eleanor would be adrift on an iceberg of her own. She wanted to cry, wanted to say "Don't go, don't go, don't go." She knew if she did that, Martha would stay and also knew it would be the worst thing she, Eleanor, had ever done to anyone.

Instead, she said, "You'll want a coat, a real one. If I really work, I could have it finished in a week."

Chapter 3

CORNELIA

MY MOTHER HAS ALWAYS BEEN a person who eschewed sentimentality, eschewed it vocally and often, and while I can hear you protest, as I myself have done—vehemently, on more than one occasion, that sentimentality is purely subjective, that what qualifies as sentimental for one person can carry honest and considerable emotional weight for another—I can tell you that the list of what qualified as sentimental for Ellie Brown was long, as was her commitment to it: long-lived and also intractable. And she didn't just disdain sentimentality for herself, but, despite her overall kind and mostly patient nature, she also found it exasperating in others. She attempted to conceal this exasperation, but as her daughter—and arguably (although I can't think of anyone apart from me who would actually argue) the most sentimental member of our family—I have cause to know that most of these attempts fell flat, occasionally spectacularly flat. But like most people who eschew sentimentality, my mother had her exceptions, her blind spots, although she would never label them either of those. If she deigned to discuss the matter at all, I'm sure she would say that those things that elicited her sentimentality weren't silly but sacred, that her attachment to them wasn't sentimentality but love.

Christmas, for instance. In my parents' house, the Christmas season always began while the Thanksgiving turkey carcass was still simmering itself into a glorious, gold-pooled broth on the stove. Before any of us had fully digested our pumpkin pie (or apple or apple crumb or apple cranberry or pecan or chocolate pecan or all of the above if you were my brothers, pie being a kind of religion in my parents' house), we would be corralled and coaxed and bullied (depending upon the child; Ollie invariably required bullying) into full hall-decking mode: lugging boxes from the attic and the basement, swapping out orange and gold for red and green, gourds for pine cones, cornucopias for Santas; hanging stockings; untangling and looping endless strands of lights and glass beads and jingle bells around every living thing in the yard, including our pets and a blue whale–size magnolia, as Christmas music and the aroma of fir-scented candles filled the house. And while my mother had a long history of ruthlessly tossing nearly all of her children's artwork—sometimes curating out the best pieces and allowing them a few days of bulletin board, refrigerator, or kitchen counter display, sometimes not—she had scrupulously hung on to every Christmas ornament we had ever made.

Although I should add that over the years, my mother's children's ornaments were more and more relegated to the dark side of the tree, edged out by those of her grandchildren. Which brings me to another item on my mother's list of sentimental exceptions. Another item? The topper, miles above even Christmas: her grandchildren. Most people love their grandchildren, but I reckon most don't keep everything the grandchildren had ever made or worn or written; every selfie they'd texted from their parents' phones; every paper napkin jotted with a tic-tac-toe or hangman game their grandfather had played with them to keep them busy at a restaurant. My mother had a huge drawer in the hallway armoire exclusively for the bits and pieces they'd shed while visiting: hair bands, rubber bracelets, baby teeth (in miniature labeled manila envelopes), socks (ranging from thumb-size to soccer socks a foot and a half long), used toothbrushes (*used toothbrushes!*), hats (some small enough for an apple to wear), and a single, very small, daffodil-yellow Croc that once belonged to my daughter Rose, the fate of its mate remaining, probably for all time, one of our family's darkest unsolved mysteries.

And now that I was back in my mother's house, sleeping in my childhood room, I discovered another item in my mother's sentimentality exceptions clause, one I'd never noticed before in all my years of visiting: books. Specifically, mine.

Obviously, my mother was not the variety of parent who freezes her children's rooms in time, preserves them as untouched sacred shrines to their childhoods, but neither was she the sort who, practically the second she got home from dropping us off at college, began cheerfully strip-mining our rooms of every trace of us. (My friend Linny claims that, just days after she left for college, before her homesickness had even begun to wear off, while she was still crying in the shower and digging out her teddy bear in the dead of night to sleep with, her otherwise loving and attentive dad had whisked away the bed, desk, and beanbag chair from her room at home, replaced it all with a table as big as multiple barn doors, and launched headfirst back into a hobby he'd zealously pursued back when he was a carefree, unmarried man in his twenties. By the time Linny came home for Thanksgiving, her room housed an entire landscape—trees, buildings, people, shiny ponds, matchstick-size telephone poles and wires, dogs and cats, even outdoor cafés with food on the plates—through which a miniature steam train wended its chugging way, and Linny slept in the guest room.)

My mother didn't make a project of it; instead, she did it gradually, organically, and over years: disappearing a few posters here, a bulletin board covered with photos and ticket stubs there. Stuffed animals; sports trophies, ribbons, and medals (of which, between the four of us, there were about ten million, none of them mine); lava lamps; Nerf basketball hoops; old perfume bottles; dried corsages;

tissue paper flowers; school pennants; framed photos: all of it, little by little, quietly ebbing away, relocated to the attic or the basement or the Salvation Army or—let's face it—the landfill, until our rooms were pleasant and tasteful and mostly anonymous, with clear surfaces and neutral wall colors.

Just before I made the books discovery, I had gotten back from visiting my mother at the rehab center. She was getting better, stronger, but it had been a hard few hours nonetheless. She'd reminded me to feed a long-dead neighbor's longer-dead cat and to bring in the neighbor's mail and newspaper while the neighbor and her family were on vacation, and, just before I left, my mother asked for the northern lights, but this time, she also grabbed my jacket sleeve and said, "I left them behind so long ago, years and years; I did. But I need you to understand I never forgot them, not for a single day," and I avowed as solemnly as I had ever avowed anything that I believed her, that I had never doubted that for a second.

When I'd gotten back to the house, I had heard my father in the kitchen, but I needed a minute. I'd slipped upstairs, taken off my shoes, sat down on the edge of my bed, shut my eyes, and let my tired mind wander. What it made its wandering way to was my mother's garden, not as it was now, in fall, tipping toward russets and golds, with scraps of scraggly, rickety, leggy loveliness abiding here and there—asters, goldenrod, calendula—with most of its splendor gone or fading. Instead, my mind entered my mother's garden in early spring, the time of year when she practically lived there. It floated easy as a cabbage butterfly over the trees with their luminous lemon-lime leaf buds; over the grass dotted with tiny, spiky, purple crocuses; amid stands of snowdrops and startling daggers of green coming up out of the dark, mulched ground. And then my mind found what it had come for: little wire cages, bell-shaped and placed over a few of the newly planted plants. Cloches, they're called, a word I remembered, of course, because of the hats. As I drifted over the cloches, I could hear my mother explaining to me how rabbits like to eat certain young plants, delicate new growth, how the cloches protect the baby plants until they mature and their stems get too tough to be worth the rabbits' bother.

And then my mind ceased meandering and zipped from the cloches straight back to my mother, her face open and sorrowful, washed with tears, her breaking voice asking for what I did not know how to give her. I did not try to erase the image of my mother's sad face from my memory. I'd done that before after a rough day, but this time, I took that face and held it in my mind, as gently as if I were taking it between my two hands, and I stared into it, right into its eyes. Her eyes, my mother's.

I wish I could drop a cloche over you, I told her.

What you should understand about us is that this was new. I had never taken care of her, had never thought of her as someone who needed taking care of. Our relationship—well, there was love, love in abundance. Every act between me and my mother was and had always been some version of love, even when it hadn't always looked like it. As I lived, I loved her and she loved me. Still, distance stretched between us, the kind of distance that stretches between people who are, in essence, different from each other. My mother had always behaved as if emotions in excess were rather like bad manners: they put other people out, made them uncomfortable. As Robert Frost said (ironically, if you ask me, but my mother never did ask me) and as my mother liked to quote, "Good fences make good neighbors," and my mother kept her emotional and psychological fences in excellent repair. While I? I didn't seem to have a fence at all, not even split rail, full of spaces. I deflected attention away from this fact with jokes and sarcasm and a studied nonchalance, but it was all a dodge, a dance, smoke and mirrors, bob and weave. Really,

I lived in a state of osmosis, every membrane permeable. I had never really minded; no, if I'm honest, I thought it was the best way to be, life at its most real. Lately, though, I had thought more than once that I could stand to grow myself a fence. Even a hedge, a low one, would be an improvement.

But there I go, winding my way back to myself. Again. Ugh, sorry. Enough. *Enough*, Cornelia.

About my mother: regarding her as fragile—a delicate, pale-green shoot in need of protecting—was something I'd never done before; it threw me off and scared me to regard my mother this way; it ached, that tender patch opening inside of me. But the chance to love in a completely new way a person you've loved forever doesn't come along every day. When one does, you need to seize it.

"I'm it," I said, firmly. "I'm your cloche."

I said this aloud in my childhood bedroom. Calmed by having made this resolution, my mind resumed wandering in my mother's garden until it drifted off to sleep.

I woke up in a sweat with gunfire in my ears, proving once again: there is no calm that can't be, in an instant, smashed all to hell.

I bolted upright, dry-mouthed, gasping, scrambling blindly for the lifeline that is my husband's voice. My scuttling hands found my phone on the bedside table, and I called him.

"Saved by the bell," he said, instead of hello, and, in the wake of those four syllables, my heart rate slowed enough for me to speak.

"Me, too," I said. "Or saved by your being saved by the bell, anyway."

"Hey," said Teo, lowering his voice, "you okay? You needed saving?"

"Just a hard moment," I said. "I wonder—are the kids around?"

"Yep, right here doing homework. That's what you saved me from. I was helping Rose—"

"Trying to help Rose," I heard Rose's voice say.

"Yeah, so it turns out differential equations are peanuts compared to fifth grade word problems."

"I'd give my right arm to talk to them for a sec," I said.

"I don't think that'll be necessary," said Teo, "since Simon is jumping up and down like a kangaroo trying to grab the phone."

And then, my little boy's panting breaths fogged the phone line for a blessed split second, before he said, "Do you know why water striders can walk on water? That's what we're supposed to call them: water striders. This one kid said they were Jesus bugs, but Mr. Clyde said that was disrespectful to people who worship Jesus or whatever, even though he knew the kid, Josh, didn't mean to be disrespectful, and it turns out Josh does worship Jesus, so, yeah. Anyway, it's *not* because they have special feet."

"Really?" I said. "How does someone walk on water without special feet?"

"Haha," said Simon. "You called bugs someone. No one does that, Mom."

"Well, they should," I said.

"It's because of this thing called surface tension," said Simon.

And he was off.

When he finished and when I finished telling him how cool I thought what he'd just told me was (and it was extremely cool), he said, "Okay, bye, Mom, love you," and was gone.

I could hear muffled voices and then Teo got back on.

"Hey," he said.

And even though I am always happy right down to my bone marrow to hear his voice, right then, his wasn't the voice I was hoping for.

"She doesn't want to talk to me, does she?" I said.

"Guys," said Teo to the kids, "I'm going outside for a minute."

"Don't be lovey-dovey on the phone!" yelled Simon and dissolved into laughter.

Once outside, Teo said, "Sorry. I tried."

"Did you tell her about the right arm offer?"

"Look, she might not talk to you, but she talks about you," he said, "and a lot of times, she totally forgets she's mad."

"I don't blame her for being mad that I'm here instead of there," I said. "I'm mad at myself. But I can't stand it if she hates me."

"She doesn't hate you. Her hating you is just not in the cards. So stop worrying about it."

I sighed.

"How is he?" I said. "He always sounds like that, just like he always has. I spoke with Dr. Joyce yesterday. She thinks he's doing great. She says kids are amazingly resilient and he's no exception. But what do you think?"

There was a small silence.

"I think he *is* doing great a lot of the time," said Teo. "And he does seem like himself. But sometimes, he seems like himself turned full volume. He goes at a fever pitch, like he's trying too hard to seem normal, maybe. But, I don't know, that could also just be me thinking he could not possibly be as okay as he seems or not wanting to take his okayness for granted. But anyway, overall, he's doing really well. Rose, too."

"What about nighttime?"

"He's stopped getting into our bed in the middle of the night."

"Really? Stopped altogether?"

Simon had always loved getting into bed with us in the very early mornings, especially on weekends. Not because he was upset, but because he just liked waking up there. But after the day in the checkout line, he'd shown up almost every night, trembling and wordless, to curl up against my back in a hard, hot knot. When I'd left, he'd kept coming to our room, and Teo would find him sleeping, his arms wrapped tightly around my pillow.

"I get the idea it started to embarrass him," said Teo. "Most nights, now, he sleeps in his own bed, but two or three nights a week, he sneaks in with his blanket and sleeps on the floor on your side of the bed. In the morning, I make a big noisy deal out of getting up to go to the bathroom and when I come back to the room, he's gone."

"You let him save face," I said. "That's just exactly like you."

"We're all good here, Cor," said Teo, gently. "We miss you. We can't wait till you're home, but we're all coming along. How about you?"

I didn't tell him about the gunshot crashing through my dreams almost every night. I didn't tell him how, when I hung up, I would fall into a deep hole of missing the three of them and would take a long time to climb out. I didn't want to hear his kindness and caretaking come through the phone to hold me. Some mothers are torn from their children. When you leave of your own accord, the last thing you should do is ask for comfort.

"I'm coming along, too," I said.

AFTER I HUNG UP, I sat on the edge of the bed, missing my family for all I was worth. When I could focus on something besides this feeling, I found myself staring at the bookshelf that stood against the wall near the foot of the bed, the same bookshelf I'd had in my room since I was seven and asked for it for Christmas. If you're thinking "Oh my, what an interesting choice for a second grader to include on her Christmas list!" you'll be even more interested when you learn it was the sole item on my list that year and I specified the height, which is towering, by saying, "I'll grow into it! Like Ollie's clothes!" Nine-year-old Ollie had widened her eyes in exaggerated excitement and said, "Santa's gonna see that and say, 'Wow, Cornelia must be such a cool girl!'" And then added: "You'll be in high school before you wear these clothes, pygmy," which was mean and culturally insensitive but also closer to accurate than you might imagine.

Distractedly, I scanned the books, starting at the top shelf and working my way down: *The Snowy Day, Make Way for Ducklings, The Little Fur Family, Bread and Jam for Francis*, all the Little House books, *The Secret Garden*, the Narnia books, the entire set of L. M. Montgomery's Anne books, Trixie Belden, Nancy Drew, the Melendy Quartet, *Little Women*, Madeleine L'Engle's time travel books, *To Kill a Mockingbird, Franny and Zooey, A Room with a View, The Collected Poems of Emily Dickinson, Middlemarch* . . . As my gaze skidded and hopscotched over the spines and from shelf to shelf, I thought, *It's like being haunted by my growing-up self, like taking a stroll through my developing brain.* And then, I thought, *Wait, what?*

Because I'd never arranged my books this way: in the order of when I'd read and loved them, beginning with picture books, moving on to chapter books, and so on. I don't think I'd ever arranged them at all. I've always been a haphazard shelver, usually deliberately so. I like the idea of books as odd and random bedfellows, keeping unexpected company with one another: Jane Austen hanging out with Zora Neale Hurston; Ann Patchett rubbing elbows with A. A. Milne; E. M. Forster cheek by jowl with Tana French. The only organizational principle I'd ever applied to this collection of books and to every collection I'd ever owned was love. I loved every volume; I lived inside them; I'd read every one over and over, often literally to pieces.

I stood up and walked over to the shelf. I narrowed my eyes. I lifted out and then put back one book, then another. Then, I shut my eyes and sought out my mother's face again.

You, I told her, wonderstruck, *are a mystery. All these years, I*

*thought I knew you and it turns out you're a mystery. You've been one
all along.*

"SHE REPLACED THEM!" I TOLD my father. "I took my set of Madeleine L'Engle to college and never brought it back. Those books are
right this second in my house at home. Narnia, too! And a bunch
of others. She *replaced* them! She walked into a bookstore and she
bought new ones!"

My father was slicing a cucumber, coolly. He didn't look surprised
at my discovery. He didn't even look up.

"Well, if she bought new ones," said my father, continuing to slice,
"she must have walked into a bookstore to do it. I hear everyone
orders online these days, but you know your mom. She believes in
supporting stores owned by flesh-and-blood people."

"But that's just it," I said, thumping the counter with the side of my
fist. "I *don't* know my mom. Not like I thought I did. And you know
what? She shelved them in order, too! Took them out and reshelved
them in the order I got them and read them. Picture books first."

My father shrugged. "I guess she wanted to remember that about
you, what you read when."

A thought hit me. "And, Dad, listen! I never told her when I took
books off that shelf and out of our house. You realize what that
means, right?"

"It means she noticed? Not a lot gets by your mother, you know."

"She noticed what was missing. And replaced it. I mean, who even
knew she was paying attention?"

My father put down the knife and looked at me with a quizzical
smile. "To you, Cornelia? When did she ever *not* pay attention to you?"

There was the tiniest reprimand in his voice, and chastened, I said,

"No, I know. She's a great mom, a prince among moms, a queen. She loves me. I just mean: nostalgia. She's just not nostalgic. She's not sentimental. She doesn't hang on to things."

"Well, no, not a lot of things. Not most things even."

"Like our artwork," I said. "The crafts we made in school. Some parents keep all of that, but she didn't."

"I guess some parents do," said my father. "But you know, you weren't really artists, were you? You, Ollie, Cam, and Toby."

"You think that's why she threw our artwork away? Because it wasn't very good? I mean, no, it wasn't. Most of it was outrageously bad, but do you think that's why?"

My father laughed.

"It was generally pretty bad," he agreed and pretended to shudder. "The stuff of nightmares, some of it. But that's not what I meant. I meant art really wasn't important to you. It wasn't who any of you were. In your case, reading was. Reading is. Your mother loves that about you, always did."

I sat down on a counter stool, considering this, considering the noticing, me-reading-loving, reshelving mystery that was my mother. Then, I looked at my father, standing in our kitchen in his UVA sweatshirt, making a salad. He'd finished with the cucumber, had put it aside in a small glass bowl as was his habit, and had started in on a glossy red pepper.

Your father and his little glass bowls.

As clearly as if she were in the kitchen with us, I could hear my mother saying the words. I couldn't remember when the conversation had taken place. Last Christmas? The one before that? Or maybe another holiday altogether. But I could recall the fondness in her voice as clear as day.

"He likes to keep all the ingredients separate until the very last second," she'd said.

When I asked her why, she'd smiled and shrugged her pretty shoulders, never taking her eyes off her husband. "It's one of his many mysteries."

"Dad?" I said.

"Yes, honey?"

During her lucid moments, of which there were many, I never asked my mother about the northern lights. I didn't know if the loss of them was rooted in her past or even in the actual world, and I wasn't at all sure that her northern lights were *the* northern lights, the natural phenomenon, because while you could leave those lights behind, no one could bring them back to you, could they? Although I had imagined it: how I'd gather them in with my hands, folding them like fabric, silk organza or maybe tulle, violet and bottle green, then would carry the shining bundle in my arms to spread out before her. But whatever the northern lights were or were not, whatever they stood for in my mother's mind, even if they were pure sundowning hallucination, her grief at losing them was sharp, fresh, unmistakably true. Her grief was real, and since it was real, there was a chance it had always been there and was still there, dormant, sleeping just beneath the surface of my clear-headed, sunup mother, and I would not risk waking it up.

But I hadn't yet mentioned the northern lights to my father, either, or to my brothers and sister, or even to Teo. Maybe it was because I worried that my mother's sundowning upset them, but maybe it was because it—especially the northern lights part of it—upset me. Maybe I'd left the subject alone for all our sakes. I took a breath and plunged.

"Can you think of any connection between Mom and the northern lights?"

The knife my dad held hovered above the cutting board, and he looked at me, lifting one eyebrow.

"You mean the actual northern lights? The aurora borealis?"

"Yes. Or maybe not. I don't know exactly. But let's start with those."

"Let's start with a connection between your mother and the aurora borealis? That's what you're saying?"

"I am. Yes."

"Well, they're both examples of nature's wonders. Obviously."

I smiled. "True."

"Or," he went on, "were you thinking she's responsible for making them happen?"

"I wouldn't put it past her."

My dad came around to my side of the counter and sat on the stool next to mine.

"Cornelia, honey, maybe you should tell me what you're talking about."

I did. I told him and did not cut corners off her sadness or gloss over her regret. I did not make it prettier than it was, even though I wanted to. When I'd finished, my father let out his breath, which I guess he'd been holding.

"I wish I could give them to her," he said.

"Same here."

"Your mother doesn't ask for much, and when a person who doesn't ask for much asks for something, you just want to give it to them."

"I know," I said.

I put my hand over my dad's then leaned my forehead against his shoulder, and he rested his other hand against the back of my head, and we stayed that way for a few quiet seconds. When I sat up again, I asked, "You think she ever saw them? Did she ever go north?"

"We've been north together to visit you and Ollie."

I laughed. "I don't think you can see the northern lights from Wilmington, Delaware, Dad. Or even from Long Island. I mean when she was younger, before us."

"I met your mom when she was twenty years old, and as far as I know, the only North she ever got to before then was Carolina. She was living there when I met her."

"Oh. Right. I forget that's where she's from," I said. "I forget she ever lived anywhere else but here."

My dad got up, went back to the other side of the counter, and began to chop pepper as if his life depended on it.

"Well, that's what kids do I guess," he said, briskly. "They think their parents' lives started when they were born."

"I don't, though," I protested. "Not with you, for instance. I still make Granny B's shortbread; I still have her rocking chair next to my fireplace. I call my cousins from your side on their birthdays. And we all grew up hearing stories from your youth."

My father grinned. "My wild and misspent youth I think you meant to say."

If ever a youth had been tame and well spent, it was my father's. As far as I or anyone else could tell, my father's, Dr. B's, young life had been a long and seamless succession of Norman Rockwell prints. Pie-eating contests, fishing holes, county fairs, debate club, church basement suppers, tennis and swimming championships, family car trips to Assateague Island and the Great Smoky Mountains.

"I know about the time you mistook the tree stump for a bear," I said. "I know about the time you and your cousin Gene switched sugar for salt in your great-aunt Cornelia's kitchen as a joke."

"That wasn't very nice of us."

"Not nice? I'm pretty sure it was the worst thing you ever did."

"I don't know," said my dad. "I turned in at least two, maybe three library books late. Shoot, maybe four."

"So, what was Mom doing down in North Carolina before she met you?"

"Awaiting my arrival, of course."

"Dad."

"The usual, I guess. She grew up in a small town near the coast. Then, she went to college."

"At UVA," I said. "Right here. After Ollie and I were born."

"Well, no," said my father. "She finished at UVA. But she started off at Cadwallader College, near Charlotte. Got through the better part of three years there before she left."

"Hold on. She did? How did no one ever tell me that?"

Instead of answering, my father grabbed two lemons from the fruit bowl on the counter and began juggling them.

"Dad, I'm not ten. You can't distract me with juggling, especially just two lemons."

While one lemon was still in the air, he snagged a third and tossed it into the mix, never missing a beat.

I cupped my hands around my mouth and pretended to bellow, "Why did she not finish at Cadwallader?"

My dad caught one lemon between his chin and shoulder and stopped juggling.

"I guess because sometimes life happens and moves you onto a different path, Cornelia."

"You know that isn't really an answer, right?"

"You know this isn't really my story to tell, right?"

"I don't know *any* stories from Mom's growing up."

My dad's face went serious. "You don't? Not one?"

Yes, one. One story.

More than ten years ago, before she was one of my best-loved beloveds, before I even knew her, my friend Viviana had struggled with bipolar disorder, a struggle that culminated in her suddenly, one dark day, stopping her car, dropping off her eleven-year-old daughter, Clare, by the side of the road, and disappearing for over two weeks. I looked up one day and there, in the middle of the café I managed at the time, stood Clare, and because Clare was alone in the world and because she was a person I'd loved practically on sight, I took her to the place where all confused, hurting, and lonely children should be taken: home. Specifically to Ellie and Dr. B's house, this very one, the homiest home I'd ever known, so that when Viviana tracked us down, after she'd gotten medication and come back to herself, it was this house she came to. Viviana would get better; she and Clare would move from Pennsylvania to live in my hometown; Clare would become the child—now the grown woman in love with my stepson, Dev (thank you, universe)—of all our hearts, and my mother would grow to love Viviana as much as she loved any of us, which I can tell you is a lot. But on that long-ago January dusk, when Viviana materialized, wan and wraithlike, sane and sad, on my mother's doorstep, my mother had gotten mad. She had flared like a torch, my ordinarily polite and warm and generous mother, and she'd stood between Viviana and Clare like an angel with a burning sword.

"I hope you don't think you can just pack her up and take her home," she'd hissed at Viviana.

And then, later, in our cozy, firelit family room still Christmas-decorated to the gills, my mother had told me about her own bipolar mother, Susan. She told me about Susan's rages, her drinking, her early death. For the space of one hour, the door to my mother's childhood was jolted open to reveal ugliness and fear and a smart, careful, wary, blue-eyed girl always awaiting the next bad thing, trying with all her might to keep her world in balance.

"I swore nothing like that would ever touch this family," my mother had told me.

And with that declaration, the moment had ended. The door to that girl and her mother and her world had slammed shut and stuck that way, and I had long ago given up on my attempts to jimmy it open.

"Is that why?" I asked my father. "Because of her mother? Is that why she dropped out of college?"

"Your mother doesn't talk about that part of her life. I trust she has her reasons, good ones. How about you let it alone, Cornelia?"

He didn't raise his voice or even sound especially angry. My father is the gentlest of men. But I sat on that kitchen stool and knew what I was seeing on the other side of the counter: the angel with the burning sword.

"Okay," I said, nodding. "Okay, Daddy. The thing is, I feel like I almost lost her and I don't really know her and I want to. But you're right about it being her story. I'm sorry."

THAT NIGHT, WHEN I WAS curled up in the velvet armchair in my room with a shiny, never-before-opened copy of *A Wrinkle in Time*, my dad came in with a Post-it-size scrap of paper in his hand.

"After I went to bed, I remembered this," he said, handing the scrap to me. "Something she keeps tucked inside her day planner."

The paper was softened with age, almost silken, ragged-edged, as if it had been torn from a larger sheet. I looked down at it, and before I understood what I was seeing, I recognized that what rested in my palm, weightless as a leaf, was an object of astonishing loveliness. Pen and ink and watercolor. Greens and purples and opal-blue, incandescent. And then, as I looked at them, the colors resolved into a scene, a place, a miniature jewel of landscape and skyscape. Black, spiny spires of evergreens in the foreground, a glimpse of snowy knoll, and the sky, more than anything the sky, a sky alive with pouring, slanting, breathing, color-charged, star-inflected light.

"This," I whispered, "is so beautiful. Where did she get it?"

My father shook his head.

"I never asked her. I never paid much attention to it. I've seen it only a few times and not for years."

"Years," I said, with wonder. "Mom gets a new day planner every year. She must move this from planner to planner, year after year after year."

"Do you think this is what she wants you to bring her?"

"Maybe," I said. "But she said she lost the northern lights a long time ago, and this is right here in her own house."

"It looks like she tore it out of something. A sketchbook. Or a letter maybe." He leaned over. "It looks like little bits of handwriting on the edges."

I held the piece of paper under the reading lamp.

"You're right. In pencil. It's too faded to read, but it's nothing you could read anyway, just tail ends or beginnings of letters."

"You could bring it to her," said my father.

I nodded.

"If this were mine, I'd want it, too," I said.

"Look at that sky," said my father.

"If I were there, on the edge of those trees, I would just stand and watch it shine," I said. "Wouldn't you?"

"You still having those nightmares?" asked my dad.

"Sometimes," I said.

And then, as if the small exchange about the nightmares hadn't happened at all, he said, "It looks pretty cold. But, yep, I probably would."

There we were, my father and I, our two heads bent over that tiny piece of beauty, imagining ourselves into its world, ourselves and Ellie Brown, too.

"Once we'd started," I said, "I bet we'd stay and stay. I bet we'd stand there all night."

Chapter 4

ELEANOR

October 1964

October 1, 1964

Dear Elsbee,

I'm here. And you know what? I just realized that when I imagined being here, I didn't really. I only imagined being gone, far away, a chicken flown the coop. I pictured, again and again, waking up in a bed that wasn't the same old bed in a room that wasn't the same old room. I imagined not living with Susan (more times than I can count!). But I never pictured what it would be like once I __got__ here. Not really. Isn't that funny?

And I didn't imagine what it would be like to be so far away from you. Which might have been on purpose because if I'd known what it would feel like—what it feels like right this minute—I might not have stepped foot on that airplane at all.

The airplane was amazing. And also not amazing. For some of it, I forgot I was even in the air, if you can believe it. I guess I thought I'd be aware of __flying__ the entire time, of whizzing through space. I definitely thought I'd at least feel high up, and I did have that sensation at takeoff, watching the buildings and trees and highways and striped fields and bodies of water drop away, get smaller and smaller. It's interesting how many bodies of water there actually are when you're up there, ponds I suppose, and lakes of the not-Great variety. But for a lot of the trip, I could have just been in a room. A weird room, to be sure, long and narrow and full of strangers sitting elbow to elbow and all facing forward. It was only now and then, if the plane dipped a bit or rumbled or if I looked out the window at the clouds (which reminded me of dollops of mashed potatoes—how's that for poetic?), that I thought: _Good gosh, we really are flying!_

Remember how you would go to slumber parties and the girls would tell ghost stories in the dead of night? Back then, I never understood it, why a person would scare herself on purpose with made-up monsters when there's more than enough scariness in everyday life. And then you would lie wide awake all night afterward and come home exhausted. I hated it. But I did that exact thing to myself on the plane! I'd find myself getting lost in my book or dozing off just as ordinary as anything, and I would jolt myself out of it by picturing the plane, that bucket of bolts, miles above the surface of Earth, endless, swirling blankness above and below, suspended there by what? Air? Wishful thinking? I shut my eyes and pictured the plane plummeting, nose first, spinning into the dead center of a lake or a cornfield.

I know it's awful to deliberately conjure up such tragic and terrible things, especially because they do actually happen, but I just wanted to _realize_ it, to feel in my bones and stomach, not exactly the danger but the _difference._ This is my chance at adventure, the first I've ever had. I want to be aware of, to be _all the way here_ for every second, my eyes wide open. You know what I mean? Don't know why I bother to ask because you always, always do. Maybe someday another person will know me so well—even half as well—as you do, but, honestly, I can't imagine it.

My new employer, David Olson, sent a car to pick me up from the airport in Duluth and to drive me to his house in Banc Rocheux, a little over a hundred miles away. I wanted to talk to the driver, whose name was Eddie, and to take in the view out the window (there's a miraculous thing in Duluth called a lift bridge that I was told in a letter from my new employer not to miss; I missed it) which I am sure was like no view I've ever seen—and you know how I just eat up views—but I was bone-tired. I'm embarrassed to say I climbed into the backseat, slumped against the window like a sack of turnips, and was out like a light.

When we got to the Olsons' house, it was nighttime. The property is tucked away in woody hills, a mile or so from the small coastal town, so it was black as ink apart from the stars, and the sky was flooded with them. Those stars broke through the tired fog inside my head, and I got the tingle in my fingers I get when I want to paint a thing. I'll do it, too, sometime soon, paint that sky. How utterly lovely and luxurious it is to think I will have beautifully empty hours in which to paint.

The house isn't grand, thank goodness (I haven't had many occasions to test this theory, but I strongly suspect that grand and I don't mix), an oversize cabin really. There were muddy boots on the porch, looking as if they'd been kicked off and left, some old white rocking chairs like we have at home, and a rake leaning against the wall, so, nervous as I was, before I'd even stepped through the door, I thought, maybe this is going to be all right.

Elaine opened the door. I used her first name in that sentence because that's what Mrs. Olson asked me to call her, straight off, and I need to get used to it. She's younger than I thought she'd be, her husband, too. Forty or so, maybe. She wore blue jeans and a ponytail. I didn't meet the kids, who were evidently banished to a neighbor's in order to give me some peace and quiet on my first night, but there are twins, May and Tessie, fifteen years old, and a boy, Elliot, twelve.

Elaine is one of those busy, bustling, chatty sorts, with a kind smile. Before I had really gotten my bearings, she'd asked Eddie to take my bags to my rooms (I liked the sound of "rooms" since I'd been picturing just one), sat me down at the big kitchen table, and placed a bowl of beef stew and a thick slice of buttered toast in front of me. I ate, but not much. Too nervous, too tired.

Mr. Olson poked his head in. His phrase, right after, "Sit, sit!" because at the sight of him, I'd stood up. "Just poking my head in to say hello." He told me to take a few days to get acclimated before I started work, which I thought was very nice of him.

After he'd gone, Elaine apologized for talking my head off and trying to stuff me full of food when I probably just wanted to see my rooms and settle in, and I couldn't even be polite and argue. I was that tired.

My "rooms" turned out to be a little cabin set in a copse of paper birches behind the big cabin. A bedroom; a windowed front room the length of the cabin with an armchair, a bentwood rocker, and a big oak table that will also serve as my desk; a bathroom; and the tiniest kitchen you've ever seen, with a scaled-down refrigerator and stove like something out of a dollhouse. There's a black woodstove in the corner, well polished and standing on its short legs like a cute, friendly, toddler-size robot. Even now, in my sorry state, I know that soon I will love this house. Imagine it (if you can, I can't quite): a place that is all mine!

But for now, my state really is quite sorry. It's morning, the first morning of the first day. I don't know if I'd call this homesickness. I don't miss our house. I don't miss Susan. She was in such a rage for so long about my leaving; if you'd heard the threats and the horrible things she called me! I think—I'm almost sure it's at least partly because she knew she would, in her own way, miss me. She gets lonely like the rest of us, although she never admits it.

She probably spends most of her life lonely. But, no, I don't miss her. I'm happy about every mile between us. I think what I feel is uprooted. Like a lost lamb, if you can imagine dark, gangly me as a lamb. I didn't expect to feel this way. But when you think about it, I've never been much of anywhere and never, ever alone. And this place—well, I've been too cowed to do more than glance out the window, even though the light is calling to me the way light does, but it's like another planet out there, one I don't know how to live on quite yet.

Mostly, though, I miss you, little sister. I realize how with you at school, I'd go weeks, even months, without setting eyes on you. But I knew I could. Turns out the knowing-I-could was what kept the ground steady under me. Now, I feel like I'm drifting on the ocean—or on this lake they have here, which is huge and more like the ocean than any lake I've ever seen—and I can't see the shoreline anywhere. You. You're my shoreline, Elsbee.

But listen to me go on and on, all this lost lamb bleating. Don't you worry. I am just having one of my dramatic moments. Before long, I'll head out on an exploring expedition and will soon bounce back to being good as new—no, better, far better—but whatever the coming days bring on this strange, starry, watery planet, I'll always be your loving sister,

Marthy

P.S. Send me some words to describe the clarity of light here, please. That is your assignment! —M.

On the way to Professor Joel Pulliam's house, Eleanor had stopped at the college post office for the fourteenth time in two weeks, and when the postmistress handed her the letter, she had wanted to laugh with joy at the sight of the envelope addressed in Martha's unmistakable hand: sculptural and severely elegant, all long strokes, slashes, and Gothic arches, her own name—*Eleanor Campbell*—jagged as a cityscape across the white envelope. She'd have torn it open and read it right there, but it was Friday afternoon, and the place was packed with chattering students, restless for their weekend to begin, standing in line to pick up packages from home. Scarves and sweaters for the cooling fall weather, Eleanor imagined, or home-baked treats for the weekend. New socks, paperbacks. Whatever normal mothers mailed off to their children at college. Eleanor decided to wait. Martha's letter deserved a quiet place.

So she had tucked the letter into the pocket of her wool jacket, gotten back on her bicycle, and pedaled like the wind. During the two-mile trip, she didn't notice the cars going by or the turning maple leaves. She patted her pocket every few minutes to be sure the letter was still there.

When she'd arrived, red-cheeked, tousled, Alice Pulliam laughed and said, "You're early! Good ride?"

And Eleanor had run a hand through her hair, grinned, and said, "I got a letter from Martha, and I'm dying to read it."

"Well, what are you standing here for?" said Alice. "Sneak out back before the wild beasts know you're here. Sit under that tree you like. I think I can manage to keep them at bay for a few minutes."

"NELNOR, WHY ARE YOU CRYING, Nelnor?"

Eleanor had been with Martha, inside her letter, in deep: on an airplane; sleeping in a car; upturned face awash in starlight; sitting in a tiny cabin, swallowed up by loneliness. The letter was like standing waist-deep at the ocean's edge: a wave of love, a wave of sadness, sentence after sentence, wave after wave. Reading the letter, she had been miles away with her sister, how far exactly she couldn't guess. A thousand miles? A light-year? But Christopher's question, delivered in a tremulous half whisper instead of his usual puppy yelp, tugged Eleanor back to the Pulliams' yard, to the giant sweet gum tree with its wide shadow and star-shaped leaves. Four-year-old Christopher and his younger sister, Kimmy, stood a few feet away, dark eyes huge, hands clasped behind their backs.

"I'm not crying," Eleanor said, smiling.

She couldn't be crying. Beginning when she was not much older than Christopher, Eleanor had learned how not to cry. Or smirk or pout or even wrinkle her brow. She'd learned how to, inside her head, take two giant steps back from nearly all her feelings. She'd learned to put on composure like a dress and do up every button.

"You're so cool," her friend Maisie had told her just days earlier. "Unflappable Eleanor."

The children didn't look worried. What filled their faces was astonishment, as if they'd trotted out into their yard and found a magical creature—a unicorn, a fairy—instead of just their nineteen-year-old babysitter with tears on her face. But she didn't have tears on her face. She couldn't.

"You *are so* crying," said Christopher, pointing.

Eleanor swiped her forefinger across her cheekbone.

"Oh," she said. "So I am."

She wiped her finger on her pants, then shrugged and made a face, tongue sideways, eyes crossed, Christopher's favorite.

"Well, that's silly of me!" she said, "I'm not even sad. Who cries when they aren't even sad?"

"No one!" yelped Christopher.

"Play now!" piped Kimmy. She said it like "pih-yay no."

Eleanor stuffed the letter into her pocket, as if it didn't matter, as if it were any old piece of paper.

"Ready or not," she said, jumping to her feet, "here I come!"

Chapter 5

CORNELIA

"WE WERE THERE TO BUY laundry baskets."

That's how I began.

But this was at nightfall as we were driving home—yes, home, because while I would have and do have other homes, the house I grew up in will forever be one of them—with a tangerine moon already pulled loose from the horizon and floating upward. And yes, I will give you the story just as I gave it to Viviana as she sat behind the wheel, with her openhearted silence and her own only partly healed-over history of letting her child down. I will get to nightfall and the ride home and the story; I promise. But I need to start with morning and the trip to my mother's childhood home (Was it still one of her homes? Was it ever?) because context matters, and my mother was my context just then. Just then? Then and all the days before and since. All my life, my story has been being written inside hers. I just didn't know it until I almost lost her.

Two days earlier, I had brought the tiny northern lights watercolor to my mother. That is, I'd brought my mother's daily planner to her, with the painting tucked into what my father said was its usual place, a slanted pocket inside the planner's front cover. I'd decided on this mode of delivery because to simply hand it over to her would have meant explaining why, and explaining why could have meant waking the grief I knew was sleeping somewhere beneath the surface of her consciousness.

"Since you'll be coming home soon," I told her cheerily, as I handed her the planner, "I thought you might want to count the days."

"Oh, thank goodness. I've been right on the verge of carving hash marks on the wall," she said.

"Which probably would've gotten you immediately thrown out of this place on your ear," I told her, scolding.

My mother narrowed her bright blue eyes and rapped her fingertips thoughtfully on the cover of the planner.

"Immediately?" she said. "Maybe I should stick with the hash mark idea after all."

She laughed, a free and easy sound, one that, on the worst days, I'd feared I'd never hear again. All of it—the joking, the laugh (like music, that laugh), the beautiful, ordinary, Ellie Brown business as usual—made me want to sing for joy. Last week, the doctor had told us she'd be home well before Christmas, and after that, whenever I looked at my mother, I saw a woman seeing the light at the end of the tunnel. I knew what the light was, too: porch light and kitchen light, green-shaded desk lamp light and morning sun gilding her yard. The light of home.

I took a red marker out of my handbag.

"Here," I said, "slash away."

The marker had been my father's idea. We were in cahoots these days, my father and I, coconspirators, plotters.

"She needs to open the planner while you're there," he'd said. "You'll want to see her see it."

After I'd gotten home that day, I told my dad, "The marker worked! She did open it! And not randomly or straight to December. She opened just the cover."

My father shot a victorious fist in the air and leaned in. "And?"

I'm not sure what we'd been expecting. Wonder? Tears? Trumpet music, confetti, and heavenly light falling from the rehab hospital's ceiling?

"Nothing," I said. "Nothing really."

My father slumped.

"Nothing? Dang. Maybe she didn't see the painting."

"No, she saw it. She even touched the corner of it, the one that sticks out a little from the pocket."

"Oh," said my dad. "Well, that seems like something."

"Except she did it so quickly and automatically and absent-mindedly I could tell it was a habit. As if every time she opens her planner, she checks to see if it's there, even though she knows it is. Teo once pointed out to me that I do the same thing with a photo of the kids I keep in my car, on the backside of the sun visor. I get in the car, flip down the visor, flip it back up, and start the car. I don't even realize I'm doing it."

I could tell my dad was disappointed and knew it was partly the disappointment of a coconspirator whose plan has come to nothing, but mostly it was the disappointment of a man who has failed to give someone he loves something they want.

"Well, clearly, the painting's important to her," he said. "Or she wouldn't check on it."

It cracked my heart a little, watching my dad kick into bright-side mode, although it didn't cost him much effort. Until my mother's accident and even most of the time after, bright-side mode was my father's natural state.

"Yes," I said.

"And it was late morning. She was completely herself. Clear as day. Maybe if she sees it when she's sundowning, she'll be more excited."

"Yes," I said and then sighed. "Maybe. I just don't think those northern lights in the watercolor are *the* northern lights. I wanted them to be, too, but I don't think they are. I feel sure I would've seen *something*, some change come over her, however unconscious or slight. But there wasn't one. She just touched that corner, then flipped to today's page in the book—December fifth—and drew a big, red slash across it."

The brightness of my father's bright-side mode dimmed, visibly.

"You're probably right, sweetheart," he said. "If she asks for the lights again, I guess we'll have our answer."

And the next day, when I visited her in the early evening, she did.

After the teasing and laughing from the day before, this asking, the urgency and pleading, her voice cracking under her freight of sorrow, hurt worse than it ever had. But this time, for reasons I can't explain, the hurt didn't make me feel weak and useless. This hurt straightened my spine and bolstered my heart. I may even have heard some trumpet music—a clarion call—of my own. I took my mother's face between my hands.

"Don't you worry anymore, my love," I told her. "I'll find them. Whatever it takes, I will find them and bring them to you. I promise."

I know what you're thinking. A reckless promise, maybe even a cruel one. How could anyone make such a promise? But truly, I didn't just say it to calm her, to give her peace of mind, if only for the moment. I said it because, suddenly, I believed it. More than believed. I felt it in my bones to be true. This thing my mother had lost I would find.

So there it was, a mission, a calling: I would bring my mother the northern lights.

But wait. That's not quite right. She was a mother and she was as much mine as anyone was ever anyone's, but those were just pieces of who she was. "My mother" was just the tip of her iceberg.

So this then: whatever space the lost northern lights had left inside this woman, inside this familiar, inscrutable, beloved, mystifying, wild wonder of a human being, I would fill. So help me, God.

God? God's help was all well and good, but I knew who I really needed. As soon as I was sitting in my car, before I pulled out of the rehab center parking lot, I called Teo.

He answered, and I didn't say hello. I said, "I need a witness."

"You got it," he said, just like that.

"Don't think I'm crazy."

"You never are."

"Not everyone would agree," I reminded Teo.

"I'm not everyone," Teo reminded me.

"You're Teo," I said. "And we're us. We're us, right?"

"Yep. What else would we be?"

"Okay, then."

"Shoot."

Deep breath.

"With you as my witness, whatever it takes, even if it takes a lifetime, I will bring Ellie Brown, whoever she is, the northern lights, whatever they are."

There was silence, and then I heard the vintage wall clock I'd found at an estate sale chiming, faintly, and I knew Teo must have been in the dining room, his de facto office, even though he had a real one in the back of the house. Teo and I had both been kids who preferred to do our homework at the dining room table instead of in our rooms, to be in the family thick of it, a still eye in a sweet storm of people talking and eating and moving around us. When we grew up, we kept preferring it. If I'd been at our house with him just then, I might have been sitting at the other end of the table; I would have had my eyes closed, listening to the Westminster chimes, the lush notes plopping, one by one, into our shared quiet, the air between us glittering for a second or two even after they'd finished.

They finished. And still: silence.

"Hey, Teo? Are you there?"

"Hold on."

More silence.

"Done," said Teo.

I felt an itch of annoyance. When you take a blood oath, even if it's over the phone and there's no actual blood involved, you want your witness to pay attention.

"Yes, I'm *done*," I said. "You seem kind of distracted. Did you hear what I said?"

"No," said my husband, "*I'm* done. Sorry, I just wanted to make sure I got it right."

He'd been writing it down.

I pictured him at our dining room table with a pen in his hand, checking over his work like the good student he'd always been, and I smiled. Leave it to Teo to bear witness to my bizarre declaration the way he'd always borne everything about me, as if it weren't bearing at all, as if it were just a normal part of love.

"You dated it, too, didn't you?" I said.

"How could it be official," said Teo, "without the date?"

"Oh, Teo," I said, "what kind of wretched person would spend even one day away from you?"

"The kind who's doing what she needs to do." He paused. "And you're the opposite of wretched. But, uh—"

"But what? Say it. I love you. Say anything."

"I'm looking at your declaration, and, you know, obviously, I'm prepared to stand by this mission for however long it takes. But it would be good if it didn't actually take a lifetime."

"I'll come home soon."

Just saying the words made my chest clench and my stomach hurt. I know how that sounds, but listen: I loved this man and our children. I can't stand it that I even have to state for the record what is the fundamental truth of my life. Loving Teo, Rose, and Simon Sandoval comprises at least two-thirds of who I am. Missing them—and I missed them every day, woke up and went to bed missing them—was like having the flu and was also like being lost in some freezing, windswept place—Neptune maybe, my stepson Dev having once told me that Neptune is the windiest place in the solar system—wandering blindly around and shouting their names. And still, the thought of living with them, in the same house (and I loved our house, I did), of taking care of them every day, sent me into a reeling, airless, stomach-punched panic.

Even so, if I could swear before Teo and all the universe to hand over the aurora borealis to the enigmatic Ellie Brown, I could promise to come home to my family. Could promise to come home *soon*. Could and should and would. So I said it.

"I promise. You can write that down, too."

"Done," said Teo.

WHEN I'D TOLD MY FATHER about my solemn vow to bring my mother the northern lights, he'd smiled and said, "I guess that would sound implausible to a lot folks, but if you swore before Teo . . ."

"He wrote it down and everything."

"Well, then, sounds to me like it's as good as done."

But when I told him I wanted to start by seeing where my mother had come from, the house she'd grown up in, he said, "How would going to her old house help you figure out why she's talking about the northern lights now, almost fifty years from when she left that place?"

He had a point.

"I don't know," I said. "I guess I just think the more I get to know about her past, the more I'll get to know her, and the more I know her, the closer I'll get to understanding what she's lost and needs to get back. The house she grew up in seems like a good place to start. It was also the only place I could think of."

"If she'd wanted you to go there, she's had fifty years to take you."

"Dad, it's just a house. Bricks and windows."

"Wood siding, actually. But that's exactly my point. You won't find her there, Cornelia."

When I told Viviana this, we were half an hour into the five-hour drive to that very same house. A cottage, my father had called it, dating from the early 1900s, one and a half stories, light blue, at 660 Moir Street.

"But he gave you the address," Viviana said. "So maybe deep down he wants you to find her there."

"Or maybe he gave it to me because he's sure I won't. He said that even before she left the house, she never really belonged to it."

"So she was living there when he met her?" asked Viviana.

I'd asked that, too.

"She was," he'd said. "But when we got engaged, she put it on the market, and I bought us a house in the next town over."

As soon as I'd absorbed what he'd said, and it took me a while, I began to babble. It likely won't surprise you to hear that when it comes to babbling, I am quite something, prodigious, a champion, superstar babbler.

"Hold on," I said to my father. "You moved in together before you got married? I mean, no judgment here obviously, since I did the same with Teo, and, shoot, I'd be fine if anyone did it, my kids included. Actually, I'd recommend to them that they do it. It's even possible that I've already recommended it, and they're ten and eight. For the future, I mean, not now. Obviously. Truthfully, I think it should be de rigueur. Did I pronounce that correctly? It's one of those phrases I always use and then immediately doubt I got right. What I mean is automatic. Required. Standard. If I ruled the world, all people would live together before marriage. So, yes, no judgment at all. But I just mean, well, wasn't that sort of thing frowned upon back then? And weren't you someone—and it's fine if you weren't—but weren't you? Someone who didn't really do frowned-upon things? Although, again, not judging. I'd even go so far as to say—"

My father put up his hand like a traffic cop.

"We did not. Calm yourself, child. She put her house on the market; I bought a new one in the next town over; and we got married a week later."

At this point in my story, Viviana said, "Well! I bet you were relieved to hear that."

"I was!" I said. "Not for the reasons some people might be. I really do believe all that stuff I said about prenuptial cohabitation."

"Of course," said Viviana. "So do I. But Dr. B is Dr. B."

"He is," I said. "He has to be. Always and forever. World without end."

"It would've been like finding out he'd once been a sword swallower or had crossed the Atlantic in a hot-air balloon. Much too jarring."

"Much," I said. "My mother's turning out to be a mystery was unexpected. It threw me for a loop. Many loops. But I'm beginning to see that she always was one; I just hadn't noticed, probably because I didn't want to notice, a fact of which I'm not proud. But Dr. B going all sphinxlike on me? Those clear waters suddenly running dark and deep? I could not have handled it."

"You could have, though," said Viviana. "And furthermore, you would have."

"Of course I would have. I'd have journeyed to his dark side, plumbed his depths, whatever the situation called for. But I was glad I didn't have to. My mystery apple cart is feeling a tad full."

"I can imagine," said Viviana. "Along with some of your other apple carts, I'll bet."

I glanced over at her, at her profile and her honey-gold hair pulled back and twisted into one of those low and careless knots that make you want to scream or notify the press. My friend Viviana looked like a woman for whom everything was easy, but I knew better. She probably had taken five seconds and one hairpin to do up her hair; she probably hadn't so much as glanced in a mirror while she'd done it, but I knew she knew a thing or two about shaky apple carts and rutted roads.

"You help," I said. "Thank you for coming with me today. Thank you for driving, which was really above and beyond."

"It's a nice day for a drive," she said, breezily.

I laughed.

"It's at least ten hours round trip," I said. "So we can stand in front of an old house and stare at it for five minutes. Is any day nice enough for that?"

"This one is just exactly that nice," she said.

I looked out the window. The stretch of highway roadside gliding by was exceptionally pretty: channels of mirror-bright water weaving through rust and gold marsh grass and stands of spiky spent cattails. I sighed.

"My dad might be right. Maybe I won't find a trace of her anywhere there. It seems kind of likely that I won't, actually. What do you think?"

After a moment, Viviana said, "The other day, I was crawling around on the floor looking for an earring, and I didn't find it, but I found a note from Gordon wedged between one of the bed legs and the wall, covered in dust. As soon as I saw it, I remembered it. He wrote it right after he moved in with me. He'd gotten up and gone into work early and left the note on his pillow so I'd see it when I woke up."

I turned to look at Viviana.

"What did it say?"

"Nothing momentous. Just: 'I like waking up next to you every morning.'"

"Sounds momentous to me," I said.

"Me, too," said Viviana.

THE HOUSE WAS GONE.

I did not immediately understand this fact because when we got to 660 Moir Street, there it was, a house, with a brass 660 shining plain as day next to the front door. We sat looking at it from the car.

"It's big for a cottage," I said. "It's big for anything."

"It's gargantuan," said Viviana, disapprovingly. "Far too large for the lot. And the street."

"And the town. And it's mint green, not blue. They must have painted it."

"Cornelia," said Viviana, gently.

"And it has a round turret with a pointed roof. You'd think my dad would've mentioned a turret."

"He would have," she said. "How could he not mention such a turret?"

"That historic part of town we drove through was Victorian. I guess this is, too?"

"This is certainly Victorian-*inspired*," said Viviana, lifting an eyebrow.

I knew. I'd known before I was ready to know. Probably, I'd known the second I'd set eyes on the house, before Viviana had even stopped the car.

"Victorian-inspired with a vengeance," I said grimly, taking in the woodwork, like Battenberg lace trim, edging the eaves. "And new.

Maybe not new-new. But this house was definitely not here seventy years ago. Or sixty."

"Or twenty," said Viviana. "I'm so sorry, honey."

"I guess we're in the right place? I'm directionally challenged, as you know. I put complete faith in my phone to get me places, but those satellite navigation systems must get it wrong sometimes, mustn't they? What if they get blown off course by a solar wind? Maybe get dinged by a passing meteorite? I'm no expert, but it does seem possible."

"I suppose," said Viviana. "But this is the right town, and there's the street sign saying Moir Street, and I'll bet it's the only Moir Street they've got."

"Two Moir Streets would be unusual," I admitted.

I looked at the house again. There was a giant Christmas wreath on the front door. It was cotton candy pink, and I cannot swear that it wasn't made of actual cotton candy.

"All right. So I get that there's a conspiracy afoot to keep me from learning about my mother's past—" I began.

Viviana nodded. "Oh, yes. It runs deep, too."

"Very deep. I get it. They had to tear down the house. What else could they do?"

"The cottage," corrected Viviana.

"The cottage, yes," I said. "But, listen, did they have to make the replacement house so godawful ugly? I mean look at that gingerbread trim. I don't think it's even real wood, although I can't think what in the world else it would be. Fiberglass? Can you think of why they felt compelled to add trim like that?"

I'd like to step in here, shame on my face, and say I am not usually one to make fun of the things other people love. For one thing I know as well as anyone that love is both sacred and personal. Love is a question that contains its own answer, the one instance of circular reasoning with which no one can argue: we love what we love because we love it. For another thing, all my life, I've loved scads of things most other people would not dream of loving. In high school, for instance, I was a living anachronism, living mostly inside films from the 1930s and 1940s, only venturing out now and then to dance around my room in a cotton day dress or wide-legged, pleated pants, Ella singing Cole Porter on my stereo, Cary and Katharine, and Clark and Carole, smiling down at me from the walls of my room. You can probably imagine how many friends this won me in ninth grade and can also imagine the derision heaped upon me by the three other Brown offspring, especially Ollie, for whom derision was and is a kind of superpower.

You see where I'm going with this: people who live in glass houses shouldn't throw stones, not even at oversize faux-Victorians. This new incarnation of 660 Moir Street was someone's home, and everything about it had clearly been deliberately (trim like that didn't happen by accident) and lovingly chosen down to the chili-powder-colored shingles on the turret and the stained-glass transom window (three pink scallop shells) above the front door. But whether the people who lived in that house loved it or not, no one should ever make fun of another person's home.

But I'd been counting on the blue cottage at 660 Moir Street. Counting on it for what I wasn't sure. Had I expected to find little Ellie Campbell there, sitting on her front porch, head bent over her homework? Had I thought she'd glance up from her math book to stare at me, answers to every question I'd ever had about her gleaming in her cottage-blue eyes?

Or maybe I believed I'd find the northern lights themselves in that cottage, beaming from the windows or unfurling, glow-stick green, out the open front door and onto the lawn?

No. I mean, okay, maybe some tiny, not entirely rational part of me held out a hope that the cottage would offer up magic. Some-times, things *do*, don't they? But mostly, I'd just wanted to see it, the house where my mother had lived before she was my or anyone's mother, the spot where her story had begun.

"Are you okay?" asked Viviana.

"I can't tell," I said.

"Do you want to just go home?"

I considered this, but then I said, "And miss out on a chance at finding a love note from Gordon?"

"That's my girl!" said Viviana, reaching out to squeeze my hand.

"What if we park?" I said. "And take a walk. And then get some-thing to eat."

"I like that plan," said Viviana.

THE TOWN WAS CHARMING, AND I know the word *charming* is overused when describing towns, especially small ones, but *charming* was the sole word in all of human language for what this town was. What was also obvious was that at some point, maybe not so long ago, the town's charm had gone from purely organic to at least partly cultivated, turned up a notch or two, in order to beguile tourists, and, as tourists, Viviana and I were duly beguiled. In the downtown strip, antique shops, cafés, bookshops, and art galleries proliferated, bedecked with hand-carved and hand-painted signs, pastel store-fronts, white picket fences (strung with magnolia-leaf garland and white twinkle lights for Christmas), colorful flags, and rocking chairs on porches. There was a candy shop called Loblollies, and a French bakery called No Pain, No Gain, which made Viviana laugh, then and for weeks afterward, every time she thought of it. Even in De-cember, it was warm enough to sit outside, which we did in order to eat elaborate and enormous vegetable/cheese/grain concoctions at a garden café called Bowlerama.

IT WASN'T UNTIL WE WERE actually making our way down to the beach that it hit me: my mother grew up near the ocean.

I'd known this, of course. But it is one thing to hear a fact in passing and file it away, and quite another to walk bodily into it, the air freshening and cooling with each step, the rhythm of the waves easing your pulse, slipping serenity into your bloodstream before you even glimpse the water, and then: broken cobblestones of shells crunching underfoot; wheeling, squawking gulls; the tang of salt.

"It has to matter, doesn't it?" I said to Viviana as we both stood on the sand. "It must shape a person in a million ways, ways they can't even name."

"I think it would have to," said Viviana.

Strips of cloud hung suspended above the horizon without touching it, so that the horizon itself was a laser-cut line stretching on and endlessly on. I considered how the border of my own childhood had been irregular, pretty, and smudged: hills overlapped like tissue paper, blue upon blue, lapis and cornflower, faded denim and pigeon gray, changing with the weather, the time of day. I'd been born into the soft lap of those patient, river-stone-smooth hills, and even when I couldn't see them, I'd known they were there.

How might it affect a person, a little girl, growing up in the presence of a line this straight and true? Or with the immense, breathing, restless ocean at the end of every road?

"I bet she swam all the time," said Viviana. "You know how she still loves to swim."

"She does," I said. "I bet she did swim. I bet she collected shells and scolded away seagulls who tried to steal her sandwich and got sunburned."

"Hmm," said Viviana. "Her skin is wonderful. I bet she wore a hat."

"Okay, so not sunburn. But freckles for sure. Hat or no hat, she still gets them every summer, across her nose."

I stood, imagining Ellie Campbell, freckled and diving into the waves like a seal.

How wind-scrubbed, how newly laundered everything seemed: the air, the white gulls, the bright sky and brighter water.

"I wonder if she came here, escaped to the seashore, when things got bad at home," I said. "I hope so. I hope she escaped somewhere."

"Do you think things got bad a lot?"

"We had one conversation about it, but, yes, I do. It was more the tone of what she said than what she said. Her voice was venomous, if you can imagine that. I'd never heard my mother speak so harshly about anyone. But what she actually said was bad, too. She told me about one drunken rage where her mother threw open the refrigerator door and yanked out the shelves, one by one. I could see her picturing it while she told me. Eggs, mayonnaise bottle, bowls of leftovers crashing to the floor. Glass shards flying. Tomato juice like blood on the linoleum. What kind of woman does that? And all while her daughter stood watching."

"What kind of woman?" said Viviana, quietly. "A very unwell one."

"Yes, and the crazy thing is that my dad said she taught Sunday school for years at the church across the street, the one my mom grew up going to. My dad said it's partly why they got married by the justice of the peace; Mom associated the church with her mother, even though her mother was dead by the time they got married. She kept the books for the church and taught Sunday school. I just can't picture that person, that lunatic, raging person standing in front of a classroom talking about Moses in the bulrushes or what have you or in a hat and dress, passing the offering plate."

When Viviana didn't say anything, I looked over at her. Her face was turned toward the ocean but her eyes were far away, seeing something else, and it was only then that I remembered what prompted my mother's refrigerator story: Viviana on her doorstep, newly emerged from her own illness, looking for the daughter she'd dropped by the side of the road and left behind. I reached over and held the cuff of Viviana's jacket sleeve.

"Oh, honey," I said, "I wasn't thinking. I'm sorry."

She turned her head and gave me a half-smile. "Don't be."

"I shouldn't have said 'lunatic,'" I said. "Who says that? What is wrong with me?"

"Nothing. You're angry on your mother's behalf. And protective and loving. And fierce, just like always."

I shook my head. "Not always. The way I'm behaving lately? Retreating? Spending weeks away from my husband and my traumatized children? Not fierce. And not exactly the picture of mental health either, let's face it."

She didn't contradict me, but she took my hand and squeezed it.

"But listen," I said, "she wasn't us. We aren't her."

"Oh, I know," said Viviana. "Not even close."

"I know she was sick. I'm not sure if she ever had a definitive diagnosis or what it was, but she certainly struggled with mental illness. And she drank, probably as a way to self-medicate. And she is deserving of compassion and understanding. Of course she is. From me and from everyone."

"Yes," said Viviana, "we all are."

"But from what my mother told me, and not just her, but my dad, too, she was violent and mean. I know she couldn't help it—"

Then, Viviana surprised me by interrupting with, "We don't know that actually. And it doesn't matter."

"We don't? It doesn't?"

"Maybe she was doing her best. But maybe not. Maybe meanness felt good. Maybe she was a psychopath. We can't know. But what we do know is she hurt her daughter. Whatever her reasons, she hurt her so much that even after she was dead, her daughter, who grew up to be a loving and decent and fair-minded person, stayed hurt and angry. The damage your grandmother did was no less damaging because she was mentally ill."

"Yes, I see what you mean," I said.

"You're right about her not being us. We have caused some damage. Or at least I know I have, and I am not letting myself off the hook. I'm accountable. But we are women who spend most of our time not causing it. And we aren't mean."

"You're the opposite of mean," I said.

Viviana nodded. "True. Most of the time."

"So what you're saying is: we should not let my grandmother off the hook."

"Yes. But also we should allow for the possibility that she was a mixed bag. So maybe she was a good Sunday school teacher. Maybe the church got the best part of her, even if your mom didn't."

As if we'd planned it, Viviana and I spun around together and began to walk away from the ocean, back toward the town.

"What if we check to see if the church is still there, right across the street, like my dad said? I was too distracted by the disappeared cottage to notice."

"It's there," said Vivian.

"The original church? Not replaced? The conspirators missed it?"

"Original. Old. Greek Revival. White clapboards and the prettiest square steeple, set not in the middle of the roof but off to the side, like the antenna on a walkie-talkie."

"It sounds like the church was important to my grandmother. And, oh, you know what? She might be buried there. It seems like she would be, doesn't it? I guess we could check?"

"You want to?"

I realized I did. I wanted to visit my grandmother's grave. Not because she was a good person because she probably wasn't so good. Not even because she was my grandmother.

"Let's do it," I said. "In honor of the mixed bag she might have been. In honor of mixed bags everywhere."

"Hear, hear," said Viviana.

And with that, we turned our faces toward Moir Street again and began to walk.

AN HOUR LATER, AFTER WE'D left the church behind, as we were driving home, Viviana said, "I wonder . . ."

"I wonder, too," I said. And even though I didn't know the specifics of her wondering and don't think I even quite knew the specifics of my own, I was still aware that both the noun and verb forms of the word—and probably a whole slew of *wonder*-rooted adjectives—applied to my present state.

Out the windshield, the remains of an operatic sunset simmered low in the sky, ember-orange and pearl-blue, with lashings of glossy buttercup.

"I wonder," repeated Viviana, "if Ellie's was a case of holding too close or, instead, of pushing away too hard."

"Oh. The people, you mean? The memories? Or the entire thing, the first twenty-plus years of her life?"

Viviana considered. "All of those. Or maybe not quite any of them. I think I mean the story. Her story. The story of whatever happened to make her leave it all so radically behind."

We sat in silence, contemplating the nature of my mother's secret keeping, if that's what it was.

"Once," I said, finally, "I mistakenly thought I'd erased all my photos from the past four years or so from my computer, and it was the worst feeling. I wasn't just sad but—I don't know. Lost. Bereft. Cut loose and drifting and not quite the person I'd been before the moment I thought I'd lost them. I guess that sounds dramatic, but it's true. And they were just photos."

"But they were photos you wanted to keep. Maybe that's the difference. Your mother didn't want to keep those years."

"Yes, but it seems so ruthless. And she's never been ruthless."

"No, never. I can't imagine she ever was. So maybe she didn't delete that part of her life. She just doesn't tell anyone about it."

"About *her*," I said. "A human being. Except it can't have been a matter of just not happening to talk about her, can it? It had to be deliberate. Because I've known my mother for over forty years, and Ollie's known her for longer than that; all of us have known her all our lives, and she's never told any of us."

"Well, except for your father. He knows at least some of her story because he was there for some of it."

I bopped the dashboard with my fist. "Right! So you see? Both of them had to purposely withhold it. There had to be how many moments? Dozens? Hundreds? When some subject came up where it would have been natural for one of them to mention something about my mother's early years, and they deliberately did not," I said.

"Not even by accident, it seems," said Viviana.

All this time, absences piling up: holes in conversations, names unnamed, places and topics swiveled away from. Gap after gap, for years. How porous, how flimsy my knowledge of my mother had always been, like a structure slapped together out of cardboard, full of spaces for the wind to whistle through.

"It must have been hard," I said, "not telling."

"Do you think?" asked Viviana. "I was thinking it was possibly easier."

I shook my head. "When you don't tell your story, when you don't put it into words and give it over, at least to the people you love best, it just hangs out there."

"Hovering," said Viviana.

"Waiting," I said. "Pending. Growing."

"You're right," she said. "Especially painful stories. My therapist says that. She says telling hard stories doesn't make them more real because they're already real. Telling takes the power away from them. It makes them yours."

"Exactly!" I said. And then, like I'd fallen and had the wind knocked out of me, I said, "Oh."

I had answered questions, so many questions. I had eked out broken, broken-hearted sentences to Teo. I'd woken up, night after feverish night, with the sound of a gunshot exploding inside my head and sobbed in Teo's arms, gasping out apologies. But I had never—in my own words, beginning at the beginning and ending at the end without end (oh, let there be an end someday)—I had never told.

"What?" said Viviana, turning sharply toward me. And then, at the sight of my face, "Oh."

We sat in silence with a delicate, indigo night falling upon the world outside the car windows, the moon on the rise like an orange balloon.

Then, Viviana said, gently, "You don't even have to be talking to me. I can just be here while you talk. If you want."

Later, I would marvel at how I just did it, conjured the words, sentence after sentence. How I didn't collect myself first or close my eyes or even reach back inside my head to press fingers to the edges of the wound, checking for tenderness. I just told.

"We were there to buy laundry baskets. I'd noticed just that morning how beat up and broken-down ours were from years of Simon playing with them. He's outgrown it now, mostly, but it used to be his favorite game. Roller coaster. He'd put stuffed animals or plastic dinosaurs inside the baskets and then half-push, half-throw them down the basement stairs, one after the other, over and over, for years. So after I picked the kids up from school, we went. We found the baskets and also managed to find all manner of other stuff, the way we always do. Flavored lip balm; headbands; socks with sloths on them; a neon-green soccer ball; what as kids we used to call a Chinese jump rope, an object I had no idea still existed; some books; a giant pack of colored markers; the kind of trail mix I'd said no to all the times before because it is actually just candy; and a shower curtain with a map of the world on it, which we absolutely did not need because we'd just bought a shower curtain with narwhals on it not three weeks earlier. It was a three-person festival of impulse buying. Except we did not, of course, buy any of it in the end. Rose pushed the cart because she loves to and because she's tall enough and careful enough not to ram into product displays or other shoppers, and Simon took it personally, the way he always does, which makes sense because it *is* personal. As a cart pusher, that child is just plain undependable. And because he was disappointed about the cart, I promised him he could put our merchandise onto the conveyor belt. He calls the grocery counter a conveyor belt, which I suppose is what it is. It was a rash promise because, honestly, he's not so great at this job either, and it takes at least three times longer than it does when I do it myself, and people behind us can get testy, but in a rash and hurried moment, I promised. When it came time to check out, I saw that one line was shorter than the others, so we got into it. The man ahead of us was buying just a bag of candy corn and a tube of natural toothpaste, details I remember because the combination struck me as funny. Because of my rash promise, Simon stood in front of me in line, ready for me to hand him our items to place on the conveyor belt, so that when the man ahead of us grabbed the person closest to him, Simon was the person. Automatically, I reached for Simon's arm to pull him back, but the man yanked him away and put him in a kind of stranglehold, and he put the gun he had in his hand, put the muzzle of the black gun, which I remember as enormous although I think it probably was not, against Simon's temple. And I yelled, 'Give me my son!' And Simon screamed, 'Mommy!' which he doesn't call me much anymore, and Rose started crying the way she does, lips closed, almost noiseless, but I could hear her anyway. And the man said, 'Shut the fuck up. He's not your son. He's my free pass out of here.' So I shut up, and Simon shut up, and Rose stopped making her quiet sounds. And I never took my eyes off Simon's eyes. I should've saved him. But I stood like a cowardly nothing and just kept eye contact and tried to make him less scared, but we were all so scared. The man shouted, 'Nobody move!' and I could hear people running away through the store behind me, but I didn't move. And the man reached across the counter and grabbed a plastic shopping bag, and he told me, 'Don't you fucking move, bitch,' and he walked from register to register, dragging Simon with him, with the gun never leaving Simon's sweet head, until they were too far away for me to see. I should have saved my son, but I just stood there, obeying the monster who had stolen him, my little boy, who was taking him farther and farther away, and then I looked behind me and saw my darling Rose shaking harder than I was, so I reached across the cart and took her hand, and whispered that it would be okay, even though it never would be again. I heard sirens, but before the police got there, I heard a shout and a gunshot. Shout, shot, that fast. And only then did I run. I screamed, 'No, you don't! No, you don't! Not Simon!' and I ran to find my son. And when I got to him, he was in a woman's arms, one of the workers in her red vest had her arms around him, and I ran and put my arms around them both. For maybe two seconds, there was nothing in the universe but the woman and me, with Simon in between. Then I knelt down and took his precious face in my hands and saw blood on his forehead, just a sprinkling, and my heart lurched, even though I knew it wasn't his. Behind us, I think the man lay on the floor. I would learn later a plainclothes police officer had shot him, and I would learn that he wasn't dead. He lived. But right then, all I could see was Simon's pale face, and I had never loved anyone so much or so uselessly, and all I could say was, 'I am so sorry, sweet boy. I am so sorry. I am so sorry. I am so sorry.' Shame overrode all other emotions, even gratitude and relief, even my useless, endless, teeming, towering tidal wave of love. Isn't that horrible? So horribly self-centered to feel shame above all right then. But I think it still might be winning out over everything else because I was and still am so desperately, hopelessly, pathetically, shamefully ashamed and sorry for how I failed my child."

VIVIANA DIDN'T SAY ANYTHING BECAUSE her only job was to be there while I talked. I didn't say anything because I'd already said it all. Almost all. As much as I could say. The guardrails and signs ticked by and the moon draped its light over the traffic and we two women rode in a silence that was like a cup filled to the brim.

WE HADN'T FOUND MY GRANDMOTHER'S grave.

By the time Viviana and I had arrived at the church on Moir Street, the sun was starting to set, and the white church standing stalwart and simple against the luminous sky looked less built than grown, something the ocean wind had spun out of sand and bone-white sea-shells and sand dollars. We'd gone straight to the back of it, to the cemetery, small with old gray, tilting stones in scarves of grass and willow trees and a low, wrought iron fence with a gate, and I knew right away that my grandmother wasn't buried there. No one who had died in this century or the one before was buried there. Then, I saw a man, young, wearing a ball cap and work boots and carrying a Weedwacker. When he saw us, he took off his cap and smiled.

"Hey, I'm Rory. I work here. Can I help you? And it's cool if you're just wandering."

"My grandmother used to go to this church," I said. "I was hoping to find her grave."

"She'll be over in the annex, the memorial park out near the entrance to the highway."

The entrance to the highway. For a moment, my mind flashed on a car driving past the memorial park, a young woman in the passenger seat, window down, breeze tugging back her brown hair, her new husband behind the wheel. Maybe she would have given the cemetery one last glance, but I hoped she'd pointed her gaze unswervingly forward. *The entrance to the highway, Ellie Brown,* I thought, cheering her on, *and the entrance to the rest of your life.*

Rory was still talking about the annex. "I mean, she's there if she died after about 1880, which I bet she did. Unless you're a lot older than you look."

I smiled. "Like a hundred years older."

"Exactly," said Rory, "and you don't look a day over a hundred and four."

I laughed. "I get that a lot. So I guess it's off to the annex, then."

"Yeah, but the annex is big. You'd think it would be smaller than this place because it's called an annex, but it's actually way bigger.

Most people who work at St. Philip's don't even call it the annex, though. We call it 'the overflow.'"

"Ah. Like parking."

Rory's expression went sheepish. "Sorry. I was forgetting your grandmother was buried there. 'Overflow' isn't very respectful, although, until right now, I never thought about how it isn't."

"It's fine," I said. "I didn't know her, my grandmother. And from what I hear, she wasn't all that nice. So I'm good with 'overflow.'"

Rory grinned. "Awesome. But hey, you want to come in? I can print you a map of the overflow, and I can do a name search on our computer. Come on in and you can wait in the coffee parlor while I look her up."

THE WORDS *COFFEE PARLOR* HAD conjured tufted velvet, picturesquely frayed Persian rugs, tea services, and Tiffany lamps, but the coffee parlor was a long, narrow room with tan carpet, a bank of windows along one wall, and a large and motley collection of framed photos hanging on the other.

"It's how it always is with churches, isn't it?" whispered Viviana. "Soaring ceilings and stained glass up front, industrial carpet and folding tables in the back."

"I loved it, though, coffee hour after church," I whispered. "We'd eat butter cookies and ham biscuits by the handful and run around like wild animals. It was awesome."

Viviana walked over to the wall of framed photographs, her hands clasped behind her back, her head tilted, her hair like knotted gold in the evening window light. I smiled at how Viviana might have been a Parisian perusing Old Masters at the Louvre; she strolled the length of the wall, with every step conferring elegance on even this most ordinary room. Suddenly, she stopped.

"Cornelia," she said, turning to me, wide-eyed. "Do you know what these are?"

"Let me guess. Pictures of Christmas pageants past, Easter flower arrangements, and maybe a vestry group portrait or two? That's what they had on my church's coffee room walls."

"Some of that, yes, but mostly—and not every year or anything, sporadically, but they definitely span decades and decades—I mean some are black-and-white, so—"

"Mostly what?" I said. But I was already walking over.

"Sunday school classes," she said.

It took me two minutes tops to find her: my mother, about six years old. And even though I'd seen exactly zero childhood photos of my mother—a fact that did not strike me until I was standing there staring at one—I recognized her at once, her big serious eyes under her dark brows, her perfect posture. She wore a plaid jumper over a blouse with a Peter Pan collar, and a barrette pulled back one side of her hair. At the other end of my mother's row stood what had to be my grandmother. Shorter than many of the children, resembling my adult mother—same eyes—but heavier, shoulders more rounded, face fuller around the chin. She wore lipstick and an inscrutable gaze. No smile. But she didn't look evil, either. She didn't look evil or kind or anything. At least in this photo, she had a blank, closed face, the kind that gave nothing away.

"That's her, isn't it?" said Viviana, resting her finger on the inscrutable woman.

"I think it has to be," I said.

"Your mother is darling, same as now," she said. "Hey, maybe they can give it to you. The photo, I mean. You should ask Rory."

I shook my head. "I don't know. *Her* mother's also in it. And my mom left her behind. I don't think I should bring her into my parents' house."

"Okay," conceded Viviana. "But at least take a photo of it with your phone."

It seemed like cheating to me, but a phone photo isn't really an object, not something solid you can hold in your hand. And suddenly, I found I wanted to keep that solemn girl with her lifted chin; I wanted to take her from this place where she'd been unhappy and carry her back with me.

Which is why the first time I saw the other girl it was on my phone screen: she was tall—the tallest child in the photo—skinny, with a cloud of curly dark hair and a gaze so direct it verged on scowl. She stood next to and slightly behind my mother, and I noticed what I had not noticed when I'd been taking in my mother's little-girl face: the tall girl had her hand on my mother's shoulder. Slowly, I lowered my phone.

"Oh, my God," I said, under my breath.

"Cornelia?" said Viviana. "What?"

"They're dressed exactly alike. The collar," I whispered, "the plaid jumper. Even the barrette. And also look how she's touching her. Look."

Viviana looked at the photo, and then she said, "Oh, my God."

"She must be," I said. "I think there's too big an age difference for them to just be friends. She has to be. Right?"

Like the girl in the photograph, Viviana placed a protective hand on my shoulder.

"I think so," she said, "I think she has to be. Your mother never told you about her?"

"She never breathed a word."

"Wow," said Viviana. "How do you never tell your children you have—"

"A sister," I said.

And then I said, "My mother has a sister."

Chapter 6

ELEANOR

December 1964

"She chose *pellucid*. Did I ever tell you that? From the word list I sent her to describe the light there," said Eleanor. "I must admit I was rooting for *pellucid*."

She was lounging, shoeless, legs tucked sideways, on the worn brocade sofa in Alice Pulliam's sewing room. Alice looked up from the dress she was letting out—Kimmy's Christmas dress that Eleanor had made for her a couple of months earlier, dark pink velvet with a satin collar and sash—and smiled at the sight of Eleanor.

"You look like the Little Mermaid sitting there," said Alice. "Like the statue in Denmark, but sitting on a raggedy old sofa instead of a rock."

"Sofas are much more comfortable," said Eleanor, snuggling catlike into the cushions. "How Martha would fuss at me for being careless. No shoes *and* feet on the furniture at someone else's house!" and then added, "The statue might be nice, but 'The Little Mermaid' is an awful story. She gives up the sea and her tail and her voice and walks around—*dances* around—in terrible pain, really makes a complete mess of her life, all for that stupid prince."

Alice stopped stitching and cocked her head, thinking. "Why, yes, I suppose it is awful, when you put it that way. I think I've always thought of it as romantic. What we sacrifice for true love and so forth. I guess you mean it's awful because he doesn't love her back."

"She was a mermaid, for heaven's sake! And she stopped being one. She just—snap!—gave up who she was. No, even if he had loved her back, it wasn't worth it. She should've let the silly boy drown."

Alice shook her head. "I wonder if poor Ronald Bancroft knows what a hardhearted wretch he's dating."

"Oh, Ronnie's an excellent swimmer," said Eleanor, airily. "He'll be fine."

"Hmm. So back to *pellucid*. I do like it. But what was the runner-up?" asked Alice.

"*Crystalline*. But Martha thought it was too solid, not liquidy enough. Which is just what I thought when I wrote it down in my letter to her. Martha is really better with words than I am; I think she uses them to paint what she sees and thinks when she can't use real paint. She just asks me to come up with words sometimes because she wants to include me, which I appreciate. Anyway, she says the pellucidity is agonizingly difficult to capture on canvas. 'Build' is how she puts it in one of her letters, which I love: building light. She's getting better at it—there ends up being quite a lot of green involved, of all things—but she says it's still agonizing. She doesn't sound agonized, though, not a bit."

"She's happy."

"Deliriously. Let Martha build a little light every day, and she's happy as a clam. Also, she's discovered smoked fish."

"To eat or paint?"

"Both, knowing her. But eat is what she meant, on crackers. Back home, everyone under the sun ate fish *except* Martha. She said it was much too fishy, with which I could not argue."

"Who could?" said Alice.

"But this smoked stuff, it's a Minnesota delicacy, she says. It's a good thing for her they don't eat smoked caterpillars up there because she'd probably gobble them like popcorn. I believe that girl is madly, head over heels in love with Minnesota or at least with the North Shore."

It was Christmas Eve. The eve of the second Christmas Eleanor would spend with the Pulliams.

A year ago, when Eleanor was halfway through her first year of college, Professor Joel Pulliam had slipped out of the Christmas Eve pageant at the Episcopal church early—if a person with an armload of loud, squirming nativity lamb can be said to slip—after the lamb's overzealous baa-ing had caused the Angel Gabriel, ten years old, to stop dead, mid-tidings-of-great-joy, and hiss, "Shut it, you brat." As Christopher's wails careened off the vaulted ceiling, stone floor, and stained glass angels, Professor Pulliam had spotted his student Eleanor standing alone in the back of the church and, after a moment of surprise, had smiled at her much more brightly than she would have expected, given the circumstances. When, after a minute or so, she could still hear the child's cries, Eleanor walked out of the nave to find them in a wide hallway, Christopher facedown on the floor and his father sitting in a chair a few feet away.

When she got to them, Joel Pulliam said, shrugging, "Sometimes, it's best just to wait it out. He'll run down after a while."

"Like a windup toy?" said Eleanor.

"Exactly."

The little boy lifted his head to look at her. His cheeks glowed strawberry red, and his wet lashes spiked stars around his eyes.

"Hello, lamb of the field," she said.

Christopher stopped crying.

"Hello," he said, breathing hard.

Professor Pulliam turned to stare at her. "How in the world did you do that?"

Eleanor crouched next to Christopher, who still lay on his stomach. "Have you ever actually stood in a field full of lambs?" she asked him.

Christopher shook his head.

"Well, I call that amazing," she said, "because I have, and I'll tell you this: lambs are loud. There is just no such thing as a quietly baa-ing lamb. Are you *sure* you've never been to a lamb field?"

Christopher rolled over like a log to sit cross-legged in front of her; he squeezed his eyes shut, thinking.

"I maybe did one time," he said, opening his eyes. "I remember— maybe."

"I just don't know how anyone who hadn't could be such a perfect lamb. But it's also possible you just have a gift for it."

Christopher nodded.

"Well, either way, you were wonderful. Wonderful! You were the best part of the pageant."

Christopher sniffed and nodded, again.

"Santa," he said, "is coming to my house."

"Well, of course he is. You're probably at the top of his list."

Christopher's entire wet face broke into a grin. "You are, too," he said.

"Hmm. I don't know about that. But I suppose I might be second. Right after you."

Christopher laughed. "No, *you're* coming to my house, too!"

Eleanor felt her cheeks flush. "Oh, well—"

"Please do," said a woman's clear voice.

"Oh," said Eleanor, getting to her feet and brushing off her coat, suddenly embarrassed in the presence of this stranger. The woman was blond and young-looking and carrying a sleeping child. "Oh, gosh, I couldn't."

"Couldn't you?" said the woman, smiling. She was pretty, with a radiant, frowny, upside-down smile, and the kind of nose that crinkled. "I'm Alice, Joel's wife, Christopher and Kimmy's mother, and we would love it if you joined us. It's just the four of us this year. Please come."

Christopher knee-walked over to Eleanor and threw his arms around her legs.

"Please, please, please!" he sang.

Joel Pulliam laughed. "My family," he said. "They believe in the art of subtle persuasion. But you probably have your own plans for Christmas Eve, Eleanor."

The child in Alice's arms stirred, and Alice bent her head, fluttering dove sounds, half-whisper, half-whistle, into the baby's ear. It was the gentlest patter of sound Eleanor had ever heard. The baby sighed and went still. Alice brushed a kiss against her child's head and then looked at Eleanor.

"Do you?" she said. "Have your own plans?"

Eleanor felt her face flushing. She had lied to—or at least deliberately misled—everyone: her roommate, her friends, her other professors. All of them thought she was going home. Only the dean of students knew she was spending the holidays in her dorm room and only because she had to ask him for permission.

Lying was old hat for Eleanor, although she didn't think of what she did—had always done from as far back as she could remember—as lying exactly. It was more like art, not like Martha's wild and gorgeous conjuring, but like decorating a room or arranging flowers: crafting a picture of her life for others to look at. And it was her right, wasn't it? Her right and her life. Every piece of it belonged to her, every piece and every choice, which pieces to display, which to leave in shadow. Sometimes, this involved outright lies—how could it not?— but more often it was sleight of hand, a combination of distraction and suggestion. Mostly it was easy. She'd found that most people— people like her friends—unthinkingly assumed other people's lives looked like their own—safe, even the most dramatic moments causing the needles of their personal Geiger counters to give only the slightest hops—especially the lives of girls with pretty clothes, forthright smiles, snappy comebacks, friendly eyes, and straight As.

This time, she had been especially meticulous, telling the dean that her mother's mother had passed away in Ohio, that their family could not afford three plane tickets, and that since her sister was much older and more responsible and also such an all-around wonderful person, she would be the greatest support and comfort to their mother (even this was not a lie because, despite Susan's meanness toward her older daughter, if anyone gave her support and even comfort, it was most certainly Martha). In her dorm room, she and her hall mate Liz, had packed together, and Eleanor had ostentatiously held up items of clothing, asking Liz questions like "How many party dresses are you bringing? Isn't it hard to decide?" At dinner, the night before everyone—everyone else—would catch their rides, planes, and trains home, she'd chatted merrily about Christmas shopping, how hard it was to buy gifts her mother would love (the truth, a sad and ugly little truth, but as true as true could be), and she'd told her friends, including the lovelorn Ronnie, how, at home, people put up Christmas trees on the beach and decorated them with shells and seaweed. "Gee, I'd love to see those trees," Ronnie had said. "Maybe next year I'll go with you!" To which Eleanor had cast her eyes down, lashes fluttering, smiled shyly, and thought, *Never. Never ever. Not on your life, buddy.*

Had she done all that only to tell these people—her psychology professor and his family, to whom she owed nothing—the truth? *Of course not, silly girl! Tell them your mother was delayed in picking you up but will be here tonight. Tell them you're catching a ride with a friend who is desperately working to finish an English paper. Make up something, anything!*

Eleanor looked from Professor Joel Pulliam, to his wife and baby, to the child with his face buried in her skirt. She pressed one hand to her hot cheek and reached down and placed the other on the boy's head. The hood of his wooly lamb costume had fallen back, and his hair was warm, his head solid and curved under her palm. She straightened and looked at Alice Pulliam.

"You know how you said it was just the four of you this year?" she said. "Well, this year, for me, it's only me."

"Is that a yes?" said Alice.

"Yes!" yelped Christopher.

"Yes," said Eleanor. "Yes and thank you."

She had surprised herself by saying this, just as later, over tea in Alice's kitchen, after the children were in bed, she would surprise herself by pouring out the story of why she was at school, alone, at Christmastime: the nightmare of Thanksgiving, how they had come home from a pleasant dinner at the minister's house, had gone to bed, and then how, in the middle of the night, Susan had banged open their bedroom door, drunk and raging, swinging a cast-iron skillet over her head, spitting insults and accusations—*ugly, stupid, lying, disgraceful, ungrateful* (*ungrateful* was her favorite, and, truly, they found very little in their mother to be grateful for), and finally screeching, "Get out, get out, get out!"

Stirring honey into her tea, Eleanor would tell Alice about Susan's darting eyes, about how the pan hit the overhead light and broke it, about Martha pulling Eleanor out of bed, forcing her behind her so that Martha's body was a shield as they sidled toward the door, Martha shouting, "We're going, you maniac!" They had left the house in their nightgowns and, barefoot, had taken the long walk to the beach, sitting at the edge of the dunes in the cold, cold, moon-washed calm until the sun edged out of the water, staining the sand pink. Eleanor would tell Alice how Martha had made her promise to stay away at Christmas, to spend all the holidays from then on, away. "You know how holidays bring out the beast in her," she'd said. "But she's better when it's just me. I think because there's still a part of her that wants you to like her, whereas me she's given up on, as she should have. You'd think wanting you to like her would make her nicer, but, like everything else, it just makes her mad. And don't you worry a second about me. I'll be fine, always am. You just stay gone."

That night in the Pulliams' kitchen, Eleanor would understand, fully, for the first time, the gravitational pull of good people; and she understood how once she'd given in to this pull, she would keep giving in, over and over. She had told Alice the story of the bad Thanksgiving, and after she did, knew she would keep telling, knew Alice and Joel would be her trusted ones, her secret keepers.

Standing there, in the church hallway, Eleanor did not quite know all this yet, but she'd felt the pull; she felt kindness tugging her forward, into the heart of this family, and she'd let it.

"I SHOULD REALLY TURN THIS over to you," said Alice, holding up Kimmy's dress and eyeing the hem. "You're a far better seamstress. But sewing has always made me happy. It's like being the eye of a storm. My house can be falling to rack and ruin, my children can be running amok, but if I sit here faithfully stitching away, all is well."

"And *I've* never liked it much, but it allowed us to have nicer clothes than we could otherwise afford. And it was one of the few things my mother taught me how to do. I think I was seven when I made my first piece of clothing, if you can call an apron clothing. When I was twelve, I made Martha a dress for her senior dinner dance at school. My first dress and she still wears it."

At the thought of Martha in the dinner dress, a half-formed sob rose in Eleanor's throat. It's how it happened sometimes: an ordinary memory, a sentence in one of Martha's letters, the sight of something she knew Martha would love (a tree with sunlight caught in its limbs, a water glass on a table casting a perfect shadow), and there it was, grief darting out of nowhere to rattle Eleanor's soul.

Alice stopped sewing and said, "Oh, darling."

"It's all right," said Eleanor. She busied her hands, fanning out Martha's letters on the sofa cushion.

"The darned mail," said Alice. "It must be hard to get her letters so long after she writes them, sometimes two weeks!"

Eleanor considered this for a moment, then said, "You know, I thought it would be hard, but I like it. Isn't that funny?"

"You do? Why?"

"I don't know if I can explain exactly why."

"Oh, I bet you can. You always can. Whatever you say about Martha, you're very handy with words yourself, you know. Ideas, too. Give yourself a minute. I'll go rustle us up some Christmas cookies. If you can't eat cookies in the middle of the day on Christmas Eve, when can you?"

Alone, Eleanor took a recent letter out of the envelope. Almost from the beginning, after that first forlorn, homesick letter, Martha's correspondence had been what Eleanor could only call exuberant, the sentences in her craggy handwriting fairly radiating off the page.

What a sight we painters must be, perched on the brown rocks in our coats, hats, and scarves like fluffed-up birds, our easels in front of us, not caring a whit about the cold or about anything but the water and sky and what's coming off the tips of our brushes.

Tonight, I heard a loon's voice, so lonely, floating out of the fog.

This morning, I went for a walk in the woods. I bent down to tie my boot, and when I stood up, there was a moose not twenty yards away.

humpbacked, long-nosed, and gangly-legged with mossy-looking antlers. I was scared and whispered "Go away, please," but then, the second it did, maneuvered all the pieces of its big self around and dissolved into the trees. I wanted it back.

Elaine and David are good people, through and through, but also they're my kind of good people: unbuttoned, funny, blunt, a little distracted, a little messy, chock-full of life, certainly not like any rich people I've ever known. David's the sort who misplaces everything, who might wear the same shirt for three days in a row without realizing it. He bakes the most delicious bread but has to set timers in different parts of the house or else he'll forget and burn it (and sometimes burns it anyway). And Elaine, well, you have to love a woman who gardens and cooks but also hikes for hours, reads absolutely everything, and swears a blue streak when she talks politics. And can they ever laugh! All of them, kids, too, laughing together like it's the most normal thing in the world.

When Eleanor had read this last bit aloud to Alice, she'd said, "Look at those Campbell sisters, grew up in screeching chaos but then got themselves folded into the nicest families ever." To which Alice replied, "I'd say those two Campbell sisters together made a pretty nice family all by themselves."

But the most recent letter troubled Eleanor. It was as rife with free-wheeling awe as the others, and, in it, Martha sang Elaine's praises again, noting especially what a great mother she was. Loving, of course, but also so truly *interested* in her children. *And she makes it look effortless, almost careless, as if she just knows how. She's a natural.*

But then, she wrote: *Whatever Elaine has I know I don't and never will. On the off chance I was born with any maternal instincts at all, I'm sure they've gotten warped and twisted from all those years with Susan. And before you get the wrong idea, I don't think the same is true for you. Not a chance! I know you're different from me. I can tell just by the way you talk about Christopher and Kimmy. Wouldn't be surprised if you were a natural like Elaine. Kids have always taken to you and you to them, even back when you were a kid yourself, helping out in the nursery at church. And if I've done anything right, it's keeping you from getting tainted by the worst of Susan's ugliness. But me? Nope. No kids for me; I wouldn't trust myself. Not that it would ever have been an issue anyway—haha. The men aren't exactly showing up in droves—which is just fine with me. I'm better alone. In fact, I am loving my independence like I've never loved anything before. I feel as if I'm drinking from the cup of freedom at long last, taking enormous gulps, and it is glorious.*

Eleanor loved the last two sentences, could have sung them from the rooftops or flung them, like the Milky Way, out across the sky, but all that came before those sentences made her want to cry, to cry for days and then to scream at the universe, at God, at their mother, at their mother especially and at the top of her lungs. Her Martha, feeling twisted and scarred and unworthy, when who had ever been more loving?

When Alice came back with the tray of tea and Christmas cookies and settled back in with her needle and thread, Eleanor said, "Okay, about my getting the letters so long after she's sent them. Why I like it."

"Yes?"

"She's ahead of me now."

Alice pondered this, then shook her head. "Say more."

"She stayed, always. Until she left at last, I didn't see it, not fully, and I'm ashamed I didn't because I love her; I do."

"I know," said Alice. "She knows."

"It's just how it always was; it was how we lived. I left and she stayed. When I was little, she protected me; she almost never left me alone. She would come straight back after school, and, oh but if you'd seen how she'd come striding through the door and right away check me over, turning me around, staring sharply into my eyes, demanding to know if I was okay. 'Right as rain?' she'd ask. 'Right as rain and sun and cinnamon toast,' I'd answer. Cinnamon toast or jump rope or dolphins or my new shoes, whatever seemed like the rightest thing in the world to me at the time. And then when I was old enough to leave the house alone, she stayed. I went to sleepovers and summer camp and to friends' houses, and she stayed home. I went on beach picnics and school trips; I swam and played tennis and did homework at the library, and she stayed home. Yes, she went to school; she had jobs, but she only left when she had to and she never stayed long."

Alice looked up and nodded. "I'm beginning to understand, I think. Go on."

"By the time I get her letters, she's moved past them. She's way ahead of me, out there in the distance, living her Martha life, on to the next thing and the next. I'm the one left behind now. And I'm so glad."

"Dear Eleanor," said Alice, "darling girl."

"She's like stars."

"Stars?"

"It's like she's in the sky, and I'm standing on the ground, and by the time her light reaches me, it's already old."

TWO DAYS AFTER NEW YEAR'S, Eleanor got a letter, written on heavy sketch paper, and, at the bottom, radiant as a jewel, was a tiny painting of the aurora borealis.

There are miracles overhead, Elsbee! Think of it: all our lives, every year, while we were going through our ordinary days, this has been happening in the sky. I could spend my life painting it and never get it right. And I think I will. I think the trying is what I was made for. I love this place. I was born for it. I am never leaving.

A week later, when she was back at school, Eleanor received another letter, just two sentences long, the rest of the paper filled with painted swirls and birds and snowfalls of color: *Elsbee, Elsbee, Elsbee, I am in love. His name is Jack.*

Chapter 7

CORNELIA

VIVIANA HAD SAID, "DR. B is Dr. B. Always and forever. World without end," and I'd agreed. But when I told my brothers Cam and Toby that our mother, our very own no-nonsense and ever reliable Ellie Brown, had a hitherto undisclosed sister, I realized how, all this time, I'd thought the same of them. Maybe everyone feels this about their closest people, that they are immutable, known, that they just are who they are. Cam and Toby were not Cam and Toby in exactly the same way Dr. B was Dr. B. They weren't stalwart and steadfast—the Grand Canyon, the *Collected Works of Shakespeare*, and the North Star all rolled into one in khakis and an elbow-patch sweater—but they were eternally themselves all the same. As familiar, unchanging, and true as—I don't know—red Solo cups. Blue swimming pools with black lane lines on the bottom. Nacho Cheese Doritos.

I'm making it sound as if they lacked gravitas, and they didn't, although, for a long time, they almost did. Until they were well into adulthood, my little brothers were boys. Guys. Dudes. The type who listen to loud Bob Marley, collect loud Hawaiian shirts, experiment with really bad facial hair, and who—thoughtlessly, gleefully—divide the objects of the world into things to climb, things to ride, things to jump off, things to kick, things to throw. When, ten years ago or so, Cam had come out to our family, Ollie had said, "Does this mean you'll stop wearing flip-flops in winter and eating ravioli out of the can?" and it had not.

Still, they'd never really been flimsy people. Goofy, yes. Laid-back (very far back, often in a hammock), definitely. Jumping at every opportunity to give their sister Cornelia crap, always. But they were both gainfully employed. They were both in thriving, healthy, long-term relationships. They both had huge reservoirs of niceness and big, open, breakable hearts. Cam and his husband, Niall, were in the process of adopting a baby. Toby had a new girlfriend and a ten-year-old son with a woman who'd dumped him while she was pregnant, smashing his heart to smithereens, and, despite all our fears, had always been a good dad, a superlative dad, treating fatherhood like the coolest adventure ever, but one in which the adventurers wore helmets, ate vegetables, and read a lot of books.

But Cam and Toby were still Cam and Toby. I *knew* them. Of course I did. They were easy to know—shiny, splashy puddles, no dark and mysterious depths—and I'd known them all their lives, hadn't I?

So when I sent a text to the sibling chat saying I'd made a surprising discovery about our mother's past and asking Cam, Toby, and Ollie to call me, I was sure I knew what my brothers would say. Not the exact language, maybe, but close. Something along the lines of: "Whoa, look at Corndog going all super-sleuth on us! Way to live out those Nancy Drew dreams, girl. So listen, you definitely need to track down that long-lost aunt, like ASAP. What if she's a billionaire? What if she's a retired rock star? What if she has a yacht? What if she has a *beach house*? Dibs on the beach house!"

I believed I knew what Ollie would say: nothing, not a peep. And because Ollie is Ollie is Ollie, as much as anyone was ever anyone or more—that's just what she did say. Ordinarily, I would have found this maddening. But given how wrong I was about Cam and Toby, I ended up finding it kind of reassuring.

Toby called first.

"Mom's a spy," he said. "Am I right? I'm right, right? Dang, I always knew she was a spy. She just has a stealthy way about her, sneaking up on you with her little feet."

"Not a spy," I said.

I told him the story of my trip to my mother's hometown, beginning with the faux Victorian, ending with the photograph on the church wall. In my humble estimation, I did a crackerjack job of telling—including vivid descriptions of the beach; the storefronts; the church steeple against the sky; the general tenor and ambience of the town; and even sliding into a passable rendition of Rory's drawl. Crackerjack but also—and this likely won't surprise you—not as direct and to the point as some tellings would have been (but not meandering either, my loopings back and detail filling in were always purposeful), and not, by most people's definitions of brief, brief. But Toby did not interrupt once. He did not interject one interjection, not a single "Rad!" or "Whoa!" into my stream of talk; he did not laugh—not even a chuckle, and Toby was a champion chuckler—at No Pain, No Gain or "overflow."

When I was finished, he said, "Huh," and I recognized the "huh" for the thrown bone it was.

"Toby! What is wrong with you? Wait, are you processing? I never do leave people time for processing, do I? Sorry about that. Process away. Take your time, but, you know, hurry."

"Um, it's okay," said Toby, not sounding as if it—whatever it referred to and I couldn't quite tell—was indeed okay.

"Anyway," I said, charging ahead, "you must be wondering whether or not I got confirmation that the girl in the photo is indeed Mom's sister."

"Confirmation. Don't you mean corroboration, detective?"

There. Finally, a touch of Toby. Except that his delivery wasn't classic Toby, not light or teasing. In fact, he sounded irritated. Not overly, or not overly for most people, but because Toby got irritated far less than most people, it was overly for Toby.

"What?" I said.

"Nothing," he said, still irritated.

"Dad confirmed it: her name is Martha."

"Well, that's a nice name," said Toby.

"It is," I said, and waited for him to say more.

When he hadn't said more after about ten seconds (not all that long, perhaps, but by normal Toby/Cornelia conversation standards, a great, gaping sonic void), I said, "Toby! For crying out loud, could you rouse yourself at least a little? This is important!"

Another silence, and then, thank heavens, a chuckle. A ghost of a chuckle really, but I'd take it.

"'Rouse,'" he said, and ghost-chuckled again.

"Toby."

He made a sound like "Errrgh," and I would have bet money he had his eyes squeezed shut and was scrubbing his head with the fingers of his right hand, as if he were washing out shampoo, even though, if he was maintaining his lifelong hygiene habits, and I'd be stunned if he wasn't, he didn't actually use shampoo, opting instead for bar soap. "Shampoo is the opiate of the masses," he'd once told me. "Besides, my hair looks pretty great anyway," and while the first sentence was obviously completely meaningless, the second was annoyingly true. But the "Errrgh" and the scrubbing were what Toby did on those vanishingly rare occasions when he found himself conflicted about what to say.

"Okay," he said. "I get that this is important to you. I guess what I just don't get is why."

"Really?"

"Yeah, I mean, why dig up all this stuff? Why does it matter who she was a long time ago? So maybe she used to have a sister named Martha—"

"If Martha's alive, she *still* has one. Dad said he met her once, just once, and he wouldn't tell me any details, none at all, but at least we know Mom had a sister after Dad met Mom. It's not like Martha died when they were kids. And I hope she's still alive out there somewhere, but even if she's not, Mom could have had a sister for years and years, even after she had all of us. And she might still."

"No offense to Martha, but who cares?"

"Toby!"

"Seriously, I just don't get why it would matter. Mom is Mom."

"You're in California, Toby. You haven't heard her ask for the northern lights. She's so sad. There's something in her life she's lost and wants back."

"You don't know that for sure. And even if it's true, she's had a lot of years to find whatever it is already. Maybe she couldn't. Or maybe she decided not to look. Or maybe she'll look herself, once she gets better and comes home."

"She asked me to find it. Over and over, she asked," I said.

"She's not herself when she asks," said Toby. And then, quietly, he said, "Are you sure this is just about what Mom wants?"

"What do you mean?"

"Maybe there's something in it for you, too," said Toby.

"What is that supposed to mean?"

"I don't mean it in a bad way, like you're in it for material gain or something. I just think it's worth thinking about."

I took a deep breath.

"We almost lost her," I said. "And one day, we will lose her. I just want to feel like I know her—really know her—before we do."

"Yeah, I know we almost lost her. Maybe that's why I don't want her to be a different person with a sister and a terrible mom and a past. I just want her to come home and be the Mom she always was because the Mom she always was was awesome. Is. Is awesome."

He sounded sad and scared and about seven years old.

"I agree. Of course I do. I love Mom," I said gently. "But I've never felt like we truly connect. There's always been some distance there."

"You and your connection obsession," said Toby, but I could hear the affection in his voice. "E. M. Forster and whatnot."

I smiled.

"My favorite writer," I said. "I didn't even know you heard me when I talked about E. M. Forster."

"How could I not hear you? Everyone heard you. Me, Cam, Ollie, Teo, the mailman, the lady next door."

"Toby, I do think she wants me to find something she's lost. But also, I just want to know her better, to feel closer to her. That's all."

"Fine, fine, whatever. Old E.M. is probably doing the happy dance in his grave."

I laughed. Then, I said, "Listen. It'll be okay, Tobe. She'll be okay. She'll come home and be Mom again."

"She has to," said Toby.

"She has to," I said. "And she will."

MY CONVERSATION WITH CAM MOVED along similar lines: I told the story, he didn't ask questions, then he sounded irritated, then I asked what was wrong, then, instead of saying the stuff Toby had said about not wanting Mom to be anyone but who she'd always been, he said this:

"What gives you the right?"

"Cam! Ouch. Jeez."

"No, I'm not being judgmental. I'm asking for real. Here's the thing: it's her life. Just because we're her kids and we love her, do we automatically have the right to know her story? Or are we invading her privacy? Like Dad said, if she'd wanted you to go to her home-town, she could've taken you, and she didn't."

I thought about telling Cam what Viviana had said about how avoiding telling the story of bad things doesn't make them not exist. I thought about the ride home, my voice in the car telling my own story, how it didn't fix everything but how it helped and was still helping, a little bit more every day. I thought about saying something about how the truth could maybe set our mom free because that's how truth worked. But suddenly, I felt tired.

"I'm about to have a kid," said Cam. "Do I want him to know about all the stupid stuff I did?" He paused. "Wait. I probably do, because a lot of it was truly rad and super-funny."

"Hmm."

"But Niall had some bad shit happen to him. His dad rejected him pretty hard there for a while. He came around, eventually, but it's still not the greatest relationship. Does our kid have the right to know about all the hard times? When he grows up, would it do anyone any good to have him go snooping into them?"

"I'm not snooping!" I said, although as I said it, I wasn't sure anymore. I felt off-balance. My goofball brothers had thrown me off-balance. Now, there was a "rad" turn of events. How had it hap-pened? I felt something close to awestruck but also forlorn and like I might cry.

"I'm not just idly curious, Cam," I said. "I honestly am not. I love Mom."

"Nah, I know that," said Cam. "Sorry. *Snooping* was the wrong word. My bad."

Sweet boy, I thought, and swallowed hard so I wouldn't cry. Cam didn't say anything, and I knew he was giving me a second to collect myself.

When I was collected at last, I said, "Who even are you and Toby, anyway? All this analysis and nuance and preoccupation with ethics. Like what the hell? What happened to 'dude' and 'word' and boneheadedness and leading the unexamined life?"

"Glitch," explained Cam. "Brain fart. We will soon return to our regularly scheduled programming. Fear not, Corndog."

WHEN I WENT TO BED, fell into it utterly exhausted, I called Teo and told him about the two conversations.

"Dang," said Teo. "The boys are getting all philosophical on us."

"Right? Thank God Ollie's still her good old self-involved, emotionally detached robot self. She still hasn't responded, not a peep."

Teo laughed. "Thank God for Ollie."

"Teo?"

"Yep."

"It really isn't for me," I said. "This digging up the past, trying to find the northern lights. It's for her, to help make her whole. You know that, right?"

After a moment, he said, carefully, "I know it's done out of love, like every single thing you ever do."

"But? Because I hear a 'but' coming."

"Not a 'but' really. More of an 'and.'"

"And?"

"I know you're doing it for your mom."

"And?"

"I also know nothing hurts you more than feeling like you've let down someone you love."

"And?"

"And I know you've been feeling that way, lately. I don't think you should. I don't think you've let anyone down at all, not Simon or Rose or anyone, not a single person. But I know you think you have."

"And?"

"And if the process of taking care of your mother also ends up helping take care of you, well, I would personally be very happy. Everyone who loves you would be happy."

"Oh," I said, and then I said, "You think maybe I'd be bringing the northern lights to all of us and that would be okay?"

"They're large lights," said Teo. "Plenty to go around."

I could hear him smiling.

"Why do I need the northern lights when I have you?" I demanded of my husband.

"Because you do," he said.

TEO WAS TEO WAS TEO.

But Ollie?

I'd gone to bed so early that the next morning, I was up before both the sun and my father. When I looked out my bedroom window, I saw the dark yard was full of fog; the trees invisible, as if they'd melted away. I went downstairs and made oatmeal with brown sugar and butter and diced apples. I'd taken one exquisite bite when I heard someone open the front door.

"Dad?" I called. "Shoot. I thought for once I'd early risered you!"

A voice said, "Not Dad," and I looked up from my bowl.

She stood in the entrance to the kitchen, a leather duffel bag in her hand, mist in her hair, her trench coat pearled with droplets, as if she hadn't walked from her car to the house but all the way from Long Island.

My sister, emerged from fog, standing before me and saying, "I came to hear about Mom."

Chapter 8

ELEANOR

January 1965

"You sure you won't join us, El? Give the books a rest and come save the world?" said Liz.

Eleanor's dorm hall mates Liz and Marge were headed to an anti-war protest at the big state university, a small protest it seemed to Eleanor, just a handful of students—including Liz's older brother Gregory—burning their draft cards. They were college boys and would almost certainly be granted deferments, even Liz had said as much—the protest was small, the burning symbolic—but then she'd added, her eyes gleaming: "But, kids, it's just the beginning!"

According to one of Martha's recent letters, Martha's Jack— Eleanor hoped Jack was Martha's because Martha was most assuredly Jack's—had said the same words about the goings-on of the world in 1965, but whereas Liz meant the beginning of something shining and bold and better (the details of which even Liz would have admitted were vague), Jack meant something darker: the beginning of the end. The end of what? Martha had seemed not altogether sure. Individual freedom seemed to figure in, although Eleanor wondered which of Jack's freedoms seemed to him particularly imperiled. He was five years older than Martha and had dropped out of college years ago. He wandered the country and out of it, working as a welder and also as an artist, crafting sculptures out of metal. No family, no children. White, able-bodied, as far as Eleanor could tell. So Eleanor had wondered if he was mostly worried about having to go to Vietnam. But in the next letter, Martha had said no.

He seems unconcerned about the war because he simply wouldn't go. He says he would never fight for something he doesn't believe in, which I think is its own kind of bravery, don't you? He wouldn't go to prison, either. He'd just disappear for a while. He says he's an expert at disappearing, and I can believe it. Even when I'm in his arms, he feels not quite there, like he's a piece of a dream. A good dream but a dream all the same. No, he is just a person who wants to live purely according to his own priorities and moral sense. He says the rules and regulations of ordinary life pervert our instincts and turn society rotten. He says people have never been more rotten than now. And then—oh, Elsbee—he looks at me with his very own eyes and says, "Except for you, Martha." And do you know, I think I've been waiting all my life to hear those words? Except for you, except for you, except for you.

Eleanor believed in civil rights, in women's rights. The war felt not quite real, like something happening in a newspaper, but she did want it to end. She hoped she was rooting for all the right things. Back in the fall, she'd attended a protest at the whites-only barbershop downtown, mostly because she'd become casual friends with a young man named Paul Lucas, one of the few Black students at her college. They had an English literature class together on Mondays and Wednesdays, and, twice a week, on their walks from class to the cafeteria, the two of them engaged in lively conversations about Blake and Wordsworth, before they parted ways to sit and have lunch with their separate friend groups. Eleanor thought having one Black friend might be the wrong reason to go to a protest, and she'd felt out of place there in the crowd of singing, chanting people. She'd brought no sign, didn't know what to do with her hands. While everyone else seemed fervent and assured, buoyed by anger, righteousness, and hope, she'd felt shaky, inexplicably on the verge of crying the entire time. She hadn't seen Paul there and was glad; if she had, she was sure she would have disgraced herself by bursting into tears.

Marge appeared next to Liz in the doorway to Eleanor's room.

"Come on, stick in the mud!" she teased.

Marge's cheeks were flushed, and Eleanor couldn't help but notice how the energy her friends buzzed with now seemed a lot like their mischievous excitement when they sneaked bottles of champagne into the dormitory or sneaked themselves out of it after hours. But the thought was uncharitable. Maybe they did like the rule-breaking, but they also cared; she knew they did.

"Don't tempt me, you devils!" said Eleanor, smiling. "Nope, I fear it's just me and the horrible Spartans this weekend. I am hopelessly behind in my reading for Ancient Greece."

"Aren't the Spartans a football team?" said Marge. "And since when are you hopelessly behind in anything? Are you sure you're not staying behind to hole up with Ronnie for the weekend?"

Eleanor gave her an impish grin, one she hoped said "You caught me!" and shrugged. For Marge and Liz, romance was a pretty good excuse to blow off anything, even saving the world, certainly a better excuse than history homework.

In fact, after some long, lovely, blessed hours alone, Eleanor had a plan to bring Ronnie sandwiches and coffee from the cafeteria later that day, to sit and eat with him in the common room of his dormitory, maybe quiz him on the battles of World War I. He was doing eleventh-hour cramming for a big exam, eleventh-hour cramming being his preferred form of studying. Ronnie was bright but also the specific brand of lazy that comes from knowing his future was secure no matter what; come hell or high water or mediocre grades or foreign wars, he would graduate, go to the same law school his father and grandfather had gone to, and work at his family's law firm. Eleanor suspected it's what she liked best about him: the thoughtless ease with which he inhabited his world. It was in everything he did: biting into a sandwich, sprawling on the grass, jamming a cap onto his head on their way out the door, grabbing her hand. Ronnie didn't go in for protests or counterculture. Liz berated him for this, but his complacency felt honest to Eleanor. And anyway, he was nice. Whereas other boys in his position might be arrogant or demanding, Ronnie was kind.

"Hmm," said Liz, then rolled her eyes and threw up her hands. "Fine, fine. Young love and all that jazz. But next time! Next time, when we head off to change the world, you're coming with us, you hear?"

"I hear," said Eleanor, blowing them kisses.

When they were gone, she stood at her window, gazing out at the campus, and thought, *But this world, this sweet world. What needs changing less?*

It was a wrong thought, selfish and small. She would have said it aloud to no one, not even Alice. But she could not help treasuring this place. Her friends chafed against the insular, old-fashioned atmosphere of the campus. They found it narrow and boring, too quiet. For them, serenity was what you went home to. Pretty, orderly rooms, low voices, families laughing over meals, forks clinking on china. But here was Eleanor's serenity: trees against the sky, lakes of green grass, conversations about books and ideas, flowers in rows, a library with high ceilings and shelves full of rhyme and reason. The card catalog alone made her heart happy—all the things of the world resting in their places.

Martha had said something similar in her last letter, how at night, tucked into her own bed in her own house with the sky flashing above, the moose long-legging their way through the woods, ponderous heads held high, the vast lake lapping in the dark, she was aware of everything—every large and tiny thing—settling into its correct and proper, its *foreordained*, place.

Jack talks and talks about leaving. A couple he met up in Canada a few months ago were going south to set up their own little utopia: artists and writers and philosophers and anyone just finished and done with what Jack calls "the soulless chaos of civilization" living together in harmony, growing their own food, neither buying nor selling, answering to no government, ruled by no laws outside the human heart, and so on and so forth. His handsome face glows like the moon when he talks about it. But then I drag him outside into the clear cold to look at the actual moon and its reflection, at all the pellucid light. And I know he feels it—who wouldn't?—the completeness, the serenity. I never, ever, ever want to leave.

"Don't leave there, Marthy, not for Jack or for anyone." Eleanor stood at her window, soaking up her own pellucid light as it swept over the grass and into her room, and whispered to her sister. "Stay right where you are."

The knocking startled her, two brisk taps shattering the sunlit silence.

She opened the door to find Patsy Fisher, one of the college receptionists, standing there, a slip of paper in her hand, anxiety in her eyes.

"Eleanor, dear, I'm sorry to bother you, but you've had a phone call from a Mrs. Caroline Cullen from back home. She'd like you to call her back as soon as you can. She says it's urgent."

ELEANOR SPENT THE FIRST HALF of the drive to what felt nothing like home angry, replaying the conversation with Mrs. Cullen, the church secretary, sentence by sentence, over and over, raging at not just her words—and her words were horrible—but also at her tone: accusatory, scolding, condescending, all rolled into one. Eleanor had no sooner said hello than the words started, in full-blown sentences and paragraphs, punctuated with dramatic pauses, as if Mrs. Cullen had rehearsed it all, which Eleanor thought she probably had.

Poor Susan began to go downhill after you two girls—her only family—left her all alone during Christmas. I hate to place blame, I really do, but it's true. We all noticed. Dear Sylvia—good minister's wife that she is—had her to their house, of course, after the Christmas Eve service and then to dinner the next day. She and the minister would never allow a parishioner to spend the holidays all on her own. But it isn't the same, is it? As being with family? The minister himself encouraged her to take some time off. She really is such a devoted worker. She makes mistakes, of course, from time to time, but with all she has always had to contend with at home, who can blame her? She stayed away from church for a while then, enjoying her well-earned rest. But a few days ago, out of the clear blue sky, the poor thing showed up to work in a state. Hair a mess, looking as if she hadn't slept in days, and not, if I'm honest, making much sense. Not babbling, exactly, but talking a mile a minute. It's possible she'd been drinking, although I hate to imagine such a thing. But, oh, when I think of her all alone in that house, who knows to what lengths she may have been driven! I sent her home, of course, told her, for heaven's sake, to get some sleep. Sylvia and I went by the next morning to check on her, and she opened the door— and I don't mean to alarm you, but it was quite a sight—she opened the door with blood, well, everywhere! Her pajamas, the floor, even a smear on her face. It gave us such a fright. She'd broken a mirror and cut her hand badly, a deep cut right across her palm. We phoned the doctor, and Sylvia asked him to come to your house, just, you know, for discretion's sake. People can be such gossips. I don't trust those flighty nurses at the hospital as far as I can throw them, and your mother was in disarray. Disarray is exactly the word that popped into my head when I saw her. There's a new doctor in town. Very young. Has to be fresh out of his medical training. Nice as can be, though. Said he had to take her to the hospital, so so much for discretion, but he drove her himself, which I thought was above and beyond. We went to see her the next day. Her hand did not require real surgery, thank heavens, just a lot of stitching. But there was Susan, her hand just a big white mitten of bandages, still looking frazzled, if a tad more like her normal self, saying she was going to jump in the car and go see you, of all things! Said she would've visited Martha, but she had no address for her. It seems Martha left her high and dry without so much as an inkling of her destination. That was just not right. Only God can judge, but that was just terribly wrong of Martha. Anyway, we talked her out of going. That was almost a week ago, and the times I've seen her—and of course I've visited the poor thing—she has seemed good, more settled. But then this morning, she told me she thought she was up for the drive to your college; she thought she'd be leaving soon. And I hate to impose on you when you must be so busy having fun at school with all your friends, but Sylvia and I agree that you need to come home immediately. We can't have your poor mother driving, and once again, we've done our best to make her see reason. But I don't know how long it'll last. She seems determined to see you. And it would be very awkward for you, wouldn't it? If she showed up there and made a scene in front of your fancy college friends.

Fury hit Eleanor in waves, boom, boom, boom. How dare they? How *dare* they?

"How dare you!" she yelled. She banged her fist on the steering wheel. "You stupid, heartless, sanctimonious old bats! Blaming us? Us? When she's been a monster for years and years? When Martha went to Sunday school with bruises? How dare you blame us? How dare you? You are all horrible people, twisted, soulless, horrible people!"

Deep down, Eleanor knew this wasn't exactly true. She knew that the church ladies weren't really heartless, not even Caroline Cullen, and she was the worst of them. If Eleanor were being fair, she would have admitted that the church ladies had simply not quite known what was happening in Eleanor's house. Susan was a consummate actress. But if Eleanor were being fair, she'd admit that it wasn't all an act. Mixed up with her meanness and manipulation was a true fragility, a lonely, childlike longing to fit in.

"Susan doesn't know how to be a person, not really" is how Martha had explained it. "And she knows it and she wishes—with every bit of her being, even though she'd never admit it—that she could be like everyone else."

When Susan showed this vulnerable side of herself to the church ladies, their soft hearts opened toward her in much the way Eleanor imagined her and Martha's father's heart must have. She asked— with every eager, tremulous smile, every cast-down gaze—to be cared for, and she was cared for. According to Martha, it was because Susan only knew how to be cared for, not how to take care of others, because she had not the smallest natural gift for motherhood and hated her daughters for making her face this fact, that she reserved her sharpest edges, her coldest glares, her most explosive tantrums for Eleanor and Martha, even as she gathered the church ladies to her and fed them sad stories about ungrateful, selfish daughters.

But also—if Eleanor were being honest—she'd acknowledge that she and Martha hadn't done a thing to ingratiate themselves to the church ladies, even the ones—and there had been several over the years—who had cautiously tried to help. Eleanor and Martha had stayed wary and silent; they'd rolled sleeves down over bruises and neatly deflected questions about how things were going at home; they'd guarded their secret life as if their lives depended on it.

But in the car, driving to the cottage on Moir Street that was not home, Eleanor was in no mood to be honest, so she ranted on and on, mile after mile, invigorated by rage.

And all the while, deep inside her, staring and scratching at her like a beady-eyed rat in a cage, was the thought that she and Martha really were to blame; they had been bad daughters, unlovable and failing to love, cruel to leave their mother alone, to go off to live their lives in beautiful places.

No, she told herself, *no, no, no. She woke us up in the middle of the night to scream at us. She started fires, for God's sake. Fires! Twice! She could have killed us, so many times. We were children, and she could have killed us!*

After Mrs. Cullen had said her piece, Eleanor had given her a terse "Thank you. I'll leave today" and had hung up, fury blasting through her like a hurricane.

The fury had propelled her out of the building and straight to Ronnie's dormitory. The truth was if she'd had her own car, she never would have gone. It would not even have occurred to her to tell him she was leaving. When she got to his dorm, college protocol demanded that she ask the person at the front desk to tell Ronnie she was there and then wait in the common room until he came down. Unlike most of her friends, she'd never balked much at this system, if only because she enjoyed having fair warning when Ronnie visited her. Eleanor was not a fan of the unannounced arrival in general, but especially not from Ronnie; she needed time to prepare for his boundless, bounding energy and affection. But today, she was relieved to see the front desk empty. The boys took turns at desk duty, and some were less vigilant than others. Eleanor ignored the sign-in sheet and slipped around to a back staircase she'd used before.

When Ronnie opened his door to find her there, he broke into a grin, pulled her into the room, and enveloped her in a bear hug. She tried to keep herself from going rigid inside his arms, but he felt her tension. He pulled back and brushed the hair away from her face with one big hand. The concern in his long-lashed hazel eyes made her go even chillier.

"Hey," he said softly, "you okay, El?"

"I'm fine," she said briskly, gently extricating herself and stepping back. "I just need to go home for a day or two, and I was hoping I could borrow your car. I'm sorry, but I wouldn't ask if it weren't important."

"Oh! Yeah, sure thing, doll," he said, "of course. But why? What's happened?"

"It's nothing," she said. "Really."

"Obviously, it's not nothing. Come on, you never just pick up and go home like this. What's wrong?"

Ronnie reached out and took her hand.

"Hey, you're freezing," he said. "What are you doing, running around without a coat? Let me get you mine."

"No." The word came out sharper than she'd intended, and Ronnie flinched.

"I'm sorry," she said, eking out a smile and touching his shirt-sleeve. "I guess I'm a bit on edge. I always am before a long car trip. You know me, little old lady behind the wheel!"

It was one of Ronnie's standing jokes about her, one she didn't particularly like and knew to be inaccurate (she was a careful but confident driver; Ronnie was a speed demon), but she tossed it like a bone to a puppy.

"Ah, that's it," said Ronnie, smiling again. "Brilliant idea!"

"I don't think I had an idea," she said, uncertainly.

But Ronnie snagged his keys from his bedside table and, with a wink, shook them in front of her until they jingled. When she reached to take them, he lifted his arm so they were out of her reach.

"Nope, nope, nope! I'll drive you! I'd say it's about time I checked out the old Campbell homestead, met your mother. She'll love me, naturally. Mothers always love me."

Eleanor was in no mood for his teasing, found it so irritating that for a moment she wanted to slap the keys right out of his hand. What kept her from doing it was the vision of Susan racing down the highway and headlong into Eleanor's snow globe world, smashing it beyond repair. Eleanor needed Ronnie's car. If she hadn't needed it . . . But she did.

Get hold of yourself, Eleanor. Choose your words, manage your tone, and, for heaven's sake, smile at him.

She smiled and then ruffled Ronnie's hair with her fingers.

"Look at you, silly boy," she said. "I'm sure mothers love you. How could they not? I bet those dimples work their magic on mothers just like they do on everyone else. So listen. You'll come home with me soon. You really and truly will. But this time I have to go by myself."

Ronnie tipped his head to the side like a puzzled Irish setter.

"But why? Is something wrong? Maybe I can help. Just tell me why you have to go."

Eleanor wanted to screech with frustration, but instead, she shook her head ruefully and shrugged. "I can't. It's personal."

Ronnie's eyes flew open wide and his face turned pink. His jaw actually dropped. For a mad second, she wondered if she *had* slapped him. He looked as if he might cry.

"What?" she said.

Keeping his eyes locked on hers, Ronnie started to pace. The dorm room was narrow and his legs were long, so he could only walk a couple of steps before turning around. He looked like a toy soldier.

"'*What?*'" he almost shouted, amiable, easygoing Ronnie who never raised his voice. When life always went your way, there was no reason to yell. "You don't get it, do you? 'It's personal'? Like that's a reason not to tell me? Me! I'm your boyfriend, Eleanor. Don't you know you're supposed to get personal with me? You're supposed to tell me stuff you don't tell other people. It's what people in love do!"

"In love?" she said, truly confused.

In the stunned few seconds of silence that followed, Eleanor realized two things she had not known until that moment: one, Ronnie was right about what people in love did, and two, she was not in love with Ronnie, was not, had never been, could never be. She'd thought she might marry him, but she had never even considered being in love with him.

"I'm sorry," she said. "Oh, Ronnie."

He stopped pacing and stood before her, his head drooping, and she bent her legs so she could see his face. She took his face between her hands. It was hot, but her hands were as cold as ever.

"Ronnie, I'm sorry I hurt you just now, and I want us to talk about this, and we will, soon. I just—"

She'd been going to say "I just have to go home," but she realized she couldn't borrow Ronnie's car now. It wouldn't be fair. She would call Mrs. Cullen and ask her to tell her mother she was taking a bus. She'd be there as soon as she could. She'd ask Mrs. Cullen to tell her mother, for God's sake, to wait for her to get there.

Ronnie shut his eyes and leaned his face into Eleanor's hands for a moment before he straightened, then he held out his own hand. The car keys sat on his palm.

"I know," he said dully. "You have to go."

"I do," she said. "But I can't take your car. Not anymore. Not under—these circumstances."

He gave her a sad smile. "Not under false pretenses, you mean? Because you don't really love me?"

His prescience startled her. Right then, Ronnie seemed very grown-up. Grown-up and sad. A sad man. She almost told him she did love him. But even she, with her long history of easy lies, understood she couldn't lie about love; if she did, she'd be lost. She nodded.

"It's okay. You don't love me, but I love you. So you should take my car," he said, with a logic so nice she wondered if she might be able to fall in love with him after all.

He moved his hand closer to her and nodded, and Eleanor whispered, "Thank you." She meant for loving her and for lending her the car, in that order, to her relief. Then, she picked up the keys from his palm and left.

DURING THE SECOND HALF OF the ride home, when her ranting, fist-banging rage at Mrs. Cullen and the church ladies had spent itself, burned itself out in the hard, white, winter sunshine blaring through the windshield and filling the car, leaving her feeling tired and scoured clean, Eleanor began to do what she'd done countless times before, to call up a certain memory like a magic spell, a memory that was really many memories, brief, bright instances spanning years distilled into a single, crystal-clear scene, her secret power source, her ace in the hole: Susan sitting with her and teaching her to sew.

In the memory, Susan was relaxed. She gave instructions in a quiet, patient voice. Yellow cotton fabric like a swatch of sunshine; yellower thread spinning off the spool, feeding the needle, stamping lines of stiches, straight and true, like little bird tracks, the sewing machine chugging like a train. When Eleanor made mistakes, Susan didn't shout or belittle but simply offered corrections. She sat so close that Eleanor could smell her: L'Air du Temps and the fine pressed powder she put on her cheeks. Sometimes, their hands brushed against each other's or their tilted heads would momentarily touch.

Eleanor did not fool herself into believing it was her daughter's presence that granted Susan these rare hours of placidity, tranquil pools in a storm-wracked forest. No, it was the sewing itself. Like Martha's jigsaw puzzles or her own bicycle rides: a clear series of movements requiring your mind to focus just enough to prevent its wandering into the dark or the complicated.

Whenever Eleanor knew she would have to spend time alone with her mother—and, thanks to Martha, it hadn't happened often—she would lift the memory from its place of safekeeping and let it sit inside her mind, slowly giving her attention to each detail, every sound and silence, every scent and touch, the yellow on yellow on yellow, Susan's tapered fingers on the fabric, her instructions oboe-low, rhythmic, almost a song. The memory opened up a space for Eleanor, one in which she could meet her mother without anger, not with love (she had not mustered love for Susan since she was a child, had long ago stopped feeling guilty about it) but with the ordinary compassionate regard she'd grant any human being, an acquaintance, a stranger, anyone. The memory didn't clean the slate; nothing could. And it didn't go so far as to make her hopeful. But it bought her some time to be civil and fair; a few hours in which they could be just two women in a house, talking.

"SO YOU CAME, DID YOU? And here you are, the invisible daughter."

Susan stood in the doorway. She'd not yet invited Eleanor in, although Eleanor knew she would. First, she had to perform her bit of drama, just like always. Her words were caustic, but her tone was reserved, decorum tinged with exhaustion, much like her attire—no skirt or dress but narrow plaid wool slacks, perfectly fitting, with an old sweater—and her hair, unstyled but clean and brushed. The bandage on her hand was white as snow, and until she felt her own relief, Eleanor hadn't realized she'd been worried it would be stained with blood. Susan wore no makeup, not even a dusting of powder, and she had always been the sort of woman who would do her brows and lashes even if the house were burning down around her.

She wants to look haggard and world-weary, so I see the devastation our abandonment of her has inflicted, but also to look pale and dignified, so I know she's rising above. Eleanor shut her eyes, briefly, resurrected the sewing memory, her mother's patient presence. It was too early to get mad. And Eleanor also knew that, however necessary, however well deserved their abandonment of her was, it had been a blow to their mother. The exhaustion in her face was probably genuine.

The worst thing, she thought as she looked at her mother, *the very worst thing anyone can do to you is to leave you alone with yourself.*

"Yes, I'm here," said Eleanor, making her voice pleasant.

Susan stepped out onto the porch. For a moment, her face, bathed in the setting sunlight slipping in under the porch roof, resembled Eleanor's own so closely, she almost gasped: heart-shaped, upward-tilting nose, big eyes. It was a resemblance she'd always resented.

"I see you've come in style," her mother said, gesturing toward Ronnie's Austin-Healey.

"It belongs to a friend."

"I'll bet. Well, since you're here, Eleanor, you may as well come in. No use standing on the porch. Caroline Cullen is probably peering at us from one of those church windows this minute."

The house smelled like lemons. Susan had never been much of a housekeeper, but Eleanor remembered what Mrs. Cullen had said about the blood on the floor, and she wondered if Susan had scrubbed it up herself, with lemon floor cleaner and her one bare hand.

Nothing inside the house had changed. The same watercolors on the walls (painted by local artists but not by Martha, not a single one), the same books on the shelves, their gold-stamped spines faded from the sun slanting through the tall front windows, the same marble-topped tables and heavy antique furniture Eleanor's father had inherited from his parents and brought east. Eleanor recognized every item, knew the precise color of the kitchen curtains (melted butter) and all the tangles in the fringe of the living room rug (she'd always wanted to comb them out) and the pale gold and white chrysanthemum-patterned wallpaper in the dining room. But none of it felt like hers; she felt not a trace of honest attachment. And she was a person who got attached to places. She loved parts of this town, for instance. Occasionally, since she'd left, she got painfully homesick for certain trees and benches in the park downtown; she'd dreamed, vividly and more than once, about the public library; and she knew that if she left right now and made her way to the shore, she would greet the ocean like a sister, but, except when she was inside the room she'd shared with Martha, in this house in which she'd lived her entire life, she felt numb, like a visitor, a sleepwalker.

Eleanor dropped her bag at the foot of the stairs and followed Susan into the kitchen, bracing herself for the berating or the interrogation she was sure would come. But Susan switched on the radio, and as "The Girl from Ipanema" filled the room, easy and mellow as evening light, she began to delicately and unconsciously samba her way through preparing dinner, shimmying her shoulders, taking short forward-backward steps and rocking her narrow hips. Susan was a natural dancer, had always been. Martha said she could remember being a child and watching her parents dance together in the living room.

"She'd dance with you, too," Martha had told Eleanor, "when you were a baby. She'd put a record on and dance all over the house with you on her hip or with her cheek pressed against yours. She'd dance and Dad would watch, smiling ear to ear."

But Eleanor couldn't remember anything like this; by the time Martha had told her—and she couldn't have been more than seven years old—she couldn't even imagine it.

Susan switched on the oven and opened the refrigerator.

"Why don't I do it?" Eleanor asked. "It's too hard with just one hand."

With her bandaged hand, Susan batted the offer away.

"It's just a casserole. One of the women from church, Eve Shields, dropped off this one, so it'll probably be decent. Some of those church ladies couldn't cook their way out of a paper bag."

She laughed.

"They've been inundating me with food: casseroles, Jell-O molds, heaps of cookies, as if I had any other mouths to feed but my own. I'm sure I don't have to tell you the Jell-O went straight into the garbage."

Eleanor didn't answer. Susan had taken a head of lettuce and a cucumber from the refrigerator and was reaching to lift a knife from the wooden block.

"I'll make the salad," said Eleanor quickly, going to the counter and getting to the knife first.

Susan gave her a mild, amused look.

"I appreciate the concern," she said. "But you needn't worry I'll chop my own arm off—or yours. I won't be slitting anyone's throat anytime soon, either. I'm back on my medication."

Eleanor tensed at Susan's words, the acid edge to her tone, the tiny, black threat tucked inside her knife jokes, but she said, neutrally, "Oh? Well, that seems like a wise decision."

"Maybe," said Susan. "I hate the stuff. Loathe it. But I promised the doctor who stitched up my hand I'd give it another go. He's a persuasive sort of man."

Eleanor gave her a sharp glance. She could never remember Susan having a boyfriend; certainly, she'd never brought a man home. But there was a particular state she'd sometimes get to—fizzing and hectic and loud—when she would engage in what could only be called flirting with almost anyone: the mailman, a teacher at her daughters' school, the minister. But now, Susan laughed.

"Not in *that* way, silly! He's cute enough, but no. He's just smart and not a showoff about it. He makes sense in a way most people don't. And he spoke without an ounce of pity or judgment, which heaven knows makes him different from everyone else who ever talks to me. So when he recommended I go back on a slightly lower dose of the damned medication, I said I would. I might not stay on it, probably won't, but for now, you don't need to hide the knives."

SUSAN WAITED UNTIL 4:00 A.M. to get crazy.

Small talk had carried them through dinner: scraps of local gossip, questions about Eleanor's classes, her friends. Eleanor bent the truth when she needed to, changed names when she felt it necessary, didn't mention Alice and her family, or Ronnie. No one spoke Martha's name. After dinner, at Susan's urging, while she took a bath, Eleanor went out into the crisp air for a walk under the streetlamps and then along the shore. She loved the beach at night, the whispering dune grass, the sand silvery and dappled with footprints, the ocean pleating quietly under the moon.

When she got back, she found Susan in one of the living room armchairs, damp-haired and looking childlike inside her pink quilted robe. On the table next to her was a cut-glass tumbler of Irish whiskey. Other parents drank Lancers wine or martinis or Tom Collins cocktails (most of the mothers seemed not to drink alcohol at all), but Susan Campbell had kept bottles of Irish whiskey on the top shelf of the pantry for as long as Eleanor could remember. She always drank it straight and from a fancy glass.

"Don't worry, dear," she said cheerfully, lifting the glass in Eleanor's direction, "I'm allowed one per day. Doctor's orders."

Eleanor doubted that the smart, young doctor had given any such orders, but she didn't say so.

"I think I'll go to bed," Eleanor said. "It was a long drive."

"No, no, sit for a while. I haven't seen you in ages."

Eleanor's heart sank, but she took off her coat, hung it in the closet near the front door, and, warily, sat.

Susan smiled and said, "Now, then. I would like you to tell me where Martha has gone."

Eleanor shook her head.

"I can't," she said.

"Can't?" said Susan, her voice still pleasant. "But you really must. I've been worried sick."

Eleanor did not believe this for a second, but she said, "Oh. Well, you can stop worrying. Martha is fine. Better than fine. She's doing wonderfully well, actually. I'd say she's flourishing."

Eleanor knew she should've stopped at "fine," knew how every word she'd said after had fed whatever ugliness was surely brewing under Susan's bland exterior, but she couldn't stop herself. And her words were true. Martha was flourishing. Martha was triumphing.

You didn't ruin her life, she thought, *despite all your best efforts.*

"Is she?" Her mother's smile hardened. "There's a man involved, obviously. Anyone could have seen it coming: poor, plain Martha having her head turned, throwing her morals to the wind the first time a man gives her a wink. What's his name, the man she ran away with?"

Eleanor wanted to get up and hurl the glass of whiskey across the room, upend the furniture, bring the whole house down around her mother's ears. The intensity of her fury frightened her, and she knew, even as the fury spilled over, out of her, to fill the room to the rafters, she knew she was angry at the woman, but also angry at the grain of truth in what she'd said. Not the part about morality, which made Eleanor want to scream. Who had less right to crow about morality than the person sitting in front of her? But the part about Martha's head being turned, well, Eleanor had to—would never, never out loud, not to her mother or to anyone—admit she was right.

In Jack's hands, I turn beautiful, Elsbee. Me. Me, of all people. Beautiful.

He's a man of moods and silences, but when he does talk, he sets the air on fire. His voice, his face. I often don't know if I agree with him: I might but I don't know. It doesn't matter, though. Sometimes, I catch myself not even hearing what he's saying because I'm too busy feeling his voice inside me.

Elaine and Mr. Olson disapprove of him. They don't say so, but I can tell. And I do see why. They're protective of me (and I love them for it), but they might be right to be when it comes to Jack: he's got a wandering, wild streak. Not wild like Mother, not unhinged, but wild like a wolf or a bear or hawk. Not quite tame. It's unsettling, but, oh Elsbee, intoxicating!

Eleanor thought she would want to protect Martha from Jack, too, but all she said to Susan was "Martha didn't run away with anyone. She's working hard and painting. She left to live her life."

Susan went rigid with anger and drew herself up the way she did before she started shouting, but then she blinked and said, "It's all right, Eleanor. You've always been loyal. Not, of course, to me, but I don't suppose most children see what goes into being a mother. You've probably never considered for one second that I'd have liked to go off and live *my* own life. But your loyalty to Martha, I've always found it adorable. I'd still like to know where she's gone, though, so please consider telling me. Tomorrow, maybe. But for now, off to bed with you! You look absolutely spent. Like death warmed over."

AT FOUR IN THE MORNING, Eleanor awoke to the sound of her bedroom door opening, two clicks and a creak, a series of sounds she'd heard and dreaded and been hyperattuned to for so many years that even in sleep, she recognized them. The sounds yanked her upright, heart racing, and she reached for the switch next to the bed, flipped it. The overhead light came on, dimly, barely diffusing the darkness with grainy yellow. She'd noticed the night before how the frosted glass globe was dusty and flecked inside with dead moths and how all but one of the three bulbs had burned out. All the furniture in the room bore a fine coating of dust, giving Eleanor the eerie sense—eerie but somehow satisfying—that she and Martha had not slept there in decades.

Susan stood near the foot of Eleanor's twin bed, and the look in her eyes wasn't crazed, as Eleanor had expected, but flat like a bird's or a reptile's.

"Good morning, Eleanor."

Her voice was as flat as her eyes, controlled and devoid of emotion. This was new. *A new kind of crazy*, thought Eleanor, a shiver running through her. *Perfect.*

"I'm giving you one more chance to be reasonable and fair," Susan said, "because I of all people have a right to know. Where. The hell. Is Martha?"

"I'll never tell you," said Eleanor, quietly. "Ever."

Her mother took a step closer and held on to the footboard of the bed with her thin hands.

Eleanor saw her chest heave, once, twice, but otherwise she stayed very still. She didn't sway or stumble. She didn't seem to be drunk, which was surprising. Not drunk, not screaming with rage. Fresh hell, a new kind of crazy, and Eleanor was struck hard by the understanding that the woman standing before her hated her. All her life, she had known her mother didn't love her. She believed her daughters belonged to her, but this belonging was not the same as love. Eleanor knew Susan had used her and Martha, especially Martha, as a target when she got crazy; knew she blamed them for her own unhappy life, but what Eleanor saw now was not just the absence of love. On Susan's white face, in the cords of her neck, and in the tendons of her hands as they gripped the bed, was pure, ice-cold, animal hatred.

"You spoiled bitch," said Susan. "You ungrateful, spoiled, stupid bitch."

Eleanor got out of bed and walked to stand a few feet from her mother, who unhooked her hands from the footboard and turned so the two of them were eye to eye.

"Do you think I care what you think of me?" said Eleanor. "You're a grown woman who has spent her life bullying little girls. But even when we were scared, we always felt sorry for you. And we never, ever, cared what you thought of us."

She meant to hurt Susan, to hurl words like rocks, but, as she did it, she understood the words were true, at least were true for her. She wasn't as sure about Martha, but Eleanor had wanted to placate her mother, to defuse her, to keep her at bay, and had never even thought of wanting her approval. Even in this weird, charged, and precarious moment, some analytical part of Eleanor's mind thought, *That's strange, isn't it? I wonder how I escaped it, wanting her to love me?*

And the answer came to her: *Because Martha loved you.*

"I'm going to leave now," said Eleanor, in a steady voice. "And I am never coming back. But you are to stay away from my sister. If I hear of you going off to find her, I will ruin your life. I will make you sorrier than you can imagine."

She saw it then, the swift crack in the ice, the flare, and when Susan lifted her hand, Eleanor caught her wrist before the slap could fly. Susan stood there in her grip, eyes blazing, and then she wrenched her arm free.

"Get out," she hissed. "I'll buy a gun. If you ever come back here, I will kill you as soon as you step through the door. I will set my house on fire with both of us inside."

"I'm not afraid of you," said Eleanor.

Susan barked a laugh. "Yes, you are," and she spun on her slippered heel, silent as a cat, and walked out of the room.

Eleanor heard her run down the steps and into the kitchen. A cabinet banged. There was the long sigh of the front door. From the window, in the moonlight, she saw her mother raise a pan, her favorite weapon, over her head with both hands and bring it down on the hood of Ronnie's car. She tossed the pan into the grass, and, in her robe and slippers, she began walking down the dark street, purposefully, taking long strides.

Eleanor looked down; her hands on the windowsill were shaking. Her teeth chattered. Susan had been right; Eleanor was afraid.

She drew the curtains, got dressed, went into the bathroom, brushed her teeth, and walked downstairs. The front door stood open, offering a rectangle of what lay beyond it: clean, salt-tinged air, moon scattering glitter on the dewy grass, a road winding on and on, away. Eleanor stepped through the door and into the world.

She would be halfway home, halfway back to school, before she would realize she'd left her coat hanging in the closet of her mother's house, but it didn't matter. She would arrive where she was going, she would sit down in her bright room, and she would make herself a new one.

THE NEXT MORNING, ELEANOR RECEIVED a letter from Martha, dated just two days after the last one she had sent. It was written across a watercolor of a hawk flying through a pale gray sky and was one sentence long: *Because above all else, I must be where he is, tomorrow, I head south, to utopia, with Jack.*

Chapter 9

CORNELIA

AFTER OLLIE'S DRAMATIC ENTRANCE, SWEEPING in with the dawn and spangled with dew, she dropped her bag, went back out to the car, and sleepwalked her son into the house. He was tall for nine and skinny, with a glorious mop of springy dark brown curls. He was wearing green fleece pajamas and red shearling slippers and dragged a blue-and-white-striped blanket behind him. With his head drooping sleepily sideways, he looked like a big shaggy flower on a thin stalk.

"Clive, we're here," said Ollie, in as gentle a voice as I'd ever heard her use. "Say hi to Aunt Cornelia."

Clive lifted his head an inch and mustered a half-smile, the dimples I'd forgotten he had suddenly popping up under each sleepy eye. He waved his free hand, and then his head lolled sideways again.

"Why don't you put him in Cam and Toby's room?" I said. "That way, you'll be right across the hall."

Ollie thought for a moment, and then said, "I think I'll put him in my old room with me. He's been having some minor sleep issues lately."

"Oh, okay," I said.

Ollie gave me a sharp look. "It's to be expected. Very developmentally normal. Nine-year-olds are starting to be more aware of the larger world and its complications, An increase in anxiety at night is typical."

I started to remind Ollie that I myself had a ten-year-old who had in fact been a nine-year-old just one short year ago, that a person didn't need umpteen degrees in genetic science and a list of publications as long as her arm to understand that kids' brains change as they grow up, and also that, jeez Ollie, all I'd said was "Oh, okay," but I battened down my rising hackles just in time. This woman had just driven all night, presumably motivated by concern (however uncharacteristic) for our mother, and was certainly exhausted. And anyway, it was too early in the morning for the Ollie-and-Cornelia sniping show to start.

"Good idea," I said. "There are clean sheets on all the beds, and you remember where the towels and everything are, right?"

I saw Ollie bristle at this reminder—which I swear was unintentional—that she didn't visit our parents very often, but maybe she recalled that her nine-year-old, anxiety-prone, half-asleep boy was standing there, or maybe she'd decided, as I had, that we should at least wait until the sun was fully up to start fighting. In any case, she just nodded, then picked up her bag, looped an arm around Clive, and walked him out of the room and up the stairs.

LATER IN THE MORNING, CLIVE came down first. For my Simon, to wake up is to be slingshotted into the world; he eschews all the typical early-morning child cuteness—not so much as an eye rub with two small fists or an arms-lifted-in-a-Y stretch or even a few bemused big-eyed blinks. He flings open his eyes, pitches himself out of bed, and smashes a loud, Simon-shaped hole through even the most tranquil morning. But the newly awakened Clive materialized noiselessly in the kitchen with his teeth brushed (a fresh smear of white toothpaste on his pajama top gave him away) and with slippers on his feet.

Earlier, when Ollie hadn't come back downstairs after taking Clive to bed, I'd gone out for a morning run. I'd taken up running late in life and was generally still more of a walker than a runner. While I am actually quite quick, I'm also short and scrawny and stick-legged, so running always makes me feel vaguely silly, like a sandpiper or a scurrying mouse, whereas walking fast engenders a sense of authority and power: Cornelia Brown striding over the earth with her arms swinging. Also, I like to look at stuff, and it's easier when you're walking. But this December morning was fifty degrees and, once the fog dissolved, snappy and color-soaked, the sort of morning when you need to tear through the air, to feel the wind zap your cheeks red and blow back your hair, even if your hair is so boy-short as to be wholly unblowable. When I was almost home, I saw my dad power walking toward me in his jogging pants and sneakers. I stopped to talk to him, but he pointed to his wrist and kept going.

"Can't stop! Need to keep up my pace or this darned watch will berate me all day!" he said.

"Ollie's here," I called after him. "And Clive."

"Yup!" he said.

"She said she came to hear all about Mom!"

"Interesting!" shouted my dad, right as always.

Without turning around, he shot a thumbs-up into the air, then disappeared around a corner.

I was standing in the kitchen, gulping water, when Clive appeared. He stood just inside the room, radiant, honey-colored, and serious, his fingers tucked up inside his sleeves.

"Momolly's still sleeping," he said. "She said it was fine if I came downstairs by myself."

I smiled. At two, for reasons he would not divulge, Clive had spontaneously begun to call his mother by her first name. When Ollie and her husband, Edmund, had encouraged him to go back to calling her Mommy, he'd settled on Momolly, which had stuck, and, apparently—and adorably—had continued to stick.

"Well, I'm glad you did because I have an important question for you," I said.

"Okay," said Clive. He looked nervous, and I realized how long it had been since we'd seen each other.

When Ollie and her family left their home on Long Island, it was usually to go on summer research trips or to scientific conferences, often to islands other than Long: Galapagos, Pitcairn, Madagascar. She and Edmund were genetic scientists, although since Clive had come on the scene, Ollie had mainly been working as an associate editor for a scientific journal. During the holidays, they traveled ("We travel," I could hear Ollie say, in a tone suggesting that to do anything but travel was unthinkable, or at least only thinkable to the small-minded, provincial, and hopelessly ordinary), often to Jamaica, where Edmund had grown up, but also to Iceland, Costa Rica, Prague, Tanzania, and any other dazzling place wherein members of Ollie's immediate family did not live. My parents made an annual visit to Ollie's house (although they stayed at an inn nearby), but I had not seen Clive in person since he was in kindergarten. No wonder the prospect of a question from me made him shift to high alert.

"Waffles or pancakes?" I said. "Or eggs and bacon? Or maybe coffee cake? I made some yesterday, loaded with apples."

Clive's shoulders relaxed, his fingers fluttered into view, he nodded, solemnly, then his face bloomed a grin full of big, square, gappy kid teeth that made me feel like I'd won a prize.

"Yes, please," he said.

OLLIE WAS HAVING COFFEE IN the kitchen with Dr. B, each ensconced in their own silence, reading, as if there weren't everything in the world to talk about, when Clive and I took our chance to steal away to the attic. I was already in need of an escape from Ollie, but my excuse for going was to find the wool Pendleton blankets my mother brought down every winter. We'd first gotten them decades ago to use during car trips to my father's uncle's cabin in the Great Smoky Mountains. There had been four of them, one for each child in our family.

When Clive and I got to the attic, without saying a word to each other, we decided to stay.

Clive was the sort of boy who finds whatever pockets of quietude a place harbors and sits in them. Arms crossed, he surveyed the attic, then tucked himself into a pie slice of sunlight sparkling with dust motes, between a bin of summer bedding and the box of Spode Christmas china, opened his book, and dove in. *Harry Potter and the Sorcerer's Stone*, one I knew he must have read before, and I thought how he was a child like I'd been, like my daughter, Rose, was still: in times of stress or displacement, reaching for a life preserver shaped like a book and hanging on for dear life. I recognized his expression: he might be in the attic of a house he hadn't visited in four years, but the boy was home.

And, here in this attic and in any attic really, so was I.

Old things pull me. Not ancient things, at least not usually. I did visit Stonehenge once and found it as moving as everyone else did, although I suspect not for the same reasons everyone else did. While the other tourists marveled aloud at how and at what distance the giant bluestones had been transported, discussed the math and magic of the summer solstice, speculated about Druids and space aliens, or simply walked around in blank astonishment, muttering words like "majestic" and "powerful," I found myself nearly weeping at what struck me as the tangible loneliness of those rocks. They'd been standing there, like big awkward children meant to be playing ring-around-the-rosy but too shy to hold hands, in the center of that windswept, slate-sky vastness, for centuries upon centuries. Yes, they had each other—and some eight hundred thousand tourists per year—for company, but they nevertheless seemed forlorn, orphaned. I found myself wanting to reach my arms around every stone, to make them sandwiches and tell them bedtime stories.

But mostly, it's the homey and human that reels me in. Objects that people—maybe generations of people—have worn, eaten off, cooked with, wrapped themselves in, lain themselves down upon, hung on their walls, placed on their bedside tables or mantels or kitchen counters, held in their hands. Sometimes, it's purely the beauty of an object that transports me, and my tastes run to the curvaceous and gleaming or the delicate and lily-like. I've been tempted to steal Bakelite radios, jadeite tumblers, cocktail shakers (one shaped like a Zepplin made my palms positively itch), my great-aunt's toaster, Edwardian amethyst hatpins, every Lalique vase I've ever encountered, and at least half the elevator doors in New York City.

But more even than beauty, it's the stories objects hold. How anything—the humblest saltshaker, the tiniest silver baby cup, a worn red-and-white-checkered tablecloth—can be endowed with secrets, the joys and sorrows of decades or centuries scratched into its patina, caught in its folds, whispering out of its worn places and cracks.

I've cobbled together a career out of my love of attics and old stuff. Ollie would scoff at the word *career* being applied to what I do, and it feels like the wrong word even to me. When I work, I am not on a trajectory, at least not an upward one, and I don't make much money. I go into people's attics and basements and back bedrooms, through their junk drawers and crawl spaces and closets, gleaning the precious from the ordinary like a miner with a pan of grit. I'm not just talking dollar-value preciousness, although there is that, if people want it. And the hope that accompanies those sorts of jobs is straight out of Cinderella: the grimy oil painting in the barn might be an Old Master, a soup spoon the work of Paul Revere! Usually, those hopes are dashed, but most of the time people don't seem to mind. The high-flying, long-shot hope itself is really the point.

But my specialty is winnowing out the stories attached to the objects, gathering them into sentences or paragraphs or even pages to be handed down the family tree just as surely as the objects themselves will be. "You help people clean out their houses" is what Ollie would say (and has said). "Get rid of all that dingy armchair-doily grandma crap." True, but it's more about what to keep and why, about understanding how one silver thimble could be worth more than a cabinet full of antique Wedgwood jasperware in pristine condition. I do talk to a lot of grandmas, to widows and elderly couples, collecting nuggets of history, family facts, and myths. It's slow work and intricate, deciding on which prompts and questions might gently unlatch the doors and windows of waning human memories. The stories can be gorgeous or bitter; some are hilarious; some burn—across decades, lifetimes—with pain.

But in the attic that morning, I realized I'd never done it for my own family, had never even considered it. My mother was not a keeper; my family was an open book. There would be nothing to find, would there? Now, I was beset by a high-flying hope of my own: a cardboard box, open, beams pouring out, the room full to the rafters with dancing arctic light.

TWO HOURS LATER, I FOUND three items I'd never seen before: two matching baby dresses—one slightly bigger than the other—in a rosebud-sprigged fabric with smocking and white ruffled collars; and what seemed to be a small blanket or a scarf, square, maybe three feet by three feet. They were in a shoebox with a rubber band around it in the very back of the attic. All three items seemed handmade, no tags or labels. The dresses were old-fashioned, classic, but the hand-loomed blanket was richly colored and fringed, lots of greens— emerald, apple, bottle, spring leaf—with stripes of lemon yellow, purple, and raspberry pink. It was a lovely and well-loved thing, thin and faded in spots where it had been handled but clean and carefully folded inside white tissue paper.

When Ollie showed up in the attic, I had the dresses and the blanket spread out before me on one of the attic rugs, a threadbare Delft-blue Persian runner that had once started its run outside my bedroom and ended it outside Ollie's. I was surprised to see her, since Ollie didn't like attics and didn't, let's be honest, like me. She used to like me; I know she did. We used to be thick as thieves, padding in our bare feet down that runner and into each other's room for years. And then, sometime around the middle of Ollie's high school years, she seemed to just stop, to stop both the padding and the liking, and it broke my little heart in two.

"Hey," I said, "looking for Clive? He was up here reading but left about fifteen minutes ago."

The fifteen minutes was just a guess, since Clive must have slipped out silent as a cat. It was only because I happened to glance at the spot where he'd been sitting that I'd noticed he had gone, a minor miracle in a room in which half the floorboards emitted some ver-sion of creak: bullfrog, groan, whine, shriek. I wondered if he had maneuvered his velvet-footed self to the attic door via pure intuition, like a quiet-child version of walking across hot coals, knowing just where to step. I said fifteen minutes because I didn't want Ollie to think I'd been ignoring her son, even though we'd been ignoring each other all morning in the happiest, most easeful kind of way.

"I know. I just saw him putting on his coat. He's going to Dashiell's Hardware with Dad," said Ollie.

She sat down on the cedar chest, long-limbed in her dark blue jeans and gray turtleneck. For the first time, I noticed how much thinner she looked than when I'd last seen her four years ago. Ollie was tall by my standards, five foot six, a full six inches taller than I am, but really just a shade over average. Still, she had always seemed taller with her rangy arms and legs, her ballerina neck, her good posture, and her imperious gaze. She'd been athletic, with broad shoulders and narrow hips and long muscles in her legs. Now, though, she might actually qualify as gaunt. Her cheekbones jutted; the sinews in her neck stood out starkly as she talked. I wondered if that accounted for the turtleneck. But she was still pretty, fairer than the rest of our family, almost blond, with Vivian Leigh brows and a supermodel forehead. Even as a kid, she'd had an adult face, a face to be taken seriously. Since I myself had spent my life fighting the small woman's battle to be taken seriously, to not be dismissed as cute, I envied her. No one could dismiss Ollie as anything; no one ever had.

"Remember how much we loved to go to Dashiell's with Dad?" I said, smiling. "It was the perfect place for the choosing game."

Ollie's face showed not one glimmer of recognition or interest, which threw me. If Ollie had forgotten the choosing game, then my hope—as faded, shopworn, and flimsy as a hope could be but a hope nonetheless—that maybe the two of us could one day act like sisters again might as well lie down and die.

We played it more times than I could name. We played it so often and for so many years that it wasn't even playing, it wasn't even a game, it was just Ollie and Cornelia being together. Sometimes, truth be told, I still play it—by myself and never without a touch of sadness. When Ollie and I found ourselves in a good choosing game spot, we didn't have to decide to play or to say a word. We'd just begin. Museums of all sorts, parks full of rows of flowers or trees, jewelry store windows, carpet stores (carpet stores were fantastic, all those colorful sample squares), city streets with row houses, Dashiell's Hardware, anyplace that had a large selection—an array—of a single item. In the Natural History Museum, it could be butterflies in a case. In Dashiell's it could be padlocks, switch plates, keys, doorknobs, hammers. The rule was that we had to choose our favorite, the one we'd take home if we could, and that was it, the whole game. Maybe simple, maybe silly, but still one of the best things I've ever gotten to do in my entire life.

"You'd home right in on your packet of seeds or your flashlight," I went on, "as if you had been carrying around an image of your perfect seed packet or flashlight since forever. And I would agonize, comparing every detail. Like: oh no, that flashlight is shinier, but this one is *yellow*!"

I laughed. Ollie did not.

Ollie said—and not in a fond *Oh, Cornelia, you're so adorably interesting* kind of way—"You remember the weirdest things."

MY MOTHER'S OLLIE THEORY: IT'S not that Ollie doesn't care about people. It's that she has to keep her feelings at bay because she knows if she gives in to caring, she'll be lost, so terribly vulnerable it scares her. So she pushes people away.

My father's Ollie theory: Ollie can only really open her heart to people who are right in front of her, part of her daily life.

Cam and Toby's Ollie theory: Ollie is a self-centered asshole, but she's our self-centered asshole.

Teo's theory: Ollie has limited active-love bandwidth, very limited, much narrower than most people's and therefore a million times narrower than yours, Cornelia. It gets smaller as she gets older, but it was pretty small to begin with. She has to use it sparingly because there's just not a lot there. It's entirely possible she can only actively love like five people in the world at any given time. When she was a kid, those five people were you and your family. Then she went out into the world and found another person, so someone fell off the list. And this kept happening.

When I asked what he meant by active love, Teo said, "Love love. Regular love. What most people mean when they say it. Love, the verb form. Love you put into action."

"So what about dormant love?" I demanded. "Are you saying Ollie has a giant stockpile of dormant love somewhere?"

"Possibly. Maybe not a giant stockpile, though, because giant stockpiles are giant. Maybe a small storage unit. Or a filing cabinet. A decent-size filing cabinet."

It should be noted, although most of the time no one does note it and in fact forgets about it completely, that before Teo and I fell in love—or before I fell in love with him because he claims he was in love with me for some time before he admitted it to me or to anyone (he keeps the exact length hazy but has hinted that it probably kicked off before the dawn of time), he was married for two years to my sister, Ollie. For Teo, it was a madcap move, a maybe-it-will-work-stranger-things-have-happened-and-the-woman-I-truly-love-will-only-ever-think-of-me-as-a-brother [wrong] move. For Ollie, it was more clinical (surprise, surprise): supposedly love-based unions ended in divorce at least half the time, whereas arranged or practicality-based ones had a better chance of survival overall, and there was also the little, incidental fact that Edmund Battle, the man she truly loved, would never love her back [wrong]. Unshockingly and almost immediately, they realized the marriage was a mistake; what's more shocking is that even Ollie—who scoffs at mistakes and all people who make them—admitted it pretty quickly. Of the two years they were married, they lived under the same roof for just a handful of unhappy and nonconsecutive months before Edmund swooped back into the scene and before I experienced the bone-jarring, soul-soaring epiphany that my lifelong pal Teo Sandoval and I belonged to each other—of course we did—body and soul, forever and always.

"I had a good run on Ollie's active love list, I guess. I mean, it all came crashing down around my ears when I was about thirteen, but it was good while it lasted. And I guess you made the list for a while there yourself," I had said to Teo.

"Not me. Nope. Not even close. But I'm pretty sure there's a very thin file out there with my name on it."

My Ollie theory is that all these other Ollie theories are probably right and also possibly wrong, but I am less concerned with why she is who she is than with, in spite of everything, how much I miss her. Oh, how I miss her. I miss her and I want her back. Phantom sister pain. It never goes away.

"I WANT TO HEAR WHAT you found out about Mom," said Ollie.

The urgency in her voice startled me. Startled me and made me hopeful. The urgency, the way she sat leaning toward me, elbows on knees, hands clasped: this was Ollie caring, the rarest of sights.

So I told her. About the northern lights, about our mother's abject grief, her bleak and desperate longing, about my trip to North Carolina and what I'd found there. I told her how our mother, the woman we'd always known, had had a sister all this time, a sister, for all our lives and all of hers.

When I finished, Ollie said this: "That's all?"

"You really didn't just say 'That's all?' There is no possibility that you actually said that, right?"

Ollie looked annoyed, not a rare sight at all. She even showed up annoyed in my dreams: arms crossed, lips thin, head tilted back toward her right shoulder, eyes cold.

"What I mean is: nothing about me?" she said. She enunciated the last three words as if she were speaking to a child or a nonnative speaker (if you're a person who speaks to children and nonnative speakers as if they are idiots).

"Another thing you could—as I sit here and live and breathe—not possibly have said," I said.

"It was just a question," said Ollie. "Why is everything always such a big deal to you?"

I bit my tongue, literally, as barbed and vicious (and completely legitimate) comebacks raced around in my head like a pack of jackals.

"I don't understand what you were expecting," I said. "What secrets would I have discovered about you? I know you. You know you. You weren't alive for twenty-plus years before you were born, living a mystery life."

Ollie heaved her chest in a sigh and lifted her eyes to the attic ceiling, as if asking the universe for forbearance, and then said, "Whatever. Forget it."

I could've laid into her. I knew how, knew just what buttons to push, even though, historically, when it came to Ollie interactions, I'd been the pushee, not the pusher. But something I saw in her stopped me, something alive and moving, flickering under the frozen pond of her disgust and scorn, alive and moving and flickering and sad. Ollie wasn't on the brink of crying; she had never been a crier; she disdained criers. But I sensed that she was on the brink of almost crying, which for some reason struck me as an even sadder brink to be on, a sadder sight to see.

"Well, here's something I found," I said, "that must have to do with you. With us."

I lifted the two small, flowered dresses, one in each hand. Ollie reached for them with more eagerness than I'm sure she meant to show, and I gave them to her. She placed one on each of her knees and smoothed them with her hands.

"I don't remember them," I said. "I don't remember ever seeing pictures of us wearing them."

"No," said Ollie, "I don't either."

"And Mom never dressed us alike that I can remember. Not any of us, not Cam and Toby either. It seems kind of un-Mom-like, too sentimental or something."

Ollie didn't answer, but I saw her take one of the ruffled collars between her thumb and two fingers and hold it. She sat stock-still and stared down at it, pensively. She seemed to be holding her breath.

"And they look handmade. Maybe Dad's mom made them? Because Mom's never sewed. She hates sewing," I said.

"Maybe they belonged to Mom and her supposed sister," said Ollie.

"No," I said, shaking my head. "I thought of that, but the people who wore these had to be pretty close in age, a baby and toddler maybe."

"Well, I don't think they're ours," said Ollie, finally, in a stony, dismissive voice.

Abruptly, she whisked the dresses off her lap and handed them back to me.

"Whose would they be, if not ours?" I said.

She shrugged, as if she didn't care, could not imagine caring about two dresses, as if she hadn't just been pondering the collar of one of them as if it held the meaning of life.

"No idea," she said. "Someone else's?"

"But she kept them," I said. "She put them in a box with tissue paper and kept them. Why would she do that?"

"I wouldn't know about that," said Ollie. "I just know they aren't ours."

"How?"

"I just do."

"You're a scientist, for Pete's sake!" I said. "What's your theory? Where's your evidence? Where the heck is your double-blind, peer-reviewed blah, blah study?"

"I just know. Let's leave it at that."

Bored Ollie I recognized. Ditto self-involved Ollie. Also snide, snippy, and contemptuous Ollie. But mercurial Ollie? Contemplative Ollie? Cryptic Ollie? Going-with-My-Gut Ollie? Those were new. I recalled articles I'd read about anole lizards, fruit flies, tawny owls, and other critters, how they went merrily along for centuries making minuscule and leisurely adjustments, until climate change threw them for a loop and straight onto an adaptation obstacle course. Suddenly, every time they turned around, it was adapt, adapt, adapt. Change color! Lengthen your toes! Swim faster! Migrate farther! And, yes, I understand my science might be shaky here, understand, too, the logical and moral pitfalls of comparing life in my family of origin to the biggest global catastrophe of our or any time, but still.

"Okay. Fine," I said. "This was in the same box. It seems even less like something Mom would own or keep than the dresses. It's artsy, kind of bohemian maybe, like it came from someplace far away."

I handed Ollie the woven blanket, and she lifted it into the air by two corners, and sunlight from the windows set it aglow. A light dawned in her eyes, followed by a wisp of a smile.

"Wait, do you recognize it?" I asked.

"I don't—" Ollie, who never faltered, faltered. She shook her head, then went on in a hushed voice. "I don't remember ever seeing it before. But for a second there, I felt—"

She faltered again. My stoic and practical sister, feeling and faltering. I waited, looking at Ollie looking at the blanket.

"You felt . . . ?" I said, softly.

I should not have pushed—I knew I should not even as I did it—but, from time to time in a person's life, sentences come along that should not be left unfinished. I believed that, for Ollie, this was one of them. But I braced myself for her to harden, to get mocking and derisive. Instead, she lowered the blanket, gathered it in her hands, and bent her head, as if she wanted to smell it or press it against her cheek. She did neither, but she lifted her face to look at me, and she finished the sentence.

"Love."

AFTER OLLIE HAD GONE—HAD BROKEN the moment with a shrug, as if she were shrugging off love, both the word and the emotion, had tossed the blanket in my direction, and then almost run down the attic stairs—I put the blanket and the dresses back inside the shoebox, inside their tissue paper nest, and, remembering why I'd come to the attic in the first place, I opened the cedar chest, where I thought the Pendleton blankets would be. I'd never actually retrieved them from the attic myself—my mother always had—but every winter, they'd borne the fragrance of cedar in their folds well into February. The blankets were there, a neat stack. I remembered an image from last Christmas: Rose; Simon; Toby's son, Jasper; and my dad cocooned in them as they sat around the backyard firepit, mugs of hot chocolate cradled in their hands. I lifted the heavy blankets out of the chest. In the bottom of the chest was a book I could not remember ever having seen before: *Birds of the Great Lakes*.

I sat down on the stack of blankets with the book on my lap and flipped through it. It was what you'd expect: an illustrated guide to birds of the Great Lakes. Kestrels and coots, grebes and goshawks, plovers and peregrines. On impulse, I held it by its spine and shook it. Nothing fell out. Then I opened the book to see the inside cover, and there was an inscription: Palmer Method handwriting, fluid and precise, faded black ink.

For Our Darling Eleanor,
because books can transport you to
faraway places, even as you stay right
here with us.
Merry Christmas and Much Love,
Alice and Joel Pulliam
Cadwallader College
December 1964

Chapter 10

ELEANOR

March 1965

February 15, 1965

Dear Elsbee,

We all have an inner landscape, a fact I did not know until I got to an outer one so far up the map it was almost Canada. The lake, its stony shore, the Sawtooth Mountains bristling with pines, sky so black, stars so thick, cold snatching your breath the second you step outside, snow and snow and snow. Oh, and the Aurora, Elsbee, sometimes, the Lights are so faint you think you're imagining them; other times, they are oceans and angels and fire. And the craziest thing is I recognized the place the instant I got there because it turns out I'd been carrying it around just under my breastbone, maybe since the second I drew my first breath.

But looking back at the first sentence of this letter, I see it's wrong. I did not know, not completely, that I had an inner landscape until I left the outer one that matched it.

Leaving was hard. I started grieving the North Shore before I'd even packed my bags. The Olsons did not want me to go; I grieved them, too. Jack said they just wanted me to stay on because I am such a good employee, but I believe they were sadder about what I would miss than about what they would. I think they love me. Who but you has ever loved me?

The Olsons didn't trust Jack. I can see why. He has broken the law: he has been to jail. Not for anything very terrible, so don't you worry. He just lives by his own laws. He has trouble holding down jobs because he loathes people telling him what to do. He has a temper. Elaine asked me once if I trusted him. I said yes, but really, I don't know if I do or don't. Trust is moot. Kindness is moot. I don't even know if he is a good man. I just belong to him, plain and simple, soul and body. I could not bear to lose him. And somehow, somehow, he wants me with him, a fact so improbable, so miraculous, I can't even look at it head-on because I'm terrified it will vanish if I do.

We live in Arkansas, in the east-west running Ouachita Mountains, on what used to be a farm. That is, I guess it used to be a farm. After all, it's called Bright Wind Farm. I can hear your voice wisely pointing out the silliness of the name, since wind, being invisible, cannot be bright, and then can hear my own voice protesting that, on the North Shore of Lake Superior, the wind was indeed bright—bright and silvery, it was, it was. But the wind isn't bright and silvery in Arkansas.

Bill and Louise Haven claim Bright Wind Farm was once a working farm, and I suppose they would know, since they are the ones who bought it two years ago. Bought it for a song, according to Jack, although I hope it wasn't a really good song because this can't ever have been—and I don't know much about farms but I do feel this to be true—a really good farm. It clings to the base of a mountain like a woodpecker to a tree trunk, and possibly someone years ago scratched some rows of corn or cotton out of its dry, shallow soil, but now it's less a farm than a field with some ramshackle structures poking up out of it. There is a farmhouse, once white, possibly once pretty, with steeply pointed gables and a wraparound porch. The Havens live in the house, the only building with electricity, but all here are quick to point out that it is really a "shared space." All the Bright Wind community members eat their evening meal together in the farmhouse. All the women take turns cooking. There is a communal refrigerator in the basement that we all have access to; it is full of communal food.

There are ten other buildings on the property, eleven if you count the barn, which is rotting to earth where it stands and isn't safe to enter. We call the other buildings "cottages." When we first got to Bright Wind, Jack speculated that the cottages once housed field-workers, but Louise gently corrected him, saying that they believed the farm was once a family compound. She said that families hadn't always lived as they do now in this country, each in its little box, cut off and isolated. She told us to imagine how much better it must have been when generations of family lived together, working the land, benefiting from one another's experience, wisdom, and skills. Later, in bed, I thought about this and thought Louise was right. The family you and I grew up in was too small, too isolated. We could've used more people watching over us, don't you think?

All of the cottages are really just one room with a bathroom. All have running water, thank goodness. Jack and I are lucky. He has known the Havens for years. I'm not sure how. He spent time in Ontario, where they're from, and, for a long time, they've been after him to help them create their utopia, to bring their vision to life, as Bill puts it. So Jack became their right-hand man immediately, and we were given the largest cottage, which has one very small extra room that could be used as a second bedroom, but which we use for storage. All the cottages have woodstoves for heat and most have propane-fueled stoves for cooking. But we use candles and lanterns for light, if you can imagine it. I thought I'd hate it, but honestly, it's quite lovely to see, the warm glow in the windows of the cottages at night. Reading by such light would be hard on the eyes, but I don't have many books here. There wasn't room in the car. I've stored most of my belongings and my finished paintings with the Olsons. They were quick to offer. I think they're hoping I'll come back.

We are a group of artists. That was part of the Havens' vision. The rest of the vision is hazier to me, although it's becoming clearer. They believe the outside world is corrupt and corrupting, and they aren't just talking about the war. They distrust the government, the medical establishment, the press, what they call the American miseducation system, consumerism. They want to live simply and in tune with the land, to which end they quote Thoreau and Emerson quite effectively. They aim to abolish hierarchies of every kind, to upend the traditional roles of men and women. In short, they are—we are, I suppose—turning their backs on the outside world in order to quietly create and thrive in peace and harmony.

That's the idea, anyway, according to the Havens. And the Havens are very good at talking about their ideas.

Jack believes. He's always believed, even before he met the Havens. When I point out what strike me as glaring inconsistencies, when I tell him I understand the what of their vision but not the why and even less the how, he gets angry and tells me to have a little faith. So I am trying. Because anyway, I'm with him. Any other whats, whys, and hows hardly matter.

As you can tell, I am breaking the rules already, writing to you, since no one seems to quite understand that you could never be part of the "outside world." You are forever inside whatever world I inhabit. So I write in secret. Jack has the only car here, apart from the Havens' truck, which I've never seen anyone use. Because the farming part of the farm hasn't quite gotten up and running. Jack makes weekly trips to town for provisions. On his next trip, I'll go, too, and I'll find a way to get to a post office to mail this. I have kept back a little cash for my own use and will rent a P.O. box so you can write back. But please don't worry if you don't hear from me often. I am painting and I am with Jack. And this landscape does not live inside my chest. but it's very pretty. There is a woman here named Peg. a weaver who used to be a nurse. She likes to ramble in the hills as much as I do. so it's possible I will even have a friend here soon. I am happy and well and grateful and I miss you like mad. my Elsbee.

Love.
Marthy

March 11, 1965
Dear Elsbee.
All is well with me. I loved your letter. ate up every crumb of it like cake! I could hear you trying not to worry and I do appreciate it. Know that I am listening to my heart and living out my adventure—wherever it takes me.

I persuaded Jack to speak to the Havens. and they have given permission for me to pass along the address of the farmhouse. should you need to reach me in an emergency. Please don't write letters to me at this address. only to the P.O. box. and do not share it with anyone else. Promise? I explained to Jack that you were my only family. He says he doesn't have any family. doesn't believe in family. but I know this is just his bitterness talking. the result of people letting him down over and over. since he was a child. I believe that deep down. he believes in family as much as anyone. I really and truly do.

Love.
Marthy

At the bottom of the letter Martha had jotted down an address.

Two letters in two months. That was all, and it wasn't even so much less frequent than usual. But in spite of the brave face she'd tried to show Martha in her letter, Eleanor was worried. She knew Martha well enough to read what her words did not say: both the ironies she intended (Eleanor could just see the flash of wry knowingness in Martha's eyes when she read "All the women take turns cooking" and "They aim to abolish hierarchies of every kind, to upend the traditional roles of men and women") and the dissonances and doubts she would not even admit to herself. Eleanor was bothered less by Jack's stint (stints?) in jail than "He gets angry" and (words to break Eleanor's heart over and over) "Who but you has ever loved me?"

And "So I write in secret" and "I'll find a way to get to a post office." These phrases made Eleanor's blood run cold. Had her sister been kidnapped? She knew she hadn't been. Martha had gone willingly. But in dark moments, Eleanor wondered if love itself could be a kind of kidnapping.

"You're strong and brave and brilliant," Eleanor whispered to Martha, across the miles and silences. "You're better than he is, better than anyone. Never forget."

LATE MARCH, BABY-BLUE SKY, SPRING breathing lemon and chartreuse over branch tips and garden beds all across Eleanor's campus. She was in short sleeves playing catch on the green with Marge, feeling nimble, sunlit, and eleven years old. While they were dating, Ronnie had given her the baseball glove, claimed to have searched the world over to find one small enough for her hand.

The night Eleanor had returned from the last (the very last) visit to her mother, she'd gone to see Ronnie, handed him his car keys, a story about a branch falling onto his car, and an IOU for the repairs. He had barely spoken, just torn the IOU in half, handed her the pieces, chucked her under the chin with one finger, and jogged away. A few days later, Eleanor had found a package in her room containing a baseball and a note from Ronnie: *You were quite a catch (haha). Wish I'd gotten to keep you, but no hard feelings. You've got a good arm for such a little person and your aim is always true. Have fun, El. Love, R*

The few times they'd run into each other on campus, Ronnie took the same gallant, lightly affectionate tone with her, talking to her, she thought, almost as if she were a kid sister. She marveled at his tact and good sportsmanship and wondered if her failure to be in love with him could be a symptom of something broken or missing inside of her. Martha believed the scars their mother had left made her unfit to be a mother herself. Maybe her own set of scars had left Eleanor unfit to be in love.

But Ronnie was right about her arm and her aim, and here she was, twenty years old, throwing a ball with her friend under the sky, freckles coming out like stars across her nose, her hair a mess, leaves and flowers snapping open around her.

She caught a zinger—leathery smack, palm stinging—and a high voice fluttered across the green behind her, "Eleanor! Eleanor, honey!"

She turned around. Patsy Fisher, the same college receptionist who'd given Eleanor Caroline Cullen's message, the one that had led to her final trip home, was trying to rush, but her narrow skirt and heeled pumps slowed her down, so Eleanor cantered over to her, the breeze catching her hair.

"There's a phone call for you," said Patsy.

"Again?"

She hadn't meant to say the word aloud, hadn't intended her voice to sound so fearful, but Patsy politely ignored what she'd said.

"A man this time," said Patsy.

"What man?" said Eleanor, confused.

"I didn't get his name. I'm sorry. I answered the phone and ran out to get you. I'd seen you playing catch through the window in my office, you see. He said it was a family matter and quite important."

Eleanor felt a flash of fear. *Jack*, she thought, *calling to say something bad has happened to Martha.* If he'd hurt her, if he'd laid one hand on her, Eleanor knew she would kill him. Her legs felt suddenly unsteady. She shut her eyes and felt Patsy Fisher take her hand.

"It'll be all right, dear," she said firmly. "His voice was very nice, very kind and steady. But let's go in. He's waiting on the line."

Patsy was right about the man's voice. As soon as Eleanor heard it, heard him say, "Hi, Miss Campbell, I'm Robert Brown," her heart rate slowed and the ground under her feet ceased its wobbling. This made no sense, because while he wasn't Jack, he could have been anyone, bearing any sort of news, but the voice steadied her nonetheless.

"Hello, Robert Brown," she said. "And I'm not Miss Campbell. I'm Eleanor," which later struck her as an odd thing to have said but which seemed completely natural at the time.

Her mother was dead.

Sylvia Whitney, the minister's wife, had called Robert Brown the evening before to say Susan had missed work again and was not answering her phone or her door, which caused Sylvia to realize she'd not seen Susan for a few days, not even coming and going from her house, although her car was safely in the garage (Sylvia had peered through the garage window to check). Sylvia feared Susan had fallen ill again, even though she'd seemed much better lately, and she'd asked Robert to go over with her to check.

"She called because I'm your mother's doctor, the one who stitched her hand."

Until he explained this, Eleanor realized she should have been confused about his identity, but she hadn't even thought to question how he, a stranger, came to be the person calling to convey such news. She'd simply listened, let the cadence and tone—familiar though she'd never heard the voice before—carry her mother's death across the miles and into the room where she sat, the baseball glove still on her hand, the glove still cradling the ball.

"Oh! She liked you," said Eleanor, remembering. "She doesn't like most people, but she liked you. Or maybe it's more that she trusted you, which is even rarer than liking for her."

"I'm glad to know that," said Robert Brown.

"How?" asked Eleanor. "How did she die?"

He didn't hesitate or ask if she was sure she wanted to know, as many men would have. He just told her.

"I found her in her bed, dressed in pajamas. When I examined her, I found bruising. I haven't been a doctor for very long, but I'd seen those bruising patterns before. I went to the garage to check, and your mother's car has pretty extensive damage to the front and to the windshield. I don't know for sure, and the police will examine the car, but my best guess is that your mother had a car accident, hit her head, drove home, went to bed, and then died sometime afterward, in her sleep, of a cerebral hemorrhage. It happens sometimes: a person can be badly damaged without realizing it. So they go home instead of to the hospital, and the injury to their brain bleeds slowly without their knowing it. They fall asleep and don't wake up."

Later, Eleanor would reflect how "a person can be badly damaged without realizing it" might be an apt description of her mother's entire life, not just of her death, but right then, she wasn't feeling reflective. She voiced the first thought that came to her.

"I'll bet she was drunk," said Eleanor. "I don't know, of course, but she probably was."

If Robert Brown was taken aback by this, he didn't show it.

"It seems possible," said Robert Brown. "There was a bottle of whiskey on the kitchen table and a glass. I wonder, though, how she could have had an accident without anyone noticing. This is a town where people notice things."

"Sometimes, my mother drinks in the middle of the night and gets the urge to drive. Sometimes, she stays out for hours. I don't know where she'd go, but she always came back afterward, before sunrise."

"I see," said Robert Brown.

"Dr. Brown?"

"Robert, please. Actually, people call me B."

"Bumble or honey?"

"The letter. Short for Bobby. Or maybe for Brown. Depending on who's saying it."

Eleanor smiled. "Because Bobby and Brown are very long names."

"Yes, exactly."

"B, I'm glad it was you who told me about my mother. Thank you."

For the first time, he hesitated, and when he spoke he sounded very young.

"Sylvia Whitney wanted to call, but—and I don't really know her—but I thought that if I had to hear this kind of news, she might not be exactly the person I'd want to hear it from."

"She's a busybody," said Eleanor. "She and the church secretary are the biggest gossips in town."

"I haven't been in town for long, but I already know enough to know that's saying something. So I told her I'd tell you myself. And also . . ."

"What?"

"She didn't see your mother. She seemed eager to get into the house, but I asked her to unlock the door for me and then to go back to the manse. I didn't know what I'd find in the house, but I thought it would be better to find it alone."

"Thank you. I can only imagine the conversations she would have had all over town if she'd actually set eyes on my mother."

"Don't, if you can help it. Don't imagine them."

"Yes, you're right. I won't. You are wise, Dr. B."

He laughed.

"Oh, gosh," said Eleanor, "I need to send word to my sister, Martha. She's—working away. And then, I'll come home. I suppose I must, right?"

"I think so, yes. Mrs. Whitney said she could come get you. She asked me to tell you."

"Well, a nice offer, but . . ."

"No, it didn't sound like the greatest idea to me, either. Is there a train you could take?" he asked.

"A train, then a bus. It takes quite a while, but I'll get there."

"Could a friend drive you?"

She thought of Alice and Joel, and then said, slowly, "I have friends who would drive me, but I don't bring people home. It's not as if I'm ashamed, exactly. I just, well, I like my life here to have nothing to do with the place I lived before I got here. I don't want the two places bumping up against each other."

"I understand," said B, and even though she didn't see how he could, she believed he did.

"So I'll take the train and the bus. Should I call you when I get there?"

"What if I come get you?" said B. "I have off tomorrow and I wouldn't mind getting out of town for the day."

Eleanor felt herself smiling, struck by his kindness. Maybe it should have at least occurred to her to say no, since she knew every busybody in her hometown would scathingly disapprove of her riding into town with a man she'd never met. The baseball slid out of her glove and landed on the floor with a thunk. She slipped off the glove and tapped her fingers against her smile.

"That would be nice," she said. "There will be gossip. But if you don't mind, I don't."

"I'll leave first thing in the morning," he said.

It was only after she'd hung up that she wondered at herself for not having expressed the smallest amount of sadness at the news of Susan's death. She didn't feel sadness, of course, did not, right then, feel much of anything, not gladness or rue or relief. Just—nothing. But Eleanor knew how to act; she understood appropriate behavior; she was accustomed—abundantly accustomed—to lying. But, during her entire conversation with Dr. B. Brown, pretending to be stunned or sad had never even occurred to her. She saw now, as she stared down at the phone, the receiver back in its cradle, how at the very least an "Oh, no" had been in order, and she knew just the shocked and hollow tone she should have delivered it in, but she found she wasn't sorry she hadn't. She was merely surprised. She knew there were people in this world to whom she felt called upon to tell only the truth. For so long, it had just been Martha, and then she'd met Alice and Joel. To lie to any of those three would be sacrilege, a low-down dirty desecration of love and friendship, but Eleanor had believed they would forever be the only ones.

Standing in Patsy Fisher's office, Eleanor wondered if she might have been wrong. She remembered how the young doctor had not seemed to expect her to be sad or fragile or anything at all but what she was. She leaned over, picked up her ball and glove, and walked back to her room to pack.

"DO YOU WANT TO TALK about your mother?"

B asked Eleanor this question as if he were asking her if she would like a cup of coffee, not encouraging or even suggesting, but just asking her what she would prefer to do.

"No, I don't think so," she said.

She glanced over at him, at his hands on the steering wheel. After the burst of spring the day before, the cold had come back, and B wore a gray sweater, slices of white shirt cuff peeking out just above his hands. They'd stopped at the post office on the way out of town so Eleanor could send a letter to Martha, telling her their mother was dead, asking her to come home.

"Do you think she'll come?" B had asked.

"I think so, if she gets my letter in time," said Eleanor. "I know she will if she possibly can."

Eleanor thought B's hands were not the hands of a boy, but he was young, nonetheless. His dark hair was freshly cut and a little too short. She watched him lift a hand from the wheel and run it quickly through the front of his hair, as if he were used to it being longer and falling onto his forehead. In that moment he was very young, younger than she was. His face was tan with dark pink on the peaks of his cheekbones, and she imagined he was a person who liked to be outside, as she did, even in the winter. There was a pale strip of skin next to his ear where the barber had shaved his hair, and it filled Eleanor with tenderness.

"No, I guess I don't feel like talking about her," Eleanor repeated. "But thank you for asking."

Then she said, "Martha remembers her holding me in her arms and dancing around the living room. And I know she saw it happen; she'd never make up a thing like that. But I can't imagine it. I can't imagine the mother I knew ever doing such a thing. The last time I was home, she told me to never come back. She said if I came back, she would shoot me and set the house on fire. I just can't make it make sense."

She talked on as B drove and as the gray sky turned pearl and then blue and bluer still, until all the clouds were gone.

HE WAS THERE WHEN SHE entered the house she'd sworn never to enter again and there when she identified her mother's body, bruised and waxen, when she looked at it and nodded and did not cry, felt as far away from crying as it was possible to be. He took her mother's car, her car now, to be repaired. He was not there when she stayed up late into the night to clean the house, empty the refrigerator, and launder all the sheets and towels, even the ones in the linen closet, but he came the next day with two bags of groceries and a loaf of bread he'd made himself. He was there when she met with the funeral home director, but was not there when she went to the church to discuss the service, not there to hear her leave all the details to the Reverend Whitney, every detail but this: he was not to use the phrase "beloved mother of," not once. It was wrong to lie about love. She would have liked to ask him not to speak her or Martha's name at all, but she thought this an unnecessarily dramatic request. They had been her daughters, after all.

Martha must have gotten her letter quickly because she sent a telegram. When Martha's telegram arrived, Eleanor was working in the garden, which Susan seemed not to have touched in years, and B, who'd just finished at the hospital, was in the kitchen making sandwiches. She heard his voice calling her name—calling it for the first time ever—and was so occupied with carefully stowing away the sound—his voice, her name—inside her head for safekeeping that she almost missed watching him walk across the grass toward her. He was tall and lean; his steps were long. She set down her trowel, placed her gloved hands on her knees, and wished the yard were bigger so she could keep watching him, on and on, all day long. When he got to her, he crouched down until he was eye level with her, and he handed her the envelope.

"Oh!" She breathed and opened it.

She knew this was the moment she would tell their children about. Not the funeral, all those chilly stares at the bad daughter, the snide words about the absent one, the shock at seeing Dr. Brown by her side. She knew what they were whispering, were twittering about over their coffee cups all over town, knew as surely as if she'd been on their porches and at their kitchen tables: *He's in and out of her house at all hours. She doesn't even have the grace to tell him to park around the corner! Opens the door to him in broad daylight, and I can't swear the car didn't stay in her driveway all night. And her poor mother's body not even cold!*

When she told the story, she would give the funeral barely a passing sentence. The visit to the lawyer's office, too. Those moments did not matter.

When she told the story, *her* story, she would focus on this: the smell of cold loam and rotting leaves, Eleanor's head bent over the telegram; Eleanor dropping her face into her soil-damp gloves and wailing, wailing, wailing; B, in an instant, sitting on the ground in his nice work clothes, wrapping her in his arms, rocking her like a child, until the sobs had torn their ransacking way through her and out of her, and then, still holding on, B getting her to her feet and, without a word, walking her into the house, not to give her tea or wrap her in blankets as most people would have, stopping only long enough to find her knit hat and to wind a scarf around her neck. He knew (how could he know?) she needed to be outside.

They walked to the beach and then along the shore, which was, as always, another world, wind-whipped white foam gliding at the waves' edge like ice floes in the Arctic. They drifted, too, the two of them, together and apart, together and apart. She held his hand, let go, held it again as the spray and tangy air washed her face and the sound of the waves shouted down her grief, grief not for Susan but for Martha, who could not get away—the typed phrase in the telegram "I can't get away" would frighten Eleanor for months—Martha, who would never have left Eleanor alone with Susan's death if she could have helped it.

Who would have the temerity, in the chilly, looming, swirling presence of death and grief, to fall in love?

"I would," she would tell her children. Their children.

They walked for hours, mostly in silence. They walked farther than she'd ever walked, which was a very long way.

"I could walk forever with you," she told B, "and never get lost."

He looked first at the horizon, then at the crushed shells, white as chalk, under their feet, and finally at her face.

"Then, that's what you should do," he said.

Chapter 11

CORNELIA

ON OUR WAY TO ALICE and Joel Pulliam's house in North Carolina, we stopped at the rehabilitation center and found our mother sitting on a bench in the garden.

"Right where you belong," I told her, kissing her cheek.

Despite the walker standing next to the bench, my mother looked staunch and self-contained inside her wool coat. And content. I wondered if this might be an incidental gift of the awful thing that had befallen her: my perpetual-motion mother learning how to rest in place, however briefly.

"Yes," she said, "although if I had my way, I'd be on my knees with my hands in the dirt. Not that there's much to do this time of year. I'd just like to breathe it in, the smell of troweled-up earth. But this. This is okay, too."

She spotted Ollie behind me and leaned sideways to wave at her. Ollie was hanging back like a shy little kid, even though I'd never known her to be shy. Aloof, distant, but not exactly shy, not shy like her son was. At his request, we'd left Clive in the car with Harry Potter. He'd said he just wanted to finish the chapter, but I could tell he was afraid to see his grandmother. He'd asked me a few times if she still looked like herself, and I'd known what he meant: not bruised or broken. I remembered being a kid who'd found vulnerability in adults I loved barely bearable, especially adults like my mother, who'd always seemed sturdy as an oak.

Ollie walked over to our mother and, after a few seconds' hesitation, leaned in and kissed her, not an air-kiss but an actual kiss on her actual cheek. My mother looked pleased and also surprised. Ollie was not—shockingly—a person prone to greeting with kisses. Or hugs. Or smiles. Or any display of interest, really, let alone affection. She wasn't much of a greeting person, period.

"These social transitions," she'd said to me once, in exasperation, "the hellos, the goodbyes, the hugs, everyone saying how good everyone looks, how nice it's been to see them. It all strikes me as a colossal waste of time."

Now, in the aftermath of the kiss, I felt the way I did when my children said "please" or "thank you" to strangers. Is it ridiculous to feel proud of an adult woman for greeting with a peck on the cheek another adult woman whom she hasn't seen in several years, who has recently suffered grievous bodily harm from which she is still recovering, and who is, on top of everything, her mother? Yes. But I felt proud anyway. It was all I could do not to whisper, "Good job, honey!" and take her out for ice cream.

I heard running footsteps on the sidewalk behind me. Clive. He stopped short next to his mother. He still held the hardcover book—at least four inches thick—in his hands. My mother eyed it.

"*The Order of the Phoenix*," said my mother. "It's a hefty one."

"It's the longest," said Clive.

"When it comes to page count, yes, I know you're right," she said. "But *The Deathly Hallows* sure seemed longer to me. Because I was so worried while I was reading it."

Clive walked a couple of steps closer.

"Worried that something bad would happen to Harry, Hermione, or Ron," he said. "Me, too."

He ducked his head and smiled, but then seemed to notice the walker for the first time, and stopped smiling. He reached out one hand, as if to touch it, but then wrapped the hand around the fat spine of the book again.

"It's purely precautionary," said my mother. "I can run circles around most of the physical therapists here, but I said to myself this morning, 'Ellie, you are all set to head home in a few days. But if you stumble and fall, they might try to make you stay longer.' It wouldn't work, of course. I'm going home come heck or high water, but I'd hate to have to stage a rebellion over it. Especially since everyone here is so nice. So I decided to give the old walker a spin."

"Makes sense," said Clive and sat down on the bench next to his grandmother.

"You're staying for Christmas, of course," said my mother to Ollie.

"Definitely," said Ollie, although when I'd asked her the same question just the night before, she'd shrugged and said she wasn't sure she was up for the three-ring circus of a Brown family Christmas.

Now, she added, "We wouldn't miss it."

I'll buy you an ice cream and *throw in a bag of Sour Patch Kids,* I thought. *Two bags.*

"Edmund, too," said my mother. "We must have Edmund."

At the mention of her husband, Ollie tensed and bugged her eyes at me, as if demanding I throw her a life preserver, but since I had no idea what she was drowning in, I didn't know which life preserver to use.

"Oh," she said, finally. "You don't want all the hubbub of a giant family Christmas."

"But that is exactly what I want," said my mother. "The gianter, the better."

And as if she'd pronounced the final word on the matter, she clapped her hands together and said, "Now, Clive, I hear Aunt Cornelia and your mom have some errands to run, so you're going to hang out with me for a bit, and Granddad's coming, too. He should be here any minute. Is that plan still okay with you?"

Clive didn't hesitate.

"Definitely," he said. "I wouldn't miss it."

OLLIE AND I WERE DRIVING to Cadwallader, North Carolina, to visit Alice and Joel Pulliam.

After I'd found *Birds of the Great Lakes* and read its inscription, I'd googled them. Joel was Professor Emeritus at Cadwallader College, and there was an email address for him on the college website. It took exactly two hours for them to write me back, both of them, first Joel, then Alice. Alice wrote that she'd taken the liberty of asking Joel for my email address and hoped I didn't mind. I didn't. Yes, they remembered Eleanor Campbell. Remembered and adored and still thought about her more often than I could imagine. Yes, they wanted to meet me. Anytime, as soon as I could get there. Yes, yes, yes, yes.

IN THE CAR, BEFORE WE'D gone a mile, her eyes riveted on the road, her hands gripping the wheel, Ollie said, "Go ahead and ask. I know you're dying to."

But before I could say a word, she said, "We're separated."

She sounded so sad it must have startled her because she added, briskly, more to soothe herself than me, "Not officially. If there is such a thing as an official separation. It's not a stepping stone to— not being married."

You can't stand to say the word divorce, I thought, and Ollie, who never sighed, sighed.

"At least, I hope not. We both hope not. He's got this rent-by-the-month apartment. We told Clive it's because his work is intense right now, which is true, and the apartment is closer to the lab. I don't know if he believes us. He's a kid who pays attention, so if he believes us, it's probably just because he wants to. But it's better than his paying attention to our fighting. And it wasn't even fighting. It was me being angry, punishing Edmund, and Edmund being confused and going silent the way he does."

"Punishing him for what?"

She shrugged and shook her head. "It's hard to explain."

"It's a long drive."

"You won't understand because it has to do with my job, my career."

I wanted to shriek that I had a job, too. I had created my own business! I was a bona fide entrepreneur, for Pete's sake. But while I knew I was a person who had a job, I also knew I wasn't a person who *was* my job, which is the person Ollie had been, so I decided self-righteous shrieking might be disingenuous. Plus, I wanted her to keep talking.

I said, "Hey, you never know. Try me."

"Fine," she said, as if she were doing me a favor.

"I don't mean the job I have now, the editing. I mean doing science the way I did for years. In the field, in the lab. I loved it. I loved the parts other people hate or find boring. I even loved being wrong and having to start over. Edmund and I loved it together. We worked together, for years, and even when we had separate projects, we talked about our work. We hashed out problems together. And not to get all sentimental—"

She broke off. Although I had been waiting for decades for my sister to get even a little sentimental and wanted to tell her to finish the damn sentence, for crying out loud, I kept mum. Some people find words of encouragement from me encouraging, but Ollie Brown-Battle was emphatically not one of those people.

"But, well, the sight of him listening to me talk about my work, really listening, with his eyes shut, perfectly still, and then nodding and drumming his fingers on the table faster and faster, as he got—truly got—what I was saying. Well, I've never felt so—"

Because I knew she'd never cough up the word herself, I supplied it: "Loved."

"Yes, fine, whatever."

"And then Clive was born."

"Right."

"Couldn't you have finagled some other way? Hired a nanny? Taken turns being at home with him? Or, I don't know, divided the work up more evenly? Would Edmund have done that?"

"Edmund would have done anything I wanted. He still would. When we first got together, we'd compete with each other, professionally. I won't lie; it could get pretty out of hand, even ugly. There were times we didn't speak for days. We'd get so caught up we'd sort of forget who the other person was. But after a while, we stopped forgetting and then we took it further. We started putting each other first."

"Wait. You did? I mean, *you* did?" I blurted it out, and then quickly followed up with, "Of course you did."

Ollie smiled a half-smile.

"Sorry," I said.

"No, I agree," she said. "Who knew I was capable of that kind of crap?"

"So I don't understand. Why haven't you switched things up? Why haven't you gone back to doing science?"

Ollie tapped her pointer finger against the steering wheel. She glanced out the rearview mirror, annoyed, brows knit, as if the answer to my question were a giant tailgating eighteen-wheeler bearing down on us, horn blaring.

Then, my sister Ollie said this: "I wanted to be like you."

I was stunned into temporary speechlessness, which, as you can probably guess, almost never happens. Her words were so out of the blue, so utterly unprecedented, I couldn't decide whether to stick my head out of the sunroof and scream "Hallelujah!" or dive into the backseat, curl into a ball, and cry.

"You know what I said a few minutes ago about you not having a career?" said Ollie.

I nodded.

"I know you have a job."

"Thank you," I said. "Wait. Why am I saying thank you because you know I have a job?"

"You started your own business. You're a businesswoman."

"Some might say 'female entrepreneur.' I don't mind that."

"Okay, I know. But I think I forget because—well, Mom once said people are your true vocation. And it's true. Relationships, of course, but not just relationships. Everything. Conversations, inter-actions, emotions, what they love and hate, their opinions, all the—whatever—*people* stuff. People are your calling, your real job."

"I can well imagine what you think of a woman with a job like that."

Ollie seemed to consider this. I don't know why in the world I'd said it. Who cares what she thought?

Oh, Cornelia, honey, when did you ever not care?

"All I know," said Ollie, "is if I had the same job as you, the people job, I'd have been fired years ago."

Again: speechless.

"Decades ago. In elementary school, probably. I can't be passion-ate about *people*. Just don't have it in me. But after I met Edmund, I realized I could be passionate about one person. And then Clive arrived and I thought: okay, two. I wanted being his mother to be enough. I planned to be better at it than I ever was at anything. I'm not a natural, like you. You just know how to love people and how to take care of them. But I'm smart; I'm good at learning; and I adore Clive, so I thought I could swing it. And I might even be doing an okay job at motherhood, but, God—"

She banged the heel of her hand on the steering wheel.

"I miss work. It's eating me up, and Edmund, he just waltzes off to do science every damned day, which makes me forget how to be nice to him."

Talking so much seemed to leave Ollie winded, so for a few minutes, she just drove and I just rode. I remembered when we were in high school and she, resentfully, had to drive me somewhere. I'd chatter on and on, telling funny stories, talking about songs on the radio, until I hit the point where I felt too much like a performing seal, an extremely desperate one, and then, we'd just ride along in silence.

"You don't want to be like me," I said.

"What do you mean?"

"I mean even as we sit in this car together, I am failing my family. Like, abysmally. Again. Or not again because it's all part of the same failure."

"I have no idea what you're talking about."

I couldn't believe this, since anyone who knew anything at all about the past few months of my life would have to know what I meant, but Ollie sounded sincere.

"Mom told you what happened to Simon."

"Yeah, and?"

"Oh, come on," I said. "*And* I didn't keep my kids safe. *And* I can't go back and fix it, ever. *And* I abandoned them right afterward. *And* I don't deserve them and never have. I only thought I did, but I didn't, as evidenced by my spectacular failure at keeping them safe."

Ollie's mouth tightened to a thin line. She looked angry. I'd failed my children, was still failing them, and Ollie was the one who was mad? What the hell.

She said, "Yeah, maybe it's all you, Cornelia. Or maybe you and your kids just got held up at gunpoint by some fucking maniac and you need a little break from being mother of the century, which I have to think is no picnic even on a boring day."

Speechless, again.

"Although leave it to you to take a break involving you taking care of yet more people," she said. "Typical you."

When I remembered how to speak, I didn't comment on what Ollie had said about me. I had no idea what to say. Instead, I said, "You should talk to Edmund. Tell him what you told me about your situation. Say it in those exact words. And then figure out with him what to do next."

"Bloody conversation. Your remedy for everything. Some people just aren't talkers, Cornelia. I'm not a talker."

"Hmm, I can tell," I said, primly.

"Don't get all smug. This is a one-off."

"Sure it is."

"Seriously, I think it's being back home. It throws me off. It always has."

"Why did you come? I'm glad you're here, but I just wondered. You may as well tell me now, while you're talking your ever-loving head off."

No steering wheel fidgeting, no glaring into the rearview mirror. She just blurted it out.

"I wanted to find out if I was adopted."

This was not what I expected her to say.

"This is not what I expected you to say," I said.

"So when you said you thought Mom was spilling secrets from the past when she was having hospital delirium, I thought I'd come see if she'd spill that one."

"Why do you suddenly think you were adopted?"

"I don't think I was adopted. I think I might have been. Or maybe it's more like I have this *feeling* that I might have been. And it's not sudden. Remember my friend Nancy, from high school? When we were in ninth grade, her parents told her she was adopted."

"You never told me that," I said.

"I never told you anything," she reminded me.

"True."

"She said as soon as they told her, everything made sense; all these thoughts and feelings and ideas she'd been having for so long . . . it all just fell into place. And when she told me about it, I realized I might have been adopted, too."

"Why?"

"Well, for one, there are no baby pictures of me and almost no toddler pictures, no young toddler pictures, anyway, while there are loads of Cam and Toby. Isn't it usually the opposite? Parents have less time with each kid; they lose interest. But I was the first. So if I was adopted, it was when I was about four. Because there are some pictures of me from when I was four."

"I think we have baby pictures of you," I said.

"There are pictures of a baby they say is me, but it could be anyone. Almost all babies look alike."

"'They say' is you? You mean our parents? B and Ellie, disseminators of fake baby pictures?"

"What about the blanket in the attic? Ellie Brown would not be caught dead with such a wacky, obviously handmade blanket. And she hid it up there in a random box."

"So?"

"So maybe I came with it. A package deal: baby Ollie and her hippie-dippie blanket."

"You've suspected you were adopted since you were fourteen? For over thirty years?"

"Look, it's not like I've been obsessed with it constantly. Back then, I asked Dad once and he denied it. Offered to show me my birth certificate."

"But you figured they could just have forged it," I said, "B and Ellie."

"I told him I didn't want to see it. Okay, so maybe even back then I didn't quite believe I was adopted, but I wanted to. I liked the idea of not really belonging to our family because I never really fit into it. So maybe I didn't demand to see the birth certificate in case it really existed."

"You fit," I said, "I'm the one who didn't fit."

Ollie ignored this.

"Not to be dismissive," I said, "but you know how completely nonsensical and crazy this sounds, right?"

Ollie almost smiled and said, "Thanks for not being dismissive."

"Ollie, you weren't adopted."

"Okay, probably not. But, you're right, it's been more than thirty years. I've spent more than three decades with this little, half-formed, niggling idea in the back of my mind, and I'm not a person who has a lot of little niggling ideas. In fact, this might be the only one. So that fact alone makes me think it's at least worth checking into. Don't you think?"

As a person whose mind is full of numberless long-standing niggling ideas, I had to take a few seconds to consider this. I imagined the interior of Ollie's head, clean and orderly, well lit and full of shiny filing cabinets.

"You have a point," I said.

"Right? And then, after Clive was born, when he was about three, I was watching him playing with an older boy in the park, and I remembered."

"Remembered what?"

"My birth family. My possible birth family. Or at least a sister. An older sister, I think. It wasn't quite a memory, not a picture. Nothing sensory. But I see sisters together and remember being the littler one. I remember the presence of a slightly older girl."

"You could do one of those birth family searches," I said. "I don't for a second think you're right about this, but if you really want to know, do one of those online data base thingamajigs. Or hire someone to find your birth family."

"Oh, come on, like I need any more family than I have," she said. "Can you picture me? 'Hey, guys, I'm Ollie, let's catch up on the last thirty years and start spending stupid Christmas together.'"

"I thought you wanted to find them."

"No. I don't think so. I mean, who knows? A large part of me does not even believe they exist. But I hate niggling ideas. I like facts. I want to *know*. And I don't think Dad will tell me. Like you said, Mom is the secretive one. Most of the time the nutball stuff you say doesn't ring true, but when you said she was keeping secrets, well, I realized you were right."

"Dad will kill you if you ask her about it. He doesn't even want Mom to know where we're going today, and he's sworn me to secrecy. She's still recovering. She's fragile."

"She doesn't seem fragile," said Ollie.

"You didn't see her before. She was so—ugh—so awfully, awfully fragile."

Ollie didn't comment on our mother's fragility.

I said, "I'm the one who was always the oddball. Not you. You're a crazy good athlete like all of them. And think about when we were growing up: you and dad talking science, medicine, sports; me with my old movies and my funny vintage clothes and my—emotions."

"You're an oddball in our family because you're an oddball everywhere. But you look exactly like Mom."

On that note, she said, "I'm finished talking."

THE PULLIAMS' HOUSE WASN'T FAR from the campus, but the place had a countryside feel. The house was pale yellow stucco, as if it were built of butter; its roof was slate. We drove down a long, tree-lined, gravel driveway. The trees were old and towered on either side of us. Sycamores, now leafless.

"Remember how we used to love to step on the curled-up pieces of sycamore bark in our neighborhood? Such a satisfying crackle," I said. "Whenever we got an especially crunchy one, we'd shoot our fists in the air and say 'Yessss!'"

"You're saying I wandered around the neighborhood with you stomping on tree bark? Why would I do that?" said Ollie.

"Because of the satisfying—" I broke off. "Oh. You know what? Maybe it was just me."

Somehow, this took the wind out of my sails. I wondered how many other activities my memory had imagined Ollie into.

"You did play the choosing game, though," I said, trying to sound snappy and playful and not forlorn and pleading.

Ollie stared straight out the windshield and said, "You're insane."

THE WOMAN WHO OPENED THE door had the kind of silvery hair only very blond people get when they age, but she looked much younger than I'd pictured, almost my mother's age. She wore jeans, a camel-colored cable-knit sweater, brown, knee-high boots, and was so much the picture of landed gentry elegance, I felt shy.

But then, she gasped in shock and fell back a little, her eyes flying open wide and filling with tears.

"Oh, gosh. Did we startle you? I'm sorry! I'm Cornelia," I said. "And this is my sister, Ollie."

Alice Pulliam smiled a frowny, upside-down smile as charming as a child's, and said, "Oh, what a goofball I am! I know who you are. I do. We are so glad you're here. But when I opened the door and saw you, I could only think: here is our darling, darling Eleanor, all grown up and come back to us."

Chapter 12

ELEANOR

November 1965

In the months that had passed since Martha's arrival in Bright Wind, her letters had dwindled, dwindled in frequency and length, but most troubling of all, in vivacity, like an evening sky slowly emptying of color. No soaring descriptions or winking humor, no sharp observations or raw honesty. She mentioned Jack's sculptures, her walks with Peg, her tiredness at the end of each day, but all in broad, vague, faded sentences that gave Eleanor nothing palpable of her life at the farm. Worst of all, she never mentioned her own art or made sketches in the margins of the letters or painted pictures with words, and until she'd stopped, Eleanor had not realized how deep art went for Martha, how much a part of her personality it was. For Martha, art wasn't a thing to do but was her own particular way of being alive.

"It's as if someone else is writing the letters," Eleanor told B on one of his visits, "as if she really has been kidnapped and someone is pretending to be her to trick me. Even her handwriting looks different, less bold and sure. I worry it's Jack. I worry he's wrung the spirit right out of her."

The letters stopped altogether in September. Eleanor waited eight weeks and then booked a plane ticket to Little Rock and mailed Martha a letter saying she was coming, giving her the specifics of her flight, asking if Martha could pick her up at the airport.

"If you can't or if you don't get this letter in time, I will take a bus, rent a car, something. I will find a way to get to you."

She hadn't asked permission. She was almost certain she would not be welcome. Still, come hell or high water or commandeering the Havens or Jack's temper, she was coming, damn it. She was going to see her sister with her own eyes.

She told no one, except B and the Pulliams. She told her friends she was going away for a weekend, but, in truth, she had no idea how long she'd be gone. She might get hopelessly behind in her classes; she might miss her winter exams, but, after a lifetime of caring about her schoolwork, she just didn't.

"You want to bring her home, don't you?" Alice asked. "You're planning on it."

"Yes. She's in a bad way. I just know it."

"Do you think she'll leave Jack?"

Eleanor's confidence faltered. But then she said, "If I tell her I need her, I think she will. She loves him, but she loved me first."

B DROVE HER TO THE airport. He had offered to come with her to Arkansas but had not seemed surprised, had made no protest when she'd said she needed to go alone. Now, as she stood in the Charlotte airport with her arms around him, she said, "Thank you for not trying to talk me out of this."

He appeared genuinely confused and said, "Why would I?"

"You," she said, shaking him, "you're doing the thing you always do."

"What's that?" he said.

"Giving me more reasons to love you, when I have quite enough already. They're really starting to pile up."

"Sorry," he said.

He kissed her.

"I'll come home soon," she whispered, pressing her cheek against his neck.

"I know," he said. "You'll do what you need to do, and then you'll come home."

ELEANOR WALKED RIGHT PAST HER.

She'd found the Little Rock airport bewildering, cavernous, and echoing and too bright. Everyone else seemed to know what they were doing, to be walking with direction and purpose. And Eleanor wasn't even sure Martha had gotten her letter. She wasn't sure she'd be there at all. So, yes, Eleanor was disoriented, fuzzy with the combination of exhaustion and adrenaline, holding on to her suitcase—the one familiar object in the room—for dear life, but even so, she would not have walked past her own sister, her entire reason for being there, had Martha looked like herself.

But Martha had not. The woman who caught her arm as she strode by was heavier than her Marthy in every sense. She'd gained weight, not a lot, but enough to alter her usually rangy silhouette. More than the new softness, though, was the way gravity seemed to pull harder on her than it used to. Her shoulders, the bags under her eyes, the corners of her mouth, the hem of her shapeless dress: all slack, all drooping closer to the earth. She looked older than her years and moved in a slow, waterlogged manner, this woman who used to, in Eleanor's eyes, shimmer with energy, whose facets reflected all the light in any room. Even Martha's marvelous hair was depleted, scraped back into a knot at the base of her skull.

"Oh, my love," said Eleanor.

She dropped her suitcase and threw her arms around her sister.

In an instant, Martha was hugging her back.

"I'm so glad you're here," whispered Martha into her ear, "so glad."

Before they could say more, long before they were ready to let go of each other, a voice broke in, resonant, clear, and compelling: "Let's get out of here. What do you say?"

Over Martha's shoulder, Eleanor saw him: older looking than she'd expected, tan and weathered, with etched lines across his forehead and faint traces of acne scars on his cheeks; tall and narrow-shouldered; a braid hanging down his back like an Indian in a movie. Martha had described him as beautiful, and Eleanor did not think she agreed, but he had a kind of appeal, with his five-o'clock shadow, heavily lashed eyes, and angled jawline. The man's voice was handsomer than the man, but the man, she decided, was handsome enough.

"If you're ready, of course," said Jack, flipping up one corner of his mouth.

On the plane, she had talked herself into giving him a chance, a fair shake, but confronted with his smirk, she felt a stab of distaste.

"Sure," said Eleanor.

Jack did not offer to carry her bag but, instead, spun on the heel of his brown work boot and began to walk away. Martha moved to pick up the suitcase, but Eleanor got to it first and then slipped her free arm through Martha's.

"I know I must be a sight," said Martha.

She patted her hair self-consciously, Martha who had always laughed at fashion and held her head up like a queen.

"A sight for sore eyes," Eleanor told her. "I have never, in all my days, been so happy to see anyone."

A smile sparked on Martha's tired face, then vanished.

"Marthy, honey, how are you?" said Eleanor. "I couldn't tell from your letters."

Martha opened her mouth as if to speak, but then seemed to think better of it. She shifted her gaze to Jack, who was getting farther and farther away with the sure gait of a man who is used to people following him. He hadn't turned around even once to check. Martha quickened her pace, tugging Eleanor along.

"We should catch up to Jack," she said.

IN THE CAR, A LONG, old one with slippery vinyl seats, Martha sat in the passenger seat next to Jack, which made perfect sense, but also made Eleanor resentful.

Martha is mine more than yours, she thought hard at the back of Jack's head, an unworthy thought, childish, but she felt like a child, sitting behind them, shivering in the unheated car, and trying not to slide back and forth on the slick bench seat.

Jack was utterly silent for the first part of the ride, and Eleanor resented this, as well, thinking his wasn't the silence of a shy man but of one who would not bother to unfurl his stirring baritone for the likes of Eleanor. Better to save it to preach half-baked politics to adoring masses or to seduce brilliant but inexperienced women.

You're not fit to breathe the same air as my Martha, you slinking, pigtailed nitwit.

She told herself it was unreasonable to dislike a person on sight, but she didn't really believe it, as she watched Martha glancing repeatedly over at Jack, as if to gauge his mood. Eleanor could feel her worry and could tell she was struggling to find the right words to appease him.

Finally, she said, "It's quite unusual for visitors to be allowed at Bright Wind, but Jack spoke with Louise and Bill and made it possible for you to come."

Eleanor wanted to scoff, *As if I wasn't coming anyway!* but she kept quiet. She supposed it had been good of Jack, after all, to smooth the way for her.

"Thank you," she said.

Jack said, "I told them Martha needed help with the baby, which is the God's honest truth. I sure hope you have more of a knack with babies than your sister here, Eleanor."

There wasn't a trace of meanness in his voice—it was flat, even weirdly so—but the words were mean, and for a few seconds, Eleanor was too enraged by them to fully absorb what he'd said.

"I try," said Martha, wearily, "I really do."

"It's not your fault," said Jack. "Some people are just not cut out to be mothers."

Eleanor fell back against the seat, stunned.

"Mothers," she said. "Are you talking about *your* baby?"

Martha darted another glance at Jack.

"Yes, my baby," she said. "I planned to tell you, and I would have. I don't know why I haven't yet; I guess I couldn't find the words."

Eleanor stared at the back of her head, at the head of this new Martha who had a baby and could not find words.

"Oh," said Eleanor. "Well, that's okay."

Martha gave her a wan smile over her shoulder and mouthed, "Sorry."

"Well, gosh, congratulations!" said Eleanor, brightly. "A boy or a girl?"

"A girl. Lisa. She's three weeks old. She came a bit ahead of schedule."

"But she's fine?"

"Yes, yes. She's small but fine. She does cry a lot."

"All the time," said Jack in the empty voice. "Day and night."

"But Peg said she's as healthy as can be," said Martha. "You remember I told you about Peg. She used to be a nurse."

"Of course."

You told me about Peg but not about being pregnant or about your daughter.

"She delivered Lisa," said Martha.

"She did? Goodness, you mean she went to the hospital with you? Was there not a doctor there?"

"Hospitals aren't places where people should be born," said Jack. "They're where people go to die. And doctors are just in it for their own profit."

Eleanor had a flash of white-hot anger on B's behalf but decided to ignore Jack.

"You had the baby at the farm?" she asked.

"Yes," said Martha.

"Oh, I bet you were wonderful. Wonderful and brave. Just like always."

Before Martha could answer, Jack said, "Babies have been born for centuries. It's not exactly an achievement. Women all over the world squat in fields, give birth, and keep on working."

He said it as if he were standing at a pulpit or a podium, handing down a pronouncement.

"Do they?" snapped Eleanor. "What fields? And what women exactly?"

But Martha had lifted her fingers to her head and had begun worrying the knot of hair at the nape of her neck, so Eleanor said, "Well, anyway, Marthy, I'm glad it was fine. I'm glad you and Lisa are just fine."

Martha—*oh, Martha*—looked over at Jack again.

Eleanor's sister, Martha, had lived with their mother for over twenty years, a woman who had screamed and threatened and belittled, who had once hit Martha square in the chest with a cast-iron skillet she'd flung across the room, and Eleanor had never once seen her look at their mother with the frightened, pleading look she now saw in her eyes when she looked at her husband, if that's what he was.

Jack must have known she was looking at him, needing a response, reassurance, but he gave her nothing. Eleanor found herself remembering Sally Fitch from sixth grade, butter-blond pretty and the meanest girl in school; when she was punishing another girl, which was often, she'd get her gang of followers to pretend the girl was invisible. Eleanor thought Jack was doing the same to Martha.

Eleanor had said she was glad Lisa and Eleanor were fine. She didn't know about Lisa, but Eleanor knew her sister, Martha, was not fine. Her Martha, her dear, her darling, the other half of her heart, was as far away from fine as she had ever been.

BRIGHT WIND FARM SQUATTED IN a flat space between two hills. When Jack turned sharply and drove the car through an opening in the trees, Eleanor had felt confusion, not understanding how this could be the entrance to anything. She'd expected a gate or a sign, but the road was nothing more than a dirt path, so narrow the branches clicked and scraped against the car windows. About twenty yards in, the headlights snagged on a kind of shack by the side of the road, a ruin with a tree growing out of its broken roof. It was after midnight, moonless, the road a sleeve of darkness, but just as Eleanor's unease began tipping over into panic, the trees fell away, and the farm, with the dirt path running through it, lay before them.

Eleanor had been bracing herself for the bizarre, an eerie ghost town from out of a book, populated by bohemians and zealots (although she wasn't sure she'd recognize either if she saw them), but what lay around them looked more like a summer camp. A scattering of small brown cabins, clotheslines, a firepit ringed with stones and surrounded by the kind of metal folding chairs people brought to the beach, the remnants of a vegetable garden—a rectangle scraped free of grass and populated by a few bean teepees. Eleanor could see a white farmhouse at the end of the drive; its porch light—firefly yellow—the only sign of electricity.

At the cabin closest to the farmhouse, Jack stopped the car and switched off the headlights. Eleanor pushed open the heavy, creaking door, got out, and stretched, grateful to have the ride over, to set her feet on the clean-swept, packed-dirt yard in front of the cabin. She thought how silly she'd been to expect the farm to be creepy. Even now, in the dead of night, it exuded ordinariness and a careworn quietude. The window of Martha and Jack's cabin held the faint warm glow of lantern light.

It was only when Martha, already standing at the cabin's door, said, "We should let Jack go on and get some sleep," that Eleanor realized he hadn't turned off the engine, still sat behind the wheel.

"Oh!" she said.

She yanked her suitcase out of the car and said, "Thanks for picking me up."

Jack grinned, waved, and said, "See you in the a.m.," and drove away, down the road and then to the right of the house. From somewhere behind the house, she heard the engine go silent.

"See you in the a.m.?" she said.

"Oh, well, Jack hasn't quite come around yet," said Martha, trying for cheerfulness, "He's been sleeping in the big house because the baby cries so much at night. But he'll get used to the idea."

"What idea? You mean his baby?"

Martha winced. Eleanor's scorn was for Jack, but it was Martha she'd hurt.

"It's complicated," said Martha. "Please don't blame him. When we left to come here, I was pregnant, but neither of us knew. It was a shock when I finally realized it. And Jack—well, he had a plan for us and it didn't include a baby. Why should it have? I had no notion of ever having children. Ever since Lisa was born, he's been different. Distant, angry. But I know he'll come around."

Eleanor wanted to lash out at Jack. She wanted to ask a thousand questions. But she saw the raw, ragged exhaustion in her sister's face and decided the questions would keep.

"I think this is the quietest place I've ever been," she said. "All those sounds you don't even realize you hear all the time are just— absent."

"It's lovely, isn't it?" said Martha, gazing back along the road they'd just driven in on. "This particular quality of quiet. It's the best part."

When she turned to open the door, Eleanor lifted her face to the sky. Above them were more stars—stars upon stars upon stars— than she had ever seen.

ALMOST AS SOON AS SHE'D done it, Eleanor wished she hadn't picked up the baby.

They walked into the cabin to find a woman in a rocking chair, reading a book, an intricately woven basket on the floor at her feet. The woman was red-haired with a pale face and freckles Eleanor could see plainly even in the subtle light of the lantern, which sat on a table next to the rocker. As Eleanor shut the door behind them, the woman stood up.

"Hello," said the woman, smiling. "I'm Peg."

Eleanor was ready to introduce herself in turn when she heard a rustle, and a sputtering sound, like a tiny, rusted engine starting up, arose from the basket. She didn't decide to pick up the baby, her body just bent over of its own accord and then her hands were around the child, who was wrapped in a colorful blanket, very soft, and she was lifting. Automatically, she dropped her face and breathed in the baby's fragrance, and then began to bend her knees, bouncing lightly up and down. The baby's rattling engine slowed and went still. With the velvety head still nestled just beneath her chin, she looked up to see the two women watching her. Peg appeared charmed. But Martha looked as if she'd had the wind knocked out of her, more wrung out than she had seemed in the airport, old and tired and as if she might cry. Her hands dangled at her sides, not reaching for the baby. Then, she mustered a rueful smile.

"You're a natural," she said. "Didn't I tell you? Not like me."

Peg put her arm around Martha's shoulders and squeezed.

"Hey, you're doing fine. You've got a fussy one on your hands. Fussy babies are hard."

"I suppose," said Martha.

Peg reached down and swept a shawl off the back of the rocker. It was as soft and as swirled with color as the baby's blanket. She draped it around her shoulders, then leaned in to kiss Martha on the cheek.

"Thank you for staying with her," said Martha.

"Anytime at all," said Peg. "Good night. And welcome, Eleanor."

When Eleanor and Martha were alone, Martha took off her coat and set it on a table near the door, then she held out her arms for Lisa.

"She'll be hungry," she said, unwinding the blanket from around Lisa. Underneath the blanket the baby wore white footie pajamas.

Martha's dress buttoned all the way down the front, and methodically, she settled herself into the rocker with Lisa on her lap, unbuttoned the dress to the waist, slid one arm out of its sleeve, lifted her bra, draped the baby's blanket over her shoulder, slipped the baby under the blanket, and tucked her against her body. Eleanor wasn't sure what to do with herself. She wasn't embarrassed, which surprised her, but the moment seemed a private one between Martha and Lisa. She started to fuss with the latches on her suitcase, but Martha said, "Sit and talk to me?"

Eleanor sat on the edge of the double bed. She kept her coat on.

Despite the old-fashioned potbelly woodstove in the corner, the room was cold. The cabin was so small that, from where she sat, she could reach out and press her hand against Martha's wan cheek.

"Now, see there?" she said to Martha. "You're a natural, too."

"It's Lisa who's the natural," said Martha. "Peg says some babies born early struggle with latching on or have a weak suck, but this one knew just what to do. Thank goodness, since I was completely at sea, all thumbs."

"I don't believe it for a second," said Eleanor.

But she noticed how Martha handled the baby. Her every movement was tentative, fearful. Each time Martha shifted her position or touched her child, she seemed to hold her breath, and Eleanor found herself remembering a day from their childhood. Eleanor couldn't have been more than six. That particular winter was a low point even in their home life full of low moments. Their mother hated winter, dreaded it every year, said the gray and cold sank into her soul. That winter, though, instead of their mother getting gloomier and sleeping all the time, her rages burned harder and hotter than ever. That day, they'd run out of the house to escape her wrath and ended up in the park, where they'd discovered a bird skeleton—a wisp of a thing, the pieces so delicately linked to one another it seemed a breath could scatter them. They decided they must bury it, give it a proper funeral, and, as Eleanor watched, Martha, round-eyed, reverent, had lifted it with her mittened hands. Eleanor remembered the tremendous weight of the moment: it was as if their lives, their safety, their happiness, depended on keeping the skeleton intact. But it had broken apart in Martha's hands, and the two of them had sat right down on the ground in the park, bereft, swallowed by grief, and stayed till nightfall.

Eleanor felt a rush of shame. What a terrible scene to call up now, as she watched her sister with her new baby.

"She is completely beautiful," declared Eleanor.

At this, a light glimmered in Martha's eyes, and she sounded almost like her old self when she said, "It is so good to see you that I don't even care who's worked up about it."

"I've caused a stir, have I?"

"Oh, it isn't personal, just the same distrust everyone feels for all outsiders. Well, not everyone. Not Peg. Not me."

"Not Lisa."

Eleanor reached out and took hold of Lisa's tiny foot, warm inside the pajamas. Lisa kicked her leg, and Eleanor was surprised by her strength and felt glad. Lisa was nothing like a bird skeleton. She was all of a piece, tightly, ingeniously knit together, sturdy and alive.

"Martha," said Eleanor, slowly, "I've brought you some cash. From Susan's estate. And there's more in a bank account Daddy's lawyer is managing. I've written down all the information and put it into the envelope with the money. I think you should—" She'd started to say "hide it," but decided on "Put it away. For you and Lisa. In case, you need it one day."

"Hide it from Jack you mean."

"Yes."

The spark she'd seen a moment ago in Martha's eyes had gone out.

"I know," she said, "I know. But he never wanted me to have her. He was honest about it, at least. He wanted me to end the pregnancy. He said he'd ask Peg to find someone who would do it."

Eleanor opened her mouth to speak, but Martha lifted her hand.

"I thought about it. I have told you what I think of me and motherhood, and I strongly considered it."

"You could have done it," said Eleanor. "Whatever Jack wanted or didn't want, you could have decided not to have the baby. Why didn't you?"

Martha shook her head.

"I don't know. Partly, I was scared. Women die sometimes. But mostly, I think I didn't so much decide as just put off making the decision until it was too late."

Eleanor considered this.

"Martha, I know you. You are decisive; you always know what you want. So you must have wanted her."

Martha averted her eyes. Her face shut like a box, became unreadable.

After a long time, she said, "I hope so. It's just—"

"What, darling? What is it?"

Martha kept her eyes turned away.

"The way I feel since she's been born, I don't think it's the way I'm supposed to feel."

ELEANOR WASHED UP IN THE closet-size bathroom, filling the chipped sink. The water was cold, but she used the bar of soap and the washcloth Martha had given her and did her best. She put on her flannel pajamas and brushed her teeth. When she came back out into the main room, Martha and the baby were both in the big bed, asleep.

As noiselessly as she could, she slipped into bed without waking Martha. She'd done it countless times before, back when they were girls together, when her own bed felt too big, when they were two against the world. But now there were three: Lisa lay between them, on her back, her arms thrown out, the fingers of both hands lightly curled inward, as if she were holding on to something as she slept. In the scant light coming through the window, Eleanor watched the baby furrow her brow, her face seeming to contract with sorrow, then relax. Eleanor was just drifting into sleep when Lisa began to cry, and, this time, the sputtering engine caught hold, and the hoarse cries became rhythmic, harsh, and full-throated. Eleanor watched the baby's body go rigid, as if her crying started in her feet and coursed upward. Martha began to sit up, her face hollow-eyed and defeated, but Eleanor said, "No, let me."

She gathered the fierce, hot, loud animal that was her niece into her arms, sat down in the rocker, and rocked until the baby at long last slid into a fitful sleep. Now it was as if not the baby but her state of sleep were the frail structure, spun out of hollow bones and wisps of feather, out of dust and air. Eleanor didn't want to risk breaking it, so she stayed in the chair, rocking, until dawn.

WHEN THEY WALKED TO HER studio the next morning, Martha carried Lisa against her chest in a fabric sling, stamped with daffodils, the likes of which Eleanor had never seen.

"Peg rigged it up for me," Martha explained. "She's a weaver and a textile artist. The first week after Lisa was born, I hardly ever took it off. It was the one place she'd settle down in. Well, sometimes, anyway. Peg made one for Missy, too. She's the other woman here with a baby, a month or so older than Lisa. Wren is her name."

Martha had thanked Eleanor over and over for allowing her a night of sleep, and she did seem refreshed, lighter of step, more lively and animated, as she and Eleanor strolled through the farm to her studio. In the morning light, the farm was even shabbier than Eleanor had thought it the night before. She could see peeling paint clinging to the cabins and skeletal vines shrouding the bean teepees in the sad little garden plot. But she also found it picturesque, like a village from a storybook, a miniature town nestled cozily between the hills.

"The farm's only half-full just now," said Martha. "Lots of people don't like it in the winter; it's colder than they expect. So they leave.

Some of them might try to come back in the spring, although Jack says the Havens usually won't allow people to return. The Havens don't believe in changes of heart and they only want the hardy here. Or so Jack says. Anyway, I'm glad because there are open cabins we can use as studios. Peg keeps her loom and her dye pots and her printing blocks in one; I use another one for painting."

As they walked, Martha waved or called hello to the other community members, who were beginning to stir outside their households, and, in a low voice, she gave Eleanor a summing-up of each one, painting verbal pictures with broad, sure strokes, as she'd done in her letters, before her letters changed.

When an older man dressed like a country gentleman from a movie—corduroy trousers and a green quilted jacket—saluted them with his fancy walking stick, Martha said, "Ted. His wife is Mitchie. We don't use last names here, for reasons unknown to me. They imagine themselves to be painters, but their work is—well, I shouldn't disparage the work of my fellow Bright Winders. Mitchie mostly plans paintings, talks constantly and quite eloquently about what she intends to paint, collects leaves and rocks that speak to her, but she doesn't seem to actually paint them. Ted makes splatter and drip paintings; I'll say no more. I suspect they're largely financing the farm—we all contribute what we can to the communal pot for art supplies and food and other essentials—because they get to do things other people don't: they get driven into town more. We are supposed to be vegetarians, but they have salami. I've seen it! And I've smelled it on Ted's breath, unfortunately. He will stand too close when he speaks to you. I've smelled alcohol, too, which we also aren't supposed to have. Peg believes Ted and Mitchie got in some legal trouble in the outside world, and they're hiding out here until it blows over. I wouldn't be surprised if she's right."

In front of another cabin, an especially run-down one, a painfully thin blond girl pinned clothing on the line. Martha called hello to her, but the girl froze, clothespin in hand, at the sight of Eleanor, and Eleanor believed she could feel the girl's suspicious gaze dogging them down the dirt path.

"Missy," said Martha. "She's very young, maybe younger than you. She and her boyfriend, Joe, are both runaways. Joe's parents were evangelicals, the obsessive sort. He ran away right before he was supposed to leave with them on a mission to Africa. Peg says Missy's history is a sorry tale of neglect and abuse; she left home when she was sixteen and left behind two younger brothers, twins. They haunt her, those boys. She talks about bringing them here, but Jack doubts the Havens would allow it. They're too young, and, from what Missy says, they're sick a lot, asthma I think."

"Missy doesn't look very hardy, herself," said Eleanor.

"No, but Missy worships the Havens, and Louise has a keen eye for spotting potential worshippers. Missy and Joe both were ripe for the picking. You can divide the Bright Winders into two types: people who are running away from their outside lives and true believers. Some people, like Missy and Joe, start out one and end up the other, heaven help them."

"Peg doesn't strike me as a true believer," said Eleanor.

"Ha. No. Peg was a nurse on the outside. But her marriage went all to hell. Her husband said he'd kill her if she left him, so she stayed. One of the women who left here at the end of last summer met Peg and told her about Bright Wind. Peg won't stay forever and it will be dreadful when she leaves, but for now, she likes it well enough. She weaves, takes long hikes, and acts as the farm nurse, although no one's needed much more than a bit of first aid."

"And you?" said Eleanor, keeping her tone light. "Are you an escapee or a true believer?"

Martha looked at her as if the answer was obvious.

"I'm here because of Jack."

ELEANOR WISHED SHE KNEW THE word for Martha's paintings. They were more than exquisite, although they were that, too. The seamless surfaces, how every color seemed to be made up of dozens of colors, the way she had somehow put the paint into motion. The northern lights glowed from every canvas—although there were only a few—and the lights moved: floated, fluttered, streamed, rippled like water, vibrated like harp strings a hand had just run across.

But, to Eleanor's eyes, what outshone the sheer beauty of the pieces was their emotional life, the thoughts and feelings as layered as the pigments. Eleanor saw Martha on every canvas, not the weary, drained, tamped-down, pent-up woman who'd met her at the airport, but the real Martha, her Martha, unleashed, abounding. Eleanor saw the truth of Martha swirled into every light-struck sky.

Thank God, she thought. *She's still in there.*

"I hadn't realized how different it is to paint from memory, rather than from life, how so much more personal it is, more interior," said Martha.

She took Lisa out of the sling and set her in a basket on the floor. It was a basket different from the one in Martha's cabin, but it was just as gorgeously made.

"Missy's work," said Martha. "Something a woman in her South Carolina town taught her to do. Missy is so fragile and displaced; I think basket weaving is the one thing she feels truly certain about."

A painting covered with a cloth sat on the easel near the window. Martha lifted off the cloth.

"This one is yours," she said.

Two wide, liquid ribbons of light, one wide and an unearthly green, the other narrower and streaked with fuchsia, pouring together down the sky toward a cabin on a hill; just over the cabin's roof, the ribbons joined together. It should have been a contrast: the operatic sky over the snug cabin with its windows beaming homey yellow light, but the two—sky and house—balanced each other; they were a wholeness. The scene was steeped in peace and as intimate as a face.

"It's us," said Eleanor.

"Yes," said Martha. "Ever since I can remember, what I wanted most was for you to be in a safe place, but I couldn't make it happen. I couldn't make our house safe, not while Susan lived there with us. And when I was in Minnesota, one day when I missed you more than usual—and even usual was a lot—I was hiking and saw a cabin in the distance. The cabin was the safest place I'd ever seen, so I put you into it. And put the northern lights over it. Even though most people think the lights exist to be watched by us, they've always struck me as being at least just as much there to watch us. To watch over."

"Like you," I said. "Big and glorious and watching over."

Eleanor took Martha's hand and squeezed it. Martha didn't squeeze hers back.

"I haven't felt big and glorious in quite some time," she said. "It's strange, seeing myself through your eyes again; it's jarring. I don't recognize the Martha you see."

She let go of Eleanor's hand and pulled her tumultuous hair back from her face. Her shirt cuffs rode up, and Eleanor saw purple marks she thought for a second must be ink. She caught one of her sister's wrists in her hand and gently pushed up her sleeve. The marks were bruises, unmistakable: four fingers and a thumb. Martha tugged her arm away.

"It's nothing. It's not at all what you think."

Eleanor stood very still, rigid with fear, not speaking, not knowing what to say.

Martha sighed, and it was as if her exhale took all her light with it.

"People get careless when they're tired. We just need to get our feet under us again. Since the baby, we are just so tired."

He isn't, Eleanor thought. *He doesn't lift a finger, except to hurt you. Oh, Marthy, you are the one who is tired.*

Martha rubbed her eyes with both hands.

"Eleanor, God, I don't know what I'm doing with a baby."

"You're a good mother, Martha."

"Even Louise, who is so distant and cool, is much better with Lisa than I am. Peg told me Bill once let slip that Louise was unable to have kids. When she's in the same room with Lisa or with Missy's baby, I can tell by her expression she's itching to reach out and take them into her arms. I don't ever feel that way, not even about my own baby."

"You're just tired. Why wouldn't you be?"

"No. It's more than being tired. When someone says the word *mother,* I picture ours ripping up my artwork in a rage. I don't think that's what most people picture. Sometimes, when I've finally gotten Lisa to stop crying and go to sleep and I'm just starting to fall asleep myself and she starts up again, I feel this emotion roll through me. It's despair, I think, but I'm worried it will turn into something worse. I'm worried what I might do."

Eleanor had never heard anyone sound so bleak, so terrified.

"You wouldn't. You would never. I swear to you, you never would."

"I don't know. I don't trust myself. I should feel more for her; I should feel overwhelming love, shouldn't I? I should hold her and feel only love. But I just feel empty."

Eleanor took Martha's hands from her face and cradled her sister's wrists in her hands, applying gentleness where Jack had applied force.

"Come home with me. Please. Let me be *your* safe place for once. Let me put you inside the cabin, you and Lisa. We'll take care of her together."

Briefly, Martha seemed to consider this, but she shook her head, back and forth, back and forth.

"I can't. I could never leave Jack. I know you don't understand why, but I am unable to leave him. He's my—I don't know what he is. I just need him. And I believe he needs me, too. He tells me I belong to him. He used to say that all the time. But Elsbee, you stay. For a week or two? I love having you here, but also you bring pieces of me back to myself. If you stayed, I think I could love her."

LOUISE HAVEN, SITTING AT ONE end of the very long dining table, reminded Eleanor of the photo of Queen Nefertiti's bust she'd seen in her Art History textbook: swan-necked, noble-nosed, a face cut like a precious stone, a mild, pleasant expression, and an effortless nobility. Louise exuded both queenliness and warmth, attributes Eleanor hadn't known could coexist in one person. She bestowed her full attention upon whomever she spoke with, open, inviting, interested regard that fell on the person like a shaft of sunlight.

Eleanor was already sitting at the table between Martha and Peg when Louise had swept in on her husband's arm, Jack on her other side. Jack had pulled her chair out for her, and Eleanor was taken aback by the display of courtliness. Jack sat down next to Louise, at her right hand, as if, Eleanor thought with exasperation, she were God and he were Jesus. Bill sat at the other end of the table. As if on cue, the talk at the table ceased, and all turned their eyes to Louise.

No hierarchies my eye! thought Eleanor.

Louise's gaze made its way to Eleanor, and Martha said, "Bill, Louise, this is my sister, Eleanor."

Louise stretched her arms, palms up, toward Eleanor, before dropping her hands to the table's edge and leaning in with a conspiratorial air.

"Do you know, I have always loved the name Eleanor," she said, in a sweet, clear voice. "I think it stems from my fascination with Eleanor of Aquitaine. Such an interesting woman, so determined, don't you think? I think Shakespeare got her wrong in *King John*. She's such a nag in that play. I think she was far more subtle than that, but she had awful taste in men!"

She laughed and shook a finger at Eleanor.

"I hope yours is better!"

"It is," said Eleanor.

"I am so relieved."

Eleanor caught Missy glaring at her across the table, broadcasting a jealousy so naked Eleanor felt sorry for her.

You can have her, Eleanor wanted to tell her. *She is all yours.*

Louise looked around her, as if just noticing everyone watching her.

"Oh, my goodness, I've been rambling on when you all must be starving," she said.

"Time to say grace, dear," said Bill.

Eleanor had the uncanny sensation of being an audience member at a play, and when Bill spoke, she could tell he was reciting his line.

Louise lifted her slim hand in the air and delivered hers: "Give thanks to whatever higher being your soul embraces," she said gaily.

"And if your soul isn't the embracing type?" intoned Jack, with a sly smile.

Louise beamed back at him, and Eleanor sensed something private pass between them. She wondered if it happened all the time; she wondered if Martha noticed it, too.

"Then give thanks to the cooks!" sang out Louise.

Over the clatter and murmur that followed, Bill boomed, "Eleanor, I understand you're in college."

Eleanor dropped a spoonful of mashed potatoes onto her plate, then passed the potatoes to Peg before she answered. She would not be part of their performance if she could possibly help it.

"I am."

Louise said, "Now my husband is going to launch into a diatribe against higher education, Eleanor."

"Why, of course I am," said Bill. "And you'll agree with every word, Louise. You know you will."

"Ha! I don't know about *every* word, but, yes, we mostly agree on the subject."

"Higher education is, excuse my language, a load of crap," said Bill. "The only way to truly learn is to live. And college isn't life. It's a holding pen, a moneymaking scheme, a place of indoctrination and deception. College is many things, but it is not life."

Eleanor wanted to slap the man's fat, red face, but she held her temper and forced herself to think about what he'd said.

"I would agree that college isn't much like real life," she said. "People use the phrase 'ivory tower,' and I see what they mean. It's its own world, full of pretty buildings and lawns and people reading and thinking and talking all day. I know the real world is far messier and more complicated. But I do think I learn in college. I would say it has accelerated my learning, actually. If I hadn't gone, I would be much further behind, years and years further behind."

"Ah," said Bill. "So tell me, what is the single most significant thing you've learned so far?"

"How to think," said Eleanor. "How to gather information and all sorts of perspectives and sort through them to come up with my own opinions."

"That sounds very pretty, doesn't it, Louise?" said Bill.

"Now, now, darling," said Louis. "No mocking."

Jack snorted. "Thinking is exactly what you don't learn in college," he said. "You learn only what they want you to know. You swallow it like a pill. You learn the opposite of how to think."

Peg stood up abruptly.

"I hear Lisa starting to fuss. Excuse me."

Louise's face lit up.

"Oh, bring her in if she's unhappy," said Louise. "I can hold her against my shoulder while I eat."

Peg didn't answer as she walked out of the room.

Lisa and Wren were sleeping in their baskets in the front room of the farmhouse. Martha had told Eleanor that she always ate her meals as fast as she could because Lisa usually started crying a few minutes into the meal. But Eleanor didn't hear any crying coming down the hallway. As she watched Peg march from the dining room, she realized the woman hated Jack, could not even stand to hear his voice. Eleanor was glad. If Martha would not come home with her, she needed an ally who saw Jack for who he was.

Eleanor wondered if she could throw her fork directly into Jack's left eye, but she knew the worst thing she could do to the man was show him how little she cared about what he thought. She shrugged.

"You have your opinion; I have mine."

She popped a bite of squash casserole into her mouth.

"Trained seals don't have opinions," said Jack.

"Jack. Did you not hear me? No mocking! Mocking will get us nowhere," said Louise.

"Are you trying to get somewhere?" said Eleanor. "I thought we were just having a conversation."

Jack's face reddened, but Louise didn't bat an eyelash.

"You're right, of course. We can get very bossy," she said. "It's a bad habit. Our apologies. However, I do truly believe—and hope you'll come to agree—that college—and not only college but also all the schooling that precedes it—only gives us the illusion of education. Experience is an infinitely better teacher. I mean authentic experience, of course, wherein we choose our own roles and ideals, instead of accepting what society hands us."

Eleanor put all the sweetness and playfulness she could muster into her smile and said, "Are you saying you learned about Eleanor of Aquitaine and Shakespeare through authentic personal experience? So you what? Bumped into them in the street?"

And there it was, a twitch of Louise's cheek, so fleeting Eleanor thought she might have imagined it. Under the table, Martha put a warning hand on Eleanor's knee. She'd seen the twitch, too. But Louise tossed her head back and laughed.

"Touché!" she said.

And the conversation ended.

Louise pointed her fork at Missy.

"Now, tell us what miracles little Wren has performed lately."

Missy pressed her hand against her heart, and Eleanor noticed her pallor, her knobby wrists, her lank, lackluster hair. Eleanor understood she was seeing malnourishment, poverty, a lifetime of every variety of hunger, and her heart ached for the unchecked reverence illuminating Missy's pinched features as she stammered to answer Louise. If Eleanor could have spoken to Missy, if there had been a hope in hell Missy would hear her, she would have told her, *Oh, sweetheart, hold out for better. You deserve so much better than her.*

THAT NIGHT MARTHA AND ELEANOR had been back at Martha's cabin for only a few minutes, when Jack walked in without knocking. Eleanor had just added a log to the fire in the stove, and Martha was leaning over the bed, undressing Lisa, who was on the edge of the mattress kicking her legs, frog-like, in rhythm to her mechanical crying. As the door opened, Eleanor turned around. She saw Martha startle at the sight of Jack, saw her straighten up and take her hands off the baby, just as Lisa gave an especially hard kick that scooted her dangerously close to the end of the bed. Before she could fall, Eleanor rushed forward and grabbed her, so suddenly that Lisa's cries stopped, as if a switch had been flipped.

Into this sudden quiet, Jack said, "You just don't know how to pay attention, Martha. And you have no instincts for this. I've told you a million times. It's a damned good thing your sister was here."

Martha dropped her head in shame and said, "You're right. I know you are."

"He is not right," said Eleanor, biting out the words. "She wouldn't have fallen. I was just being overly cautious."

She wasn't sure if this was true, but she had to say it. She would've said anything to keep Martha from falling further into shame.

"Sure," said Jack. "Whatever you say, sister Eleanor."

He dropped a basket covered with a napkin on the table by the door—their breakfast for the next morning—and left without shutting the door behind him.

Eleanor wanted to run after him and beat him with her fists. She wanted to grab Martha and Lisa and run away home. She had to find a way to persuade Martha to leave with her. There had to be a way. But she had seen the way Martha had looked at Jack during the car ride from the airport, across the table at dinner, even now, as she watched his back recede into the darkness outside. Martha looked at Jack the way Missy looked at Louise Haven. Enthralled, lost. She looked at him as if he weren't a cruel and selfish man or any kind of man at all, but as if he were her only hope, her sun, her religion.

Chapter 13

CORNELIA

EVEN WITH EVERYTHING WE LEARNED about my mother's life from Alice and Joel Pulliam, what won the day, what outweighed and outshone every other fact, was their love for her.

"Nowadays, you'd say she was our person. Our grandchildren use that phrase: he is my person, she is my person," said Alice Pulliam. "Eleanor was our babysitter, our friend, Joel's student, but most of all, she was just *ours*. And we—all four of us—were surely hers."

"Still are," said Joel. "We've been out of the picture, but we have been her people for over fifty years."

"We talk about her still now and then. Funny things she said and did, how wonderful she was with Kimmy and Chris. They were so little you wouldn't think they'd remember, but they do. She was, oh, a bright star of a girl."

We sat in the Pulliams' living room. The evidence of a life well lived was everywhere you looked: in their faces; in the photos of their children and grandchildren; in the well-loved furniture and the artwork on their walls and the books on shelves that went clear to the ceiling. I sat trying to think of what they and their house reminded me of, and then I realized it was my parents and their house.

"Thank you," I said. "For loving her, for stepping in and being her people. We'll never take the measure of what a difference you made in how her life went after she met you, but I know it was huge. Your kindness and your example of a happy family went a long, long way, all the way to our lives and the lives of our children. I just know it did."

Alice said, "Oh!" and I waited for her or for Joel to be flustered or embarrassed, to dismiss what I'd said, but it didn't happen.

Alice said, "You know, if that is even a little bit true, and I know I speak for Joel, too, it numbers among the great honors of our lives."

"It does, indeed," said Joel.

Alice reached over the arm of the sofa and lay a brown paper shopping bag on its side on the coffee table.

"After we got your email, I did some poking around in the guest room closet and found this. I knew I'd saved it. I'd given most everything else away years and years ago, to neighborhood children or my younger brother's two girls, but would never, not for love or money, have parted with this."

From the shopping bag, she slid something wrapped loosely in white tissue paper. It was a dress for a very small girl, dark pink velvet and satin, a lovely little garment.

"Your mother made it for Kimmy. It was her Christmas dress. And I can tell you, the child was really very vain about it, spun and spun around the house to make the skirt bell out. She'd have slept in it if we'd let her," said Alice.

Ollie and Cornelia looked at each other.

Ollie said, "But our mother doesn't sew. She never has."

"Well, how interesting," said Joel. "Because she was a real whiz at it."

"She counted sewing as the one good thing Susan, her mother, ever gave her," said Alice. "A shame she stopped, but, really, I don't think she ever loved it. When Martha went off to Minnesota, Eleanor whipped her up a coat the likes of which you'd see in a fancy store; worked on it day and night. And, you know, she set up a sewing corner in her dorm room and would hem a dance dress or mend a tear here and there for her friends. But I think the sewing was really for Martha, something between the two sisters."

"Minnesota?" I said. "As I explained in one of my emails, we really know nothing about Martha. But she moved away, I guess, while my mother was in college?"

Alice started to speak, then pressed her lips together and looked up at her husband. I could feel tension passing back and forth between them.

"Joel," said Alice, taking his hand, "it's been fifty years."

"Still," said Joel.

Alice turned to us.

"We were her secret keepers, you see. She'd call us that."

"Her trusted ones, she'd say, and, yes, her secret keepers. The two of us and, later, your father," said Joel.

"But, Joel, you know Martha wasn't a secret. All Eleanor's friends knew about her; some of them had even met her."

"But Eleanor never told her children about Martha," said Joel. "She surely had reasons for that. If she wanted to tell them, she could have. And their father never told them, either. He's still honoring her secrets."

"Our father," said Ollie. "Did you ever meet him?"

"Oh, yes," said Alice. "After Susan died, he came often to visit. The summer after, Eleanor stayed here with us, at our house, and he would come see her. He'd sleep at a hotel but would come here and spend time with Eleanor. He was great with Kimmy and Chris. They loved him. We all did. A kind, kind man, quiet, but funny when you got to know him. And he adored Eleanor."

"She adored him, too," said Joel. "They were just—happy."

"They were in harmony with each other. When they were together, they were home. We used to say they reminded us—" She paused, waiting for Joel to finish her thought.

"Of us," he said.

"But we aren't quite in harmony about talking to Eleanor's daughters, now, are we?" said Alice. Her tone was teasing.

He shook his head at her. "You, you're like a dog with a bone."

"My father said the same thing," said Cornelia. "If she'd wanted us to know, she would have told us."

"There," said Joel.

"But—" said Cornelia.

"There's a but!" said Alice to Joel.

"He can't tell us, and he's made me promise not to ask my mother. He says she's too fragile; he's afraid it would be too much for her. But I believe he wants us to find out. He's helped, in little ways, slipped us clues, nudged us in the right direction. We love her. We almost lost her," I said. "And we just want to know her."

"Oh," said Joel. "Well, I don't know."

"Also—" said Cornelia.

"There's an also, too!" said Alice to Joel.

I told them about the sundowning, about how I know she's grieving the loss of something, how I'd made a solemn vow to find it for her and give it back.

"Maybe it's Martha, the something lost," said Joel. "Is that what you think?"

"Oh, it breaks my heart to know the two of them didn't stay close," said Alice. "They were just special together; theirs was one of the best friendships I've ever come across to this day. How could such a thing happen? Honestly, I can't bear it."

"Maybe my mother can't bear it either," I said. "Whatever she's lost, however deep she's tried to bury her grief at losing it, the grief is there, alive and raw and awful, even after so many years. I just want to help her."

"Joel," said Alice, "under these circumstances, we should tell what we know. Don't you think?"

"Yes," said Joel. "How could we do otherwise?"

AND THEN THEY TOLD US the story of two sisters, a love story if ever I've heard one, marked by courage, triumph, sorrow, hope, heroism, loss, and joy, as I suppose all love stories are, if they last long enough. All the years Martha spent placing herself—burning sword slashing—between my mother and the powers of darkness that lived inside Susan; Martha breaking free, rising victorious, claiming her true self and her real home, with my mother cheering her on, even as her heart broke from missing her.

When Alice got to the part where Jack asked Martha to leave for Arkansas with him, I blurted out, "Oh, no! Don't do it, Martha. Don't go!" and Ollie said, "Please say she didn't go."

But Martha did go, of course. And when she couldn't stand it anymore, our mother went after her, swearing she'd bring her home.

"I bet she had a burning sword stuffed into her luggage," I said.

When Alice looked up, startled, Ollie explained, "She just does that, says weird, completely random things."

"I just meant she was ready for a fight."

"Oh, yes, I knew what you meant," said Alice. "It sounded so like something our Eleanor would've said it took me aback. And you're right. The child was on fire. About a week later, we got a letter from her. She'd written it while she was at the farm, but she must have mailed it just before she left there. We didn't realize it at the time, but by the time we got it, she was already back home."

Alice reached into the shopping bag once more and took out an envelope. I recognized the handwriting right away and had a moment's amazement at what I'd already known but hadn't fully until

I'd seen the hard evidence, understood: *that* Eleanor, the old Eleanor, was also *our* Eleanor, the new and ongoing and forever Ellie Brown. Alice handed me the letter. I read it aloud, my mother's words in my voice filling the room.

Dear Alice and Joel,

There is no other way to say this but to say it, although I wish I were there with you in person to say it because I think ink on paper will make it seem dramatic in a way it isn't really. My Martha is still herself and this baby is just part of our story. Because there is a baby: four weeks ago, Martha gave birth to a daughter, Lisa. She is ravishing and healthy and <u>loud</u> and full of life. She kicks like nobody's business, has a nose like the world's most perfect button, and the beginnings of hair I can already tell will be curly. I love her already. Already and for all time.

    Jack is horrible. I loathe the sight of him. He has no interest in the baby, wishes she hadn't been born, and he does all he can to shake Martha's already shaky faith in her ability to be a mother. Martha said he was good to her back in Minnesota before she got pregnant. He admired her intelligence and her paintings. She said he once told her she was his one chance at living a good life. But that changed when Lisa came along, and his friendship with the Havens, the couple who run the farm, doesn't help. Now he is so full of himself and so angry at Martha. He is swaggering and cruel and worse than we ever imagined. This place is not what I'd expected. Like a broken-down camp in the middle of nowhere. Louise and Bill Haven are a piece of work.

charismatic but untrustworthy to the core and slippery as eels. And Jack is their henchman.

Martha is low. low. low. Worn to a frazzle and terrified she'll be like Susan and hurt her baby. She won't. She never could. And I know she will be fine. She'll come back to herself. All I need is to get her away from Jack and from this place and bring her home. It won't be easy. When it comes to Jack, Martha is like a religious zealot and an opium addict rolled into one. Her eyes when she looks at him—well. I can't bear it. But I will persevere. I have to. I will bring Martha and her baby home.

With all my heart,
Eleanor

Ollie and I looked at each other, wonderstruck.

"A baby," I said. "An actual baby."

"And we never knew," said Ollie, "any of it. Why would she keep it a secret, keep them a secret, two entire humans, for so long? I think it can't have been good, whatever the reason was."

"What happened?" I asked the Pulliams. "Please say what happened next. Did she bring them home?"

Alice drooped sideways against the arm of the sofa, looking much older than the woman who had met us at the door. Her husband took her hand between his.

"We don't know," he said. "We never saw her again."

"She called us," said Alice. "She said she wouldn't be coming back to school. She couldn't tell us why, not just yet, but she hoped to be able to, soon. It wasn't her story to tell. She was loving, apologetic, but firm. Eleanor could be very firm. Disciplined beyond her years. She asked if we could have her things packed up and sent, even her sewing machine, which she knew wouldn't be easy. I offered to—I begged her to let us—drive it all down to her, but she said no. She said it very kindly, but she meant it. She told us she was fine, not to worry. And she said she loved us, but we knew that. We never doubted it. We did worry, despite her telling us not to, but back then, we thought we'd see her again before long."

Oh, Mom. How could you walk away from these good people? How could you leave them behind?

"About a month later, we got another letter. I tried to find it, but I couldn't. I'm sorry. I was upset, which is maybe why I didn't keep track of the letter. Joel and I talked about it yesterday, trying to piece together just what she'd said. You go ahead, Joel."

"She said she was getting married to B, moving to a new town. She said she hoped to finish school someday but didn't think it would be at Cadwallader. She thanked us, with very touching and beautiful language—Eleanor could write her personality into a letter so well—for our friendship, but she asked us not to get in touch. She said because of what had happened at the farm, she needed a clean slate, a fresh start. But she loved us and would love us forever. Chris and Kimmy, too. It felt like a final goodbye, which I guess it was. We were sad but not angry. We knew Eleanor. We never doubted that she had her reasons."

BEFORE WE LEFT, AS WE were standing on the Pulliams' front porch, Alice took my hand into her long and elegant one. The years had fallen off her again. There had been a moment in her living room when I'd almost regretted coming because it seemed that telling the story had broken her heart all over again. But in the mild early evening light, her eyes were bright and young. She looked happy.

She said, "It means so much to us to have met you two. Eleanor's daughters—imagine that! We understand you made a promise to your father, dear B, to not tell Eleanor you met us. But if there is ever a time when you decide you can, please say that Alice and Joel love her. Love her *big*. Tell her we never stopped for a single second. And say we would be over the moon, we would jump at the chance, to see her again."

WHEN WE GOT BACK TO our parents' house it was after eleven at night. My dad and Clive were in bed. Ollie and I didn't say much to each other; we'd barely spoken during the car ride home, both of us lost inside our own heads, feeling the afterglow and aftershocks, both, of the visit and of the story we'd been told. We turned off the lights my father had left on for us and went to bed. I couldn't sleep and was standing at my bookshelf, trying to decide which book might have the best chance of quieting my mind, when someone knocked at my door.

Ollie.

She held her laptop, open, in her hands, and from the expression on her face, I knew whatever she'd found inside it, it wasn't a happy ending. She sat heavily down in the armchair at the foot of my bed.

"I found just one mention of Bright Wind Farm," she said. "In an excerpt from a newspaper article in someone's PhD thesis on utopian communities. Only a few sentences, hardly any details. The events seem to have happened right around the time Mom was there or just after. The original source, an article from a local paper in rural Arkansas, would've been more reliable than this brief mention and might have contained more details. Ideally, we would get our information directly from that, but I couldn't find it online."

"Ollie, I understand you usually hold your research to more rigorous academic standards, but for Pete's sake, just tell me."

The words came out snippier than I'd intended. But Ollie seemed to take no notice.

"There was a police investigation into the commune at Bright Wind Farm over allegations surrounding the death of an infant. Apparently, the investigation didn't get far because somehow the residents got wind of it and abandoned the farm."

Ollie read from the screen: "'The commune dissolved, disappeared overnight, and Louise and Bill Haven, Bright Wind's founders, disappeared, too. Police said the place was gone as if it had never existed.'"

"Oh, God," I said. "Oh, no. An infant."

"We can't know for sure. There are no names in this excerpt. But it could explain what happened between Mom and Martha, why they fell out of each other's lives."

"The baby with the button nose and curly hair," I said. "I can't stand it if Martha ended up—"

"It could have been Jack," said Ollie. "But either way, I can't stand it."

AFTER OLLIE LEFT, I TURNED off the light and lay awake in the dark. I'd thrown out the idea of finding a book to read. No book in the world could quiet my mind that night. I lay there, grieving a child I'd never met, and I kept hearing in my head, over and over again, the line from my mother's letter to Alice: "I love her already. Already and for all time."

I knew what it was to fail to keep a child safe.

And I was haunted by another line, a phrase from the article.

"Gone as if it had never existed": the farm, the baby, the love between two sisters. All of it gone, gone, transformed into silence, into a story my mother would never tell.

THE NEXT DAY, OLLIE AND I hunkered down in our own separate cocoons (this is no time to tell me one cannot actually hunker in a cocoon) and dosed ourselves with tea and books and crossword puzzles like invalids. I told myself I was taking an intentional pause, a mini-staycation to meditate and practice self-compassion in the wake of all the recent revelations and before our mother's arrival home the following day. I am generally no fan of trendy lingo, but I employed all the self-care parlance I could think of to justify my position, while deep down knowing I was really only avoiding and indulging. In my defense, or to my regret, or maybe despite all my best efforts, or *something*, none of it worked. I thought about Eleanor and Martha, Martha and Jack, Martha and Lisa (oh, Lisa!) all day long.

That night, after everyone was in bed, I needed to run. I had spent so many hours steeping in the stories I'd been told that lines between other people's pasts and my present had gone fuzzy. I couldn't tell where stories ended and real life began. I was tired and wired and teeming with emotions and seeing ghosts. I missed my husband and my children, and I needed to tug cold air into my lungs and whack solid ground with my shoe soles and let the night stream by me on either side. So I put on my running clothes and a nifty knit watch cap with a built-in headlamp Teo had given me because he loved me and wanted me not to run headfirst into a tree.

I was standing in the kitchen, zipping up my jacket when I heard the sound of a car door slamming. One, two, three slams. I ran to the front door and what I found when I opened it wasn't stories, or letters, or the past, but the flushed and eager here and now, in sneakers and winter coats, with its hair in shapes that meant it had just been sleeping. Rose, solemn and hopeful. Simon, bouncing on the balls of his feet, all grins, dimples flashing.

My heart flung open its doors, and I gathered them into me. I put my arms all the way around them. Then, I lowered myself to the top step and sat and held them some more.

Chapter 14

ELEANOR

November 1965

Peg said it was the baby blues.

"Having a newborn in winter, a colicky one who doesn't like to sleep, in a place that doesn't yet feel like home. And with a father who's . . ."

"Oh, yes," Eleanor said. "I can think of a lot of words for what he is and not one of them is 'father.'"

Peg smiled at this, but Eleanor could feel her anger, an anger matching her own.

"Reluctant," finished Peg. "We'll go with 'reluctant.' Well, it's hard. And the hormones don't help a bit. But the dust will settle. Soon enough, Martha will have motherhood down pat."

Eleanor wanted to say it was more than just the baby blues. She considered telling Peg about Susan, how scared Martha was that she was simply wired wrong or had been corrupted by their childhood. More than scared, she was convinced, or almost. But Eleanor thought telling would be a betrayal. She worried it would color the way Peg saw Martha, would cause her to doubt her, and, if Martha stuck to her refusal to come home—she wouldn't, she couldn't, but if she did—Eleanor needed someone here with faith in her, someone to balance out Jack and his corrosive cruelty.

But maybe Peg was right. Eleanor believed she could see some life easing back into Martha, now that she had some relief from caring for Lisa, now that she was getting more sleep. Eleanor had not previously understood how lack of sleep could break a person down. She had been at the farm for five days and had stayed up with Lisa every night. Just five nights, but already she felt less steady, light-headed, and nearly constantly on the verge of tears. Martha had made her promise to stay at the farm for two weeks. But Eleanor hoped they'd leave before then, the three of them together. She wasn't sure how she would manage their escape, but if they had to walk every step of the way to the airport, if she had to carry them both on her back, she'd make sure they got away.

Eleanor had gone to dinner in the farmhouse just once after her first time and was grateful—both for her sake and for poor jealous Missy's—when, apart from an ostentatiously kind greeting from Louise, she was mostly ignored. The other nights, she stayed in the cabin with Lisa, and Martha brought dinner back for her to eat by lantern light in the rocker, or, on one especially warm night, by starlight at the communal wooden picnic table outside. Eleanor didn't believe Martha enjoyed the farmhouse dinners any more than she did, but some days, it was the only sustained time she had with Jack. Or not with him, because he hardly spoke to her, but in his presence. Martha drank up Jack's presence like a person dying of thirst.

But on the sixth night, because Martha and Peg had cooked the meal, Eleanor decided to eat at the farmhouse. She sternly reminded herself to avoid being drawn into conversation with the Havens. In her sleep-deprived, scattered state, she had no energy for argument, but mostly, she didn't want to be viewed as a threat by Missy, of whom she'd come to feel inordinately protective.

But when she sat down at the table, Missy's and Joe's seats were empty. Under her breath, Peg told her that Wren was sick, listless, coughing, refusing to nurse. At dinner the night before, Peg had instructed the couple to let her know if the symptoms worsened and to especially keep an eye on the baby's breathing, but Bill had overheard this and waved it away. "Missy, darling, it's a cold. Babies have gotten colds and recovered from them for centuries. Don't you worry." And Peg could tell Missy had taken the words as the gospel truth.

But at the end of dinner on Eleanor's sixth night, Joe arrived to ask for some food to bring back to the cabin. Martha was already in the kitchen, cleaning up, and Peg left the table to put a basket together for the boy. Eleanor could tell he was beside himself with worry. Faltering, he explained that the baby seemed sicker.

"Wrennie was born early, and the doctor told us her lungs might be weak. Missy's brothers have asthma, and she's seen what hard going it is for them. So she wants to be especially careful. If Wren gets worse, we might want to take her to the hospital."

Alarm flickered in Louise's eyes, and she seemed about to speak when Bill cut her off with a wave of his napkin.

"Son, the last place—and I mean the very last place—you want to take the child is to a hospital," he said. "The goal of hospitals is to keep people coming back to hospitals. Let the baby's natural immune system fight the illness, and I promise you she will be stronger for it."

"Yes, sir," said Joe, cheerfully. But when he turned to leave, Eleanor saw his smile drop from his face, as if it had been slapped away.

When he was sure Joe had gone, Bill said, in a conspiratorial tone, "Even when hospitals manage to keep people alive, they're not really well. Missy's younger brothers are a case in point, chronic invalids, it sounds like they are. Weak and bound to get weaker. It's often kinder to let nature take its course."

His meaning hit Eleanor like a blow. Horrified, she scanned the faces of the other people at the table, but Mitchie and Ted were nodding. Louise had dropped her gaze to her plate.

"Don't you agree, Louise," said Jack, sharply.

Louise straightened and looked him in the eye.

"Of course," she said, coolly.

"Wait. Surely you don't mean—" said Eleanor.

Louise cut her off.

"My husband can be a bit heedless when it comes to saying things no one likes to hear," she said, smooth as silk. "But science is science, Eleanor. Although I can see why you might not know about survival of the fittest. Perhaps Darwin is one of those unpalatable writers whose books your sweet little college chooses not to teach."

"Darwin only *describes* natural selection," said Eleanor, "he doesn't recommend it. No one with a heart would apply it to human beings."

"Oh, heart," said Louise. "I think listening to one's heart is actually quite admirable in young people. However, 'The heart has its reasons which reason knows nothing of.' And as you grow up, you'll find most adults prefer to base their decisions on reason."

Eleanor was much too tired for this sort of sparring, but she couldn't stand the patronizing smirk on Louise Haven's face.

"Finish the quotation," Eleanor said.

Louise flushed.

"Excuse me?"

"There's actually quite a lot more after that line, and obviously, there are some variations in the translations to English, but eventually Pascal gets to this: 'We know the truth not only by the reason, but by the heart.'"

She had to admire her own bravado, since Eleanor knew almost nothing about Pascal (although she vaguely recalled something about probability), but she'd once heard two classmates have a very similar argument in the dining hall, and the bit about truth, well, it had rung true for her. Luckily, she saw by the expression on Louise's face that she knew even less than Eleanor did.

Eleanor stood, tossed her napkin onto her plate, and walked out of the house. She considered leaving the door standing open, as Jack had done when he'd stomped out of the cabin, but she shut it noiselessly behind her. As soon as she'd run down the front steps, away from the house and into the yard, she burst into tears, clamping a hand over her mouth because she would be damned if she'd let Louise and Bill Haven hear her cry.

THAT NIGHT, AS IF SHE understood Eleanor was at the end of her rope, Lisa fell asleep quickly and also soundly enough so Eleanor could lay her on the bed and climb into it herself. So later, when the noise coming from the yard awakened her, Eleanor didn't wonder what the noise might be, but thought only, *For God's sake, the baby's sleeping!*

It was Martha who recognized the voices.

"It's Joe," she whispered, "arguing with Jack, and heaven help the boy because Jack sounds drunk. He can be a mean drunk."

He can be a mean everything, thought Eleanor. Aloud, she said, "I'm going out there."

"Please don't," said Martha. "It's better to stay out of the way when he's like this."

The baby woke with a start, eyes like saucers, and began to wail. Martha picked her up and pulled down the top of her nightgown to nurse her, and Eleanor got out of bed and opened the door to the cabin.

Joe said, "Please, just give me the keys, sir. It'll put Missy's mind at ease to take her in just to be sure she's okay. And, pardon my saying so, you're in no state to drive."

Joe was exhausted, hollow-eyed and gaunt, obviously desperate, but he was as polite and respectful as a schoolboy speaking to a teacher. Next to Jack, he looked terribly young and frail, so tired he was shaking. Eleanor thought he, too, looked in no state to drive.

"Don't you tell me what I'm in a state for," said Jack.

His voice was flat and dangerous. Eleanor noticed he held, by its slender neck, a half-full bottle of whiskey. Swinging the bottle, he started toward Joe, who stood his ground.

"I'll drive them," said Eleanor.

Her voice rang out in the darkness like a bell.

Jack spun around.

"You. Jesus Christ. Go the hell back to bed!"

He spit on the ground and then turned and began walking unsteadily toward the farmhouse. With his back to them, he shouted, "All of you go the hell back to bed!"

Joe looked as if he would run after Jack, but, instead, he began trudging away. Eleanor marveled at how he could give up so easily, could just take Jack's refusal as final and make his hangdog way back to his wife and sick baby. But immediately, she felt awful for judging him harshly. She couldn't know what he and Missy had come from, what tide had carried them here. They'd washed up like flotsam on the beach of Bright Wind. Louise and Bill, and by extension Jack (for Eleanor had come to understand that Jack ruled Bright Wind as surely as Bill Haven ever had, perhaps more), had scooped them up and artfully, cunningly, had turned their gratitude into a cage. Eleanor caught up with Joe and took him gently by the arm.

"It'll be okay, Joe," she said. "Come with me. We'll get Peg to look in on your Wren."

WHILE PEG WAS WITH JOE, Missy, and Wren in their cabin, Eleanor sat on the ground outside the door, leaning against the rough boards, waiting. She didn't have to wait long. In minutes, Peg flew out into the yard.

"It's bad," she said. "She's struggling to breathe. They're packing their bags. They may have to stay at the hospital overnight, possibly longer. Let's go."

Eleanor didn't ask where they were going, just scrambled up, and the two women ran together down the narrow road, their feet pounding the dirt, Peg looking to Eleanor like a bird in flight, with her bright shawl streaming out behind her. When they got to the porch of the farmhouse, Peg said, "Are you ready?"

In answer to her question, Eleanor began banging on the front door with both fists. A ghost of a smile passed over Peg's face, and she started shouting in rhythm to Eleanor's bangs.

"Open the damned door! Now! Now! Now!"

Louise yanked the door open so forcefully Eleanor nearly fell face-first into the house, but she caught herself in time. Louise's dark hair fell over her shoulders; she wore a white silk dressing gown. Eleanor could see Bill standing behind her, looking half-asleep and scratching his head.

"We need the car," said Eleanor.

"How dare you come pounding on my door, invading our privacy in the dead of night!" said Louise.

Suddenly, Jack was there, too, shirtless, his hair long and loose. He set a hand on Bill's shoulder.

"I'll handle these two," he said, and Bill nodded and shuffled off down the hallway.

"You'll handle us, will you?" said Eleanor. "I don't think so. You'll give us the damned keys is what you'll do."

Eleanor shoved her way past Louise and into the house, flipping the switch next to the door. The light in the hallway flared on, and in its glare, Louise looked suddenly old. Behind her, Jack stood as if frozen, rage in his eyes.

"I'll kill you," he said.

Eleanor hated him, hated him more than anyone, more even than she'd hated her mother; she hated his long, scrawny, eely chest and his stupid hair and his bullying, and her hatred made her calm.

"I've heard that before," she told him. "And she didn't kill me, either. Now, give me the keys so we can drive Joe, Missy, and their sick baby to the goddamned hospital."

"If you don't want that child to die right here in your utopia, Louise, you'll tell him to give us the keys," said Peg.

"Die?" said Louise, her eyes widening. "Wren?"

"She's full of shit," hissed Jack. "Only an idiot would listen to her."

Eleanor rested a hand on Louise's arm.

"Baby Wren is terribly sick, Louise," she said.

"Shut up," said Jack.

Louise's cheek twitched, and she stared down at the floor, her hair falling like curtains on either side of her face.

"She's struggling to breathe," said Eleanor. "She's running out of time."

Louise twitched her arm out of Eleanor's grasp but turned to Jack.

"Do it, Jack," she said.

"What the hell are you—" said Jack.

Louise walked up to him, slapped her two hands onto his chest, and shoved.

"Do it!"

Jack stood in the hallway, breathing hard, chest heaving, as if he'd been running; then, he took the car keys from his pocket, threw them onto the floor at Louise's feet, and left.

LATER, ELEANOR WOULD REMEMBER THE car ride the way she remembered dreams. Speed, skeletal trees, moonlight like milk on the road. Peg giving her directions from the back. Joe in the passenger seat. Missy's dull weeping. The baby's rasping breaths. Missy saying,

"Peg, was Louise very mad? About the hospital? Was she very mad?" and Joe's voice slicing through the car, saying, "Stop it, Miss. Louise can go to hell, do you hear me? They can all go straight to hell." His face when he said it—wide awake, as if a spell had been broken—was the clearest part, the only clear part of the ride.

SHE DIED. THEY HADN'T BEEN there half an hour, the four of them slumped in the brutal light of the hospital waiting room, when the doctor came to tell them she was dead. It's what seemed most unbelievable to Eleanor: how it hadn't taken any time at all, how an entire life could go out just like that, like a candle, how just like that, a baby who had been there, had *been*, wasn't there, or being, anymore.

"They'll pay," Joe said, rocking Missy in his arms. "They'll pay, they'll pay, they'll pay."

Missy and Joe weren't going back. Neither was Peg.

"But your loom," said Eleanor.

"I don't care," said Peg. "I can't go back. I think I'd commit murder if I did." When she hugged Eleanor goodbye, she said, "Get them away from him and take them home. Whatever you have to say or do."

"Yes," said Eleanor. "I will, I will, I will."

JUST AS ELEANOR TURNED THE car onto the dirt road, a figure slipped from the ruined shack with the tree through its roof and stood in the road waving its arms, caught in her headlights like a ghost. Eleanor slammed on the brakes harder than she'd needed to, her heart in her throat.

Martha.

Chapter 15

CORNELIA

FOR MY MONEY, THE ONLY experience more soul-lifting than watching a child you love cradle a bowl-size mug of hot chocolate between his two hands is watching him do it while also listening to him rattle off college basketball rankings and prognostications with such exuberance he barely remembers to sip his drink.

When I'd stepped back to let Simon and Rose run full tilt into their grandparents' house, I found myself face-to-face with Piper, and I saw right away she was in full queen bee mode, fiery and grand, able to smite mere humans with her eyes alone. I admired her in spite of myself, in spite of knowing I was almost certainly the human she would smite.

"It was time," she said. "High time. I know Teo is bringing them back next week for Christmas, but this could not wait a moment more. We will stay for the weekend."

"You could have told me you were coming," I said.

She tipped her head to one side, the points of her bob gleaming like scimitars in the porch light, and eyed me.

"Could I?" she said. "I really didn't know. I was not prepared for a conversation that would involve my talking you into being with your own children."

And she swept into the house, trailing clouds of indignation as she went.

MY KIDS, WITH CLIVE, WHO had woken up—everyone had woken up, Ollie grumpily, my father as gleeful as if he'd won the lottery—between them, sat at the kitchen table, slurping hot chocolate and eating fat slabs of the chocolate cake Thomas and Katie Hall had brought over the day before, eating with a gusto suggesting they'd never before seen chocolate or had been sweets-deprived for weeks. If Piper alone had been in charge of feeding Rose and Simon, this might almost have been true, but I knew Teo to be a dessert pushover from way back with a gargantuan sweet tooth of his own, and ever since he'd discovered Ghirardelli brownie mix, he'd been unstoppable, baking brownies at all hours and making them (by my purist baked goods standards) radically indigestible by throwing into the mix whatever struck his fancy in the moment: gummy worms, blueberries, whole Oreos, cornflakes, bananas, red hots, marshmallows, potato chips, spoonsful of strawberry jam, globs of peanut butter.

I sat across from my kids and feasted my eyes on them, sappily gulping back tears at the pure physical poetry of their hands cupping mugs. Simon was a torrent of energy and animation, talking not just basketball but football and Christmas and how his math teacher had leaned over and they'd all seen his butt crack and how Piper had driven over the speed limit practically the whole way there. Piper shot him a glare, but my boy wasn't fooled. He knows who adores him and how much, and Piper was elbowing me, Teo, and Rose for a place at the top of the list. But I, who recognize all his tells—the pitch of his voice turned up a manic notch, his hand tugging at the hair on the back of his head—knew, chocolate or no, he would crash soon. Rose, my wary, watchful, wise-owl Rose, hardly spoke at all, and her eyes never left my face.

IT WAS AFTER MIDNIGHT WHEN we all gave in and went to bed, Rose and Simon in the room they always slept in when they stayed here. But not an hour later, as if they'd intuited my heart's desire (which they frequently do), first one, then, ten minutes later, the other got into my bed, one on either side. They didn't say a word, just lay down and plunged, cannonballed straight into sleep. They smelled like soap.

Asleep, my children appear—and are as all sleeping children are—unbearably vulnerable. The old panic stirred, and I knew it would take flight inside me any minute like a flock of clacking crows. But then something happened: the panic didn't. I could feel it nearby, gleaming black and beady-eyed, but I ignored it, listening, for all I was worth, to the shushing, whisk-broom music, the lullaby of my children's breaths.

THE NEXT MORNING, I STAYED home with the kids while Ollie and B picked up my mother and brought her home. My son inhaled pancakes and told me how Piper's stepson Peter had faked being an adult, filled out an application, and adopted a dog on the internet, and how Piper had marched over to the shelter to give the workers there a piece of her mind and had marched back with not one but two dogs she called "a pair of ridiculous mangy mutts" even though they didn't have mange at all.

Rose said, "Maybe when you come home, we can get a dog."

I almost gave in to the temptation of promising her puppies to win back her trust, but I knew it would take much more than that.

"We might be able to," I said. "Hey, how did your social studies presentation go? The one you told me about."

"Good," said Rose. "Dad let me do it for him and gave me pointers, even though he used to be just the math homework guy."

"I could help with the next one," I said.

Rose shrugged.

"I guess we'll have to see," she said.

But then, not a half hour later, while I was arranging a vase of flowers, Rose came into the kitchen and said, "Hey, remember when we used to have dance parties?"

And this wasn't another reminder that I had abandoned her, because we hadn't had dance parties in at least two years. Back when Simon was in kindergarten and Rose was in second grade, mornings had become fraught: Simon, going through his brief picky-eater phase, living according to his own internal clock, which, in the mornings, ticked with glacial slowness, and insisting on tying his own shoes; Rose trying on multiple outfits and fretting endlessly over her hair, inciting me to worry about crippling self-consciousness and appearance-obsession and low self-esteem and anorexia because wasn't seven too young to care how you looked? One morning, out of sheer desperation, I plopped a new tradition smack into the middle of our mornings: the drop-everything-and-dance party. Five minutes of blaring music and crazy gyrations in the living room and we danced our blues and fears away and danced ourselves into people who liked each other again and who could get into the damned car and drive to school.

Now, in my parents' kitchen, I set down my scissors, left the rose-scattered countertop to fend for itself, and turned on the music.

We danced. Simon pogoing and head wagging like a punk rocker of old; Rose doing actual dance moves she'd learned online; me ball-rooming at warp speed with an imaginary partner. When the song ended, we played another one, and when we'd finished dancing, I said, "Rose, what a great idea you had," and Rose said, "Yup."

It wasn't all better. I wasn't deluded enough to think it was. But we—my girl and I—were inching closer.

WHEN MY MOTHER GOT HOME, I'd half expected fanfare and fire-works, a parade through the center of town, a choir of angels singing their heads off. Instead, my mother walked, of her own accord, into her house, and the house settled into place around her. A radiance descending, circling around, putting its arms around us all.

"She's like the jar in Tennessee," I said to Ollie.

"Here we go," said Ollie.

"You know, in the Wallace Stevens poem. This guy—I'm only guessing it was a guy—set a jar down on a hilltop in Tennessee, and as soon as he did, the wilderness surrounding the jar arranged itself around it and became orderly, harmonious, I guess you could say. I mean, that's how I read it anyway."

"This," said Ollie, "is why nobody likes you."

WE WOULD HAVE FED HER caviar and quail's eggs, manna from heaven or the nectar of the gods, but she wanted pizza from her favorite place. After we all ate, she shooed me, Piper, and Ollie out the back door so she and my father could have the kids to themselves. When I looked through the family room window, Clive was on one side of her, Rose was on the other, and Simon, wearing the vintage Ralph Sampson Virginia Cavaliers jersey my mother had scoured eBay for and given him for his birthday, sat on the floor at her feet, all of them downing popcorn by the fistful and engrossed in *The In-credibles*, except for my father, who sat in his armchair with wonder on his face, engrossed in all of them.

BECAUSE I TRUSTED—AND HAD TRUSTED, more than once—Piper with my life, I told her about our trip to visit Alice and Joel Pulliam.

And Ollie told her about what she'd found online, about the baby who had died. I worried Piper would say terrible things about Martha, but she didn't.

She said, "Here we are, working our brains out to make them safe, to keep out all the bad stuff. And God knows, there is so much bad stuff out there. But imagine if the danger weren't outside. Imagine if it were inside us."

I did not intend to say what I said next, the part of my story I hadn't told anyone, not Viviana in our drive back from my mother's hometown, not Teo, the part of my story so shameful, I had barely told it to myself.

"The danger did come from inside me," I said, "in the checkout line."

"Don't be ridiculous," snapped Piper. "Some thieving, degenerate lunatic threatened your children. That's about as far from your fault as it can be. You just went to a store."

"I went to a store; I shopped with my kids; and when I went to get into a line to check out, I noticed him. Everyone noticed him. He wore a black sweatshirt with the hood up and the sleeves cut off. His arms were covered with tattoos. He even had a tattoo on his face. Words. On his cheek. I don't know what they said. And he was jittery. Impatient."

"Like I said: degenerate," said Piper.

"No one was standing behind him. The place was packed, every single line was endless. But he had maybe two people in front of him and no one behind him. It was by far the shortest line in the store. And I felt bad no one wanted to stand behind him, just because of the way he looked. I felt bad *I* didn't want to. I told myself he could be a good person; good people come in all sorts of packages. And I, well, I just had to take a stand, didn't I? I had to stand up for some stupid, misguided principle, so, I got in line—I put my two children in line—behind him. And he wasn't a good person. He was the worst person imaginable."

After I finished confessing, after I'd dragged out and slapped this ugliest piece of my life down onto the universe's table, I didn't feel good, but I felt less disgusting to myself. *This is why they call it coming clean*, I thought.

Ollie said, "'Nobody expects the Spanish Inquisition.'"

Piper and I stared at her.

"It's a quote from a Monty Python skit," said Ollie.

We continued to stare.

"What? You think you're the only one who can spit out the movie quotes like a freaking slot machine, Cornelia?" said Ollie.

"She doesn't really do that so much anymore, the spitting," observed Piper.

"I don't?" I said. "Oh. I guess I don't."

"God, when I met you, it was nonstop whoever. Those Hepburn people. Kelly Lombard. Irene whatsit. Jerry Grant."

I laughed, which is what I knew Piper had intended.

"Audrey and Katharine. Carole Lombard. Irene Dunne. Cary Grant," I said, even though I knew she knew already.

"I knew the last one, actually," said Piper. "It's just such a ridiculous name for a man."

"His real name was Archibald Leach," I said.

"Well, of course it was," said Piper. "What else would it be? Out of the ridiculous frying pan, into the ridiculous fire. Anyway, you slowed down with the quote spitting after Rose was born. Because who has time for silver screen crap when someone is throwing up sour milk all over you every day."

"You know, I think you're right," I said.

"I am always right," said Piper.

"But back to the Spanish Inquisition," I said to Ollie.

"Edmund loves Monty Python. Laughs like a maniac at all their, what do you call them? Sketches? They have movies, too, I think. Anyway, all you really need to know is there's a scene where a guy is being questioned about something and he gets huffy and says, 'I didn't expect the Spanish Inquisition,' and then the door bursts open and three men in these red—I don't know—Inquisition robes, I guess, jump into the room and shout, 'Nobody expects the Spanish Inquisition!'"

"I'm having trouble connecting the dots between the Monty Python skit and my getting behind the crazed gunman in the checkout line," I said.

"Yes, well, it's not so much the skit itself. It's how we've come to use it in our family. Like a guy is driving and beeps at someone, and the person they beeped at goes nuts and runs them off the road. The guy who beeped is not to blame, even if he was mad and beeping a lot, because—"

"'Nobody expects the Spanish Inquisition,'" I said. "I think I get it. No one can be expected to expect the completely out-of-left-field terrible or crazy thing. Not even Piper."

"Piper might expect it more than most, but yes."

"I'm actually sitting right here," said Piper, raising her hand. "But even I see what you're saying. And I agree."

"It started because my friend Maria told me someone sent her teenaged daughter Allie a photo of Allie's boyfriend with another girl, and Allie broke up with him," said Ollie.

"As she should have!" said Piper.

What I thought was: *Ollie has friends and they get together and talk about their kids? Where was the Ollie I knew?* But I didn't say this.

"But then someone discovered that a boy who liked Allie himself had found online a picture of another guy with a girl, photoshopped the boyfriend's face onto it, and sent it out into the world. The boyfriend was mad at Allie for not trusting him and wouldn't get back together. I told the story to Edmund, and he said he thought the boyfriend should take the girl back because . . ."

She waved her hand in the air, filling in the punch line.

"Would you have gotten in line behind the tattoo-sleeve guy, Ollie?" I asked.

She thought about it.

"Probably. I don't really notice people," she said, sounding exactly like the Ollie I knew.

"Piper, you know you wouldn't have gotten into that line," I said.

"Oh, I could have. At that particular store, I get in Maggie's line, no matter who's in it, no matter how long it is. I try to only go when I know she'll be there—"

"You know her work schedule?" I said.

"One day, I asked her to give it to me. I would have preferred a paper copy, but she just told me, and I stood there and put it into my phone calendar, right away."

"That's not crazy," I said. "At all. I can't believe she gave it to you."

"'Nobody expects the Spanish Inquisition,'" said Ollie.

I laughed.

"*Anyway*," said Piper, "if Maggie's not there, it's Jeremiah's line all the way. Have anyone else check you out and you may as well smash your bread with your laundry detergent yourself before you even get in line, just to save them the trouble."

"Piper. You wouldn't have done it."

"Smashed the bread?" she said.

"He had a tattoo on his face," I said.

"Fine. You're right. I wouldn't have. And it's maybe the one example of how not being more like you is a good thing."

"I don't know," said Ollie. "I can probably come up with other examples. One or two."

· "You're generous," said Piper. "You give people the benefit of the doubt. You treat every person like a human being, blah blah blah. It's one of the reasons everybody likes you, for crying out loud. The goodwill you've stacked up for all these years outweighs by a ton the one time it backfired. How about all the yammering you do about forgiveness and love? Maybe put your money where your mouth is and show yourself a little of both?"

Before we went back inside the house, when Ollie had already stepped through the door, Piper pulled me aside and said, "I could not take them back tomorrow. Teo could work it out with the school. At their age, there's not much happening the last week before break."

When she said this, I felt the flock of crows who had been biding their black-feathered, sharp-beaked time begin to stir inside my chest.

I said, "You know, I think I'll just wait for Teo to bring them. I need to get my mother settled."

"Your mother looks pretty settled in there with her grandchildren all around her."

"Pipe."

"Okay. You're probably right."

I should have realized then. Piper saying I or anyone was probably right should've been a tipoff. But I was so guilt-ridden and relieved, I didn't pay attention.

THE NEXT MORNING, WHEN I woke up and slipped out from between my two sleeping children and went downstairs, Piper was gone.

My mother sat at the kitchen table, with a cup of coffee, the newspaper spread out before her.

"Piper's gone," I said.

"I thought maybe she was," said my mother.

"Did you see her go this morning?"

"No, and I've been up for quite a while. She must've hopped it in the dead of night. You have to admire her stealth," said my mother.

I sat down heavily in a chair next to her.

"She asked me if she should leave the kids instead of bringing them home this morning, and I said no."

My mother nodded and turned a page of the newspaper.

"Honey," she said, without looking up from the paper, "why do you think you've stayed here for so long? I have an idea or two about it, but I'd like to hear it from you."

"Well, you had your accident and—"

"Nope. That won't fly. We love you and are grateful for your help, but nope."

I groaned.

"There are a lot of hard-ass women in my life, do you know that?" I said. "And I don't use the word *hard-ass* lightly. In fact, I think I've never used it at all before now."

"No, I don't believe I've ever heard you. But getting back to my question . . ."

"See? Hard-assed. Persistent."

Gracefully, my mother turned another page of the newspaper.

"I didn't mean to stay away for so long," I said. "I didn't plan it. But then, I came and the days went by, and I really don't think—and I've thought about this quite a lot—I really don't think it was just avoidance."

My mother lifted her head and looked at me.

"When I was back home with them," I said, "it was always there. I'd be putting them to bed or talking to them about something normal, and it was always there in the room with us."

"The memory of that terrible man?" asked my mother. "What he did?"

I shook my head.

"No. I mean, yes, especially at first. I did keep seeing him pulling Simon away from me; I kept hearing his voice. But I mean me. What I did. What I didn't do. It was always there. So at home, I could never find the space or the quiet to make peace with what I'd done. But here, I could. I mean, it's taking a while, obviously, but I think I'm almost there."

My mother frowned.

"You? With what *you've* done? What do you mean?"

"Oh, come on, Mom. You know what I mean."

"Tell me."

"Do I actually need to spell this out for you?"

"Yes."

"I didn't keep them safe," I said flatly. "I am their mother. I am supposed to keep them safe from horrible things, but when the horrible thing arrived, I didn't."

I suppose I had expected sympathy, but my mother clucked her tongue in irritation.

"Keep them safe? So that's what mothers are supposed to do? Well, I'm sorry, but keeping them safe is impossible. Can't be done."

"But you did. You kept us safe. That's what motherhood is, the most basic part of the job description, and you did it."

"Oh, Cornelia."

She sounded even more irritated.

"Listen," she said, "motherhood is a phantom. No one wants to say this or hear it, but it's true. There is no such thing as motherhood. You can't fail at what doesn't exist, but you also can't succeed at it. So forget about it. Forget motherhood. It's a losing proposition."

She slapped the table gently and stood up.

"Those kids of yours—Clive, too—are going to wake up ravenous. It's not their fault. They're growing like weeds. But I think we should get moving on breakfast, don't you?"

Forget motherhood. It's a losing proposition.

A losing proposition?

I believed, I *knew*, because no way could she be talking about herself (who had ever won more at motherhood than my mother?), I knew she was talking about Martha.

MY FATHER, MY KIDS, CLIVE, and I were bringing the Christmas decorations down from the attic and up from the basement. It was evening. Earlier in the day, my father had taken Rose, Simon, and Clive to a local farm to chop down their own tree, and it sat in a corner of the family room, filling the house with its fragrance.

My mother sat on the sofa with Ollie, watching us as if we were a beautiful sight, a marvel.

My dad and I were in the middle of untangling the strands of lights and glass beads when Ollie said, "Mom, I need to ask this. I've been wondering for a long, long time, and I need to ask. Am I adopted?"

Clive and Simon had gone outside, but Rose was going through the box of tree ornaments, picking out her favorites, and I saw her go still.

My dad said, "Not now, Ollie."

"If I was adopted, I know it wasn't when I was a baby, because I remember my other family, what I think must have been my other family. A sister, older than me. I remember her, Mom. I know I do. She was real. So could you please tell me the truth?"

"That's it," said my dad. "Enough. She just got home."

"Dad!" said Ollie. "Enough is right. Enough with the secrets. This is my life we're talking about, not just yours and Mom's. I want to know."

My mother lifted her hand, as if to touch Ollie, but she was too far away.

"Oh, Ollie. I never knew you thought that, and I'm so sorry."

"Ellie," said my dad.

My mother seemed not to hear. She had eyes only for Ollie.

She said, "Honey, you weren't adopted. She was."

Chapter 16

CORNELIA

"ONCE, A LONG TIME AGO," said my mother, "I had a big sister, too."

"This can wait," said my father. "You're still getting your strength back."

She took his hand, pressed it to her cheek, and smiled up at him with as much open tenderness as I'd ever seen her display, her or anyone.

"It's fine, B," she said, "I want to. I don't know why, but since my accident, she has been more with me. Sometimes, in the rehab center, I'd wake up confused, and there she was, her voice inside my head, sharp and joking, laughing down the demons, like she used to do when we were kids. So I want to talk about Martha, now."

She said to us, her girls, Ollie, Rose, and me, "That was her name, Martha."

Ollie and I looked at each other, checking in to see if we should jump in to confess we'd been doing some investigating, but my father caught my eye and gave the slightest shake of his head. We would tell her, but we would listen first.

We listened.

They took care of each other, the sisters. They became a family of two.

"While we were living with our mother, we never told anyone what she did or what she was. At the time, we considered it a point of pride, but I see now how we were actually ashamed. We got very good at lying and even better at distracting people from the truth."

She looked wryly from me to Ollie. "I guess I stayed good at those things, although the person I was most desperate to distract was myself."

She told us how Martha got away from their mother, finally, and how, for a while, she'd fallen passionately in love with her life.

"I missed her so much I felt some days I couldn't breathe. But I never wished her back. How could I? She was soaring. She was living the life she had always deserved, on the edge of a lake as shining and deep as she was. I should have known it would take a big, beautiful, glittering place like that to contain my sister. But then—"

My mother stopped to pull her sweatshirt sleeve down over her fingers so she could dab at her suddenly brimming eyes.

"Back then, I didn't understand how it could have happened, how she could have given it all up for a man—his name was Jack; I never knew his last name—who wasn't fit to live in even the tiniest corner of her shadow. He wasn't just not good enough for her. He wasn't good at all. He was selfish and cruel and arrogant, and she just wrecked herself for him. It was like he reached out for her, and instantly, she collapsed herself small enough for him to put inside his hand.

"But now, I think I understand better. Men had never paid attention to her, and she had never seemed to care. I'd always thought it was because she was beyond them and she knew it. But she was a girl, and I think she'd wanted to be in love, just as most people want it. And when I think about it, she hadn't been loved enough, period, except by me. Our mother was a monster, of course. She loved no one. And Martha was always too caught up in taking care of me and keeping all our secrets to let anyone get close. People liked her, but she'd never had real friends. So I can see now why she fell so hard."

She lifted her chin and her face hardened.

"But I could have killed Jack. I wish someone had."

Then, she caught herself and laughed.

"With any luck, someone did. Who knows?"

She told us about how Martha had disappeared into Bright Wind, her letters getting shorter and less frequent, her radiant words dulling and petering out.

"So off I went to rescue her."

She told us about the farm. She told us about Peg and the Havens.

When she told us about the painting Martha had made for her—a cabin in the snow with the northern lights above it—my heart gave a leap.

Mostly, she told us about the baby. Lisa. I found myself holding my breath. Ollie's left knee was bobbing—a nervous tell I'd all but forgotten. We waited for the terrible news, the heart-shattering moment we knew would come.

But it never did.

What did happen was terrible, too, and shattered plenty of hearts, my mother's included. But it was another baby who died, and afterward, with the grief of Wren's parents still raw and echoing inside my mother's ears, my mother drove back to Bright Wind to get Martha and Lisa and bring them home with her.

When my mother described that part of the night—or it was early morning, really—so cast backward into the past was she, we watched her disappear. She wasn't seeing us, her family, wasn't sitting on her family room sofa in the house she'd inhabited for over forty years, wasn't even detectably sitting inside the body she'd inhabited for nearly seventy. She wasn't our mother at all, but Eleanor, standing in tree-filtered moonlight on a dirt road that snaked off into black-ness. Her sister, Martha, was there, too.

WHEN SHE SWITCHED OFF THE car and got out, the energy that had propelled her back toward Bright Wind to rescue Martha and Lisa deserted her. She sagged forward, her arms wrapped around her mid-dle, and Martha came, pulled her sister into her, and held on.

"She died," wailed Eleanor. "She was just a baby and she was all they had and she died anyway."

"Shh," said Martha, her hand on the back of Eleanor's head. "Shh, my love, my sweet girl," and, for an instant, they were the old Martha and Eleanor.

When Eleanor's sorrow quieted, Martha let go of her and ges-tured down the road toward the farm.

"You can't go back there," she said, "Jack is on a rampage, and Louise is stoking his fire the way she does."

"But—"

"Hush," said Martha. "Wait here."

She went into the ruined shack and came out cradling Lisa's sleep-ing basket, the one Missy had made for her, in her arms.

"Lisa can't stay here, not even for one night more," she said.

Relief whooshed through Eleanor like a spring rainstorm, fresh and clean.

"No, I know! I know. I came back for you both," she said.

Martha settled the basket on the ground. Moonlight landed softly on the baby's smooth cheek.

"Not me," said Martha. "I'm not leaving."

"You are," said Eleanor. "It's why I'm here, to bring you home. We'll take care of Lisa, you and I together."

"Oh, Eleanor, I would only end up hurting her."

"No. Never. Jack wants you to think that because he's horrible, but he's wrong. You are the best person I know. Kind and strong and gentle."

Martha took a step back, away from the basket on the ground.

"It's not Jack. It's me. I look at Lisa and feel nothing but fear. That's not right."

"Once we're together, away from here, everything will be different."

In frustration, Martha pulled her hair away from her pale face. This time, Eleanor couldn't see the bruises on her wrists, but she knew they were there. And when those faded, there would be more.

"Listen to me," said Martha. "Listen. You know what I realized tonight?"

She stabbed her own chest with her forefinger.

"I would have done the same as Missy and Joe. If Jack had told me not to take Lisa to the hospital, I would have obeyed. I would have waited until it was too late."

Her voice was harsh. Eleanor hated to hear anyone speak of Martha in a voice like that.

"No! No, no, no," said Eleanor. "You would have trusted your instincts."

Martha reeled away from her, her nightgown flaring. When she spoke next, she was almost shouting.

"I don't have any instincts! Not maternal ones and maybe not any of any kind anymore! That's what I'm trying to tell you."

Eleanor's arms fell to her sides. Martha wouldn't come. She wouldn't come, and Eleanor was going to have to take her child and leave her there.

Martha was talking.

"I have your bag and a bag for the baby. Take Jack's car, go to the airport, and fly home with the baby."

"How can I leave you, Martha?"

"Because you know it's the right thing. I can't be a mother."

"I will only leave if you promise you'll come as soon as you can, as soon as you feel like yourself again. You can't stay with Jack. He hurts you."

"Please, just go, Elsbee."

She put her arms around Eleanor, and the two of them clung to each other, and because Eleanor did not know how to let go, she waited for Martha to do it.

Martha didn't pick up her daughter or kiss her goodbye. She just leaned over, rubbed the back of her index finger down the hill of her cheek, and turned to go.

Walking away, she said, "Don't judge me too harshly if you can possibly help it."

"I love you. I don't judge you at all. Come home. Come home, soon."

Because there was nothing else to do, Eleanor lifted the basket and tucked it behind the passenger seat, then put the bags Martha had brought into the trunk of the car.

From behind the wheel, Eleanor saw Martha had begun to run down the dirt road. In a matter of seconds, the darkness absorbed her.

"I will see you soon," said Eleanor, and she started the car.

AND THEN ELEANOR WAS ELLIE again, our mother, her hands in her lap, one palm up, the other curled inside it like a nesting bird.

"I hadn't been back to our town since my mother's funeral and I'd sworn I was finished with it for good. But I didn't see how I could go back to my dormitory with an infant in tow."

"What did people in your town think when you showed up with a baby?" asked Ollie.

"Your dad and I had been an item for nearly a year—a story for another time. He'd been visiting me at college, which caused the gossip mongers to just about lose their minds. So people assumed I'd gotten pregnant and stayed away at college—or hopefully someplace worse—until the baby was born. They thought Lisa was our love child."

She spoke this last sentence in a funny, dramatic voice, but she also reached out instinctively toward my father, and he held her hand.

"And she was," he said.

"Of course she was," said my mother.

For a few seconds, they were the only two people in the room. Then, my mother turned to us.

"I'd phoned your dad from the airport to see if he could pick us up, and I didn't explain about the baby. It felt like days since I'd slept and the story was so long. He walked up and saw me there, looking a mess, I'm sure, like I'd been blown in by a hurricane, with a tiny, squalling baby in my arms. I wouldn't have blamed him if he'd done what a lot of men would have and run for the hills."

"Ha. Who are you kidding? You would've blamed me," said my dad.

She laughed. "I would have for sure. But I knew it wouldn't happen. I didn't know he'd do what he did, though."

"Which was what?" I asked.

"He walked up and asked me to marry him."

We stared at my father.

"You did that?" said Ollie. "When you didn't even know whose baby she was holding or why?"

My father shrugged. "I saw Eleanor standing there with a baby and I thought: B, there's your life."

We gave this the dazzled moment of silence it deserved, and then my mother began again.

"I was sure Martha would show up any day—" She broke off.

"Well, maybe I wasn't sure about *any day*, not entirely. She had post-partum depression. I see that now. But also, she believed growing up with our mother had twisted her into someone who should never have children. I knew she was wrong. She'd raised me, hadn't she? But when she was with Lisa, I could tell she didn't trust herself not to hurt her. She was terrified of it. And that evil, soulless *shithead* Jack fed her terror. Between him and the depression, my poor Martha was lost."

"Mom, do you want to stop for a while? Maybe pick up in the morning?" I said.

"Just because I said 'shithead' doesn't mean I'm coming unhinged, sweetheart."

My mother. Telling the tale of the heartbreak of her life and still funny.

A WEEK WENT BY. THEN, another. And Martha didn't come.

My mother put her mother's house on the market. My father bought a house two towns south, nearly an hour away, close enough for him to commute to work, far enough to feel they were leaving the wreckage of my mother's childhood and the mean and gleeful gossips of the town behind. The new house was white clapboard with a wide porch and a backyard perfect for a garden: large and level with bright open spots and also, in an ancient oak's wide skirt of shade, spots good for woodland plants like Virginia bluebells and astilbe and bleeding hearts. With the front windows open, you could smell the ocean.

One morning, Eleanor and B went to the justice of the peace and married. My mother held Lisa in her arms, grateful to have the baby there because she was herself and also because she was a piece of Martha.

They moved.

"I left my new phone number and address with the lawyer who'd set up Martha's trust, believing she'd call any day, any day. She didn't. We hadn't been in the new house two months when I found out I was pregnant with you, Ollie. Remember that day, B?"

"Yup. We put the radio on the kitchen windowsill and danced in the backyard with Lisa between us. Like lunatics."

"Happy lunatics."

My mother smiled at Ollie.

"You two. You were thick as thieves. The day I left for the hospital to have you, Lisa was thirteen months old and not quite walking. Still holding on to the furniture. But the day we brought you back, I was sitting on a chair with you in my lap, and she walked to see you. Just let go of the coffee table and sauntered on over. When she got to my chair, she held on to my knee with one hand and reached for you with the other. She set her fat little hand against your cheek, so gently and carefully, even though she was kind of a headlong, high-energy child most of the time. I said, 'Lisa, this is your sister, Olivia,' and she patted your cheek and said, 'LaLa.' And you were her LaLa from that moment on. LaLa and 'mine.' Those were the words she used for you. For those four years, I had almost no pictures of you by yourself because she was always right there."

Ollie sat very still, her expression private, turned inward. Then, she said, "You called us sisters?"

My mother tensed, and I saw my father turn his vigilance up a notch, his eyes never leaving her face. Slowly, my mother nodded.

"We didn't plan to. We hadn't discussed it at all, which I suppose would be unthinkable these days. The best I can explain it is we knew the truth when we saw it, and Lisa was your sister."

"You let me love her," said Ollie. She didn't sound angry or accusatory, not really, but my mother flushed.

"We couldn't have stopped either of you if we'd tried," she said. "But, no, we didn't try."

"We were in uncharted territory," said my father. "We were making it up as we went along. Not even making it up. We were just living, going with the flow, I guess. Doing our best."

My mother straightened.

"Listen, we didn't fall in love with her, because we loved her from the second we stood together in the airport: your father with his arms around us both. But she became our daughter. How could we stop it? She was this little baby girl, and we were the only people there. When she could talk, she called me 'Mama' because I could not stand for this beautiful child to think she didn't have one. But also it was true. A fact. She just was ours. We were a family. I don't see how I can apologize for a fact."

Her voice broke, and she shut her eyes, until her breath steadied.

"Apologize?" I said. "You two loved her. Who could ever think you should apologize? Who could possibly blame you? You *loved* her."

My mother looked at me and said, "My Cornelia, who thinks love is always reason enough."

Then, she told us who could blame them, could and had, possibly forever.

Martha came back.

"Your father got the job here in Charlottesville, and we were packing up to move. By then, there were three of you, of course. Three daughters. Lisa was five, ready to start school in our new town in the fall. I was packing plates into boxes, and your dad was upstairs giving you three a bath, putting you to bed. When he was home in the evenings, he always wanted to be the one to do bedtime. The doorbell rang, and I opened it. It was the first week of June, the very early edge of summer and one of those clear, pearly evenings with a delicate moon. I opened the door and Martha was standing on our porch. Just standing there with the porch light on her curly hair, and I couldn't speak. I just put my arms around her, and after a second, she hugged me back. I could have hung on to her all night, maybe partly because I was afraid, even then when we hadn't spoken a word, of what would happen next."

She sat, remembering, gathering strength to tell what happened next. When she spoke, it was very softly and in the dull tone of a person who just wants to get the telling over with. Rose sat on the floor, leaning against my legs, and I bent to drop a kiss on the top of her head, which was still damp and smelled like jasmine shampoo, and she caught the side of my face with her hand so she could whisper to me, "I worry this will be sad."

"It might be," I whispered. "So you don't have to stay if you don't want."

"But it's sad from a long time ago, right?"

I considered this. Some of the sad was almost certainly still here, with us in this room; some kinds of sad hold on forever.

"Well, I don't know, but all of this happened a long time ago. From when I was too little to remember it."

She nodded and stayed.

"Martha looked beautiful," my mother said. "Clear-eyed. Fit. Younger than when I'd seen her at the farm. Self-possessed. She was restless like a cat in a cage, nervous, and something else, too. Not exactly angry, not then. But sort of coiled, poised to react. I'd expected our reunion to be pure joy, but it was a very . . . complicated moment.

"She said, 'I know you must be dying to ask where I've been. And I do owe you an explanation.'

"I said, truthfully, 'I guess. But just now, I was just thinking how wonderful you look.'

"Martha looked surprised and then she softened.

"'Thank you. I suppose I am wonderful,' she said. 'It took me a long time, but I'm strong and healthy. I live in a good place; I'm working. I'm painting.'

"'What good place?' I asked her.

"Instead of answering the question, she said, 'And Jack is out of my life. He's been out of it for a long time. Getting him out of my head took longer. But the bastard is gone.'

"'Good,' I said. 'He was monstrous.'

"She agreed, but she blamed herself, too. She said she'd made choices and had done some awful things for him, even after she'd seen him for who he really was. She said she'd even gone to jail for a while because Jack stole from people, and she'd helped him get away with it. She said she was still working on letting go of the shame of that.

"I could tell she expected me to be ashamed of her, too, but I wasn't. I said, 'Did you think I would care about such a thing? I'm so glad you're here, Marthy. I've missed you so much.'

"Your father came down then, and Martha stared at him, suddenly flushed and wild-eyed. What is the reaction animals have when they're threatened?"

"Fight or flight," said Ollie.

"She was like a cornered animal, but it was all fight. I couldn't understand it. You see, in my head, she'd come home to stay. I had dreamed about her coming back over and over, for years, and I knew I would ask her to live with us. It would be hard, an adjustment, but I felt we could make it work. I'd gotten so used to this plan in my head, I assumed she'd want the same thing.

"Anyway, your father came down, and I introduced them, and he took a step toward her, to hug her maybe or at least shake her hand, but she backed away and said, 'Do you have children?' And my throat went dry as sandpaper. So your father said, 'Two girls,' which sounded terribly, terribly wrong to my ear, and I just felt filled with panic. I'll never forget it. Right then, I'd have chosen flight over fight. I'd have run upstairs and grabbed all three girls and taken off into the night.

"And then Martha seemed suddenly to notice the packing boxes and the bare walls, and she said, 'You're moving?' And I said yes, and she said, 'You weren't going to tell me?'

"I was going to. I meant to leave word with the lawyer, but I had forgotten. I would've remembered and done it right after we'd moved. But I could tell she didn't believe me.

"Then, she started asking for Lisa in a loud voice. And I automatically shushed her because it's what you do when you're the mother of bad sleepers. It's a habit. But it set her off. She started yelling, 'You're telling me to be quiet? Do you know how long I've waited to see her? My child? My daughter? Did you forget she was mine?'

"I shouldn't have said what I said next. I just got so scared. I lost it. I said, 'Did *you*? You left her for *five years*! You never wrote so much as a letter.' And it was as if I'd thrown gasoline onto a fire. She began shouting about how dare I judge her, how with my perfect life, the life she'd worked to give me, I couldn't know what she'd gone through.

"She said, 'You don't know how time can slip away when you're trying to rescue yourself! You wake up one day, finally whole enough to realize you're ready. And you know when that day was? Yesterday! I didn't waste a second.'

"And then—"

My mother pressed her hand to her mouth and shook her head.

"What happened?" said Ollie.

"Lisa," said my father, and I could tell he was back there, in the living room of our old house, seeing Lisa. "She'd come downstairs without us hearing, and she was standing at the entrance to the room in her flowered nightgown, her curls tangled around her face.

She looked dazed, the way kids do when they get startled awake, but also scared, and then she said, 'Mama?'"

"She was talking to me," said my mother. "Who else would she be talking to? And she ran over and buried her face in my legs. I looked at Martha's face, stunned and hurt and angry, and I knew—as well as I'd ever known anything—I knew we would lose her."

Almost silently, my mother began to cry, her shoulders rising and falling, and my dad got up and sat next to her, and took her in his arms, and her head dropped against his chest.

"I know," he said softly. "I know."

When my mother could speak, she said, "She took her. That night. I can't—I can't talk about it. But we moved here and, until Cam was born, everyone knew us as a family of four. I couldn't bear it. I wanted to die."

I felt Rose's hand wrap around my ankle and I kissed the top of her head again.

"Oh, Mom," I said.

"No, no, not the way you're thinking. I would never have left my family. Never in a million years. But I was in so much pain. I had lost them both. I could hardly stand to get out of bed some days, and it happened on and off for years. And you, Ollie, my sweet girl, you were heartbroken. I know very small children can grieve because we watched you do it.

"So one day, a dark, dark, rock-bottom day, I decided to take it and lock it away. Martha, Lisa, huge chunks of the first twenty years of my life. It was as if I'd torn pages out of a book. I know now it was very wrong, unhealthy. But then, God help me, it felt like I was saving myself, saving all of us. Your father didn't want to. He thought it was better just to go through it, to feel what we felt, and to carry it all with us. I just couldn't. Or I thought I couldn't. But I was wrong, and, Ollie, I know what I did hurt you. For a long time, I thought it hadn't. The bad dreams stopped; the questions about her dwindled and finally went away. But denying her left a hole in you, didn't it?"

Ollie said, "It's okay. I know now."

"I worry it's made it hard for you to let people in. Maybe especially the people in this family."

"Maybe," said Ollie. "Maybe I'm just—crotchety."

"But, listen, we're all still here," I said. "We can fix it now."

"I hope so," said my mother.

"And, Mom, what if we try to find them?" I said. "Martha and Lisa."

"Find Lisa," said my mother, looking dazed. "Well, I don't know."

"And Martha, too," I said. "Maybe those lawyers know where she is."

But I understood, as I said it, what must be coming, and it came.

"They did. They contacted me and told me. Close to twenty years ago now. It was cancer. My Martha has been gone for twenty years."

Chapter 17

CORNELIA

SHE WANTED ALL OF IT. Every carol and side dish; every permutation of pie and category of Christmas cookie; every sweets-riddled kid screeching and running around in circles; football on television and in the yard; *It's a Wonderful Life* in an endless loop; and the Whos singing their sweet nonsense words around their empty Christmas tree. She wanted both Christmas Eve and Christmas Day full-blown and riotous. She wanted everything. Every person, too. Every person *more*. So they all came: Cam and Niall; Toby and Jasper and Toby's new girlfriend, Anya; Teo's parents, Ingrid and Rudy; Viviana and Gordon; Dev and Clare, in love and duly radiant, trailing clouds of glory; Clare's step-grandfather, John Waterland; and my Teo, with his goldenness and his bottle-green eyes and his voice like the hum of my personal universe, walking into the house to quicken my pulse and steady my soul.

We let it carry us, the lovely, loving tumult of Christmas, a rushing, splashing current, a merry-go-round, the best kind of blur. Rampant, if frequently interrupted, storytelling; someone or other cooking in the kitchen at all hours; children loud and underfoot (even Clive screeching like a banshee); my brothers wrestling on the rug, playing catch with anything throwable, turning various people upside down and dangling them by their feet, teasing me without mercy. The blur and lightness were exactly what we all seemed to need, especially my mother, whose face could only be called rapt as she soaked in every second, but now and then in those two days, little moments floated up out of the breathless rush of sound and images, moments as clear and real as moments ever get.

Moment One:

Christmas Eve early, early morning. I woke up, not with gunfire smashing through my dreams, but at the sound of my son, my Simon, laughing in his sleep. I waited for his face to settle, gradually, like a pond with the ripples disappearing, then I went downstairs to find my mother already up and sitting in the dark kitchen. Her chair was turned toward the French doors that led out into the yard, a piece of pie and a cup of coffee—steaming, fragrant—on the table in front of her. When she heard me, she turned and whispered, "I dug into a pie ahead of schedule. What's that Toby used to say when I caught him out? 'Busted!'"

"I won't tell," I whispered back. "And we have a truly ludicrous number of pies."

In a normal voice, she said, "I think this is one of yours. Pumpkin cream with chocolate shavings on top."

"Ooh, yes, that's a good one."

"It's sheer heaven," she said. "Sitting here in my kitchen, with my pie, watching the light come up in my garden seems to me the best thing to have happened in the history of the world."

"To me, too," I said.

There was something about the grainy darkness inside and the lightening outside and the smell of coffee that made it easy to say things, so I said, "Mom, I have something to tell you, if it's okay."

"Oh, honey. Don't worry." She reached out and patted my hand. "Dad told me how you did some—research—into my life before you were born. Is that it?"

"I promise I was going to tell you. Right after you told us about Lisa, I was going to tell you everything. But he asked me to leave it to him."

"He thought I needed handling with special care," she said, smiling.

"And special care is his specialty, especially when it's you," I said. "I hope you aren't mad at me. I just almost lost you, and I wanted to know you."

I did not mention the northern lights or my solemn vow to search the world over and bring them to her. My mother seemed as replete and settled as I'd ever seen her, but I wasn't taking any chances. I'd learned a little about handling with care myself.

"Oh, gosh, no," she said, "I don't mind. There would've been a time not long ago when I think I would've minded quite a bit. But maybe it's what you said: I could have left you, without any of you ever knowing about Martha and Lisa, and how wrong that would have been. I know your father never would have told you; he'd have kept my secrets. It was long past time for the Martha and Lisa story to see the light of day."

"I've been learning myself that stories are always better off when you yank 'em out into the sunshine. I'm glad you're not mad. But I was going to tell you something else. May I?"

"Tell me anything. I'm feeling reckless." She laughed.

"I got a text last night from Alice Pulliam," I said. "Dad told you we met them?"

"Yes. My sweet friend Alice."

"The thing is, they want to come here, to drop by on Christmas Day, but Alice said they'd understand with all their hearts if you'd prefer they didn't."

"Oh."

Her silence stretched on and on, and I worried I'd made a mistake.

"I didn't do right by them," she said quietly. "I should have told them the truth from the very first: everything that happened at Bright Wind, how Martha sent me home with Lisa. They had earned my trust, and I should have trusted them with this. But her decision to hand Lisa over to me just felt so wrong, and I didn't want anyone to know she'd given away her own child. It felt like her secret, not mine, and I didn't want Alice and Joel or anyone to judge her harshly. To be honest, I wasn't even sure that what Martha had done was legal. I wanted so much to protect her."

"And you thought she would come back," I said.

"Yes, I didn't think I was saying goodbye to Alice and Joel forever. I thought Martha would come home and then I'd let Alice and Joel back into my life. But then years went by, and I suppose I didn't want anyone else in our lives to know Lisa wasn't really our baby. So I let the distance between me and the Pulliams grow and grow. And I didn't allow myself to think how this must have hurt them. All of which was wrong of me."

"Maybe. But they still love you. And they want to see you."

"But they live hours away," my mother said, confused. "Or have they moved?"

"They still live in the same town, in the same house as they did when you knew them."

Her face lit up.

"Oh, thank goodness! Inside my head, they have never left it, not in all these years, and look how they really haven't! It was a wonderful house, the first place in the world that felt like home to me. It wasn't a place anyone should ever move away from."

"They are spending Christmas Eve with relatives outside of Washington, D.C., and they are hoping to drop by here on their way home. But only if you're up for it."

She took a sip of her coffee, thinking, then said, bright-eyed,

"We've opened the door, haven't we? It was shut for so long, but we've opened it."

"Yes, we have."

"So there's only one thing to do."

"Open it wider and wider."

"As wide as it will go," she said happily. "We should just take the darned thing off its hinges and let everyone in."

Moment Two:

Just before we started to eat Christmas Eve dinner, just after Clare clinked her knife against her wineglass and the room went still, there was the sound of the front door opening, then footsteps, then Edmund Battle standing in our dining room with snow in his hair. Clive shouted "Daddy!" and ran at him like a linebacker, and Edmund scooped him up as if he weighed nothing at all. Edmund, tall and broad-shouldered and starkly handsome, brilliant, ever-confident Edmund, was nervous, his shy gaze moving from one face to the next, then settling on Ollie. He started to speak, then cleared his throat and tried again.

"I hope it's okay," he said.

We all watched her, her entire family's collective gaze boring into her, but I could tell Ollie didn't see any of us. She just sat staring at her husband, and tears filled her eyes, the eyes of my sister who never cried, and she started to nod, first slowly, then more emphatically, and Edmund blew out a sigh and said, "Phew!" And then Teo was up and slapping him on the shoulder before taking his coat; my father was heading to the storage room to get another chair, people were up and moving their plates to clear a space at the table; and I was rummaging in the china cabinet to set another place.

Moment Three:

When we'd all settled back into our seats, Clare clinked her knife against her wineglass again, and the room went still, or my family's version of still, which is full of rustling noise. Clare stood up, wineglass in hand, and said, "The first toast has to be to our magnificent, endlessly loved, lion-hearted, unsinkable Ellie Brown."

And everyone shouted, "Hear! Hear!" as my mother, all modesty, did her best Queen Elizabeth wave, before bestowing blown kisses upon us all.

And when the noise had settled into a simmer, Dev said, "And what about the second toast of the evening, Clare?"

"Oh, right. So, yesterday morning, while we were right in the middle of packing to come here—and I'm talking about I had my actual hands full of actual socks—Dev asked me a question—" She broke off, considering. "Not a question. Really, it was more like a dare."

"Definitely a dare," said Dev.

"You used the word 'dare,' so yes," said Clare. "'I double-dog dare you' I believe was the exact phrase. Words to melt any girl's heart."

"A question opens up the possibility of no," said Dev. "But when could Clare ever resist a dare?"

"Never," said Viviana.

"No!" scoffed Clare, rolling her pretty eyes, as if the word were the most ridiculous thing in the world.

Then Clare turned her back on us, fished around inside the pocket of her jeans, spun back around, lifted her long, slender left hand into the air, palm-side out, and, as we all held our breaths, flipped it, voilà-fashion, and I swear every bit of light from the big chandelier over the table swooped down upon her engagement ring and threw spangles over us all.

Moment Four:

Christmas morning, 9:00 a.m., all of us were up and up to our ankles in wrapping paper and ribbon, my parents the only ones not still in pajamas. Some of us were nursing coffees and mild hangovers from all the toasting at Christmas Eve dinner and the eggnog and hot toddies around the firepit afterward; some of us were practically climbing the walls, amped up on hot chocolate and Christmas; some of us were already cooking for another day of relentless eating, when Simon charged into the kitchen from the front hallway to bellow, "These two old people are standing at the front door!"

"Well, why don't you let them in?" said my mother.

"They didn't knock," said Simon. "Maybe they just want to stand there."

"Why would anyone want to just stand on the front steps?" said Teo.

"Who knows?" said Simon, shrugging dramatically, arms thrown out. "I don't even know them."

I growled at Simon, straightened my pajama top, and said, "I'll go."

It was Katie and Thomas Hall, dressed in smart winter coats, backed by morning sun, their white hair halo-bright, their faces bearing identical expressions of anxiety. Katie wore oven mitts on her hands and carried a pan of something gorgeous-smelling.

"Here's how it went," said Katie. "A few days ago, we'd finally scraped together the courage to come and meet your dear mother face-to-face, and then, at the eleventh hour—"

"We were actually on our way over," said Thomas.

"At the eleventh hour, as we were heading over, our courage failed us. I'm embarrassed to say it, but it's the truth. And then, last night, we decided we would not interrupt your Christmas this morning, but would drop off a little something, just leave it on your porch and send you a text message to let you know."

"We're heading to Baltimore to see our kids. Nice, clear day for it, too," said Thomas.

"And we were all set to do just exactly what we'd come to do, when the little boy spied us out one of the front-door sidelight windows, and, well, that threw a spanner of sorts into the works," she said.

"It seemed rude to leave, then, and maybe even sort of sneaky, just to slink away," said Thomas. "But also it seemed rude to knock on Christmas Day."

"And we can't deny it: we're nervous to see your mother," said Katie. "We've never caused injury to anyone before, and it's just a bit— I guess we don't know if we have the right to see her at all."

"So here you are," I said. "Standing on the front steps."

"Frozen in place," agreed Katie.

"That looks heavy," I said, "and it smells heavenly. Why don't you bring it on inside? I should warn you, it's utter chaos, and everyone is in pajamas."

My mother was perched on a kitchen counter stool, the jar in Tennessee, the still point around which everything turned, all the sprawling, talking, laughing, chasing, yelping that was her family. When she saw Katie and Thomas, she stood up and came from behind the counter to greet them.

"Mom, these are Thomas and Katie Hall. You remember I told you about them," I said carefully.

My father came over, gently took the pan from Katie, and set it on the counter.

"Merry Christmas to you both," he said.

My mother snapped her fingers.

"Oh, I know you," she said to Katie. "I've seen you in your front garden dozens of times. You've got the loveliest espaliered apple tree in your side yard, just the prettiest diamond pattern."

"Oh, yes," said Katie, her face brightening. "It's called a Belgian fence. Years ago, I took a series of classes on espaliering at Mount Lima, and I am just fascinated by the process."

"I really had to work at my magnolia against the garage wall," said my mother. "But I'm thrilled with how it's thrived. Haven't tried a fruit tree, though, but I would love to. Does it bear?"

And there they went: off into the leafy, blossoming, loamy, fragrant, fruit-bearing deep green thicket of gardening talk, a place where guilt and atonement and even forgiveness shake loose like dandelion silk and blow away. The rest of us, following their lead of not standing on ceremony even the tiniest bit, fell upon the pan of still-warm cinnamon rolls—cream cheese frosting!—like ravening wolves. Some of us, my husband and my brother Cam and even the famously fastidious Ollie Brown–Battle, did not even bother with plates.

Moment Five:

My mother was sitting in her garden, in one of the wrought iron chairs she'd pulled from the table into the center of the yard, when the Pulliams arrived. Despite her age and her tininess and her lack of natural insulation, perhaps because of her state of near-perpetual motion, she had never been bothered much by the cold, but in the days following her accident, I'd often caught her shivering. There were times, in the rehab center, when I'd seen her teeth actually chattering, and I'd wanted to fold every blanket I'd ever owned around her and then wrap her in my arms. Because I'd known that as soon as she got home, nothing in the world could keep her from going outside, even on the coldest days, I'd given her for Christmas one of those voluminous, full-length puffer coats, a sleeping bag of a coat, with a faux-fur trimmed hood. The sleeves came down over her fingertips, and the hem covered all but the toes of her shoes. She wore it now, hood up, and looked remarkably like the caterpillar in *Alice in Wonderland*, minus the hookah pipe and creepiness. At such moments, I could see how people might think of my mother as adorable (one of the nurses at the hospital had repeatedly called her "a cutie," which made me want to scream, until I discovered the nurse to be one of the kindest people I'd ever met), but I never could. To me, she was a force of nature, large and containing multitudes, more goddess than kitty cat, only adorable in as much as I adored her.

I carried over a chair and sat down next to her. The garden, so lush and rife with color much of the year, was run-down and rotting, a bloomless, black- and straw-colored wreckage of bent stems and moldering leaves.

"Does it make you sad to see it now, when it's all fallen to rack and ruin?"

My mother seemed surprised.

"Oh, no, not at all. For one thing, the dead stems and leaf litter are full of sleeping insects and egg sacs; they make good food for birds all winter, and in the spring, the rest of them will pop to life and the nuthatches and bluebirds will have a field day. The predatory bugs are in there, too, and I need them to gobble up the pests. I'm honored to give them safe harbor all winter. But also, it's got its own kind of elegance, don't you think? Such a privilege to see a thing through all its ages and temperaments."

You are freaking amazing, I wanted to tell her, but her shooing away the compliment would've broken the mood, so I sat silent for a minute, taking in the muted, ramshackle beauty of my mother's garden.

"They're here," I said softly. "Alice and Joel. Shall I bring them out?"

"Oh!" My mother pressed her gloved hand to her heart. "Yes, please do."

I HAD PLACED CHAIRS NEXT to my mother's, but when Alice Pulliam came out into the yard to see her friend Eleanor for the first time in fifty years, she sat in neither. Alice half ran to stand before my mother in her chair, then, painstakingly, got down on one knee before my mother, clasped my mother's hands between her own, and rested her cheek against them.

"Oh, my darling girl," said Alice, her voice choked with tears, "I have missed you every second."

"I am so sorry. I'm so sorry I disappeared. I missed you, too," said my mother.

She put her arms around Alice and leaned over until her forehead rested against Alice's head, and the two women sat curved into each other for what felt like minutes, before my mother laughed.

"Get up, you goose, and let me look at you!" she said, wiping away her tears.

Joel Pulliam, who'd been standing quietly to the side, allowing the two women their private reunion, his head bowed, his hands in his coat pockets, now stepped forward.

"You get up, too," he said to my mother. "And let me look at you."

My mother stood and spun around, grinning ear to ear. Joel caught hold of her two hands and held them.

"Eleanor Campbell," he said. "The only person who could run our children ragged. You sure played a mean game of tag."

My mother's eyes twinkled at him.

"Still do," she said.

"Well, of course you do," said Joel. "It was just yesterday, wasn't it?"

"Definitely yesterday," she said. "Oh, those summer nights. We'd run around in the yard till it got dark and the fireflies started to bubble up out of the grass. Remember that?"

"And you and the kids would watch bats. You'd slather them in citronella and the three of you would lie on your backs on the picnic blanket and watch the bats zip around for what seemed like hours," said Alice. "Chris still talks about it: you, Kimmy, the bats, and the smell of citronella."

My mother gasped and then said, "They remember me? They still talk about me?"

"Of course they do," said Alice. "Chris, especially. I'm not sure Kimmy has actual memories, not detailed memories. But she remembers the—" She turned to her husband. "What do I mean, Joel?"

"The gist of you," said Joel.

"Yes," said Alice. "The goodness of you."

My mother took her hands from Joel's and put them over her face.

"Even though I left them like I did," she said. "Left all of you. I'm so sorry. I should have at least explained."

Alice's arms went around my mother.

"Hey, now," said Joel, "none of that."

My mother took her hands away and wiped her eyes.

"I don't know why I didn't. I trusted you. You must not think I didn't trust you. I worried the story reflected poorly on Martha, and I felt especially protective, I guess, after seeing her so broken down. I was going to tell you when she came back, when she was back home with me and Lisa and B and the story had a happy ending, but she didn't come back, not for years."

Alice stared at my mother.

"Lisa?"

"Oh, listen to me go on, when you can have no idea what I'm talking about," said my mother. "I should tell you everything. I want to."

"And we want to hear everything," said Alice. "Honestly, I'm dying to hear and I know Joel is, too. But it's Christmas, and we don't want to keep you from your family any longer."

"You're not going?" said my mother.

"No!" said Alice. "Wild horses couldn't drag us away, at least not for an hour or two. We want to meet your family, and Joel was eyeing the pie, as he does. But let's save the story for next time."

"Which better be soon," said Joel. "This had better be just the beginning."

My mother smiled and said, "I was thinking precisely the same thing."

"Now," said Alice, taking my mother's hand, "let's go inside. We've got a few surprises for you."

When we walked out of the sleeping garden into the house, the house seemed louder and jollier and more crowded than ever. And it *was* more crowded: because folded into the fray, as naturally as if they'd been there all along, were Chris and Kimmy and their spouses and their children. And never, if I live to be a thousand, will I forget my mother's face when she saw them.

Moment Six:

Late Christmas night, the dishes done, my parents and the children in bed—Simon and Rose having a sleepover in their room with Clive and Jasper—Ollie and Edmund in the small, book-lined den off the front hallway talking and talking about what I hoped was their future together, Cam, Niall, Toby, and Anya playing a marathon game of Monopoly at the kitchen table, Teo and I stole an hour alone by the firepit.

"What a day," said Teo. "You did a very cool thing, bringing the Pulliams back to your mom."

"Yes, I think so. I just— I wish she'd never lost them. If I ruled the world, people who love each other would always keep each other. Keeping would be the top of my list of rules."

"You *should* rule the world. Actually, I think I always thought you did."

"Sometimes, we lose people. We can't help it. But if we can possibly help it, I think we should hold on like snapping turtles."

"Yeah, but I can see how it happened. She thought it would be temporary, and then, life just carried her. Marriage and babies. And then she lost Lisa and thought she had to sever all ties with the past just to live with the loss. Who knows? Maybe she did. Maybe it was the only way."

"I understand how cutting loose and leaving can feel like saving ourselves, but I don't believe it really works," I said. "I think it doesn't."

A faraway train horn filled the dark yard with its chime-and-fade, chime-and-fade harmonica song. When it ended, the only sound was the fire snapping and purring.

"Teo, I need to tell you something," I said, "a thing I just recently realized. I'd say it counts as an epiphany except it wasn't really sudden. Do epiphanies have to be sudden?"

"Are there rules about epiphanies?"

"I think there might be. But they aren't my rules. Anyway, can I tell you about it?"

I shivered and stretched my open hands toward the flames. Teo stoked the glowing coals, then reached for more logs and added them to the fire.

"Tell me anything," he said as the flames curled around the logs and caught, and I thought how this was the essential Teo, beautiful under the sky, keeping me warm, saying *tell me anything* and meaning it.

"Okay. So. When the terrible thing happened to Simon, to Simon and to Rose, too—"

"And to you," said Teo.

"Yes, to me, too. But when it happened to Simon and Rose, I felt so wretched, felt such rock-bottom despair because I hadn't kept them safe. I got lost in those feelings. I lost myself."

The light from the fire was wavering and amber, and in it, Teo's face was inscrutable and crossed with shadows.

"But here's what I realized, what Viviana and my mother and Martha and Ollie and Piper and Thomas Hall and all these days I've been living again in my parents' house and you and Rose and Simon—maybe especially Rose and Simon—have taught me: I didn't keep them safe that day in the checkout line, but—and here's the thing—" I leaned forward, toward my beloved man, with the fire between us, my elbows on my knees. "I never did keep them safe. I never had."

Teo looked confused and started to speak, probably to tell me I was wrong, but I said, "Wait."

"Okay," said Teo.

"I tried. I loved them—the very bones of them—with every single bit of me, and I wanted more than anything to keep them safe. And I tried. But—and this is the thing I just came to understand—every time they were safe, for all those days and years before the checkout line, every time they went to school or rode in a car or rode their bikes down the street or kicked a ball or ate a meal or caught a cold or danced in the living room with me or waited in a checkout line with me, danger was right there, brushing past them, parting to let them by, or swerving away just in time. It was right there. But before the checkout line day, they were safe, and I helped, you helped, we did our best, but mostly it was pure grace. Luck. We do what we can, but luck tips the scales in the end. Every time they were ever safe, they could just as easily have not been. Do you see what I mean?"

"I think maybe I do," said Teo. "I think I almost get it. But are you saying this is comforting?"

"Not comforting, exactly. But clarifying. And humbling. How arrogant to believe we are in control of what happens to the people we love, good or bad, when there's this giant, teeming universe of forces at work out there: biology, society, economics, physics, grief, greed, the Spanish Inquisition, meanness, illness, drugs, love, weather, accidents, randomness. Do you see what I mean?"

Slowly, Teo nodded. "I do. I mean, I have some questions about an item or two on that list. But I do get it."

"It doesn't mean we're off the hook. If we are horribly selfish, if we deliberately hurt people, we fail. But our only job is to do our best to love the people who are ours to love. It's a big thing to be on the hook for, a huge thing, but if we do our best at it, we're doing okay."

"You do your best," said Teo. "You are really, really good at loving people, especially us."

"Thank you," I said.

"But—" said Teo.

Teo began poking the fire again, hunching over, really focusing on it, and I tried to see his eyes and couldn't—he had his face turned deliberately downward—but what I saw instead was how much— despite all his patience—how much pain I'd caused him by leaving him alone for so long.

"I'm not an expert on epiphanies," he said, "but I wish we could have tried to get to this one together. I bet we could have. It was hard, having you gone, hard for Rose and Simon and me."

"I'm sorry," I said. "I should have asked you for help. Even if I had to get away for a while to figure things out, we should have made that decision together."

"We should have been together more throughout this whole thing," he said. "That's how we do things."

"I know."

We sat for a moment, watching the fire, and then Teo looked at me, with an uncertain smile that hurt my heart.

"So in light of this epiphany," he said, "however gradual and possibly atypical it was, what's next?"

I recognized this as the million-dollar question it was, and, although the Adirondack chair I sat in was heavy and firmly planted on the ground, I was up out of it so fast, I almost sent it flying. I walked behind Teo's chair, put my arms around him, and pressed my lips to the side of his neck.

"Next, I go home with you and Simon and Rose," I told him. "I pack up and I go home and I stay forever."

Final Tiny Moment:

I was in the bathroom putting on face cream, when the door opened and my mother came in. Her cheeks were flushed, her eyes wide open, dilated, hectic; she was tense and trembling, and in a split second, time accordioned, and I was back in the rehab center, where she was frail and fervent, delirious and pleading, sundowning. Fear struck, and I turned to face her, to face whatever was about to happen.

But then she took a breath, a sharp in and out, and I saw she was only excited, on fire with urgency, and she said, "I want us to go see her. I know you'll say it's too soon for me to travel, but if the accident taught me anything, it's that there is not a moment to lose. So we need to find her and ask her if we can come, and then, Cornelia, right away, as soon as we can, I want to go to wherever she is."

Chapter 18

CORNELIA

MY MOTHER ASKED THE DRIVER to take the scenic route, and, almost before the words were out of her mouth, Ollie was leaping in to agree: *We're here, so we should see as much as we can, because you're right, it's scenic inasmuch as it's known for the scenery and the lake and the wildlife, et cetera, and anyway, there's plenty of time, she said anytime this afternoon, she'll be ready whenever, "ready when you are" were her exact words, right, Cornelia, so obviously we're fine, we've got plenty of time . . .*

"Sure," said Kaki Corliss, the driver, when Ollie paused to catch her breath. Kaki appeared unbothered by my sister's manic tumble of words, her highly uncharacteristic volubility. Of course, she didn't know the volubility was highly uncharacteristic, but even if she had, I believe she would have been unbothered. If an immense sinkhole had yawned open in the road before her and frogs had begun plummeting from the sky, she would have remained unbothered. Behind her black Wayfarers, as she navigated traffic and icy patches and blinding, sunlit-snow-flanked roads, she radiated the sort of ancient peace usually reserved for tortoises or giant redwoods. Ollie spouting gibberish would not flap the unflappable Kaki, but I wasn't Kaki, not even close, and because Ollie was starting to freak me out, I turned around to check on her.

Ollie and my mother sat together in the backseat, their faces pale in the blue snow-light coming in through the windows, my mother studiously staring out one window, Ollie studiously staring out the other, so it was almost as if they hadn't noticed that, across the gap in the seat between them, they were holding hands.

IT HAD BEEN EASY TO find her. My mother had simply contacted the law firm that had handled first her father's estate and then her mother's. The lawyer she spoke to wouldn't give her Lisa's current address, but she did agree to pass my mother's contact information along to Lisa, and, two days later, Lisa sent this email:

Thank you for getting in touch, and, yes, my family and I would welcome a visit from you and your daughters. We would be happy to show you my mother's studio, too, if you like. My husband and I own and run a resort, a log lodge plus some cabins, right on a lake. It's very pretty, even in winter, and we hope you'll consider staying here when you come, free of charge, of course.

The minute she got the email, my mother called to tell me. She spoke in bright, adrenaline-fueled, staccato bursts, and I knew I should have been overjoyed at how easy it had all been. Certainly, I was happy. More than happy, I could have wept with relief. When my mother had told me she'd sent Lisa the email, I'd regretted instantly not having offered to do it for her because the thought of her waiting—tiny, taut, and fragile, her eyes huge and frantic the way they'd been when she knocked on the door of the bathroom on Christmas night—frightened me. I pictured her on pins and needles, not sleeping, waiting for their landline to ring, checking and rechecking her email, her cell phone, with, all the while, Lisa's possible rejection dangling above her, ready to come crashing down. And it was a short and awful jump to remembering her as she'd been weeks ago, asking for the northern lights, all her agitated longing, her hands clutching the edge of her blanket. When I phoned my father to check on her, he sounded more worried than he had since she'd left the hospital.

"She's not eating much, can't sleep. And what if Lisa doesn't respond at all?" he said. "I don't know what will happen to her then. Ollie, too. She's called four times already, checking."

"She'll respond," I told him. "If she doesn't, we won't let it go. I will march right up to her door, wherever the hell her door may be. But she'll respond. She has to."

So when she did, and so quickly, scarcely forty-eight hours later, I should have been overjoyed. But sadness cast its shadow over all of it, not sadness at Lisa having emailed back, but at how easy it had been, how the knowledge of Lisa's whereabouts had been so close all along, so within reach, so discoverable.

"What a waste," I said to Teo. "She could have found her years ago. She could have found Martha."

"Maybe she couldn't, though," said Teo. "Maybe she wasn't ready. I know what you mean, and I don't disagree. But maybe she was too afraid."

"Maybe," I said. "I know a thing or two about fear. Fear can throw you for a loop. It can stop you dead in your tracks."

Then, I had a thought.

"But you know what? She's not stopped in her tracks, now."

"Nope," said Teo.

"Yes, she could have found Lisa years ago, but also, she could never have found her. She could have chosen to never even look."

"She looked," said Teo.

She had. My mother had looked and found and would fly all the way to the top of the country, and Ollie and I would go with her.

When I looked at Lisa's Minnesota town on the map, I found it was just eighteen miles south of the one Martha had moved to all those years ago, her heart's home, her world of spiky trees and water and wild light.

THE DAY AFTER CHRISTMAS, AS her children—including her younger daughter Cornelia, the lingerer, the hanger-on—and grandchildren had been packing and readying themselves to head to their respective homes, my mother had asked my father for a stepladder.

"I know what you've got in mind," he'd said sternly, "and I'll bring the stepladder, but you will not be standing on it."

She'd eyed him, considering whether or not to stand her ground. She shrugged.

"Fine," she'd said. "Then, you'll have to."

I'D BEEN IN THE ATTIC, putting away Christmas decorations. My parents would leave the tree and the outside lights up until New Year's Day, but I'd taken down and boxed up most everything else. Oddly, it was a task I loved, dismantling, folding, unhooking, wrapping in bubble wrap, putting away, bringing the house back to its daily self. Because its daily self was good. To my way of thinking, the only thing better than a good house during the holidays is a good house every other day. I couldn't wait to get back to my own, to my own sweet and holy normal.

I had heard the attic stairs creak and first my mother had appeared, then, a step behind her, Ollie. My mother carried a shoebox, rose-pink, held closed with a rubber band. I moved some boxes from the top of an old steamer trunk so she could sit.

"Martha's letters," said my mother, her eyes shining. "Your father got them down for me."

We'd read them together, out loud, taking turns, and when we'd finished, I told my mother how the last time I'd been in the attic, I'd been searching.

"For you, I guess," I told my mother. "I found the two dresses and the blanket and the book, the way I told you. But what I'd pictured was finding a box of light. I imagined opening it. I imagined the light leaping out and throwing itself all around the room."

"Well, that's a normal expectation," said Ollie. "Not weird at all."

"Okay, but here it is happening," I said, "because, oh, these letters. These letters and this *person*. I'm just—I'm enraptured. She spins light out of words."

"True," said Ollie.

"She had so many gifts, my Marthy," my mother had said, closing the box. "She could make something breathtaking out of anything or out of nothing at all. Her paintings, they were as alive as people."

ICE.

Ice like no ice we had ever seen. Ice draped over every rock and surface, ice humped, ice fluted, ice bubbled, ice fringed along its hem like a curtain, ice in edgy, slick shards like a giant broken plate.

Kaki had taken us down a scenic offshoot of the scenic byway and parked, and we stood at the edge of the seemingly infinite lake, staring at ice. Kaki stood with her arms crossed, her legs wide apart, her boots firmly planted on the snow. Outside her car, she was still unflappable, but she was also proprietary, commanding, magnificent.

"It's Narnia," I said, breathless.

"Oh, brother," said Ollie, rolling her eyes. "Always with the Narnia."

"We get Narnia a lot," said Kaki.

I stuck out my tongue at Ollie.

"We get Narnia. We get *Frozen*. We get *The Shining*, minus the horror. We get the ice planet Hoth. We get any number of Christmas shows, of course," said Kaki.

"'Santa Claus Is Coming to Town,'" I said, "'Frosty the Snowman.'"

"You cried at the melting scene every single year," said my mother.

"We all did," said Kaki. "We get wedding cake. We get cottage cheese, which I can't say I see myself. We get meringue. One woman even made the leap to pavlova. 'It's like standing on a ginormous pavlova' she said."

"Standing on a ginormous ballerina?" said Ollie, blinking. "What?"

That Ollie would display even the tiniest bit of bafflement while demonstrating at least a working knowledge of Russian ballet while also saying, aloud, for what I would bet money was the first time in her life, the word *ginormous*, seemed further evidence, as if we needed any, that we had flown across the country and landed, smack, in an alien world.

"Dessert," said Kaki. "Don't feel bad. I had to google it myself. We get hot tub, if you can believe it."

"Hot tub?" said my mother.

"Because of the sea smoke, which isn't occurring just now."

We stood a few minutes more, wondering, each inside her own silence, at the dazzling kingdom of ice, the wealth of metaphors it inspired, the concept of sea smoke. The air we breathed crackled inside our chests, and ghosted from our mouths, and put roses in our cheeks.

Kaki clapped her hands.

"Should we get back to the car now, ladies?" she said. "We're almost to the lodge."

At this, I saw my mother and sister startle, stiffen, lock eyes.

"Oh," said Ollie. "Maybe we can stay a few more minutes?"

"Yes, maybe just a little while more?" said my mother, although her teeth were beginning to chatter.

It'll be okay, I wanted to tell them. *She'll know you; she'll remember you; she'll embrace you; everything will unfold exactly the way you want it to; I just know it.*

But I didn't know it. All I had to go on was a lone email, one I'd sat with for a long time after my mother had forwarded it to me. I'd sat with it, and then, I'd shown it to Teo.

"How does this strike you?" I'd asked him. "Tonally."

He'd read the email and said, "Guarded? Even a little cold?"

"She feels sort of—absent, doesn't she? Maybe because there's not even one sentence starting with 'I.'"

"You're right. Like she's a corporation, the corporate 'we.' The email seems businesslike. And she ends with 'free of charge.' Ouch."

"She signed it 'Best, Lisa Dyer-Fellows.' Best? And her last name? That hyphen somehow sticks like a, I don't know, a staple in my soul. Because, Teo, they can't get their hearts broken," I said. "They just can't."

"Well, look, she invited them to come. It'll be okay."

But I knew Ollie and my mother wanted much more than okay. They wanted deep recognition, immediate connection. They wanted voids to fill in and years to vanish. They wanted love. They wanted magic.

So, standing in the snow, in that everywhere of ice, I couldn't promise them they'd get what they wanted, so I just said, softly, to the woman shaking inside her black caterpillar coat, "You've come so far. You've come all this way."

My mother reached out and grabbed Ollie's hand.

"It's time, darlings," she said. "It's time to go."

THE LODGE WAS A LONG, low structure built out of honey-colored logs. A gray ribbon of smoke uncurled out of its stone chimney. I

could imagine the wide, now bare porch in spring, scattered with
bentwood rockers and unpainted Adirondack chairs, with tables covered in checkerboards and iced tea glasses and Mason jars full of
wildflowers. In summer, the lake would bloom with colorful kayaks,
green and red canoes. Now, the lodge rested easy in the snow, bare
and welcoming.

Let us be welcomed, I thought, *please,* and I opened the big green
door. The huge room was resplendent in the sunlight, all golden-
brown wood and windows, comfortable furniture, a great stone fireplace. A dark-haired girl sat at the desk, her head bent over a book.

When she saw us, she stood and said, "Hey, there. You're here!"

Then, she peered at us.

"I mean, you are here, right?"

She shook her head, setting her curls in motion, and waved her
hand, erasing what she'd just said; she couldn't have been more than
seventeen.

"Nope, what I mean is you're *you*, right? Because obviously, you're
here."

"We are," said my mother, her eyes twinkling, "we are us."

"Phew!" said the girl. "I'm Amelia. Let me text Mom. She's back in
the office, working. I could shout, but she'll yell at me."

Amelia. Lisa's daughter. Martha's granddaughter. I felt my mother
standing very, very still beside me.

"Better text then," I said, smiling at Amelia.

"Actually, she probably wouldn't yell in front of you guys, at least
not so soon after you got here. But why risk it, right? I'll text. Please
have a seat, make yourselves comfy."

We did sit, but I can't say there was much comfort involved. My
mother and Ollie sat together, twitchy as cats, on the sofa, jittering
their knees. Ollie thrummed her fingers against the seat cushion, and
my mother reached out automatically and covered her hand with

hers. Ever since my mother had told us about Martha and Lisa, thus giving Ollie's vague but unshakable, nearly lifelong, piece of emptiness a shape and a name, something new and tender had grown up between my mother and Ollie. They touched more, and my father had told me Ollie had taken to calling my mother once a day, which meant that in the two weeks since we'd all left my parents' house, she'd called more times than she had in two years. Two years? Three. Possibly four.

Ollie had texted even me, not once, not twice, but three times, once to tell me she was going back to work in the lab, and then two more times to clarify that my conversation with her about going back to work in the lab had in no way influenced her decision to go back to work in the lab. Still, my sister of the hard heart and icy disposition was softening and melting with time-lapse speed, and while I'd been waiting since forever for her to show some vulnerability, right now, as we awaited Lisa's arrival, as the possible dashing or coming to fruition of decades' worth of hopes and longings stood just on the other side of a door, I would've given my eyeteeth to see at least a glimpse of the caustic sister of days gone by.

"So hold on," I said. "Is Amelia our second cousin? Or is it first cousin once removed? Or, hell, is it second cousin once removed? You know what I suspect the answer is? Nobody knows. Nobody in the history of the world, including the history of genealogy and—what do you call it—consanguinity, if such an unspellable, unpronounceable thing can have a history, knows. The entire cousin-tracking business is just a conspiracy to make us all feel stupid."

I waited to see if Ollie would take the bait, because if there is one thing Ollie wants everyone to know it's that she knows everything about something about which everyone else knows nothing. For a few bone-chilling seconds there, I thought maybe caustic, omniscient Ollie might be lost for good, but then she stopped knee-jiggling,

looked me dead in the eye, and said, "The degree indicates the min-
imum number of generations between both cousins and the nearest
common ancestor, minus one. The remove indicates the number of
generations, if any, separating the two cousins from each other."

"Ah. Got it," I said.

"Oh, good. So I'm sure you know the number and degree of Amelia's cousinship, now," she said, in a tone suggesting I knew no such
thing and never, if I lived to be a hundred, would, which may have
been accurate but was also infuriatingly smug. But I wasn't infuri-
ated. I wanted to hug her and not only—or even chiefly—because I
knew it would annoy her.

My mother and Ollie were facing the reception desk and the door
next to it, which I assumed led to the office and through which Lisa
would walk, through that door, right out of my mother's story and
into our lives. They faced the door, and I faced them, my mother and
sister, an arrangement holding metaphorical significance, because
while I was eager to meet Lisa, I harbored no personal memories of
her, despite having, once I'd learned of her existence, rifled through
my memory bank more than once. I did not even seem to have hid-
den away in some dusty memory drawer what Joel Pulliam had described, poetically I thought, as the "gist" of her. I'd been two when
she'd left. I did not have an emotional horse in this race, apart from
the two women in front of me, skittery as thoroughbreds, whom I
loved with all my heart. I thought of myself as a handler, a buffer,
even an interpreter. If Ollie were to turn into a marshmallow in Lisa's
presence and start tossing out words like *ginormous*, someone had to
be there to say, "She doesn't usually talk like that."

Also, of course, I was poised to shift into full-out angel-with-the-
burning-sword mode, should the occasion for such a mode present
itself.

In any case, they were facing the door, I was facing them, so that when Lisa came walking toward us, I saw her arrive on their faces before I saw her arrive. Daunted. My girls looked daunted, and we'd only just gotten here.

"Courage, dear hearts," I whispered, but they were already collecting themselves, lifting themselves stiffly to their feet, and they didn't hear me. I turned around.

My first reaction was "Oh. She doesn't look like Ollie at all." Which made no sense because (A) Lisa was not actually Ollie's sister; and (B) I was actually Ollie's sister, and I didn't look a thing like her. But without realizing it, I'd been hoping for Ollie's sake there'd be a resemblance. Ollie, sandy-haired and fair and tall-seeming, always feeling out of place with her dark and tiny female family members who were lookalikes, apart from our eye color, a set of impractically small salt-and-pepper shakers. I'd been hoping Ollie would find her doppelganger, the other half of her matched set.

But this woman was truly tall, perhaps five ten, with dark brown, gray-streaked curls just brushing her shoulders, and a long, narrow, suntanned, red-cheeked face. She had an outdoorsy, effortless, wind-burned/blown air about her and a long, fur-lined-boot stride. I thought about the little smocked dresses I'd found in the attic. How jarring to imagine this woman and the dress-wearing child to be one and the same, and if it were jarring for me . . .

I glanced sideways at my mother, and my heart cracked at the bemused expression on her face, but then, as quick as a wink, she transformed into the woman I'd recognize anywhere, the Ellie Brown for whom social grace was reflexive and real, whose warmth went from her eyes to her fingertips. It was this Ellie Brown who offered her hand to Lisa Dyer-Fellows.

"What a pretty place this is!" she said. "We're very glad to be here. I'm Ellie."

And in the presence of the disarming Ellie Brown, like countless others before her, Lisa became disarmed. Not entirely, not even close, but I saw her hesitate just a moment, taking my mother in, before she took her hand.

"I'm glad you think it's pretty," she said. "Not everyone would say so in the winter. I'm Lisa."

"This is my younger daughter, Cornelia," said my mother, "and this is Ollie."

Lisa nodded at me and then her gaze shifted to Ollie, and I braced myself for a display of emotion—Ollie getting teary-eyed perhaps or falling into Lisa's arms, but I saw my sister had transformed, too. Transformed *back*. Perfect posture, distant eyes, every visible shred of anxiety fallen away. I understood the anxiety couldn't be gone, but to the untrained eye, the Ollie Brown-Battle of old was back with a vengeance, aloof as an empress. And in a flash, as I watched the two women standing there, holding each other in cool regard, I saw the resemblance after all.

Oh, you two, I thought, *so high and mighty, but you're just two turtles ducking into your shells, two armadillos balling up, two possums playing possum.*

"Our house is on the property, just a few hundred yards away," said Lisa. "Why don't you all come with me and have some coffee and something to eat? Amelia can take your bags to your rooms."

Amelia waved at us from her spot behind the desk and threw up her arms in a muscleman pose.

"She has a luggage cart," said her mother, drily, but I saw the corners of her lips twitch.

THE HOUSE WHERE LISA LIVED with her family wasn't a log house but was crafted out of wood the same amber color as the lodge. Like the lodge, it seemed a natural object, a manifestation of earth and sky, but it was newer than the lodge and the rare sort of modern that you know won't ever feel dated. Perfectly symmetrical, single-storied, the front part of the house had a peaked roof and was narrow, the width of one very large room with long windows on either side of the front door and three more windows on each of its sides. Two symmetrical wings, also long and narrow, also sluiced with windows, jutted out from either side of the middle section. The house struck me as honest, as simple and graceful, but also as being unlike any building I'd ever seen.

"What a marvelous-looking house," I said when we'd stopped at its front door, which was flush with the walkway in front of it.

"Thank you," said Lisa, in as warm a tone as I'd yet heard her use. "We love this place."

Inside, the room was one long sweep, with a kitchen and dining table on the left and a living space on the right. It was spacious but not too spacious, all the furniture fitting neatly into place, as if it had been designed to belong to the house, which it probably had. Large paintings hung between and on either side of the windows. In the back of the house, I saw a door that was directly across from—and a mirror image of—the one we'd just entered through.

I turned to my mother to see what she thought of the house, but she'd already left my side and was standing, statue-still, in front of one of the paintings, a rectangular canvas so large that if it had been a window, my mother could have stepped right through it. Ollie and I walked over to look, too. Sunrise-tinged fog, pearl and shell-pink, rising in great billows out of water, a little lighthouse nearly lost, seemingly ungrounded, suspended in the fog's midst. The painting's surface was silken and glowed like a candled egg.

"Sea smoke," I said, because I didn't have to ever have seen sea smoke to know the painting could not have been of anything else.

My mother seemed hardly to hear.

"It's hers," she said. Her voice was almost a whisper.

"They're all hers," said Lisa, who had come to stand just behind us.

Then, silently, the four of us moved from painting to painting. A rocky slope, spiked with fir trees; a snowy field under a black sky plush with pinpoint stars; a forest with light sliding through it, tree shadows striping the ground; orange sun-stained cliffs; an island and its reflection, both ink-blot black, in the center of a lake. In other hands, the subject matter might have been grand, majestic, Ansel Adams—awesome, and the paintings were definitely awe-inspiring, but it was an awe born of an intimacy so intense it was palpable. These landscapes bespoke precise and delicate emotions, gradations of joy and sorrow, and the longer I looked the less they seemed like landscapes at all. Each was more like a painting of a human face.

The last painting *was* of a human face. A man's face, brown and high-cheekboned, his black eyes lively, amused, his mouth about to speak. He was assiduously human but also seemed ageless and ancient, the peaks and valleys of his face carved by wind and water.

Landscapes like portraits, portraits like landscapes. Martha had a mind I'd have loved to stroll through like a museum.

"That's Ring," said Lisa.

We looked at her. She was smiling a smile so sweet and natural and unself-conscious, it transformed her entire person.

"Ringgold Dyer," she said, "an architect. He's famous in the Great Lakes region, but he grew up in Houston, and all of his designs echo the shotgun houses in his family's ward. He said most people would not have supposed his would've been a happy childhood, living where he did, but he said it was glorious, love in every yard and on every porch. Every building he ever created was a tribute to that childhood."

"Oh! He designed this house, didn't he?" I said.

"Yes," said Lisa. "Ring was what most people would call my step-father, except that would suggest I had a father before him, and I never did, just a rat bastard who hurt my mother terribly for years before he disappeared."

"Oh. Oh, I'm so glad she found someone. He was a good man? He deserved her?" said my mother.

"He was magnificent. The best man I've ever known," said Lisa. "They deserved each other."

"Thank God," said my mother. "I met him, you know. The rat bastard."

"I know," said Lisa, nodding. "I know everything, the entire story. I grew up knowing it. You, your mother, the blue house, the rat bastard, the farm that wasn't a farm, the baby dying, my mother sending me away with you to keep me safe, my mother going to jail, my mother working so hard to build herself back, to discover how to trust herself, and then coming back to get me."

"Wow," said Ollie.

The wow came out clipped and barbed. Ollie sounded jealous, and I knew she was wondering how different her life might have been if she'd grown up with the story, too.

I put a hand on my mother's back, and she leaned, ever so slightly, into my touch, allowing me to hold her up, and as if Lisa sensed the tension her words had caused, she jumped in to amend them.

"She didn't tell me all of it at once," she said. "The story sort of grew as I did. She filled in more details over the years, saved some of the darker stuff—the abuse she suffered at the hands of her mother and the rat bastard, the jail stint—"

She broke off and then just said, "Other things. Until she thought I was old enough to understand. And I did. I did understand. But, really, the story didn't make much difference in my life, if that makes sense, because I was so used to it. It just got woven into everything else, into the everyday, I guess."

No one spoke, a silence so clogged and crowded with feeling, I couldn't breathe it in for long.

"How did your mother meet Ring?" I asked.

Lisa smiled the unself-conscious smile again. I thought she probably smiled it every time she thought of Ring.

"Listen. Why don't I feed you and we'll talk?" said Lisa. "You must be starving."

"Oh, we're fine," said my mother.

But as soon as Lisa set the food in front of us, we were starving. There was a huge and ravishing charcuterie platter, a kind of landscape in itself, with pots of chili-spiked honey and ramekins of sour cherry jam blooming between the rounds and piles and pathways of cheese and the slices of sausage; fat, halved fresh figs arranged like flower petals; and hillocks of nuts and dried fruit rising here and there. Also, there was fragrant homemade bread; wedge-shaped shortbread cookies, also homemade; bowls of chicken stew; a green salad with pumpkin seeds and apple slices.

"I wasn't sure what you'd be in the mood for, a meal or snack, so I just went with, well, everything under the sun," Lisa said.

We threw all caution and resistance and most of our table manners to the wind and dug in, and somehow, our undignified chowing down was just what the occasion called for. It broke the ice, or at least thawed it a bit, even the ice-queen ice of Lisa and Ollie.

As we ate, Lisa talked about her mother. She told the story in the manner of one who has had it told to her, possibly many times over. Some of the phrases felt passed down, smoothed and grooved from years of handling, part of Lisa's family vernacular.

"As soon as she got to town, she found a therapist and a job, in that order. The family she'd worked for the first time she lived here had moved away by then. She'd never planned to ask for her job back, but she'd wanted to tell them how sorry she was for leaving the way she'd done. Didn't get the chance, though. The bookkeeper here at the resort had just announced she was pulling up stakes and moving back to Saint Paul, and my mother claims it was out of sheer desperation that the owners, Marnie and Douglas, hired her, but I know it's because they saw something special in her. She lived right there in the lodge, in one of the first-floor rooms. In the two and a half years that went by before she brought me home, her job expanded to include more and more, so when Marnie got pregnant with her third child and decided to stop working, it was natural for my mother to step in to manage the place.

"We lived in the lodge for the first six months or so after I got here. Marnie and Douglas had a son my age, a boy named Walker, and we'd play together. Walker and I would eat our breakfast at the kitchen counter every morning and would wait on the porch for the school bus together. It was nice.

"But eventually, we moved to town. We rented the second floor of a house right in the thick of things, well, as much as such a small town has a thick of things, and we were close enough to school for my mother to walk me there. But by the time I was in first grade, I was walking with a group of other children, to school, to the playground after school, to the library, everywhere. The librarian called us a band of merry travelers, but really she meant loud. The town was a place where everyone knew everyone, everyone looked out for one another. Our lives were full of people scolding and joking and watching over, standing on porches and in the doorways of shops telling us to step it up or we'd be late for school or dinner. Sometimes, when we were walking to school, Ann Smith at the bakery would give us bags of day-old sticky buns or cheese Danishes and we'd divvy them up and eat them while we walked. It's what my mother wanted, what had been her plan ever since she moved back here: an entire town to raise me."

"It sounds sort of like our neighborhood," I said. "We ran in packs and in and out of each other's houses, letting screen doors slam behind us. We ate wherever we ended up when it was mealtime. Other people's moms would ask me how my history test went. If a kid fell while we were out playing, we'd just go to the closest house to get a Band-Aid."

Lisa looked at my mother, thoughtfully, as if really seeing her for the first time since we'd arrived.

"So you wanted the same thing she did," she said. "The opposite of how things were for the two of you."

"That's right," said my mother. "We grew up keeping secrets, keeping everyone at a distance. Of course, the isolation only made everything worse."

"Those were her reasons, too," said Lisa, and I was taken aback by the note of defiance that entered her voice. Just like that, she'd become the angel with the burning sword. With her wilderness of hair, her wiry strength, and flashing black eyes, she made a good one.

"It wasn't because she didn't trust herself to be alone with me," she said. "She told me—and told you, too—how scared she'd always been of being a bad mother, and how Jack had fed those fears, but, by the time she brought me home, she'd come so far, she wasn't afraid anymore. She never doubted herself as a mother, not in all the time I knew her."

My mother held Lisa's gaze, and when she spoke it wasn't as anyone's mother, but as Martha's sister. While her voice was gentle, she met Lisa's ferocity, word for word, sword stroke for sword stroke.

"My Martha was fiercely kind and good. Always. Never would she have hurt a child. I have not, for a single second of my life, no matter what she said or how she worried, believed she was capable of it."

I knew my mother had come to this place wanting something from Lisa, wanting it with a starved desperation I could barely stand to witness, a link, a hard nugget of immutable love left over from those five years, an acknowledgment of who they'd been to each other. But maybe this is what she'd get instead: a link born of their love not for each other, but for Martha.

Oh, Mom, I thought, *I hope that will be enough.*

"When I was nine," Lisa said, "my mother met Ring. Winter here can be crazy—this one is actually mild by our standards—and the winter before Ring came into our lives was even worse than usual. My mother was back to painting, and Douglas, who loved her work, had given her a shed on the property to use as a studio. We spent a lot of time on the weekends here; she painted, and I played with Walker or we did homework together. The two of us loved to explore; we walked for miles in the woods. Sometimes, I helped Douglas around the resort, maintaining the trails down to the water or cooking in the kitchen. This place has been my second home since as far back as I can remember.

"But one morning, during the awful winter, after a big storm, my mother found her studio in ruins. The weight of the snow had caved the roof in. She lost a lot of work. She claims she didn't mind so much; back then, she was just starting to show and sell paintings. Mostly, it was about process, she said. The hours spent trying to bring her ideas to life were more the point than the finished work. She says she saw the ruined paintings as a reason to start fresh, to take new risks. But Douglas felt terrible. That spring, he met Ring, who was working with a rich family in Duluth to build their summer home. Douglas went crazy for Ring's work. Back then, all there was of the resort was the lodge, so Douglas hired Ring to design the cottages and a studio for my mother. Ring asked her to give him ideas, and that's how they fell in love, over making something together."

"What a perfect way to begin," I said.

"And it's pretty much how the rest of their relationship went: they fell in love over making things together, over and over, again and again, for twenty years."

She looked across the room at his portrait and said, "He died two years ago. Up until then, I saw him at least once a week. The kids adored him. I have a son, Wes, a senior at UW; he and his granddad would Facetime almost every day, even if it was just for a few minutes. The other day, Wes said he just filled out the online form for graduation tickets and automatically put down four, when it's just me, Walker, and Amelia now. I think none of us can quite get our minds around the fact that Ring's gone."

"Walker?" said Ollie. "Douglas and Marnie's Walker? You married him?"

"I did!" said Lisa. "There were two or three other boyfriends over the years before I realized no one else would do. I was trying to get excited about this graduate program I'd just started in ecology and evolutionary biology out east when I realized what I really loved was just being in the woods. So I came home and started working here at the resort, leading hikes and kayaking expeditions, giving wildlife tours, and when Walker moved back a few months later, I saw the man with new eyes."

When Lisa laughed, a lovely, loose, ringing sound, her reserve dropped away completely, and I heard my mother, who sat next to me, gasp. On her face was an expression I couldn't read, but I thought, *She remembers it, the laugh. It hasn't changed.*

"I brought some pictures," said my mother, suddenly, "of you when you lived with us. I wasn't sure if you'd want to see them, and, of course, it's fine if you don't. I just thought . . ."

She blushed and trailed off.

"Oh," said Lisa.

Her shoulders rose and fell.

"Oh."

She stood and began to collect up the wreckage from our feeding frenzy, and Ollie rose, too, to help her. I watched them together in the kitchen, the two of them standing at the double sink, the ease of it, their elbows bumping, and I wondered if there was a kind of muscle memory at work there, if they were still the two girls who'd slept in the same bed, who'd sprawled on the rug to play. My instinct was to help them, but in more than one way, there wasn't room, and, anyway, my mother next to me was staring down at her hands folded in her lap. I decided to stay where I was. I put my hand on her knee and squeezed. The clatter of plates and chime of silverware were the only sounds.

After what felt like ages, but was probably three minutes, Lisa came back to the table wielding a sponge, but instead of wiping up, she dropped down into her chair.

"I do," she said. "I want to see the pictures. I really, really do."

My mother didn't reach into her bag to get them. She knew more was coming.

Lisa said, "I lied. When I said my mother never doubted herself as a mother."

Whatever I'd expected her to say, it wasn't this. But my mother was nodding.

"It's okay," she said. "I can see why you would."

"I can't remember what happened right after she brought me here, brought me home," said Lisa.

She sighed a giant sigh, and, after a long moment, continued.

"But later, I never wanted to go to sleepovers. I had lots of friends, but whenever they invited me, I made up reasons why I couldn't go. And my mother never tried to persuade me. If there was a birthday party, I'd go to the party and stay until maybe ten at night, and then she or, later, Ring would pick me up and bring me home. The thought of sleeping somewhere other than my own house terrified me. I'd shake; I'd feel sick to my stomach. So then, in the spring of fifth grade, we had a field trip to Duluth. Two nights in a hotel. The field trip was a huge deal at my school, a rite of passage from elementary school to middle school. The teachers really talked it up. All my friends had been looking forward to it for years, and I couldn't figure out how not to go without humiliating myself."

She raised her eyebrows and said, wryly, "Which turned out to be ironic, because I ended up humiliating myself a thousand times more than I would have by not going."

"Oh, gosh," said my mother.

"Yeah," said Lisa. "It was like a bomb detonating, a giant humiliation bomb. At bedtime, when I was supposed to go sleep in the room I was sharing with three other girls, I lost it. Ended up literally on the bathroom floor in the fetal position, sobbing. My friends walked me down the hall to one of the chaperone's rooms—the music teacher, Mrs. Schlegel—and I cried the entire trip through the halls of the hotel. Cried audibly. Very audibly. I was in hysterics. I ended up sleeping in the double bed with Mrs. Schlegel, who was so nice to me I almost could not bear it. The next morning, before the other kids were up and around, my mother picked me up. And I remember I kept saying why. Why am I like this? How did I get this way? So she told me."

Lisa wiped her eyes, impatiently, with her long, tan fingers.

"Simply put, when she brought me home with her, I had a five-year-old's version of a nervous breakdown, and it lasted a year. I was so shattered, so deep in my grief that I didn't even go to kindergarten consistently, not for the first few months. I did take the bus with Walker, but a lot of days my mother would pick me up early. Some weeks, I didn't go at all. Mom would just work with me at home. I was ahead of most of the kids, anyway."

She lifted her eyes to my mother and said, "You and your husband taught me how to read."

"Oh, well, you just wanted to so much all we really had to do was get out of your way," said my mother.

"My mom did all she could to help me. She got me a therapist, and this was back when not many children went to therapists. I went to her for years. My mother was so deliberate about love; she showed me she loved me in a thousand ways, like folding my napkins into swans or putting a pink-tinted bulb in my bedside lamp. She was always trying to think of what might make me feel safe and at home. And eventually, I got happy. I thrived. I loved my mom and my life here. But I think I was afraid for years that if I slept someplace else, I might have to stay there and never go home."

"Oh, sweetheart," said my mom.

"I got over it," she said, brightening. "But my mom never really shook off the guilt at taking me away from you, from all of you. Even though she knew she had to take me, because I was her daughter. The guilt came back from time to time, for a very long time. It would blindside her, and I hated to have her feel bad. So I didn't ask questions about my life before I lived here. And sometimes, I'd be visited by these tiny, hazy memories, little memory ghosts, mostly of you, Ollie."

Ollie wrapped her arms around her middle and said, "Really? You did?"

"Yes, but I never told my mother. I needed her to feel sure she'd been right to take me back. Even though she'd been gone for twenty years when I got your email, I almost didn't answer. It felt disloyal to want to meet you, to be interested in my life before I lived with my mom. But I am interested. I want to fill in some of those blanks."

"Ollie was heartbroken, too," said my mother. "It was so sad to watch a four-year-old mourn. It was unbearable."

We all looked down, not speaking, for a moment, in tribute to the grief of children.

"Maybe," said Ollie to Lisa, "we could look at the pictures together."

"Would that be okay?" Lisa asked my mother. "We could go see my mother's studio later? In an hour or so?"

"Of course," said my mother.

She got a manila envelope out of her bag, stood up, walked over to Ollie, and handed it to her.

"I should have shown you these a long time ago," she said.

"It's okay," said Ollie. "It really is."

And my sister got to her feet and hugged Ellie Brown, who, like her sister, Martha, had done every single thing she'd ever done because of love.

I stood up, too, and said, "If it's okay with all of you, I think I'll go back to the lodge to call Teo and the kids."

I wanted to hear my children's voices. I'd hated to leave them, however briefly, and my missing them was a full-body experience, a longing in my hands, an ache at the back of my throat. But also, I know when a moment isn't mine.

And even though I could tell she wanted so badly to stay there with Lisa, just to be near her, my mother said she'd leave with me. As we walked to the front door, I glanced over my shoulder and saw Ollie and Lisa sitting side by side, setting the photos, carefully, one by one, like tarot cards, on the table before them, two women filling in their blanks, together.

Chapter 19

CORNELIA

WE WALKED IN PAIRS, FAIRY-TALE fashion, down the path to Martha's studio, Ollie and Lisa up ahead, my mother and I maybe fifty yards behind. The path was clear, salted, and completely free of ice, but I'd insisted my mother hold fast to my arm, and she'd complied. It wasn't a long walk, but it was through a grove of young trees, paper birches, lithe and coming up out of the snow straight as pencils. The late afternoon sun turned the white trunks incandescent and threw a latticework of shadow onto the path before us.

"Ollie seems lighter, don't you think?" said my mother.

I watched my sister move up the path next to Lisa. Her right hand was lifted and animated, so I knew she was talking.

"She does," I said. "So what do you think they're talking about? From the way Ollie's hand is twisting, I'd say science. She always does the adamant hand thing when it's science."

"Ecosystems," said my mother, agreeing. "Adaptations. Et cetera. Funny how their interests intersect, isn't it? A happy accident."

"Sounds like Ollie's version of light, all right: strolling through an enchanted forest talking about climate change."

My mother laughed.

"Are you okay?" I asked her.

"Yes," said my mother, "I think I am."

And because her words rang true, I decided to say something I hadn't yet said to her.

"I want to tell you something," I said.

"Of course," said my mother.

"Okay. We've told you about the sundowning. In the rehab center."

"Yes."

"What I haven't told you is that you would ask me, over and over and so sadly, to bring you the northern lights. You would say you hadn't meant to leave them. I promised you; I promised Dad and Teo and myself, too, I'd find what you were missing. I'd figure out what the northern lights meant and I'd find them and bring them back to you, no matter what. And now, I understand maybe you meant the painting Martha made for you, of the cabin and the northern lights, the one you left behind at Bright Wind."

My mother slowed her pace, thinking. Then, she said, "I don't remember asking you for it, but I was very sad about losing the painting. Not right away. There were too many other things to think about the night I left with Lisa and the days following. But later, I regretted its loss. There were times over the years when I wished I had it."

"Yes, I'm sure. But what you were missing, the way you asked for it, the rawness of your sorrow, well, it seems to me it was—it is—more than the painting, bigger."

"Ah," said my mother, evenly. "What do you think it is?"

Suddenly, I realized I was crying. I'm not sure when it had started, but my face was wet with tears.

"Lisa," I said, "you wanted her back. And I promised. And here we are with her, but it's not how I thought it would be. It's not how I thought you would want it to be."

My mother reached into her pocket and pulled out the kind of tiny pack of tissues I didn't know existed anymore. I let go of her arm to extricate one and wipe my eyes.

"You and your tissues, always and forever," I said. "You and your bottomless pockets full of tissues and Band-Aids and peppermints and whatever we need."

"You think you haven't found my northern lights for me," said my mother, "but you have."

We both stopped walking, then. Lisa and Ollie were out of sight. A breeze kicked up and dust devils of snow spun on the side of the path, and all around us, the birches whispered. I worried my mother would be too cold, but I saw her head was tipped backward as she watched the slender branches sway overhead, and their shadows danced on the planes of her face. When she brought her head upright again, we were eye to eye, and she took hold of my shoulders with both her hands.

"Yes, I wanted Lisa to remember me. It would have been nice if she'd loved me on sight."

"She might still end up loving you," I said, "eventually. The person she is now might love the person you are now. How could she not?"

"Good point," said my mother, "and that'll be nice, too. But I've already gotten what I've wanted all these years, the thing I've been missing. You've already given it to me."

"I have?" I said. "I don't see how. What was it?"

My mother rested her gloved hand against my cheek.

"You know what? It *was* the painting. Or the meaning it held for me and Martha. The quiet cabin with light in its windows and the glorious sky watching over it. It's the same thing I've always wanted for all of you."

If there was one thing I knew, it was what my mother wanted for all of us. The mystery of the northern lights wasn't a mystery at all.

"You wanted to know they ended up happy," I said.

AT FIRST GLANCE, IT WAS the sheer number of them. Twenty? Thirty? Small, rectangular, identical in size. They covered the entire back wall of the gallery.

When we got closer, it was the luminosity. Each canvas pouring out color and light.

"The work of years," said Lisa. "Seven? Eight? She couldn't stop. Her agent begged her to let her sell them, but she refused to let a single one go. She wouldn't even exhibit them. She wanted them all to herself."

"The same scene over and over," I said, in wonderment. "Like Monet and his haystacks."

Each painting had its own mood, its own palette—cool pearl, fiery opal, pigeon-throat iridescent, a squiggle of fuchsia or red wine or royal purple, greens verging on neon. Each sky was different from the next. Sometimes, there was snow on the ground, sometimes not.

But in each painting, the composition was the same: a cabin with lit windows under the northern lights.

I had my arm around my mother. She gave a brief cry and drooped, as if her knees were giving way. I held her up, and she leaned into me, her hands over her face.

"She thought about me," she said in a thin voice. "She still loved me."

And Lisa was there, in front of her, holding her by her shoulders, just as, minutes ago, outside among the trees, my mother had held me.

"You thought she'd stopped?" she said. "I never imagined. I should have told you. I should have told you right away. Of course she loved you. All her life, she talked about you."

Ollie was there with a chair she'd brought from the other side of the room. Together, we settled my mother into it.

"I hoped," said my mother, "she was my Marthy, after all. But it's easy to be afraid, to think dark thoughts when you never see a person. I hoped but I didn't know."

When my mother had caught her breath, Lisa said, "There's one more painting in the series. The last one. Would you like to see it?"

"Yes," said my mother.

Lisa started off across the gallery, with my mother walking next to her. Ollie and I stayed in front of the wall of paintings for a few seconds more, and right before we left them, Ollie pointed to one and said, "I choose this one."

I covered my smile with my hand.

"I need more time," I said.

"I know," said Ollie. "You always did."

WHEN WE'D ENTERED, LISA HAD led us straight to the back of the studio. Now, she'd led us to the front. On the wall to the right of the front door was another painting, a very large one hanging all by itself. The composition was the same as the others, with the northern lights sweeping across the sky, but in place of the cabin was a house. A redbrick Colonial with a tree in front of it.

"Lean in," said Lisa. "Look closely."

A small boy playing catch with a woman in a summer dress, both of them in baseball mitts. A piñata shaped like an alligator dangling from one of the tree's limbs and a girl straddling the limb, as if she'd just tied it there. A man with another boy on his shoulders, standing under the piñata, looking up at the girl in the tree. And a second girl, sitting on the front steps reading a book.

I was the second girl.

The house was our house.

"The day of Cam's birthday party," said Ollie, in a hushed voice. "I'm not sure how old he was turning—six?—but I remember tying the piñata."

"Martha was there," said my mother. "Martha was at our house."

She looked up at Lisa, her eyes huge with amazement.

"I was thirteen," said Lisa. "Two years after my field trip meltdown, and she finally felt okay about leaving me for a few days."

"Oh, my. My, my, my. We might even have seen her without realizing it," said my mother.

"When she got home, I asked her if she'd talked to you, but she said no," said Lisa.

Lisa sounded worried, as if she thought my mother must be upset by this. But when my mother answered, she didn't sound upset at all.

"She didn't have to talk to me. What matters is she came," said my mother. "She was there."

"She said the same thing," said Lisa, surprised.

The four of us looked at the painting of our happy family with the impossibly delicate, tissue-thin northern lights streaming and arabesqueing and keeping watch above us.

"She said she'd gotten what she went there for," said Lisa. "She'd seen all she needed to see."

EPILOGUE

WE ARE STANDING ON THE shore of the lake—Ollie and Lisa, Ellie Brown and I—four women caught between two radiances: the glittering blue-white snow beneath our feet, the sky unfurling its purple and green wings over our heads.

Heads back, eyes upward, faces stained with light.

I watch Ollie slip her arm through Lisa's and think it is the bravest thing I've ever seen her do.

In my lifetime, I have traveled to farther-flung places than this one, but because this landscape is nothing like the one I carry with me—the layers of soft blue mountains, circling—I believe myself farther away from home than I have ever been. I believe we stand in a specific place but also in the center of a vast, pellucid loneliness.

I miss my children and my husband. I miss my father, my brothers, Clive, Edmund, Dev, Clare, Piper, Viviana, Thomas and Katie Hall, Alice and Joel and Christopher and Kimmy. And then I cast the net of missing farther, cast it wider, into the past, into lives and stories other than my own. I miss my mother's sister, Martha, who built light. I miss Ring. I miss Peg and baby Wren. I miss Missy and Joe. I miss the other babies I hope they had.

I would put my arms around them all, around them and so many more, not to keep them safe, which I can never do, but because holding on is who I am.

Instead, I'll put my arms around this woman next to me, around all the girls and women she has ever been: Eleanor Campbell, Ellie

Brown, Elsbee, my mother. She's tiny but she contains us all; she is a garden; she is the cabin and the sky keeping watch.

We watch the northern lights, but if I were the sort of woman who spoke to skies, I'd tell the lights they should be watching us.

Just look at us, I'd say to them. We shine, too.

ACKNOWLEDGMENTS

I am grateful to:

the indispensable Jennifer Carlson, my brilliant agent and true friend of nearly two decades;

Jennifer Brehl, all-around lovely person and my insightful, straight-shooting editor;

the incredible team at William Morrow, especially Francie Crawford, Emily Fisher, Lisa Glover, Nate Lanman, Bonni Leon-Berman, Elsie Lyons, Marie Rossi, and Shelly Perron;

my beloved friends June Alt, Karen Ballotta, Helen Boulos, Jon Brilliant, Sherry Brilliant, Susan Davis, Dan Fertel, Susan Finizio, Dawn Manley, Jim Manley, John Nowaczyk, Ciara O'Connell, Kirsten Olson, and Kristina de los Santos—in my cozy cabin under the dazzling sky, there is forever a room for each of you;

my Minnesota friend Ann Morken, who helped me write a place I have never been (yet!);

my dad, Arturo de los Santos, who loves me through everything, and for my mom, Mary de los Santos, who does, too, even though she's gone;

my tiny, tick-tock-tail guys and perfect persons, Huxley and Finny, whose ears, paws, and boundless goodness brighten every minute;

Charles and Annabel Teague, brave and smart and ridiculously funny—you are everywhere I am or have ever been or have ever dreamed of going, and I love to watch you shine;

and for David Teague, my Blue Ridge, my backyard, my quiet woods, and my northern lights forever and ever and ever.